All Washed Up
And Nowhere to Run

Rosamund Snow

© Copyright Rosamund Snow 2016

Rosamund Snow has asserted her right to be identified as the author of this work.

All rights are reserved. No part of this publication may be reproduced, stored in a retrieval system or transmitted in any form or by any means, electronic, mechanical, photocopying, recording or otherwise, without prior permission of the publishers.

This is a work of fiction. Names, characters, businesses, places, events and incidents are either the products of the author's imagination or used in a fictitious manner. Any resemblance to actual persons, living or dead, or actual events is purely coincidental.

ISBN-13: 978-1720776369
ISBN-10: 1720776369

www.RosamundSnow.com

Contents

Leaving	5
Freedom	31
New Zealand	52
Tauranga	64
Dangerous Waters	67
Cabin Fever	91
Alone	102
Arrival	120
The Island	140
The Man in The Sand	161
Caught	184
Wild	208
Unforgivable	227
Exile	242
Karma	269
Abandoned	284
Confessions	311
The Storm	327
It's Never Forever	339
Brave	362
Worth the Wait	380
Three	389
Hope	402
Gone	419
The Letter	430
Promises	444
Lizzy	463

1
Leaving

The clock was ticking. It was ticking ridiculously slowly. It ticked slowly every day, even more so it seemed after her lunch break. And just like with every other day, Lara Adams was having her post-four-o'clock countdown until the end of her shift.

Just another hour and a half to go, she thought.

Lara hated her job. She worked as a secretary for the legal firm: Richards & Richards, which consisted of two solicitors. They were brothers in fact, and were the two most grumpy, pompous and humourless people Lara could ever imagine working for. She had worked there now for over five years after having started shortly after graduating from University with a graphic design degree.

The position had started off as an unexciting doorstop in her career to pay the bills whilst she found her dream job, of which she still had yet to find. What had started as a practical post however had now turned into a source of great bitterness in her life. Her salary was basic and the office she shared with her accountant co-worker and best friend Lizzy Edwards was small and perpetually dull. It was a small and windowless room with dim electric lights, threadbare grey carpet and a sad and dusty plastic pot plant that sat directly opposite

Lara's desk, beside a filing cabinet that she thought she wasn't wrong in guessing had been there since the eighties.

Between the under-stimulating work environment and the blatantly plain tedium of her actual workload, the nine-to-five hours seemed to stretch on further and further with every passing day.

The only thing that helped make the daily clock-watching any easier to endure was the fact that she wasn't really looking forward to going home either. For waiting at home would be her boyfriend Alan, also of five years, whom she had grown to dislike just as much as her mind numbingly boring job.

Lara had met Alan shortly after starting at Richards & Richards at a Christmas party that her then brand-new co-worker Lizzy had invited her to. Lara wasn't too keen on attending a small house party held by someone she had never met, but not wanting to seem unfriendly to her new colleague, she went along anyway. The party was being held in a small semi-detached house in a slightly less desirable area of town.

Lizzy had enthusiastically introduced her to as many of her friends as she could, shouting names Lara knew she wouldn't remember even ten minutes later, over the overwhelming bass of the music emanating from a stereo somewhere.

An hour or so into the party Lara had been cornered by a decidedly drunk man whose name she hadn't quite heard, although she had been sure he was the postman for her mother's area.

After having a very awkward and stuttered conversation over the beat of a lively clubbing track, she had made what she thought was a creatively subtle excuse about getting one of the bowls of nibbles from the battered, wooden coffee table next to them, refilled.

As she slipped past him into the kitchen, she remembered thinking to herself he probably wouldn't last that long in his profession if he was to drink so much on a regular occasion. And by the casually familiar way in which he took another beer from the six-pack on the same coffee table, she was sure he probably made a habit out of it.

Once alone in the kitchen Lara had ditched the almost empty bowl on the worktop and stepped through the door which lead to the dark and relatively quiet garden. She had thought of perhaps getting a five-minute break before she returned to face the deafening party inside.

Once outside, Lara had immediately leaned with her back against the cold, rough brick wall facing the small overgrown garden. She had stood there for a moment, deeply breathing in the bitterly cold air, before she had become aware that she wasn't the only person who had gone to seek some much needed sanctuary from the rowdy festivities inside. She had realized that a man was standing in the corner to her right. He too, it seemed, had been standing taking in the wintry chill and at the same time, avoiding the drunken party-goers inside.

Lara had eyed him warily at this point, wondering if she was going to want to invent another reason to be somewhere else a moment later. Even in the inky-blue, winter light, she had still been able to take in his appearance from the harsh yellow, electric light that glared through the gaps in the blinds of the kitchen window. He had medium brown hair rather similar to Lara's, although he had a fuller, roundish face in contrast to her thinner one. He also had light hazel eyes in contrast to her bright green ones and she had also noticed he was quite tall too, which she found attractive in a man. She had also quickly noticed that, like her, he hadn't seemed drunk at all, in fact it seemed as though he had hardly touched his drink, which stood beside him in its tacky red plastic, holly-decorated cup on the decking rail. After a moment's awkward silence, he introduced himself as Alan Shaw.

The conversation hadn't exactly flowed at first, but after about half an hour they had gotten to know each other enough to realize that they had actually a few things in common. They had then gone on to date each other, start a relationship and eventually Lara had moved into his apartment in a quiet part of the town.

It was now over five years later, and not much had changed since then. They still shared the same apartment in the same part of town and it still looked much the same as it had done when she moved in. Alan had been unwilling to accept any of her suggestions as far as décor and furnishings were concerned. He had clung onto his black, brown and grey patternless colour scheme. The living room was minimalist, dark and consisted only of 'the essentials' as Alan had pointed out.

Lara often imagined the place from an outside perspective; the way that her occasional guests would see it (which in all honesty were mostly her mother and Lizzy) and she always came to the conclusion that it still looked like a bachelor pad. The only evidence in the living room that a woman even lived there at all was the addition of a small handful of her DVD's in the entertainment centre that housed the fifty-five inch television that were, according to Alan: "soppy women's films".

She thought of him now as she, completely on autopilot, filled in an invoice to be sent to a client who was in the process of purchasing a fourth house, and knew with a kind of certainty that only comes from knowing someone for so long just exactly how he would have spent his day so far.

Alan, unlike Lara did not have to work on Saturday's and was most likely spending the afternoon watching as many sporting events on television as he could, whilst stuffing himself full of family-sized bags of crisps and an assortment of sweets to keep himself full enough to be able to endure the wait for Lara to come home from work and make them both dinner. How he wasn't overweight, or diabetic Lara didn't understand.

Her heart sank a little as she conjured this

mental image of him in her mind as she sat, now preparing to print the client's invoice. The truth was that her heart sank every time she thought of Alan lately; if she was honest, this had been true for a long time. She was younger when she had first met him and although she was still embarrassed to admit it due to the fact that she was twenty-one at the time, he had been, and still was in fact, her first boyfriend.

The relationship had been new and exciting at first, not simply because of the novelty factor for her, but because they had gotten along so well and had so much in common and as a result, had enjoyed some good times together. Back in the earlier days of their relationship, Lara often used to think how lucky it was that they had met each other, seemingly fatefully by escaping the same party, at the same time, through the same door.

She felt slightly embarrassed by this thought now, for the simple reason that she was now approaching twenty-six and felt much more wise and experienced than she had done before Alan. She had also slowly realized that he had plenty of flaws in his personality that for years it seemed had only been noticed by a quietly nagging voice in the back of her head.

Now every fibre of her conscious mind made a very loud and permanent note of every irritating habit, mistake and blatant act of wrongdoing that he committed. And there was certainly plenty to make a note of, particularly recently it seemed too.

It may have been the case that Lara had simply never noticed one of them before, or perhaps it was a recent addition to Alan's repertoire of infuriating things he did, but he made a regular habit of looking at other women. He didn't seem to have a particular type he liked to stare at either, it seemed any woman would do as eye-fodder, particularly if her choice of outfit showed off any amount of flesh. This seemed to make his head swivel the fastest.

Again Lara was astounded that his body allowed him to partake this practice without any kind of injury, because the speed he sent these women glances at she was sure he should be at the very least, sustaining some kind of mild whiplash.

This habit in particular riled Lara. And it certainly was a habit because it happened virtually every time they went out, so much so that Lara now dreaded going anywhere with him. It made her feel insecure.

Lara herself, was what she would call a conservative dresser. She certainly didn't dress in a frumpy way, but she always styled herself in what she thought were normal, trendy and stylish clothes she felt comfortable wearing and which she had been under the impression Alan liked.

After all, Alan always complimented her outfit choice, in fact he'd even chosen quite a few of them himself even though Lara had pointed out they weren't necessarily a colour or style she would usually go for. So why was he so interested in women on the other side of the street, wearing outfits most people probably cringed at? Lara knew they certainly made her cringe...

At first she had been upset by this behaviour of Alan's, even humiliated, especially if someone they both knew saw him doing this, but now it just made her angry.

She had for over a month now decided that if he found other women so much more interesting than her, then he was welcome to them. What she really wanted now was to end their relationship, but at the same time, knew that it was going to take a lot of strength, courage, energy and expense to initiate it. Particularly after having lived together the same way for so many years.

Every time she seriously considered what the first practical step to splitting up with him was, she found herself reasoning that she could make her move another day when it was a more convenient time, or when she had saved up more money for a deposit on a new place. Then, in the face of such a daunting task of telling him it was over, actually finding a new apartment, arranging to move out, getting settled into a new home and eventually even finding someone new Lara found she tried to convince herself he wasn't so bad after all.

If any of those tasks involved in saying goodbye to Alan had seemed the most daunting, it was the 'finding someone new' part. Before she had met Alan, Lara had hated dating more than anything else. She had found the process itself frustrating. It was also humiliating and ultimately, invariably fruitless. Not to mention having to experience the ensuing loneliness that came afterwards.

What she had found herself wishing, after trawling what she was sure to have been hundreds of online dating profiles, was that she could somehow skip the dating part and just be in a genuine, loving relationship. She had thought she had found that with Alan, but it had turned out that she had been wrong.

Lara looked at the white plastic clock above the filing cabinet again. Just one more hour she thought as Lizzy dealt with a vaguely familiar client that had just left the elder Mr Richards office behind Lara, handing him paperwork to sign as she engaged him brightly in small talk.

Now Lara accessed her house buying client's file from her computer so she could print an address label to affix to the front of the envelope.

She stared absent-mindedly at the address on the screen whilst the physical version was materializing beside her in the printer output tray. The client lived at an address in Paris. This conjured a sudden pang of regret in Lara and also another reason to resent Alan. For around three years ago Alan, along with her parents, had talked her out of pursuing a promising job offer that was located in Paris, no less.

Lara had never travelled, and had been excited, although admittedly rather intimidated, by this rare opportunity to have a taste of life in another country. Alan, along with her mother and father (although it was mainly her mother) had managed to convince her to listen to her doubts and insecurities and successfully talked her out of taking the offer.

She had been certainly disappointed at the time, and felt like she had really missed out on a great chance to make her life different; special even. But she had been too scared to stand up against, and disagree with everyone she knew and disappear to another country where she didn't speak the language and knew nobody. She had imagined, with some thanks to Alan of course, how bad she would feel if it hadn't of worked out in Paris how she would have to go back to her dull life in England having given up her steady job, her even steadier boyfriend and even her home, to be told by her friends and family that they already knew it wasn't going to work out for her.

Lara regretted this decision now, and over the last three years found herself wondering every now and then what her life would have been like if she had simply taken the plunge. Thanks to Alan however, she would never know.

Lara peeled the printed label from its sheet and stuck it on the envelope whilst listening to Lizzy talking to her client animatedly now about a trip to New Zealand that it seemed she had been planning forever, as Lizzy stapled a sizeable set of sheets of paper together.

It had certainly seemed that she had been telling

anyone who would listen about it for a long time anyway; at least a year. In fact, Lara was sure Lizzy had told this particular client about the visit to the unique geothermal park she was planning the last time he had visited the office.

Lara had to suppress a smile at this thought as she glanced across the room and confirmed her suspicion, as she took in the glazed over expression he had on his face.

Lizzy, who was still babbling on enthusiastically, stapler in one hand, more documents in the other, seemed not to have noticed. Her long dark blonde and natural curly hair bouncing as she excitedly continued sharing her plans with the client.

Lara felt a slight tingle of annoyance towards him, he could have at least pretended to look a little more interested in what Lizzy was saying, she was only being friendly after all. Although she thought she was perhaps asking too much since this client was one of the grumpiest they dealt with on a regular basis.

After being best friends with her for five years, Lara knew very well this was just Lizzy's way of dealing with nerves. She would keep on talking to keep the mood light, no matter how awkward the customer was being. Working in a solicitor's office, this was a good thing to remember.

Lara's mind was still on her would-have-been life had she accepted the job offer in Paris while she franked the newly addressed envelope. Bits and pieces of Lizzy's monologue broke through as she did so.

Lara was happy for Lizzy that she was planning such an exciting sounding holiday. As she had told Lara lots of times, it was a month long trip and she was planning to start in one part of the country and stay several days in various parts, taking in as much as she could while she was there.

Lizzy had invited Lara to join her on numerous occasions, but Lara had declined since it sounded as though it would be expensive due to the fact that Lizzy had been saving up for it for almost two years.

Even if she had of been able to afford it, she didn't think that Alan would be best pleased if she disappeared for a month long holiday without him. She was a little envious that Lizzy was confident enough to plan and embark on such an adventure alone, and wondered what she would be doing right now if she had brimmed with that kind of confidence three years ago...

It was with this thought, that Lara had decided that if her best friend can travel halfway around the world alone, then she herself should be able to find enough strength to end a relationship she could see no future in. Her mind was set now, and she felt a surge of confidence as she decided that she would talk to Alan tonight when she got home and finally end things between them.

Even though she hadn't actually done anything yet, Lara felt a great sense of relief as she finished off her day's work at her desk. She found she was actually excited at the thought of embarking on a life without Alan. She was sure that if she felt such little regret at the prospect of ending their relationship, then he must at least feel somewhat similarly and so he shouldn't take it too hard this evening when she finally made it happen.

The final forty-five minutes seemed to pass much more quickly now that Lara was in a much more positive mindset and had such an important task to complete when she got home, and it wasn't long before she was shutting down her computer for the weekend and saying goodbye to Lizzy before making the short fifteen-minute walk to her and Alan's apartment. Although she thought, as she walked along the already-dark street, it would soon be only his apartment again, making it truly the bachelor pad he seemed so reluctant to let go of.

Lara let herself into the apartment, stepping forward into the waft of dark, warm air that welcomed her. She shut the door behind her. Usually the familiar scent of home was comforting and put her at ease the moment she walked through the door; it had always told her that this was a safe place, a place to escape and unwind after a hard day's work or a night or day out in town.

But now she felt a tinge of guilt, along with the feeling that she was somehow betraying that specific smell of home that had brought her so many years of comfort, by what she was planning to do at some point this evening. Was she really doing the right thing?

She hung her coat and bag up on the hooks on the back of the door that she had only managed to get Alan to put up after a whole year of nagging him; Lara noticed it already hosted his coat this evening before she felt for the light switch and flicked it on.

To an outsider it would perhaps have seemed as though nobody was home. However, now that she had settled slightly into the familiar surroundings of home, Lara paused just inside of the door nestled slightly in the hanging coats. She was sure she could hear the sound of a roaring football crowd floating towards her down the hallway. She knew all too well that Alan would be so absorbed in his Saturday football match that he hadn't even realized that the room around him, or indeed, the rest of the apartment he shared with Lara had gotten gradually dark.

It actually took Lara to switch on a light herself for his consciousness to be pulled out of the game long enough to realize this.

'Hey babe.' he called from the living room, without making any attempt to get up to greet her in a way that might cost him any amount of effort.

She cringed inwardly at his supposed term of endearment; it always reminded her of a film about a pig.

With a deep breath and what felt like great effort, Lara removed herself from the coats and walked along the hall, stopping in the doorway of the living room. She stood and looked to her right; a large black leather sofa was backed onto this wall, directly facing the television, upon which (as she had already surmised) a football game was taking place. And sat squarely in the middle of the sofa, surrounded by several empty crisp packets, sweet wrappers and a half-eaten chocolate bar was Alan.

'Hi,' she said, in what she was surprised to hear sounded like an overly-cheery voice that didn't sound like her usual tone. Alan took his attention away from the television for a moment to look at her and give her a vaguely welcoming smile.

She wasn't sure what to say next, so she cast around for a casual topic. 'Good game?' she asked quickly.

'S'ok I guess,' he shrugged, turning back to the match. 'We're only up one goal, though like.'

She looked at him for a moment whilst standing in the doorway. Unlike the apartment around him Alan had undergone some amount of change since their relationship had started. He had in fact gained a few extra pounds from his couch potato lifestyle, and he didn't make as much of an effort with his general appearance either.

In their earlier days he had always dressed smarter, taken more pride in his hair, opted for smart shirts over the simple t-shirts he wore all the time now. He had even for a while seemed to iron his clothes before each of their dates. Now Lara suspected he did not even know where the iron was kept these days. To add to the effect, his hair was even going a little prematurely thin on top, despite still only being in his late twenties.

Still not sure how to start the important discussion that lay ahead of them, Lara looked at the digital clock on the DVD player in the media station and thought realistically that she should probably just make dinner for now.

She was certainly hungry, not having eaten since lunch time, and as this was going to be a life-changing evening for them both. There was surely going to be a lot to sort out. She was certain they would both feel a lot better if they didn't have to do it on an empty stomach.

'Listen, I'll just go and start dinner shall I?' she said turning in the doorway.

'Hang on a second' Alan called, reeling her back.

Lara turned back towards him inquiringly.

'Haven't you forgotten something?'

She looked back at him blankly.

'Don't I get a kiss these days?' He looked at her expectantly.

Not seeing how she could avoid doing this without giving anything away until after dinner, Lara walked over to him. She carefully stepped around his can of cola set down on the thick brown carpet and leaned over and kissed him briefly on the lips. She thought she caught a slight look of surprise at the almost chaste peck she gave him, before she turned on her heel and walked towards the kitchen which was adjacent to the living room. Not for the first time, she was glad the apartment was not open plan.

In the narrow little kitchen, Lara automatically grabbed two frozen pizzas from the freezer she knew would be there, without having to do even the slightest bit of rummaging around for them, and hastily slid them in the oven.

Saturday night was always pizza night, and had been so ever since Alan had declared so years ago.

Lara had tried to make other suggestions for more adventurous dishes, but Alan had always rejected them, unless they were loaded with cheese which he seemed to look upon as a food group in itself.

In the end, Lara decided it would be simpler just to back down and stick with his choice; it kept Alan happy, and as a result kept the peace.

She just wished her boyfriend was more interested in trying some more exciting cuisine once in awhile. After all, variety was the spice of life right? Alan wasn't even interested in trying different toppings and religiously stuck to the same one.

Although, Lara thought to herself, loyalty is a good trait in a partner. It probably meant he would be less likely to cheat on her, so that was admittedly one good thing about him.

Lara had to mentally shake herself as she realized she was starting to talk herself into keeping things as they were. She looked out of the window and saw a few stray snowflakes float past in the wintry blue gloom. Yes it was easier to stay here. She knew Alan, they had spent years together and they were comfortable with each other. Well, Lara was as comfortable as she could be considering the fact he had all of Alan's annoying little habits and flaws that she had come to notice over the period of their relationship. And she was noticing more all the time.

This was one thing, but there was also the fact that when she was younger, she had vaguely imagined what her partner in the future would be like and the truth was that Alan was nothing like him. The image of this other man she had kept nurtured at the back of her mind as far back as she could remember was physically the classic tall, dark and handsome outline, but with a face Lara couldn't picture. Personality-wise he was similarly idealised; he was charming and polite and his world revolved around her.

Yes, Alan was certainly far from being this man. This man who certainly wouldn't find humour in only slapstick comedy films, who wouldn't reject her suggestion of a walk in the countryside in favour of lounging on the sofa, who wouldn't have his eye on other women when he was out with her, or indeed at any other time.

Sometimes Lara felt guilty about ending her relationship with Alan for a wild dream of finding her imaginary love. Although the truth was she also felt so oppressed by Alan that she was happy for that little glimmer of hope to settle in her heart and keep her dream alive.

She wasn't happy now and if she stayed with Alan for any amount of time, she was sure she wasn't going to get any happier. With this thought, she strengthened her resolve. She would finally tell Alan what she had been yearning to for so long. She just hoped he would take it well.

Although they got on reasonably well, their relationship hadn't exactly been a passionate romance. It wasn't like they were desperately in love with each other so it shouldn't come as that much of a surprise to him.

As usual, Alan finished first and continued to sit at the table squashed into the corner of the living room, whilst Lara finished. He was watching his football match over her shoulder.

Tonight he hadn't had to wait too long though, owing to the fact that Lara was in a hurry to get their important chat started.

'Blimey, you were hungry,' He said watching her gulp down some water to wash the greasy meal down.

Lara set down her glass. It was now or never, she thought. She looked him straight in the eye and took a deep breath.

'I think we should split up.'

Alan froze with a look of absolute shock on his face. 'What?'

Lara was pleased to see that he seemed to have totally forgotten about the television now.

'We've both been unhappy for a long time now and I think we should be honest with each other over how we feel.'

Alan was still staring at her in total surprise, so she carried on. 'There's no point in going on like this, not when we both know that it's not really working and we don't have a future together.'

Alan seemed to pull himself together enough that he could speak, '"We both"' he repeated blankly. 'What do you mean "we both"! 'I thought everything was fine!' he finished heatedly.

Lara opened her mouth to speak, but he cut across her 'I don't understand where this is coming from,' he said shaking his head.

A look of realisation suddenly spread across his face. 'Is this because of a few weeks ago?' he asked.

'A few weeks ago?' Lara tried to think what he meant.

'Yeah - when we had that picnic down at the river? When you went and overreacted over nothing!' He said the last part rather defensively.

Lara realised what he was talking about now. He was of course, referring to a trip to the local castle grounds in town they had taken together. It had been Alan's idea. They had spent a nice sunny, albeit chilly winter morning touring the castle and then strolling through the grounds and along the river together hand in hand like they used to in the beginning. It would have been a nice day out, had they left and gone home at that point.

However, they decided to stop and have the packed lunch Lara had made for them at a wooden picnic bench overlooking the river. Everything was going very well, even if Lara had a few times found herself wishing they could talk about something a little more meaningful than television shows they had and hadn't watched lately.

But part way through the tuna sandwiches which Lara had tried to liven up with some olives and chopped red peppers (which Alan seemed not to even notice) Lara found that Alan's attention had been drawn somewhere else. He was blatantly not listening to her, despite the fact she was halfway through answering a question he had asked her about a box set she suspected he was planning to get her for Christmas. She followed his gaze to a group of young women twenty yards away at another bench who were certainly not dressed to avoid the winter chill...

Not wanting to cause a scene, Lara had finished eating her lunch without saying another word to Alan, and didn't even bother to finish the half answered question he seemed to totally have forgotten he had asked her.

When they had gotten home however she had pointed out the error of his ways and told him just how upset he had made her. Alan's way of dealing with the situation was to flatly deny he had done anything wrong at all and even tried to make Lara believe that he thought that the two of them were the only people beside the river during that period.

'No, that's not it,' she said quickly. She then realised what she had just said. 'Well, it sort of is...' she added.

Then seeing the indignant look upon his face, and his mouth opening to give her what she was sure was going to be more assurances of his innocence, Lara decided to interject, 'That incident a few weeks ago wasn't the first time you have done something like that, and it's not just the fact you are always looking at other women...it's just everything...

'You like different things from me, you like sports and go-karting and... and those stand up comedian's I just don't get... I like the outdoors and reading and the theatre and – well – I want to go out and maybe actually live life, rather than just watch it on a television screen–' Alan folded his arms at this '-We used to have quite a bit in common, but that was when we first met, over five years ago now. I've changed – I'm different now than when I was twenty-one, but you're still just the same. You haven't really, well...grown up I guess - I'm not blaming you or anything. We're just not really that well matched when you think about it. And, well, maybe it's not you that's got the problem – it's me–'

Alan scoffed at this last remark and even Lara had to inwardly cringe at the unintended cliché, but she wasn't going to let it stop her now that she was in full flow and saying what she had wanted to for so long. 'I think we just want different things from life – that's all,' she went on. 'We won't be happy staying with each other just for the sake of it. Maybe we would be a bit happier if we both find someone we're more...um...kind of...well suited too?'

Alan, who had been listening to all this with quiet disbelief, shaking his head after every other sentence now had a definite look of faint anger across his simple features. 'You've found someone else have you?!'

'No - of course not!' Lara sighed, he wasn't taking this half as well as she had hoped, 'I don't think you're really listening to what I'm saying. I just think we've grown apart that's all. This change will be a good thing for both of us. I thought you would understand…Wouldn't you like to find someone who actually likes sport rather than someone who absolutely detests it? Then maybe you could kind of...I don't know, go to sport events together? And that sort of thing–'

'Oh, so now you're planning my new girlfriend for me now are you? How thoughtful!' he spat, his voice rising erratically. 'Maybe you've even got someone lined up for me?!' he went on. 'So when do I get to meet her?!' he finished, half yelling now.

'Now you are just being silly. This is exactly what I am talking about. I'm trying to have an adult conversation with you and you are just being childish. I might as well be talking to myself – as usual – because you never listen to me-'

Alan was quick with his retort, 'I'm always listening to you!' he shouted at her. You're always banging on about this and that...how I never clean the flat, or how I never cook the dinner – it's like I told you isn't it? You're just better at cooking than me!–'

Now it was Lara's turn to interject, 'I wouldn't exactly call putting a couple of frozen pizzas in the oven "cooking". It's really not that hard. I'm sure you could have managed it once in awhile – if you could have dragged yourself away from the television long enough–'

He chose to ignore this, '–Or how I'm always looking around at other women! It's like I've told you before, it's all just in your head! You just need to calm down a bit, like! Stop being so paranoid and that all the time!'

'I certainly don't imagine it Alan.' Lara said in a voice of determined calm. 'Everyone can see what you're doing – it's embarrassing.'

Alan opened his mouth to object, but Lara got there first, 'I don't want you to deny it any more. That wasn't the only reason - as I've already told you. It doesn't matter now anyway, I've already made my mind up.'

'Oh right, don't mind me then!' he yelled. 'And you bang on saying it's me that doesn't listen to you!'

He really didn't seem to get it at all. This was just getting them nowhere, and if there was one thing that Lara really hated it was arguing. 'Listen,

I think you need some time to calm down and think about what I've said this evening. I'm going to go and stay at my mum's tonight and give you some space, OK? We can talk about this again tomorrow...and start sorting things out.'

With this last statement, Lara got up from the table and left for the bedroom. Alan still looked enraged and like he wanted to shout at her some more. But Lara was surprised and relieved, when he didn't get up and follow her.

In the bedroom, Lara grabbed an empty blue canvas backpack from on top of the wardrobe that she had once taken on a camping trip with Alan and started hastily stuffing it with more clothes, underwear and wash things than she needed for a single night away. She wasn't sure if just one night was enough for Alan to calm down and knew from far too much experience that it was pointless talking to him when he was like this.

After collecting a few of her things from the bathroom, she zipped up the bag and threw it over her shoulder, before returning to the living room where Alan still sat in the same position as when she had left him ten minutes earlier.

He was still facing the television, with his eyes slightly unfocused as though he was still watching it although it was now switched off.

'I'll see you tomorrow then?' she said cautiously, not sure if it was strictly true or not.

'Yeah...whatever...' he said vaguely.

Lara was relieved to hear his voice was much

calmer now than it had been before. Perhaps it was starting to sink in for him.

Lara started towards the front door, but had only made it to the living doorway when he spoke again, 'Hey Lara - do you know what I won't miss?'

Lara turned to face him.

He still looked quite calm, but had a kind of bitterness in his voice as he went on, 'Is you banging on about how I crushed your dreams and stopped you from moving to France.' He chuckled to himself at this.

If she had needed convincing that breaking up with Alan was the right thing to do, then this last remark certainly did it for her. She felt the solid steel of certainty constrict in her chest and felt empowered by it. Without saying another word, Lara turned around and walked straight down the hallway and out of the door, to continue the rest of her life without him.

2
Freedom

Lara awoke the next morning with a stream of bright winter sunshine glowing through her eyelids. She opened her eyes and looked at the window at the side of her bed and saw that someone had drawn and tied back the curtains, which were now neatly contained within matching purple, floral tie-backs.

It took a split second before the details of yesterday came flooding back to her. Now, with a rush of warm relief she remembered she was free of Alan.

After leaving the apartment yesterday evening, she had taken the journey to her mother's house on foot. Whilst that journey would usually have taken twenty minutes, last night it had taken forty-five, owing to the fact that Lara had wanted to clear her head and prepare herself emotionally before arriving, she was to be no doubt given the third degree by her mother for ending the relationship which she had so often seemed to approve of.

She hadn't been wrong either, her mother had seemed to take the news almost as badly as Alan had. As a result, Lara and her mother had spent all night talking until the early hours of the morning when they both agreed they were too tired to discuss it any more.

The conversation had mostly consisted of her

mother trying to convince Lara to make it up with Alan. Her mother had seemed to be under the impression that Lara and Alan were just having a trivial argument, and that Lara had walked out simply because she was overreacting.

In any case, they had just gone over the same points over and over again, with Lara becoming ever more frustrated as she tried to make her point understood; that Alan had different interests, he was unadventurous and above all she didn't love him, making him surely not right for her.

She now lay nestled in the double bed which was awash with grape tones in her mother's guest room and wondered if the news had finally sunk in with her yet, or if she would still insist on her making some attempt to go back to Alan.

Lara didn't know, but she got up, dressed and went downstairs anyway.

As she crossed the threshold to the kitchen she was hit with the inviting aroma of cooked breakfast. As with the guest room above it, the kitchen was lit up with the unusually bright winter sunshine, making the magnolia walls glow almost gold.

To add to this homely image, a pan of bacon and sausages was sizzling over on the stove next to a pan of eggs and mushrooms being prodded with a spatula by her mother.

This being Lara's favourite breakfast, she took this to mean that her mother had perhaps started to accept her decision about moving forward without

Alan and maybe this was her way of showing her support. Although Lara would be very surprised if last night was the last time the subject was going to be discussed. She knew her mother too well to hope for that.

Eileen Adams was a small, broad woman shorter than Lara and now in her late fifties. She had medium length hair, which since having started turning grey a few years ago, was now religiously coloured dark blonde; prior to this it had been exactly the same shade of medium brown as Lara's. This was about the only physical feature she had passed onto her daughter, who otherwise most closely resembled her father, inheriting his thin face, green eyes and slender frame.

Lara took a seat at the already-laid, pine table in the middle of the kitchen and poured herself some orange juice before taking a sip. Not having realised that the juice wasn't her mother's usual brand and this premium one contained real bits of orange, Lara had quite a surprise when she now found herself with a mouth full of small bits of fruit.

'Did you sleep well dear?' her mother asked, without turning away from the cooker.

'Yes, not bad.' Lara replied, trying to chew and swallow the tiny bits of orange. It was unusual of her mother to use a premium brand of anything, always having chosen a more cheap and cheerful alternative.

Lara looked at her, her tone seemed light, and

she seemed pleasant enough, so she decided to stay away from the topic of last night's discussion and cast around for something else to say instead, 'It's a lovely morning isn't it?'

Her mother was still occupied with cooking and replied with a vague 'Hmm,'

She couldn't think of anything better just now, so she continued, 'Hey do you want to go into town after breakfast? I thought we could do a bit of shopping? You know, get some-' She stopped short. She was about to say 'retail therapy', but thought better of it, '-get some - some nice new things - you know, for the new year?' she finished, in what she hoped was a casual fashion.

'Oh yes, we could do. That sounds nice dear.' her mother replied, now flipping the eggs over.

Lara thought her answers still seemed a little short, and realised it was going to take her a little while to adjust to Lara's new 'single' status.

'Great!' Lara said overly enthusiastically trying to keep the talk light. Perhaps their little outing together would take her mind off things. She was excited about updating her wardrobe for her fresh new start. She looked at the time on the microwave on the other side of the room; it was only just past eight o'clock.

Despite the fact she had been a housewife with no formal employer or working times for thirty years, Lara's mother had always made sure the household was awake before seven every morning, even during school holiday times.

This was something that had always irritated Lara, but since it was the complete opposite of what Alan liked to do, which was to only consider getting out of bed after eleven-thirty at weekends, she was more than happy to be awake at the current time. Although compared to her mother's usual standards, this was actually a lie in.

A few minutes later two plates generously laden with bacon, eggs, sausages, mushrooms and hash browns now sat on the table.

Lara inwardly smiled to herself, her mother never missed an opportunity to try and fatten her up. Only just realising how hungry she was, she poured a little ketchup onto her plate from what she noticed to be a gourmet bottle of tomato sauce.

Again, her subconscious registered this unusual addition to the breakfast table, but Lara began eating enthusiastically and didn't voice her surprise.

After two sausages and a hash brown, Lara took a slice of bread from the loaf on the table and started making herself a folded sandwich of bacon. Thinking of their arranged shopping trip later as she did so, she said, 'Hey mum, there's a new fashion-boutique kind of shop that opened in town a few weeks ago, I don't know if you've seen it?

No answer.

'Maybe you can see if you can find yourself a nice handbag from there later in the January sales? I think that place is right up your street. You said you needed a new one on the phone last week didn't you?'

'Oh, I already ordered myself one online the other day.' she replied.

'Oh, right,' Lara's eyes seemed to automatically find this said item as soon as she was given this snippet of information. She hadn't noticed it last night, but it was sitting still half-wrapped in its white tissue paper and black box on the chair at the end of the table. Something about the way it was packaged seemed to imply that it had a premium air about it that told Lara it had carried a high-end price tag.

Seeing the slight look of disappointment on Lara's face, she added, 'But we can still drop into that place later if you like? I still haven't found some shoes to match my new coat for the spring yet.' She indicated through the open kitchen door to the hallway to the coat stand, where there was indeed, a brand new, long, cream coloured coat Lara had never before seen her mother wear. Along with the other recent additions to the house, this too looked expensive.

The niggling thoughts in the back of Lara's head came to the fore now, and she decided to voice them, 'Um, mum? Where are you getting the money from to buy all of these things?' For some reason she gestured mainly to the ketchup and orange juice rather than the clearly much more expensive handbag that was sitting at the end of the table.

'Oh, didn't I tell you dear? The money from the

divorce came through this week.' She had tried to sound casual with this statement, but hadn't quite managed it. She knew full well that she hadn't made any attempt to mention it at all.

'No, you didn't.'

'Well, that's why I texted you yesterday,' her mother replied, getting up from the table and taking a white envelope out of the drawer, before handing it to Lara who opened it and took out a cheque for fifteen-thousand pounds.

'I thought I would give you a little gift - you and Alan that is. I thought you could maybe use it for a nice wedding? Or put it towards a house together. But then...well...last night you come here and you tell me you two have had a little falling out,'

'It's not a "falling out",' Lara interjected irritatedly, 'I've left him. That's it - it's over.' She wished that she could have sounded a little firmer whilst saying this, because she obviously had not made herself clear enough last night.

'I know, you already said that Lara dear.' she said gently, obviously hoping to avoid any heated words.

But Lara was not interested in having another discussion about Alan just now, and was thinking of her parents. 'I didn't realise the divorce would be over so soon.' she said, whilst at the same time absent-mindedly fiddling with the envelope still in front of her; it still had Lara's and Alan's names in her mother's decorative handwriting on the front. She had the strong urge to cross out the ampersand that connected their two names.

Although she was a grown woman, Lara had been rather unsettled by her parents getting divorced after over thirty years of marriage. Their constant relationship was something she had always taken for granted.

Now the house she currently sat in was no longer her parents house, it was now simply 'her mother's house'. It looked much different from her memories of it too having undergone much colourful redecoration, particularly in recent years.

Her father on the other hand had been forced to take an apartment nearby after he was rather unceremoniously dumped by his wife one day several months ago. After over three decades of marriage, Lara was sure she was not the only person who was upset to see this happen.

Her mother's response was the same as it usually was whenever Lara tried to discuss their divorce: short, cold and distant, as if trying to avoid further questioning or having to go into any amount of detail. Her response now was equally simple, 'Well there wasn't that much to sort out...and most of the time he's been cooperative.'

Lara didn't answer so her mother swiftly changed the subject, her voice becoming slightly warmer again, 'Why don't we clear up here dear, and then we can get going on that shopping trip, eh?' she said, starting to stack their plates and carry them towards the dishwasher.

Lara obliged, and decided not to push the

subject. Perhaps they could have a few hours without any talk of their less-than-ideal love lives. They both could do with focusing on something else for a change.

*

It turned out to be a very enjoyable morning. Both Lara and her mother managed to immerse themselves completely in their outing.

Lara observed a few uncharacteristic traits as she shopped with her mother; she thought them unusual. But then she thought that many things she had noticed recently were most unlike her mother too. Lara supposed she was just trying to find a new image now that she was successfully divorced from the man she had spent the best part of her life with.

The suggestion of visiting the new boutique in town seemed to go down well with her mother, who had found one complete outfit as well as a pair of shoes that matched her new coat nicely. She seemed to have thoroughly enjoyed herself. Although at one point she had looked slightly distracted as she had hastily stuffed her phone back into her handbag when Lara had emerged from a changing room modelling a white lace top her mother had insisted she must try on.

Lara on the other hand had struggled to find anything she really liked. A top in one shop had caught her attention, and she even started rummaging on the rail for her size, until she had found herself thinking that it was something Alan would have liked.

Horrified, she had abandoned her flicking through the coat hangers in front of her, moved onto a sale rail nearby and found a pair of khaki trousers she was satisfied he wouldn't have approved of and immediately decided to purchase them.

They sat briefly at the window table in the coffee shop on the high street and each had a square of maple and walnut cake and a mocha before perusing a few more shops and then driving back to the house.

They were now in the kitchen again, except that the sun had sunk behind some clouds. This time the kitchen table was laden with shopping bags rather than food and now her mother was making them both a cup of tea, whilst Lara was finding and cutting the labels from her single purchase.

Although they were not something she would usually have chosen, and they were purchased mainly to prove to herself that Alan didn't influence her wardrobe any more, Lara actually quite liked them.

Her mother now handed her a cup of steaming hot tea, Lara took a sip before finding a place to set it down on the already overcrowded table.

Lara handed her the scissors, so she could cut the labels from her many purchases. She started with a short-sleeved top covered completely in sequins Lara had spotted in the boutique.

'I thought that would be really nice for an

evening out somewhere,' Lara said. 'Hey, we could go out for dinner tonight if you want? Then you can wear it this evening,' she suggested, thinking it would round the day off nicely.

Her mother on the other hand didn't seem to be so keen on the idea, 'Oh...I'm a bit tired after all this shopping,' she said. 'We can have something here instead. I've got a nice lamb shoulder for us,' she added. 'I'll have to start that off when we've sorted this lot out.' She gestured at the table strewn with bags.

'Oh,' said Lara, slightly taken aback by this answer. 'I guess it's a good thing we only had a light lunch then...How come you've got that?' she asked.

'I got that the other day dear, when I thought you and Alan would maybe come over this weekend for dinner.' She was now peeling labels from the bottom of some shoes in another bag.

'Right,' Lara replied, disappointed she had managed to get Alan's name mentioned. She quickly moved on, 'That's not the easiest thing to make if you're worn out already. You can let me help. I can get it started for you if you like?'

'No that's OK, I can manage,' she replied whilst rummaging in another bag, 'Why don't you wear this top tonight, dear?' she said, pulling out the white lace top she had made her try on earlier that day.

Lara was again taken aback; she hadn't even realised her mother had bought it. 'Oh.' was all she managed to say.

'We can still dress up a bit, even if we aren't going out, eh? I'll wear that new top you chose for me too. We can make an evening of it.'

'Erm, OK.' Lara said, thinking this was quite unusual. She hadn't really liked the top, but her mother had already taken the tags off before Lara could say anything and she didn't want to hurt her feelings, so she took it without argument when it was handed across the table to her.

Looking at the elegant, lace garment in her hands Lara felt something stir in her memory. She moved her hand underneath one of the translucent short sleeves and remembered a rather one-sided conversation she had been part of with her mother a few months ago.

At the time of their hurried talk on the phone Lara had only been half-listening because she was getting ready for work, but her mother had insisted on recounting a magazine segment on how wearing white can prompt your partner to propose.

Lara felt her heart sink now, as the suspicion that her mother was still intent on Alan joining them for a weekend dinner formed in her mind.

She hoped she was wrong, so voiced her suspicions carefully, 'Erm, mum? It is just going to be us here this evening isn't it?'

'Yes dear.' she replied, sounding surprised and busying herself further in de-labelling the contents of the bags.

The problem was she sounded a little too

surprised.

Lara decided to try a more direct approach, 'We're not having any guests joining us, are we?'

Her mother now looked decidedly under pressure. A little flush appeared in her cheeks. 'Well, I have invited one person over, Lara dear...'

Lara didn't need to ask who had been invited. 'Why can't you just accept that my relationship with him is over?' she said firmly.

'I just think you're making a mistake, that's all dear,' her mother said earnestly. 'No man is perfect, and Alan is a nice chap - you'd be hard pressed to find another one like him-'

'I'd like to think so!' Lara retorted, a little more loudly than she had intended to.

Her mother ignored her, 'He's always been good to you and he's always so polite when I see him. And he's got a good, steady job at the bank-'

Lara had to interrupt her, 'We've been over all of this already! He's always looking at other women-'

Her mother scoffed. 'All men do that dear!' she said exasperatedly.

Now it was Lara's turn to press on, 'We have nothing in common. He's obsessed with football and sport-' Her mother looked like she was going to interrupt again, so Lara raised her voice slightly and continued more hurriedly, 'We have NOTHING-in-common any more.'

Her mother just shook her head at this obviously not able to think of a quick enough retort.

'I just don't love him. And I don't want to spend

thirty years of my life with him before I realise it.' she finished in a quieter voice.

If her mother hadn't known what to say a moment ago, she definitely didn't now. She wasn't shaking her head any more and had put down the scissors, along with the new scarf she had still been attempting to de-label, and now just stared at the table.

There was a moment where Lara had thought she had perhaps gone a little too far. But thinking about how her mother had arranged Alan's invite so sneakily behind her back when she thought they were just having a nice, relationship-stress free day, she found she had enough strength to pull herself out of the situation and allow herself some alone time.

Telling her mother she was going to have a lie down for a little while, she turned to go upstairs to the guest room, taking her handbag and new trousers up with her. She was almost through the kitchen door, when her mother spoke.

'I just want what's best for you dear,' She smiled a weak, but warm smile as she said this, making her light blue eyes twinkle slightly.

Lara paused in the doorway. Since she had changed both her hair colour and style and totally transformed the way that she dressed, her mother had made herself almost completely unrecognisable from when Lara was younger.

All of Lara's childhood photographs depicted someone much different. Countless sunny beach shots, snaps of endless summer days of strawberry picking, hiking and camping, building snowmen in the garden in winter; they all depicted a more energetic, fun-loving brown-haired woman that loved getting involved, playing alongside her daughter whilst planning the next adventure for them all.

Going over these memories in her mind, Lara had a hard time connecting the image of the woman in her head, with the slightly over-made-up, bottle-blonde woman that now stood on the other side of the table. The only thing the two had in common were the eyes.

Not knowing what to say, Lara continued through the door and up the stairs.

Once in the guest room, Lara hastily retrieved her phone from her handbag and sent a hasty SOS text to Lizzy, hoping to have somewhere totally different to be for when Alan arrived later.

She lay back on the bed and stared out of the window. The weather seemed to have changed along with the mood in the house. The sun had disappeared and thick, heavy looking grey clouds were now rolling quickly along the sky outside.

The house was quiet. Lara wondered what her mother was doing now. She lay on her back staring out the window, thinking it all over.

More than anything, she was disappointed by the lack of support she was being given by the one person who should have been on her side more than anyone. But if anything it seemed that her mother was, in every respect, taking Alan's side for some reason.

Mulling it over further, she supposed that if her mother had been as unhappy as she claimed to have been with Lara's father, then this could be to blame for her personality transformation over the years. If this was true, then she thought that her mother should have been even more understanding of her decision to leave Alan and start what she hoped would be a happier life without him.

Lizzy had thankfully answered Lara's cry for help almost immediately, and suggested meeting up an hour later in a pub not too far away.

Lara had arrived after less than a thirty minute walk, managing to arrive to gratefully see Lizzy already sitting at a table in the corner having ordered them both drinks just as heavy rain started outside.

Lara spent a few minutes filling Lizzy in on what had happened over the last twenty-four hours. When she finished, she realised she felt much better. She was also very satisfied and relieved to see that Lizzy at least was taking her side and agreeing that she had done the right thing.

'Sounds like he just needs some time to let it all sink in Lara, hon,' Lizzy said, setting her drink down on the coaster in front of her and looking thoughtfully at it.

'Alan's one thing, but what about my mum?' Lara said, 'Not only has she taken *his* side, she's also trying to get me to go back to him. She just won't listen. Like today, it's like she thought if she could get us in the same room together, we would just fall into each other's arms or something and I'd admit how silly I've been and we'd both live happily ever after.'

Lara looked at Lizzy after finishing her rant and was surprised to see a broad smile had spread across her face. 'What?' she asked, perplexed.

'Sounds like your mum had her fingers crossed for a wedding,' Lizzy said, suppressing a small laugh.

Lara thought back to the conversation she had with her mother over breakfast. 'Oh yes, she tried to give me some of the divorce settlement, so I could spend it on marrying him,' she said with a disgusted look.

'*Tried* to give you some of the settlement?'

'Yes, she gave me a cheque.' Lara replied, for the first time remembering the little slip of paper she had received at breakfast time, which now lay forgotten at the bottom of her handbag. She reached underneath the table now and her fingers found it folded in half underneath her purse. She pulled it out and dropped it in front of Lizzy, who unfolded and looked at it, her mouth dropping open slightly as she did so.

'Wow, that's pretty generous of your mum.' Lizzy said, picking up her drink. 'Yep, definitely desperate to marry you off all right.' She winked, and smiled again.

'That explains why she's so disappointed then. It's going to take her ages to get over this. Alan will have gotten over it before she has.'

At that moment, Lara felt her phone vibrate in her bag next to her ankle. She took it out automatically and checked it to find that she had received a text from her mother.

Her mother was asking where Lara was, and whether she was going to join her and Alan. As she looked at the screen certain words jumped out at her. Alan apparently was 'waiting' and still very 'distraught'. He was also 'enthusiastic' to get back together with Lara.

Lara couldn't think how to respond to this, so she just dropped her phone onto the table in front of her, took another sip of drink and tried to dispel the image of her mother and Alan sitting at the kitchen table with a large roast dinner in front of them, hoping she was about to walk in through the door.

'I thought breakups were supposed to be easier than this.' Lara said, setting her drink down and fiddling with the edges of her coaster.

'Nope, they never are.' Lizzy said with a knowing shake of her head. 'You should have asked me before, I could have told you that.' She looked at Lara, who was still staring at her place mat, her mind miles away. 'You've done the right thing though. The storm will die down eventually, you just have to wait. They'll get over it soon enough, you'll see.' she said kindly.

'It doesn't feel like it.' Lara replied. 'I wish my mum thought so. I thought I could stay with her until I found a new apartment, but I get the feeling it wouldn't be an easy time.' She absent-mindedly adjusted her phone on the table, checking the time. 'I don't suppose you know any places I can hide for a few weeks?' she asked jokingly. To her surprise, a smile once again spread across Lizzy's face.

'What?' Lara asked.

'Oh Lara, I know a great place where no one you know will bother you.' she said, smiling even more now. 'Except for me of course.' she added.

Lara suddenly realised what Lizzy was talking about. 'New Zealand,' she said slowly, nodding. 'I can't do that.'

'Why not?' Lizzy asked, looking for some reason, totally crestfallen. Hadn't Lara told her so many times why she couldn't go with her?

'Well I...' Lara paused. She realised all of the reasons she had given Lizzy previously were now completely invalid.

'Don't have the money?' Lizzy said cheekily, sliding the cheque still on the table towards Lara.

'I can't do that,' she said again, realising what Lizzy was suggesting. Although even as she said it, she felt a nervous jolt of excitement at realising she was now certainly financially capable.

'You can do whatever you want Lara, you're a free agent now, remember?'

Just then Lara's phone started buzzing again, only this time it was because her mother was actually calling her.

Lara picked it up and stared at it nervously. She looked up at Lizzy, uncertain.

Lizzy seemed to read her thoughts, 'One month. No nagging mum trying to push you into marrying a guy you can't stand.' She set her drink down. 'Plus - there's no guy you can't stand...' she added, her smile returning again now.

Lara's phone started buzzing with the vibration of a second call.

'It'll be just us. You won't have to deal with any of this-' Lizzy pointed at Lara's phone, '-until you get back. And even then, they will both have had a month to forget about it a bit. Think about it. You can move all of your stuff into my place so you don't have to worry about finding somewhere to move to before you leave either. It's perfect!' Lizzy seemed genuinely excited now, and it was infectious.

Lara sat, nervous excitement flooding through her at the thought of what her and Lizzy were planning to do. The previous times Lizzy had tried to convince her to go along on this trip Lara had turned her down, either because of a lack of funds, or because Alan wouldn't have liked to have been left behind.

Now, in the last twenty-four hours both of those reasons had expired. There was no one and nothing to hold her back now. The only person who could stop her now was herself, and there was no way she was going to let another opportunity pass her by.

Lara pressed the reject-call button on her phone and switched it off completely before she looked up at Lizzy again, 'OK then,' she said. 'Let's do it.'

3
New Zealand

Lara awoke excitedly, remembering straight away with a smile why she wasn't in her own bed in England.

Looking sideways, she realised Lizzy wasn't there. At the same moment, she heard what sounded like the shower in the adjacent hotel room.

Deciding she could really use a wash too and eager to get on with the day's activities, Lara got up and rummaged in her still-unpacked bag for her wash things and some clean clothes before entering the en-suite bathroom to wash off days of travelling.

When she came out feeling fully cleansed and refreshed she found Lizzy in much the same condition, looking much more alert than she had done yesterday. She was sitting cross-legged on the bed looking through the leaflets as Lara had done yesterday.

'You look much better than you did last night,' Lara told her, 'You must have been tired.'

'Thanks,' she replied, 'I don't even remember what happened. All I know is I'm waking up this morning and wondering what happened in that news item with Cedric the cat.'

Lara laughed. 'I think it all worked out OK in the end.' she assured her.

'Did you sleep OK?' Lizzy asked, putting aside

her pile of advertising.

'Yes, very well. I was right behind you. I don't think I've slept that well for ages.' Lara said, stretching. 'If nothing else, all that flying is a great cure for insomnia.'

Lizzy smiled, 'Yeah, not that will be a problem for us for the next few weeks. I'm planning on keeping us pretty busy. Speaking of which, are you hungry?' Lizzy asked, checking her watch. 'If we go and have breakfast downstairs now we can get going afterwards.'

'Great, I can certainly eat,' Lara replied.

They set off together downstairs. Breakfast was served buffet style in a brightly decorated room at their hotel.

Lara helped herself to spoonfuls of scrambled egg, bacon, tomatoes, toast, and a croissant along with miniature breakfast tarts to her plate.

Lizzy served herself a similar selection and they both sat down at a table near the window to eat.

Not long afterwards, both feeling a little more full than they would have liked, they were getting into their car and driving to the first tourist attraction they had planned to visit: The Buried Village of Te Wairoa.

The village itself was fascinating and definitely came under the heading of 'things Lara had no idea existed'.

The whole place had a peaceful, countryside feel to it and basically consisted of a woodland, except that every now and then there was a building from a village in the 1800's that had been excavated after a nearby volcano had buried it.

Lara and Lizzy walked between each information stand, reading about the history of the place.

Bright sunshine was falling on the luscious green trees and ferns that grew tall on either side of the gravelled path, and the gentle breeze around them was fresh, making it difficult to imagine that a sinister surge of Lava once flowed over the area they were now walking in.

Although when Lara got to one of the last information boards, she saw there was a rather vivid artist's impression of the eruption that had destroyed the village.

Before they left, they visited the gift shop which was stacked with an assortment of books and cases of carved wooden and stone adornments and trinkets.

Lara was somewhat tempted by a wooden, tribal-style ornament, but decided she didn't want to be carrying around with her for the remainder of her holiday. Instead, she decided to be patient and find some souvenirs from the journey that she felt were a little more memorable.

Lizzy on the other hand didn't seem to be concerned by any such thoughts, and left the shop having purchased both a carved stone bowl in the same tribal style, along with a hardback book with a more in-depth detail of the history of the village.

Once they got back into the car, Lizzy deposited

her newly acquired treasures safely in the glove box. After their overly large breakfast, they both agreed that they weren't at all ready to think about food for a while and decided to continue to their next destination: Lake Tikitapu.

The pair took a tour of the lake. They spent several hours of gentle-paced walking, taking in their surroundings and stopping every few minutes so that Lizzy could take photographs. They eventually found their woodland path merging with the white sand of the busy beach they had started from. Hot from their walk, they decided to take off their shoes and socks and cool their feet in the sun-warmed, shallow edges of the cerulean lake.

Lara looked down at the water lapping around her overly-white ankles, and felt the gentle breeze lifting her hair around her shoulders.

Next to her, Lizzy had gotten her camera out again and was attempting to photograph the lake at water level.

Lara amused herself thinking of how many photos Lizzy was going to end up with when they got home. It seemed almost pointless that she had brought her own camera, since Lizzy was making sure she well and truly had their trip documented in thousands of images. Aside from not wanting to end up with virtually the same set of pictures as Lizzy, Lara hadn't yet been completely inspired by anything she had seen to want to own the image of it forever.

The next day Lara and Lizzy followed almost the same pattern of waking, showering, dressing and breakfast as they had the day before, except that this time Lizzy had managed to wake up in her own bed.

After again eating a little too much for breakfast, they both set off for the day's area of visit - a nearby geothermal park.

The park was much more vast than the previous day's points of interest, and after pausing briefly at the entrance sign for Lizzy's obligatory photographs, they started off on their tour.

They passed an array of different natural wonders. There were steaming geysers; hot mud pits; pools of sulphur and a green acid lake. Lara thought the place had a slightly sinister feel to it; it was so grey and barren looking. She was glad when near the end of the trail, they came to a more friendly looking area with an energetic waterfall surrounded by green plants. She soon realised however, that this was a hot waterfall, and what she had initially mistaken for water vapour rising in clouds from the surge of water, was in fact steam.

The day after this, the pair checked out of their hotel and set off for their next destination.

They drove for over an hour and a half through a rich, dense forest. This time Lara wasn't disappointed that she wasn't able to drive, since their journey was more than scenic and she made the most of the images flashing past the window.

They again arrived at another geothermal park, but this one was much more friendly looking in Lara's opinion. As soon as they started off on the wooden-planked path, they were met with a green and luscious expanse stretching out before them; small clouds of steam were rising here and there on either side of the path.

After they had felt they had explored the park enough, they drove a short way to the next attraction: Huka Falls.

This place was yet more attractive again and comprised of a rapid river, culminating in a huge, impossibly-bright-crystal-blue waterfall which the two viewed from a large wooden-railed platform, along with several other tourists.

This time, Lara joined Lizzy and the other visitors in taking pictures.

They took the full tour of the river and falls, stopping at every viewing point along the way. After several hours, Lara was more than aware of the amount of walking she had done over the last few days and was glad when they checked into their hotel in Lake Taupo that evening.

The hotel itself was basic and not as modern as their last, but just as with the first one there were fantastic views of the lake from both rooms.

They ventured out into the town to find somewhere to get dinner and discovered a charming, little French restaurant that served a delicious two-course meal that recharged both Lara and Lizzy's energy levels enough for them to explore the town a little before they returned to the hotel for the evening.

Most of the shops were shut for the day, so they instead had fun exploring the streets by the dusky evening light, perusing the various window displays, making mental notes of which ones to return to the next day when they would be open.

The next day's point of call was a short, twenty-minute drive away to Mine Bay. This was a place Lizzy had been most excited about visiting, and Lara had heard many pieces of trivia about it when she had been sitting at her desk back in England.

Lizzy now seemed just as enthusiastic as Lara was that she wasn't going to make this visit alone.

When they arrived however, the sky was grey and cloudy which made the water sloshing around the sides of 'The Adventurer' look a dark, foreboding green as Lara peered over the metal railing.

The captain gave the dozen passengers on board a thorough tour of the lake, ending with a close up view of the Maori carvings etched into the cliffs near where they set off.

When all of the passengers were returned to the dock, well-versed in the full history of the lake Lara and Lizzy separated from them and drove into Taupo town.

They found a small, but modern café where Lara had a roast chicken and avocado sandwich washed down with a ginger hot chocolate.

Lizzy on the other hand, after nagging Lara to

do the same, chose an Irish-cream hot chocolate to wash down her potato salad and large chunk of chocolate cake.

'Oh Lara, you need to live a little!' Lizzy said jovially, as they took their seats in the window.

They spent the rest of the afternoon retracing their steps from last night and visiting the shops that had caught their attention.

Their first port of call was a promising looking clothes shop where Lara found a black, strappy dress she quite liked the look of, even if she couldn't decide exactly where she would ever wear it.

As she was scrutinising the lace-up back, Lizzy did a double-take at the item in Lara's hands and piped up, 'Ooh, that'd look really pretty on you,' she said approvingly.

'I don't know...It's quite nice, but where's the rest of it?'

Lizzy abandoned the rail she was rummaging through and pulled Lara over to the full length mirror behind them and held up the dress in front of her.

'You have to get it.' Lizzy said determinedly.

'Where would I even wear it?' Lara replied doubtfully.

'As soon as we find a decent bar on our travels, we'll go to it. The ones in the last few towns have been a little ropey.'

Lara studied her reflection, trying to imagine what the dress would look like on her.

'Come on Lara, just get it. You think too much, that's always been your problem. Sometimes you just need to just go for it.'

Although Lizzy was only being her usual, bouncy self there was something about her comment that Lara didn't like. She thought she was being made to feel a little, well, boring. This feeling was what made her decision for her.

'All right then, I'll get it. And we can wear it the next time we go for an evening out.'

Lizzy looked delighted, 'Hey great! You promise you won't change your mind? Now we can be little black dress buddies.'

'Only if you promise not to use that phrase.' Lara laughed.

'No problem, we'll be batting all the guys away.' She mimicked the action of using a bat.

'Right,' Lara said. She hadn't even thought about finding another man yet, it still felt a little too soon.

After making her impulsive purchase, Lara accompanied Lizzy to a shoe shop further down the street.

Here Lizzy looked for some new walking shoes she needed quite urgently, since her current ones were starting to develop holes.

'How come you didn't you get some new ones before we left?' Lara asked.

'These are my lucky shoes,' Lizzy said, pointing at her feet whilst examining random shoes from the shelves and frowning as though Lara had asked a silly question. 'I wanted to wear them as long as I could. I would have thought they would have lasted a little longer though, until we got back to England at least.'

'Why are they lucky?' She hadn't known Lizzy was so superstitious.

'Well when I first went abroad when I was nineteen, I was wearing these shoes for the first time and the lace on the left shoe came undone. I was on my way to catch a train at the time, by the way. So I sat on a bench and tied it back up again, but then some guy came up next to me and ran off with my backpack that I'd put on the ground at the side of me.'

'That doesn't sound very lucky.'

'You haven't let me finish!' Lizzy said quickly, now sitting on a small, leather sofa and trying on a pair of black hiking boots she was considering. 'The security guard in the station caught the guy as he was running off, so I got my bag back - but because I had to spend half-a-ruddy-hour in the security room at the train station I ended up missing my train.'

Lara still looked confused as she joined Lizzy on the sofa, before Lizzy added dramatically, 'I never caught the next few trains either - because that train I missed derailed a few stops down the line.'

Lara hadn't expected to hear such a revelation whilst simply out shoe shopping.

Lizzy had usually been forthcoming with stories

of her previous trips to foreign lands, but she had never shared this one with her before.

Lizzy now stood examining the new shoes she was trying out from every angle she could arrange herself in with a slight frown, moving in front of the full-length mirror to get a better view. 'Aww, I'll miss my lucky shoes.' There was a definite note of disappointment in her voice.

'They're getting a hole in the bottom though. You won't miss them next time it rains.'

'Yeah, I guess,' Lizzy replied, cheering up a little.

'And anyway, you don't know if it was your shoes that were lucky. It's just as likely it was your backpack. And that's still going strong, isn't it?'

'It certainly is. You're using it.' Lizzy replied, her reflection giving Lara a wink.

'Oh. I didn't realise it was that old...'

Lizzy scoffed. 'It wasn't that long ago - I'll have you know!'

'I didn't mean it like that.' Lara said smiling too, realising what she just said. 'I just meant, well...I didn't know it had that much history.'

'Likely story,' Lizzy muttered, before disappearing down the nearest aisle and returning a moment later with a pair of shiny, silver, high-heeled shoes.

'I wouldn't say those are all that practical for walking in,' Lara said sarcastically, eyeing the shoes Lizzy now dropped them in front of her.

'They're not for me, Lara hon, they're for you -

to go with your new dress. Try them on.'

Lara picked up one of the shoes and eyed the tall heel warily. 'I'm not sure they're really my thing...'

'Trust me, they'll go really nicely with that dress. What other's have you got to wear with it?'

Lara looked at the shoes she was wearing. They were practical and great for everyday wear, but Lizzy was right, she needed another pair if she wanted to wear that dress.

But did she actually want to wear it? The dress and shoes combination she now saw herself wearing in her mind's eye made her feel a little uncomfortable. But maybe that was a good thing, she thought. After all, hadn't she embarked on this trip to break out of the routines and habits that had held her back her entire life?

A few minutes later, Lara and Lizzy stepped onto the high-street carrying their new purchases in a crisp, white shopping bag each.

Lara felt flushed with a kind of confidence that felt unfamiliar, if not a little reckless.

4
Tauranga

Glorious sunshine streamed into Lara's hotel room from where she had left the curtains open the night before, enjoying the view of the moonlight reflected on the oddly calm ocean.

This morning however, the ocean was somewhat more active and slightly more defined waves were rolling into the bay.

Lara got out of bed and slid open the French windows, stepping onto the small balcony. She took a deep breath of the fresh sea air, basking in the warm sun and hearing the sound of seagulls. It was nice to finally be at a coastal location. She felt it had a much more relaxing atmosphere, reminding her of holidays she had taken as a child with her parents. Her parents. She forcibly snapped herself from her thoughts, turning back into her room and focusing now on getting washed and ready for the day.

She met Lizzy walking out of her room next door at the same time she was, and they went together to the dining room on the ground floor.

They enjoyed a usually large breakfast buffet made up of both cooked and continental fare. They ate guilt-free today however, since afterwards they were going to trek up the small mountain that dominates this part of the town.

Once they had finally made it to the top

sweating and quite out of breath, Mount Maunganui presented beautiful vistas of the minuscule looking town down below and the land connected to it, as well as the open ocean beyond. The bright colour of the cloudless blue sky was reflected in the sea below.

The journey to the top hadn't consisted completely of relentless exercise. Lizzy had stopped to take photographs every few minutes, and Lara had even joined her a couple of times too. Although she had skipped shots of the signposts and the close ups of the plants by the path side.

Now that they were at the top however, Lara had to admit the view was beautiful. From every angle, the scene looked just like a picture-postcard from somewhere exotic thanks to the palm trees, light sand and bright blue ocean. To top it all off, the sun was beating down making everything look stunningly bright and vivid.

Lara presumed the sun was giving off as much heat as it was before they scaled the mountain, but she couldn't feel it. The fresh sea wind was cooling her, lifting her hair from her shoulders and blowing it in all directions until she tied it up in a hasty bun.

She explored the top of the mountain with Lizzy, making the most of the scenery and the fresh air, since they both agreed that they didn't feel like they would want to take the walk up again.

They set off together after they were satisfied they had seen enough and ventured back down, following the same path they had hiked up on.

The warmer air was returning the further they descended, as they were busily discussing where they could find something exciting for lunch before investigating the city's shops.

As they reached ground level Lara's attention

was drawn to the slipway on her right where a dark-haired shirtless man was helping pull a small rowing boat out of the water with two other men.

As he lifted a crate from under one the seats with one of the others, Lara noticed he was the tallest of the three. She also noticed how handsome he was.

The sun highlighted the sheen on his tanned skin which seemed to emphasise his slender, toned torso.

As the two men dropped the crate into the back of a four-wheeled-drive parked next to the slipway, Lara noticed that the man carrying the other side of it exchanged a brief, flirty smile with Lizzy as they walked passed.

Lara could feel Lizzy grinning as they continued into town, but when Lara gave her a questioning smirk Lizzy just shrugged and gave her a look back that said, 'Why not?'

5
Dangerous Waters

The next day, Lara and Lizzy decided to spend the day exploring Tauranga further. They set off after breakfast and visited the city's art gallery, before doing a little window shopping.

They made up their own picnic-lunch which included items they had found from a quaint, little gourmet shop in the city from yesterday's shopping trip. They had fun attempting to spread little tiny pots of ruby grapefruit marmalade and olive pate alternatively on crusty French bread with a plastic knife whilst sitting in the sand, hearing the crashing waves of the ocean before them.

They spent the rest of the afternoon on the beach, walking the length of it and swimming, before sitting back in the sand near the mountain and drying off a little, whilst discussing where they were going to next on their trip.

'There are some really nice waterfalls near here,' Lizzy said, scrolling on her phone as Lara absent-mindedly watched some jet-skiers bouncing across the waves.

That sounds nice,' Lara said, 'Maybe you can finally find something to take a photo of,' she added, unable to keep a straight face.

Lizzy gave a mock laugh. 'Very funny, Lara. You'll be glad I took all those pictures when we get home. It'll help us remember everywhere we've been.'

'I kind of prefer using my own memory. Especially when it's somewhere...well - memorable.' Lara said, shrugging.

Lizzy put her phone away and turned to Lara. 'Speaking of memorable,' she said, leaning back on her elbows, 'How about this evening we go to that nice restaurant-bar we saw yesterday? We could have a fancy dinner there, then have a few drinks afterwards?'

'I don't see why not.' Lara replied. 'I would probably class that place as decent.'

'There you are,' Lizzy said, 'You can wear your new dress!'

'Um, OK.' Lara replied, suddenly a little less enthusiastic about their dinner plans.

Lizzy noticed her sudden change in tone, 'Lara, you'll be fine. It's like I always tell you - just live a little. It'll be just the two of us. We'll have fun.'

Lara wasn't exactly sure what Lizzy had in mind when she used the word "fun", but she didn't want to let Lizzy down or be told she was boring either so she didn't argue. Maybe Lizzy was right, maybe she did need to relax a little more.

With that thought in mind, Lara obediently got ready to go out a couple of hours later in her hotel room.

After showering and slipping into the black dress she had admittedly been slightly coerced into buying she applied her usual makeup, adding a little extra eyeliner than usual around her bright green eyes to turn the style into what she thought was more of an evening look. She left her hair loose, letting it fall naturally around her shoulders.

When she had finished, she looked in the mirror near the door to her room, standing back a little to see the full effect. She was surprised, and a little relieved to see that her reflection looked less naked than she felt in her new garment.

Lizzy came in at that moment, joining Lara next to the mirror.

'Looking good hon,' she said admiringly, looking at the Lara in the mirror.

Lizzy was wearing a black evening dress too, except that hers had thicker straps that sat just off the shoulder, and the back had a curve that dipped slightly. She had also opted to loosely plait her blonde curls, resting them over one bare shoulder.

'Thanks,' Lara said with a slightly nervous smile. 'You're not so bad yourself,'

'Yeah, I scrub up pretty well don't I?' she replied with a giggle. 'Let's go then.'

When they arrived the place was already pretty busy, so they took seats at the shiny marble bar rather than joining the lengthy queue for a table. They both ordered drinks and a shared starter, whilst they took in the atmosphere.

The décor was modern and glossy. The whole room was well lit with hanging golden lights which were reflected in every shiny surface. The place certainly seemed popular with the locals and tourists alike.

Lara and Lizzy had fun trying to guess the scenarios of the people around them over sips of drinks whilst they waited for their food.

One couple who were at a table on the opposite side of the room, were clearly on a first date; the man's mannerisms were overly polite and he was making an obvious attempt to listen to whatever the woman opposite him was talking about.

'It's a shame they don't stay like that, isn't it?' Lizzy said bitterly.

'Amen to that,' Lara said, clinking her glass with Lizzy's.

It wasn't long before they were enjoying their food. Everything was delicious and very well presented, stacked neatly and drizzled with interesting sauces.

They had finished their main course and were waiting for their desserts, when they resumed their earlier game.

Lizzy was trying to decide whether a group seated at a table near the door who looked as though they were related, were celebrating an engagement in the family or a promotion.

'I'm going to say promotion.' Lara said.

'It's definitely an engagement,' Lizzy said confidently, 'They're all so giddy.'

'That's because one of them is about to be paid more.' Lara pointed out. She took another sip of her drink, her gaze sliding across to a table near the corner of the room she hadn't looked at before.

She swallowed a larger mouthful than she had

intended to when she realised that the two men seated at the table that were now being served drinks were the same men they had seen unloading the rowing boat yesterday.

Lara looked at Lizzy, who seemed to have noticed this at the same time and was now looking over, rather too obviously in their direction.

When the man who had shared a brief smile with Lizzy looked up from his drink, he gave a small smile and a wave and said something to his previously-shirtless companion, who looked now that Lara was focusing on his face like he could be his younger brother.

He stood up from the table and started moving in their direction.

'Erm, what are you doing?' Lara muttered to Lizzy. '

'Trying to get their attention,' Lizzy said simply.

'I can see that.' Lara hissed hurriedly. 'I thought you said it was just going to be the two of us?'

'Yeah, I know. I also said we were going out to have some fun.'. She took a half-glance at Lara, seeing her panicked expression she added, 'Lara just relax. Follow my lead OK?'

There was no time to discuss it any further, as the younger man now emerged from behind a few of the family members Lara and Lizzy had been discussing, who were carrying more drinks to their table.

'Hello,' he said, drawing level with Lara and Lizzy, looking from one to the other.

For a second, Lara actually thought his cologne got there before he did, but then she thought that it wasn't actually unpleasant.

He was dressed smartly in a slim, dark purple shirt with black trousers and shiny black boots. His black hair was neater than it was yesterday too and was swept back in a way that seemed to make his high cheekbones and dark eyes stand out more.

'Hi,' Lizzy said in the most girly voice Lara had ever heard her use.

The man smiled, 'My brother and I-' he gestured vaguely behind him '-we were wondering - if you like - would you join us at our table?' His accent was heavy, but Lara couldn't quite identify it for sure. English didn't seem to be his first language.

'We'd love to,' said Lizzy, again in her unusually sweet voice. She told the bartender where to send their desserts before she followed the man over to the table, pulling Lara subtly by the wrist as she did so.

When they arrived at the table, the other man stood up and gave them a nod as they took their seats. He was dressed much the same as his brother was, except that he wore a navy blue shirt instead. Lizzy sat next to him, whilst Lara sat at the only other available seat next to the previously-shirtless man, whilst trying to push that mental image of him out of her mind.

'Hello,' the older brother said. 'My name is Matías, and this my younger brother Alexis,' he said gesturing to the man next to him. His English flowed much better than Alexis's, as though he was more used to speaking in it.

'-Half-brother,' Alexis interrupted.

'As he always reminds me…' Matías said, raising his glass to Alexis in a mock-toast, before taking a sip.

'Hi Matías,' Lizzy responded, 'I'm Lizzy and this is Lara.'

'Are you two sisters?' Alexis asked.

'No. We're just friends.' Lara replied nervously. She'd always found it hard talking to men in her younger years and it wasn't any easier now. She really didn't know what to say. 'We're here on holiday...' she added.

'I just am loving your accent. Where is it you are from?' Alexis asked Lara, leaning forward on his elbows on the table.

She was strongly reminded of the first-date-guy she and Lizzy had watched earlier.

'Well, we're from England.' Lara replied. 'We've been travelling around New Zealand for the last two weeks,' she added, feeling a little more confident now.

'Two weeks?' Matías nodded impressively. 'You are positively a local. We have only been here a couple of times.'

'Where is it you're from Matías?' Lizzy asked, still in her annoyingly flirtatious voice.

Alexis started to answer, 'We are from Argentina at first, but now-'

'-Now we travel.' Matías interjected quickly,

with an almost imperceptibly small glare at his brother.

Something about that look bothered Lara. There seemed to be a hardness in his eyes that didn't match-up with his apparently polite demeanour.

'Are you here on business?' Lizzy asked Matías.

'Yes,' he replied. 'We have done our business here for now. Tonight we set off for our next destination - the Cook Islands.'

'Ohhh, I've always wanted to go there.' Lizzy said, remembering her love for travel and forgetting her flirtatious tone. 'It looks so beautiful...'

Alexis piped up again, 'Yes it is a paradise there. The water is the clearest in the world, and the sand the whitest...'

'How are you getting there?' Lara asked.

'We are sailing there,' Matías replied.

'You have a boat?' Lizzy asked, adopting her girly tone again.

'Yes. We have a very large yacht.' Alexis said, making a vague gesture with his hands. 'It is staying here in the bay for when we leave here tonight.'

'Oh, you're so lucky, getting to cruise to the Cook Islands by yacht,' Lizzy said dreamily. 'I'd love to do that.'

'Then come with us,' Alexis said abruptly, smiling and again looking from Lizzy to Lara.

Lara froze, she hadn't expected that response.

Neither it seemed did Lizzy.

'You're joking?' Lizzy said, laughing.

'No, I really, I am serious,' he said, leaning forward more on the table. 'We have plenty of space on board our yacht.'

'Especially for two beautiful ladies such as yourselves.' Matías added, smiling.

Lizzy looked to Lara, who wasn't sure what to say. They had only just met these men and now they were inviting them to go sailing on their private yacht? It made her feel more than a little uneasy. She was just thinking of how to politely voice the word 'no' when Lizzy answered for them both.

'Go on then, you're on.' she said.

Lara kicked her under the table, giving her a pointed look. 'Can I talk to you for a second?' she said without looking at the two men and getting up from the table.

'Will you excuse us for a second, gentlemen?' Lizzy said hurriedly.

The two men quickly stood from their seats as the two women left theirs. If nothing else, they certainly were polite Lara thought, even if they were a little forward...

Lara walked across the room and stepped behind a pillar. She turned around and faced Lizzy who was right behind her.

'What are you doing?!' Lara asked her exasperatedly.

'What are *you* doing, more like!' Lizzy said, as though she was astounded Lara was considering not accepting a crazy offer from two random strangers.

'We can't just get on a boat with two random guys we've only just met.' Lara said, gesturing wildly. She was glad they were having this conversation behind their private pillar.

'Why not?' Lizzy said. 'They're OK. They're just a couple of businessmen on some kind of business trip and now they're going to one of the most beautiful places in the world and they're inviting us to go with them!' Now it was Lizzy's turn to gesture. 'This is a once in a lifetime opportunity. It's a free cruise on a huge yacht! To top it all off, they're both really hot!' she said the last bit in a hurried whisper. 'Come on Lara, I saw you checking Alexis out yesterday. You like him.'

Lara didn't know what to say to that. 'That's not the point.' she said, blushing slightly. She was struggling to think of reasons why this wasn't a good idea.

She thought of the sudden hint of coldness in Matías's eyes when he stopped his brother giving away a snippet of information he didn't want him to. What was he trying to hide? 'We don't even know what they do anyway.' she said. 'What kind of business are they in, anyway?'

'I don't know!' Lizzy said shrugging. 'They're probably yacht salesmen, or internet millionaire guys or something...What difference does it make?'

Lara shrugged. 'We just don't know very much about them, that's all. And you want to get on a boat and go sailing off with them.'

'Lara, what did I tell you? You just worry about everything too much. You do this with everything. You just need to relax a little. Whenever there is something nice or fun, you just come up with a list reasons not to do it. You're doing it now.'

Lara thought Lizzy was right, but she didn't want to admit it. She had always been indecisive, and never able to just do anything impulsively. She found her mind forming another excuse. 'I'm just not ready yet.' she said, 'You know, after...well...my previous relationship.' She just couldn't bring herself to say his name.

Lizzy's expression softened a little and she took half a step towards Lara. 'Just trust me,' she said, her tone much softer too, 'It'll be fine. Lara, you've only ever been with one guy. Doing this is the best way to get over him for good. That is what you want isn't it?'

'Of course.'

'He's still got a hold over you if you're letting him influence your decisions now,' Lizzy pointed out.

Something in that comment stirred Lara. She wasn't going to let Alan affect her life any more. She didn't want to waste another second even thinking about him. Here she was on the other side of the world, thinking of the man who had stolen five years of her life whilst she was surrounded by people who were getting on with their lives, not worrying about the past. Lizzy was right - she needed to do this.

Lara looked at Lizzy and nodded. Her decision was made, and she knew what she was going to do next, even if she still had a niggling doubt in the back of her mind as she walked back to the table with Lizzy.

Lara smiled at the two men as she sat down again. 'We'd love to join you.' she said in a voice she hardly recognised. 'When do we leave?'

Matías and Alexis accompanied Lara and Lizzy to their hotel a few blocks away to retrieve their belongings and check out, before the four of them walked together, along the streetlight-lined pavement to the slipway where they had first caught sight of each other.

The two men helped Lara and Lizzy into the same rowing boat they had seen yesterday. It was a little awkward in the partial-darkness, and Lara couldn't quite see the seat she was sitting on, she could just feel the rough wooden texture against the back of her bare knee.

Matías took charge of rowing the short distance to their yacht through the dark water. There was no light at all until they pulled up beside a large, white triple-decker yacht. Warm, golden light shone from several of the windows, illuminating the choppy water around the sides of the boat. Even in the darkness the vessel seemed to gleam brilliant white.

Matías steered the rowing boat around to a

narrow wooden staircase at the side of the yacht. Alexis stepped fluidly out of the small boat and onto the square platform at the bottom of the staircase and held out his hand to Lizzy who was nearest so she could climb aboard.

He then did the same for Lara, who stepped onto the platform and followed her friend up the stairs, grasping the metal handrail tightly, very aware of how loud her heels sounded on each of the hard steps as she ascended onto the brightly-lit deck.

Lara felt slightly odd. She had the lingering sense that she and Lizzy were trapping themselves on this boat. Though they were only meters away from the shore, Lara was more than aware that the only way back relied upon their hosts. She tried to push this unwanted thought to the back of her mind, trying to mimic Lizzy's upbeat attitude.

Lara looked around her surroundings. The whole floor of the deck was smooth and white, making it seem overly bright in the darkness. The top level seemed to be the captain's cabin; it was just visible through the large glass windows where a group of three men were sitting talking to one another. They were so engrossed in conversation they seemed not to have noticed the new arrivals. Beneath that was a much larger room lined with slightly darkened glass windows that looked like a lounge and dining room.

It certainly was a luxurious yacht. Whatever the men did for a living it certainly paid well, Lara thought as she tried to relax her body language into something that didn't say 'I want to get out of here'.

They didn't have to wait long before they were joined by Matías and Alexis who gestured for them to go through the tinted glass doors that lead to the lounge.

The lounge was a wide, spacious room composed mainly of two modern sofas facing each other on opposite walls. Beyond those was a winding staircase that lead to the lower deck. Tucked behind the staircase was a smaller dining area. The décor was modern and downlights shone down on everything from the ceiling.

Alexis invited them to sit down and made them drinks whilst Matías excused himself so that he could go and talk to the crew to tell them they can set sail.

Lara sat down on the squishy, cream sofa scattered with cushions opposite Lizzy who sat on one identical running along the other wall.

Alexis returned a minute later handing them both a drink before sitting down with his next to Lara, a little closer than she had anticipated.

Lara thanked him with a smile she really had to force, taking a subtle deep breath to try to calm the butterflies in her stomach. This didn't help much, and she found she only inhaled more of his fragrance.

'What do you think of our boat?' he asked Lara, resting his arm along the back of the sofa behind her just as Matías entered the room, sliding the glass door shut behind him.

'It's beautiful,' Lara replied, taking a sip of her drink. She was regretting having already had two drinks in the bar. Now that she was in this circumstance, even though everything seemed perfectly clear, she would have preferred to have been more confident that she had all of her wits about her.

She felt she needed to elaborate more so she went on, 'You must be in a profitable business if you can afford such an expensive boat.'

Lara thought she saw Matías give Alexis a sharp glance, before he answered the question for him.

'It's not bad,' he said slowly pouring himself a drink and taking a seat next to Lizzy. 'I started when I was very young. Alexis started working for me several years ago now. Our mother insisted I should take care of him.'

Alexis interjected, 'I am not working under him, you know,' he insisted looking at Lara, 'It is more of working together - a partnership.' he added earnestly.

Matías looked at him with his head tilted slightly to one side, as though considering his merits. 'Yes, he has made some bold changes to the way we operate, but they have been profitable, I must agree.'

Alexis seemed pleased with this. He raised his glass to his brother with a smile, the same way Matías had done with him earlier.

Just then the roar of the engine shuddering to life vibrated through everything in the room, before there was a definite sense of movement as the boat started to move.

'Off we go then!' Lizzy said excitedly, raising her glass to initiate a toast.

Everyone else joined her and clinked their glasses together.

The small talk continued for several hours as they sailed further and further from the bay of Tauranga.

Although she felt much better than earlier, Lara was still nervous. Her hands were slightly clammy as she gripped her glass. She nursed the drink, only taking half sips occasionally, so as to not be offered a second refill.

Lizzy on the other hand didn't seem to be thinking this way at all. She was just being poured her third drink, and she was merrily chatting away with Matías seemingly without a care in the world.

After the first few minutes of awkward conversation, Lara realised that Alexis wasn't that difficult to talk to. What puzzled her the most was how different his level of English was compared to his brother's. Lara presumed this was all down to the fact they were only half-siblings, probably having each had a different upbringing.

They'd spoken briefly about his interests and Lara's and Lizzy's travels so far. He'd also talked about their destination, since he had been there once before. According to Alexis they should arrive at the islands in around three days time, with the crew taking care of the sailing day and night.

Matías drained his glass and set it down on the low table in between the two sofas.

Lizzy did the same.

'Hey Alexis,' he said to his brother, 'Why don't we give the ladies a tour of our boat?'

'Ooh that'd be great,' Lizzy said enthusiastically. She looked a little more flushed in the cheeks than usual.

'Sure,' Lara said.

Matías took Lizzy's hand and stood up, guiding her out of the glass doors and out onto the deck. Alexis followed suit and took Lara's hand in his, following his brother.

This did nothing to dispel her nerves. She hoped he wouldn't notice how her hands had broken out in a cold sweat, despite the warmish evening air. They walked to the front of the boat and up the narrow white staircase up into the cabin where the crew were sitting in the padded cream-leather seats.

They looked up from the controls as the group walked in through the door.

Matías did some brief introductions and explained how the boat basically sailed. He seemed to know how to sail, even though he had a full crew taking care of everything for him.

Lara presumed this was because he had owned another yacht at some point. She looked out of the windows above all of the screens and controls at the captain's view; it was nothing but dark ocean. The horizon wasn't visible through the window that was faintly reflecting the view of the cabin.

They moved on quickly from this area, returning to the lounge and this time being briefly shown the small dining room before they descended the stairs onto the lower deck.

The kitchen was down here, along with a larger outdoor dining area.

They moved along the wide, carpeted hall, both couples still hand-in-hand.

'And here we come to the bedrooms. This is mine,' Matías stopped in front of a door and opened it, standing back so that everyone could see inside. It was a large room with a king size bed inside. As with all of the other places in the yacht, this room was lit with downlights.

'Not too shabby Matías,' Lizzy said playfully, pulling him by the hand over the threshold.

Lara and Alexis stayed in the doorway.

'Let's call it a night shall we?' Lizzy added, giggling.

Matías tried, and failed, to suppress his smirk as he turned to the two outside the door. 'I believe this is where I bid you two good night.' he said with a curt nod as he shut the door behind him, leaving Lara and Alexis alone in the hallway.

Alexis turned to Lara, 'Come,' he said, 'I will show you my room.' He pulled her gently by the hand to the next room along, causing a fresh wave of butterflies to rise in her stomach.

Once inside, he released his gentle grip on her hand and shut the door behind him.

This room didn't look that much different to the one next-door. It was a spacious room with a door leading to an en-suite bathroom in the corner, a sofa much like those on the deck above and just as with the room next door, the main focus of the room was the king size bed.

'Do you like it?' Alexis asked.

'Like what?' Lara asked, unable to think what he meant.

Alexis gave a half-laugh, 'My room,' he said smiling, waiting for the comprehension to sink in.

'Oh, right. Um, yes it's lovely - very modern.' Lara replied smiling too, the heat rising slightly in her face.

Her mild embarrassment quickly turned to plain nervousness again as she realised that Alexis was moving towards her now, closing the already-small gap between them, a more serious look on his face.

His hands cupped her face as he leaned in to kiss her.

Lara automatically froze as he did so, causing him to pull back with a questioning look on his face.

'Lara, relax OK?' he said with a small smile, brushing her cheeks with his thumbs.

'Sure, I'm fine,' she said, noticing again her voice didn't sound like it usually did.

He leaned in again, brushing his lips against hers.

This time it was Lara who pulled back.

A look of confusion spread across Alexis's

attractive features. 'What is it?' he asked, 'Are you feeling uncomfortable?'

'I'm sorry,' Lara said, 'This is just happening a little too fast. I mean, I only just met you a few hours ago.'

Alexis sat down on the end of the bed and nodded.

He didn't say anything, so Lara quickly went on, 'I don't usually do this sort of thing. It was Lizzy that got me to buy this dress. I wouldn't usually wear this sort of thing.' It seemed important to tell Alexis this, so that he didn't get the wrong idea about her. *As if he hadn't already*, Lara thought darkly to herself.

'I understand,' he said.

Lara was slightly relieved to see that he wasn't angry, on the contrary, he seemed to look slightly relieved himself.

'I am not doing this much either. I am not bringing all women back to my room all of the time.' he said, leaning back on his hands and giving a small laugh.

He took her by the hand again and guided her into a sitting position next to him on the end of the bed. 'If you like, we will wait. We can get to know each other first if it's what you want?'

'OK then,'

'Maybe you will feel differently when we get to the islands,' he went on, putting his arm around her and kissing her on the cheek.

'Are you OK sleeping in here tonight?' he asked,

'It is just our crew are using all up all the other rooms.'

'Yes, sure, that'll be fine.' she said giving him a reassuring smile.

Lara got changed into a white t-shirt for sleeping in the en-suite bathroom before she returned, slipping into the bed next to Alexis who was already under the covers having changed into a slim-fitting black t-shirt. He had switched off the overhead lights and now only a lamp on his bedside table lit the room.

The clock on the other tiny bedside table told Lara it was already the early hours of the morning, making her realise all of a sudden how tired she was. It was a good thing that she was so exhausted, since she knew it would have been far more difficult to get to sleep in this strange place with an almost complete stranger.

The motion of the boat and the distant noise of the powerful engine was far more obvious now that she was lying down, but instead of keeping her awake Lara found it helped relax her.

Alexis reached for the lamp switch on his side of the bed, he paused with his hand on it for a moment and leaned over to Lara to whisper in her ear, 'Lara, I have to tell you - you do wear your dress very nicely.'

He kissed her again on the cheek before clicking off the light.

It had taken Lara a moment before she

remembered where she was when she woke up the next morning. She had awoken in exactly the same position she had fallen asleep in to find Alexis's arm around her.

Alexis had waited in the bedroom whilst Lara got washed and dressed in the bathroom.

They had gone together to the outside dining area further along their deck for breakfast, where they found Lizzy and Matías already seated at the table so busily engaged in a kiss they hadn't noticed the new arrivals for a moment. They had all had breakfast together at the sunny table, the fresh ocean air cooling them as they ate.

The rest of the day passed in much the same way. The boat was constantly moving day and night, powered by the crew and never stopped. There wasn't all that much to do to pass the time of the journey other than sit around in various parts of the yacht talking and in everyone's case except for Lara's, drinking.

Lara was trying to avoid alcohol, mindful that she wanted to have her judgement intact, even if Lizzy had told her it was holding her back.

At some point in the afternoon, the four of them went up to the control cabin for Matías to show them how the boat sailed. He even let Lizzy have a go at steering for a few minutes.

The crew kept to themselves and didn't say much. Lara assumed they didn't have much of a grasp of English.

While their hosts were friendly and welcoming,

Lara couldn't help but feel a little awkward. It didn't help that Lizzy and Matías were all over each other at every available opportunity.

Lara had to admit she felt ever-so-slightly betrayed by her friend. She knew that Lizzy was trying to make their holiday ever so much more memorable with a trip to the Cook Islands, but now this had led to Lara staying in close quarters with Alexis.

Lara couldn't deny she had initially felt slightly attracted to him when they had first met, but if she was honest she felt it was still far too soon to enter into any kind of relationship with another man, no matter how brief it may be. For this reason Lara felt she would be glad when they reached their destination.

It was just after midnight when both couples agreed it was time to retire to their cabins for the night.

Just as with the night before, Lara got changed in the bathroom before getting into the bed next to Alexis who was already under the covers. Lara had run out of clean t-shirts for sleeping in, so Alexis had given her one of his. She felt a little reluctant, but he had politely insisted. It was a long sleeved white shirt, that fitted her rather well due to his slim build.

And just as with the night before he leaned over to her before switching off the bedside lamp. This time however he leaned in to kiss her on the lips. His kiss was gentle, as though he was testing the waters.

Lara felt herself tense up slightly. Alexis seemed to feel this too, he pulled away. 'It's all right,' he said, 'We will wait,' he said with a reassuring smile before clicking off the light.

6
Cabin Fever

Lara woke up with a start the next morning. She looked around briefly wondering what had woken her. She thought she had heard a loud crash nearby. She turned her head to the side and realised that Alexis wasn't there.

She put a hand on the bed where he had been. Feeling that it was still warm, she decided that he couldn't have long left the bed.

She then realised that the boat wasn't moving. They had stopped. Surely they couldn't be at the Cook islands yet? Alexis had told her they shouldn't be there for at least another day...

Before she had the chance to think anything else, Lizzy burst into the room with a look of utter panic on her face.

'Lara! You - you need to get up!' she said in a terrified voice.

Her anxious tone cut through Lara's drowsy state immediately. She suddenly felt wide awake. 'What's the matter?' she said, throwing back the covers and running to her friend.

'It's M-Matías. He's got a gun - they both have!' she shrieked.

'What?!' Lara said as a jolt of fear pierced her. 'What do they have guns for? Have they hurt you?'

'No! They went up to go and meet the people on the other boat!' Lizzy said, hopping from one foot to the other and stepping back every few seconds to peer out of the cabin door and down the hall.

Lara was confused, 'What other boat?'

'The other boat!' Lizzy implored, gesturing frantically with her hands as though Lara should already know what she was talking about. 'Another boat has turned up. One of the crew came and told Matías that they came aboard and want to talk to him. He told me to wait down here…' She stepped all the way out into the hallway this time and looked down it, before looking at Lara again. 'When I asked him what was going on, he said it's a "business thing" - that he'll deal with it and I should wait here. He took a gun out the draw and got Alexis up to go with him.

'I thought I heard a gunshot just now. I don't know what to do - he told me to wait here, while he and Alexis went and dealt with the people. That's the thing - he used the phrase "deal with" - what does that mean?!'

'Don't panic,' Lara told her, holding her by the shoulders to try and calm her down, or at least keep her still for a second whilst she thought of what to do.

'It would be easier to figure out what was going on if we knew what kind of business they were in.' Lara said, 'But you said we shouldn't ask.' she added, a little more bitterly than she had intended.

Lizzy froze. '*I think they might be drug*

couriers,' she said in a half-whisper.

Lara didn't want to hear that answer, but she believed it straight away; it fitted in with everything she had found out about the brothers and their lifestyle.

They'd been careful to keep the talk about their business limited, but that in itself only added to the possibility of Lizzy's claim being true.

'Lara I'm sorry - you were right! We should never have gone with them. Now what are we going to do?' Lizzy's lip trembled slightly. It was unusual to see her so shaken; it unnerved Lara to see her like this. She had obviously gotten dressed in a hurry; she had only buttoned her shirt up halfway over her tank top and her feet were still bare.

Lara looked down at what she was wearing, she was still in Alexis's white shirt. 'OK,' she said with surprising authority. 'We can't do anything like this. We should get dressed and then...and then go up onto the main deck and see what is ha-'

Lara was interrupted mid-sentence by what was unmistakably a gunshot coming from somewhere above them.

'Oh my god…' Lizzy said in a tiny voice. Her frightened wide eyes shined with tears now. She suddenly darted into the hallway, Lara quickly jumped forward and grabbed her by the elbow.

'What are you doing?' Lara asked her urgently pulling Lizzy back as she struggled towards the stairs at the end of the hallway. She had the feeling they shouldn't go anywhere near the top deck right now.

'We have to see what's going on! We can't just stay down here…'

Lara bit her lip; she had no idea what they should do. The situation sounded as though it had gotten dangerous upstairs. Maybe they should just wait here for a while…

Before she could do anything else however she was suddenly aware of footsteps descending the stairs just a few feet from them.

Lara and Lizzy both froze.

Lara still had hold of Lizzy's arm in her attempt to pull her back. They waited for the footsteps to transform into a person, and hopefully one they recognised.

No such luck.

A heavily-built man dressed all in black stepped off the spiral staircase and into the hallway. His hair was pulled into a ponytail, every bit of skin that was visible was covered in tattoos and he had a definite air of danger about him.

Lara briefly took in his hard appearance before her eyes were drawn to his right hand, noticing that a silver gun hung loosely in his grip. The filigree pattern along the barrel glinted in a sinister way in the light.

The man allowed himself a leering grin at finding two women in front of him, one of whom was very obviously only half dressed.

Just then the sound of the engine roaring into

life shuddered through the hallway.

Both Lara and Lizzy and the menacing man paused for a moment, looking at each other as if wondering what to do next.

There was a moment where they all stood motionless and no one spoke.

Then all of a sudden Lizzy grabbed Lara by the wrist and started to run down the hall for a cabin at the end. They had hardly ventured two steps however, when the man caught up with them in a few heavy strides, shouting at them in his own language.

He grabbed Lara painfully by the hair causing her to cry out in pain and forcing the pair to come to a sudden stop. His other hand thrust the gun into Lizzy's neck.

Lizzy screamed and started pleading with him not to hurt them.

He ignored them. Lara couldn't tell if he understood English or not. She was vaguely aware that the boat was now moving again and was sailing at some speed.

The man started directing the two women down the hallway back towards the stairs, still pulling Lara by the hair and steering Lizzy at gunpoint.

Again, they had only gone a few steps before chaos reigned. The boat gave an erratic jolt that split the trio apart.

Lara was slammed into the wall and the man lost his grip on her as the force threw him through the open door of the cabin behind her. Lara looked around. Lizzy had been thrust against the doorway of the cabin and was regaining her balance and backing away from the man on the cabin floor who was trying to scramble to his feet.

'Quick!' Lara shouted at her, throwing herself into a run at the staircase. She took the stairs two at a time, tripping on the second-to-top-step and had to frantically push herself up from the thick-carpeted floor of the lounge with her hands.

She sprinted through the sliding glass door and onto the deck; it looked deserted.

She had no idea what she planned now that they were out here. She guessed the rest of the men were in the control room with Matías and Alexis. Lara turned around to convey this to Lizzy, suddenly realising that Lizzy wasn't there.

Lara felt her stomach drop - she thought Lizzy had been right behind her. Where had she gone?

She looked back through the glass lounge door.

There was no sign of either Lizzy or the man.

Lara hovered in the doorway, unsure of what to do. The man was obviously in pursuit of Lizzy and that was why he hadn't followed Lara up here.

She wanted to go back down to the lower deck to her friends aid, but had no idea how to fight an armed man that was easily twice her size.

She wondered what the situation was in the control room. Had the two brothers managed to overcome the newcomers yet? Or had the gunshots come from the opposing side?

Lara bent low and ran across the deck to see if

she could get a better view of what was going on inside.

Now that she was closer she could hear men's voices shouting in their language over the sound of the engine and the breaking water the yacht was crashing through. She recognised one of the voices to be Matías's

From this new viewpoint she could now see another boat in front, leading the way and bouncing off the waves as it went; it was slightly larger and had a much more unfriendly look to it, although Lara couldn't specifically say why.

Lara's heart was thundering in her ears and adrenaline was pumping through her veins as she remained crouched, wondering what she was going to do next. They were in the middle of the ocean with no way of getting back to land without the boat. But the boat seemed to be under the control of armed men.

Lara had no idea how many there were, but Matías and Alexis didn't seem to be in charge any more.

Lara assumed that the new men must be some kind of rival or competitor.

Matías's words about how Alexis had made some changes to the way he did business now rang in her ears. Whatever changes they had made had affected the status-quo as well as the cost of doing business, and now they were all paying the price...

Lara suddenly became aware again that all she was wearing was Alexis's white shirt with just her underwear underneath, leaving her legs bare. She was glad she had decided to keep her bra on to sleep in, but she still felt ridiculously exposed and vulnerable.

The sun was shining fully bright, making the deck eye-wateringly brilliant white, but a fresh sea wind blew through the railings on the top deck of the boat making Lara shiver.

Suddenly a muffled scream coming from the lower deck broke her from any indecision. She forgot all about staying hidden and ran as fast as she could back into the lounge and down the spiral staircase. Her heels thudded hard on the wooden steps as she thundered down them.

As soon as she reached the bottom, she was met with the sight of Lizzy being dragged by the hair towards her.

The man gestured with the gun for Lara to go back up the stairs. He didn't say a word in either his own language or theirs, but his actions were clear communication enough.

Lara gripped the gold, metal handrail as she ascended the stairs. Her hand was slippery with cold sweat. She could hear Lizzy whimpering behind her. She had no idea what was going to happen to them now. She wondered if she should try and communicate with the man somehow.

Maybe if she could get the message across to him that they had only just met the two brothers, then they would let them go. Even as she thought it, she knew that wasn't going to happen, so she followed the man's directions in silence as he gestured for her to go out onto the deck through the open glass door.

As she stepped out onto the deck with the man with Lizzy drawing level with her, two more men she didn't recognise were coming down the steps from the control room. They said something in their language to the man holding Lizzy.

Without question, he dragged Lizzy forward into the middle of the deck and threw her roughly to the floor. She landed with a thud at his feet before he drew back, raising his gun as he did so.

Lara knew what he was about to do before he did it but had no time to react.

He pulled the trigger. A single shot rang out, seeming deafening, even over the sound of the engine and the ocean.

Lizzy slumped motionless on the floor, and Lara knew she was dead.

Lara had a rushing noise in her ears that she knew had nothing to do with the wind or the crashing waves the boat was skipping over. Each breath she took was shallow and rapid and tears were blurring her vision.

As she blinked them away, the image that was now in front of her seemed to appear in slow motion.

The gunman was stepping over Lizzy and walking towards Lara, raising the gun again.

A rush of panic filled her and breathing seemed so difficult she felt like she was going to suffocate.

She was vaguely aware that she was backing away, her feet stumbling slightly on the cold, white deck.

The man was going to shoot her just like he had just shot Lizzy. Lizzy was her best friend. She was gone. They were on holiday together. They had gotten on a yacht with two men they hardly knew.

Lara's brain was frantically trying to put it all together and form a solution, but there was none to be had.

This was the end. They should never have gotten on the boat.

Lara only remembered that she was still backing away when her back collided painfully with the metal railing of the corner of the boat. The hard metal felt like it had bruised her spine.

The man was just a few feet from her now and had almost raised the gun to shooting height. Just like with Lizzy, he was aiming for a head shot.

A sudden rush of adrenaline surged through Lara, and she felt so outside herself that it was as though she simply watched as she spun around. Her arms lifted her as she vaulted over the rail she had just collided with, sending her dropping into the water below.

Confused images of dark blue and streams of bubbles met her now that she frantically fought her way to the surface.

The unexpected chill of the water made her gasp for air. She drew laboured breaths as she struggled to keep her head above the rough surface.

Lara looked in the direction of the two boats as they skipped over the waves, leaving a fan-shaped trail of white water behind them. She thought she saw one of the men's silhouettes give her a mock wave as the boat she had left rapidly became smaller as it sailed on into the blazing sunshine, leaving Lara alone in the water.

7
Alone

Lara struggled to keep her head above the water that was swirling and crashing around it. She tried desperately to remember her few childhood swimming lessons that had briefly taught her how to tread water. She had never imagined that she would ever have to use the knowledge in a real-life situation, and certainly not one like this. It was decidedly much more difficult as an adult.

She felt heavier, and found herself having to take panicked breaths in between waves of water rushing above her ears and stinging her eyes.

Lara was starting to regret having jumped. Although it wasn't as if she had been given any choice. In reality she had only had two choices: jump, or be murdered in cold blood. That wasn't a choice at all.

She couldn't believe Lizzy was gone. A numb sense of disbelief settled high in Lara's chest and clouded her brain, denying the reality of her friend's fate to sink in.

Lara looked around her, twisting her neck in every direction, still frantically trying to stay afloat. Since the boat had sailed off, there was nothing but endless ocean in every direction. The sun was bright and high in the sky. Lara could feel its warmth on her face contrasting to the rest of her body which was being cooled by the deep, blue water.

She accidentally breathed in a mouthful of salty water, causing her to cough and splutter.

Lara decided there must be another way to stay buoyant, she leaned backwards, trying to manoeuvre herself into a floating position.

This was better she thought, as she now faced the bright-blue, cloudless sky. Her ears were submerged and the water lapped around her face as she floated on her back, but she was more stable in this position and it took a lot less effort to stay in it. She even thought it felt slightly warmer.

Lara lay in her new position, the sound of the bubbles and the waves in her ears as she thought hopelessly about her options. She had no idea where she was, only that she must be somewhere on the route to the Cook Islands. There wasn't any sign of land in any direction.

The only people who knew she was anywhere in this region were on the boat that had sailed away without her and that was getting further away with every passing second.

She had no idea what had happened to Alexis and Matías. Had they managed to reason with the other men on the boat? Was it possible they could yet overpower them and regain control of the yacht? Or had they simply been shot too? Somehow Lara thought the latter was the most likely outcome, and that wasn't going to help her now.

She continued to float on her back, staring up at

the sky; Alexis's white shirt billowed soaking wet and translucent around her. As she mulled everything over, the one hopeless thought that drifted to the forefront of her mind above all the others was that *no one was going to come looking for her.*

Lara shivered as the weight of this thought caused a cold, uncomfortable feeling to steel itself in her chest.

Lara and Lizzy had been travelling to a casual plan they had made together, and they had told no one that they were about to set off on a spur-of-the-moment cruise with two men they had only just met in a bar.

Lara felt an overwhelming surge of anger and regret at how stupid this decision had turned out to be. And she had known it was a bad idea in the bar. Why hadn't she listened to her instincts? She could have - *no* - she *should* have been more adamant that they weren't going to get on a boat with Alexis and Matías, no matter how alluring the opportunity may have seemed.

Lara's eyes stung with hot tears that ran sideways down her cool cheeks and into the water surrounding her.

Her only hope now was if another boat came sailing by and noticed her. Surely other boats would sail through these waters? Other boats with legitimate passengers simply enjoying a cruise in the South Pacific would surely journey past here soon.

Lara decided she would just have to bide her time until then. She could conserve energy whilst she waited by floating on her back. It had been working rather well so far. And even though her ears were underwater, she would definitely hear a boat if it got anywhere near her. Yes, that's what she was going to do. It was the most logical thing to do, and it must surely just be a matter of time before rescue came...

Lara shivered again. She had no idea how long she had been in the water, but it felt like hours. In that time, the sun had travelled across the sky from one side to another. Despite the fact that the same bright sun was blazing above her, Lara was starting to feel cold. The deep water that surrounded her in every direction was draining heat from her body rapidly, and she was shivering more frequently now.

The harsh reality that there would be no hope of rescue in the form of a passing boat sank into Lara's consciousness like a stone. She felt overwhelmingly annoyed with herself that she had even had such a thought. It had been more than wishful thinking. Lara thought that she had been hoping for a miracle.

This is it, she thought. *I'm going to drown... I'm going to drown and nobody will even know what happened to me*, she thought hopelessly.

She thought of how it would seem to her mother and father when she didn't return to England with

Lizzy in less than two weeks time. They would presume that she had simply gone missing in New Zealand somewhere. They would never dream that she had gotten on a yacht with several drug couriers and jumped ship halfway to another part of the world.

Lara thought of how upset her parents would be and wished with a pang of sincere regret that they wouldn't have to go through that heartache they had yet to experience at guessing what their daughter's fate had been.

Then she thought of Alan. He would probably hear the news too, most likely from Lara's mother since they seem to be on such close terms. A vague image of the two of them and the telephone conversation they would have on the matter formed in front of Lara's eyes as she stared up at the blank, blue sky above her.

Her mother was crying and trying to get her words out in between sobs as she dabbed her eyes with a tissue. Alan was sitting on his brown-leather sofa, his mobile phone pressed to his ear as he stared dumbly at the television, trying to think of what to say to console his ex-girlfriend's mother about the demise of the very woman who had left him alone in England, while she went off an impromptu adventure without him.

Lara thought he wouldn't be upset. The thing that was bothering him most in her vision was the fact he had to deal with a hysterical, crying woman over the phone. He had never been good in those sorts of situations.

Lara found herself hoping that he wouldn't just hang up on her mother when she called to tell him the news. She felt a stab of anger for the extra pain that the imaginary-Alan may potentially cause her mother.

Lara really did hate him. Not only had he stolen five of what should have been the best years of her life, he had also been responsible for her impulsive decision to take the trip with Lizzy in the first place.

In fact now that she thought about it, this was all his fault - Lizzy's death, and the awful situation Lara was in now.

Some nagging voice in the back of her mind told Lara that she was being slightly unreasonable blaming Alan for everything, but it felt good to blame him and she couldn't admit that any of this had happened because of any bad decisions on her part.

A hot burning hatred like she had never known before started to seep through Lara's veins. For a moment it took her mind off how cold she was. She thought of everything Alan had ever done wrong, everything that had ever irritated her about him. To top it all off, he was also going to be responsible for her being lost at sea.

Lara started to shake with what she thought was rage, then she realised that she was actually shivering uncontrollably. The cold from the deep, vast ocean around her had been slowly penetrating her muscles from every angle and there was no escape from it.

No, said a determined voice in her head. *Not like this. Not because of him...*

There was only one thing Lara could think of to combat her dropping temperature, and that was to start swimming.

She moved back into her treading-water position, this time doing a slightly better job of keeping her head above the waves and looked around her.

Using the sun as a guide she tried to determine which way the boat had sailed on to. The best idea she had was to start swimming in the direction of the boat and hope that she ended up finding land, or at least some kind of rescue.

Lara couldn't be sure if the boat had altered course during the takeover, but if it hadn't then that meant it was still heading in the direction of the Cook Islands. Alexis had told her that they should arrive today, so they probably hadn't been that far away at all.

Lara weighed up this plan. How far would she be able to swim? She had been a pretty strong swimmer as a child...

Even if she didn't make it to the islands themselves, she should at least be able to get near enough that she could have a better chance of being saved by smaller boats on day trips perhaps?

Since it was either this, or wait here and freeze to death waiting for an unlikely passer-by to spot her, Lara decided to take her chances and start moving.

She launched herself forward into the waves. Lara gratefully noticed that they seemed slightly calmer than they were earlier, helping her to make her progress through the water.

Swimming seemed so much harder than she remembered from when she was younger. She found her basic overarm technique was the most familiar, and it seemed to be propelling her at quite a pace.

Lara felt tiny in the huge mass of water around her, and it suddenly occurred to her that since there were no landmarks on the horizon, there was no way of knowing how much headway she was making. It didn't matter however, she just felt so much better that she was actively doing something positive.

After around twenty minutes of solid swimming, Lara reluctantly decided to stop momentarily and float on her back get her breath back. She had hoped that she would have been able to keep going for longer, but exhaustion and breathlessness had forced her to take a break.

She inwardly cursed herself for having such a sedentary job back home and never making any effort to take any exercise. The last couple of weeks of outdoor exploration had probably increased her fitness level slightly, but it hadn't made years of living such a desk-bound lifestyle disappear.

After just a few minutes, she set off again. She hadn't completely recovered, but determination was spurring her on, she didn't want to be out here any longer than she had to be. Not only this, but Lara also had the feeling that she was drifting when she was at a standstill.

Again, she stopped after a period of swimming, gasping for air. Salty water splashed into her mouth. This time she had tried to swim faster and she didn't stop for a rest until she was satisfied it had definitely been a longer session than the last one.

She set off again.

Lara continued this pattern of swimming and resting for what felt like hours. She felt like this was the workout of her life.

She briefly glanced around at the sun's position during one of the breaks. It had moved slightly further west, giving her an indication of how much time had passed.

It was truly exhausting. What was perhaps the hardest part of all of this was that there was no fixed goal in sight. Lara could only hope that she was swimming in the right direction, and that the boat was sailing in it too.

She floated on her back again. This time she had only managed around ten minutes before she had conceded defeat.

She lay on her back with her eyes shut, expanding her chest to its fullest as she tried to draw in air. She wasn't shivering so much any more, but she still felt quite numb around the edges, in her fingers and her toes.

She was thirsty and felt completely drained of energy, and found herself wishing that she could have woken earlier and had breakfast before the yacht was commandeered.

Lara could see the sun blazing through her eyelids. She kept them shut. After a minute of this however she suddenly opened them when a shadow moved across her face; for a second it had blocked the sun.

She immediately saw what had made the shadow; it was just a sea bird gliding low over the water. Nothing at all to do with a rescue boat.

Lara continued floating on her back and watched the bird glumly. It seemed to be hunting for fish. It had an air of preparing to dive any second; hardly a moment after Lara had this thought, did the bird suddenly fold its wings into its body and launch itself beneath the waves, which now that she observed them, seemed slightly calmer than earlier.

Perhaps a passing storm had caused the more violent waves she saw earlier, she thought.

All thoughts of ocean weather suddenly evaporated from Lara's mind as her attention was drawn to the space above where the bird had disappeared from.

There was land.

It looked distant and small, but there was no mistaking it was definitely there.

Lara's heart gave a jolt and a sudden surge of

wild excitement flooded through her. She wondered how long it had been visible for and mentally kicked herself for not noticing it sooner.

She smoothly revolved back into her swimming position and immediately set off in the direction of this new image of hope.

She was splashing a little more than she had done earlier in her frantic hurry to approach her new destination, but she didn't care. Her exhausted limbs burned and ached as she forced them to move her as quickly as possible.

Lara was determined to get there in one burst, but she was forced to stop when she simply couldn't choke in enough air to continue.

Her arms and legs were aching and felt like rubber. She took in deep breaths, determined to recover as fast as possible, her eyes firmly fixed upon her goal. She felt like if she lost sight of the land then it might simply disappear.

A nagging doubt in the back of her mind made her think that it could be some kind of cruel illusion. Although she felt in her heart that it wasn't, she never let it out of her sight just in case, forcing herself to believe it was real.

Lara set off again, too impatient to wait for her breathing to return back to normal.

The land was becoming larger as she pushed on forward; she could tell now that it was definitely real. Lara could just about make out sand with trees above it; it was an island.

She thought this must be one of the Cook

Islands. Although thinking it was slightly odd that there wasn't any sign of any other islands anywhere nearby, she pressed on anyway, deciding that they must be more spread out than she had imagined when Alexis had described them.

A sudden attack of cramp in her left leg forced Lara to a stop in the water.

Frustrated, she frantically tried to shake it off before deciding that she should probably take another break and tread water for a few minutes. She avoided floating on her back for fear of drifting further away.

She scrutinised the distance between her and the land now as more gentle waves broke around her neck. She could probably make it in one last push...

Her breathing had almost returned to normal now. She was just bracing herself to set off again, when she felt something brush against her bare thigh.

Lara froze, horrified. Her heart was pounding in fear now rather than exertion. Whatever it was it was rough, almost like sandpaper.

She glanced around her body through the blue water, but couldn't see anything. She thought it must perhaps have been a fish, but it didn't matter now because there was no sign of it.

Lara looked back up towards the land again, worried that the current was causing her to drift further away without her realising it. She was exhausted from having struggled to keep her head above the water for so long and was anxious to reach her destination without being dragged further away by the tide.

Lara tried to push the mysterious underwater object out of her mind as she found the energy to launch herself forward for one final burst of effort.

She was still slightly breathless from the last session and her aching muscles were screaming for her to stop and rest for longer but she pushed on, driven by sheer determination and desperation. She was cold, tired, hungry and thirsty and needed more than anything to rest.

The island was much closer now. It spread out in front of her as she swam ever closer.

Lara could now make out a mass of dark green palm trees above a stretch of bright, white sand. To her right, a span of dark rocks jutted out into the ocean towards her. She was tempted to swim in their direction and get out of the water more quickly, but even in her fatigued state, her logic told her that the waves were breaking against it a little too vigorously than she thought was safe.

Instead, Lara swam, panting and struggling to make each forced stroke.

As the water became clearer and calmer, it also became warmer.

Lara's cold body noticed and welcomed this change in temperature immediately.

Lara could see her arms making each movement in front of her much more clearly now. They looked a little more pale than she had expected and they were starting to tingle painfully, as though a little circulation was returning to them.

Lara was overjoyed when she could see that she was just a hundred yards away from the beach.

Her legs took her weight and her feet sank into the soft, gritty sand of the warm, shallow water.

As she waded up onto the beach she began to feel extremely heavy, as though gravity was stronger than normal. Alexis's white shirt clung to her.

Once she was definitely clear of the sea Lara allowed herself to drop into the hot, dry sand of the island beach.

She turned her head to the side and lay there with her eyes shut, completely exhausted. She felt relieved as the rough grains of sand rubbed against her cheek as she tried to get her breathing back to normal.

Exhaustion took over her and she couldn't move. She just lay fixed in the same position, still shivering and conserving energy and attempting to recover.

She grasped handfuls of sand, as though proving to herself that she had made it - she was finally out of the water.

Water. Lara was incredibly thirsty. She hadn't had anything to drink since last night. Her throbbing thirst made the nagging hunger in her stomach pale into comparison.

She wondered where the hotel was on this island. From her initial impression of it, it only seemed big enough to accommodate just the one hotel. The only problem was she couldn't get up to go and find it. She couldn't remember ever being so tired and weak.

Lara wondered if any of the hotel guests or tourists would come across her on the beach soon. Perhaps a honeymooning couple out for a romantic hand-in-hand stroll before dinner would see her slumped in the sand and rush to her aid? Or perhaps it would be a billionaire tycoon?

How long would it be before anyone came? The beach had looked perfectly pleasant and attractive enough to warrant frequent visits from holidaymakers, but what if she wasn't found until the next day?

Lara tried to get herself together and command her body to carry her over one last hurdle to find some help. After all, the island wasn't that huge so she wouldn't have to walk that far. Maybe half an hour maximum?

It was no good, she had already used every last ounce of energy her body possessed in fighting against the relentless waves just to get here. Now her body seemed to have given up taking orders from her brain and insisted that she just rested.

The warm sand was so comforting after being in the cold ocean for so long. Lara was more than willing to give in to her tiredness and sink further into the sand for a while longer.

She was starting to feel drowsy and images of the last twelve hours flashed in front of her eyes, before her mind started to clear of all thoughts as she felt herself drifting off to sleep.

Lara had no idea how long she lay there for before a sudden shout cut through her drowsy state.

She opened her eyes and stared ahead. With her cheek still pressed against the ground, all she could see was white sand immediately in front of her and then beyond that was a stretch of deserted beach.

That was odd, for a second she thought she had heard someone shout something. Perhaps she was just imagining it, all she could hear now was the sound of the gentle waves behind her.

She heard it again. This time it was slightly louder and seemed somehow nearer. The beach however was still deserted.

Lara's confused brain couldn't work it out. She felt slightly annoyed that she had been pulled back from the slumber she had almost slipped into.

Her eyes closed and she immediately started drifting back into sleep, still shivering against the sand.

She heard the shout again, this time much closer but still couldn't figure out what it was saying. Maybe it was a foreign language...Why wasn't it letting her sleep, when that was what she needed to do the most?

All of a sudden, she felt, rather than heard rapid, heavy footsteps pounding against the earth underneath her ear.

A warm hand brushed the wet hair back from

her face, the other felt clumsily on her neck for a pulse.

Lara didn't have the energy to lift her eyelids, so her eyes stayed shut.

She felt paralysed, but wanted to communicate that she was alive. She realised that her freezing cold skin and motionless state looked like she was dead. She didn't want to be left here.

Lara forced the command down to her fingers to move. They managed to grip the gritty sand slightly. She couldn't see her potential rescuer to tell if he had seen this cry for help, but her question was answered almost immediately when he shouted again.

'JACE!' the man yelled behind him.

No sooner than he had shouted, a second pair of thundering footsteps sprinted up to join them.

'Go get some water!' the first man shouted again. 'Hurry!' the man yelled after the retreating footsteps.

Lara had no sense of time as she lay slumped on the ground, feeling the warmth from the stranger's hands on her back and her arm. It seemed like only a second or two passed before she heard the other man approaching again.

The strong, warm hands pulled her gently into a sitting position and she was able to open her eyes briefly to see a large wooden cup of water being guided to her mouth. Lara gulped the whole lot down without pausing. She had never been so thirsty

Then, as if she had used her absolute last reserves of energy, Lara felt herself slipping off into blackness still in the stranger's arms.

This time his alarmed voice couldn't snap her back to consciousness.

8
Arrival

Lara instantly became aware that every muscle in her body was aching. She felt warm now, unlike how she remembered she had been before…For some reason she had felt cold, but couldn't remember exactly why. She couldn't feel the motion of the yacht any more…That was odd, she thought.

She opened her bleary eyes and stared at the ceiling with a slight frown on her face.

The ceiling looked odd too…It appeared to be made up of large, cylindrical, bamboo-like sticks.

Lara's confused brain struggled to comprehend this. She wondered where on the boat could have a ceiling like the one now above her. And now she came to think of it, why did the ocean sound so nearby? Every room on the yacht was very well soundproofed against the conditions outside. So why could Lara hear waves rolling and crashing so close at hand?

She turned her head and looked around the small room she now found herself in. Now that she looked at it, she realised that the whole thing was made up of the sticks; they formed the walls and floor, as well as the ceiling.

This didn't help provide her with any clues as to where she was, or what had happened. It only caused more questions to form in her mind.

How long had she been asleep for? And where was Alexis?

Something tugged in Lara's memory. Alexis had left with Matías...Matías had a gun...They had gone up to the top deck - her brain struggled to retrieve the information - because there were people...people from another boat...Lizzy had been shot in front of her...

Suddenly everything came rushing back to Lara. Images flashed rapidly in front of her eyes as the full horror of yesterday flooded back to her in a split second. She saw Lizzy looking frantic, them both being chased down the hallway, Lara being dragged by the hair, Lizzy being thrown to the floor, Lizzy being shot, relentless waves almost drowning her, endless ocean before spotting land in the distance.

Lara strained to search for more memories beyond that and couldn't recall anything further than swimming as fast as she could, desperately forcing her muscles and gasping for air as she drew closer to the island.

Lara supposed that must be where she was now. She looked around the room again. It looked very simple; it didn't look like something a typical tourist would choose to stay in. It looked decidedly hand-made. The bed she was lying on seemed to be part of a flat, bench-like seat that lined three of the walls and was made up of the sticks too.

There were objects underneath the bench on the longest wall, jars and pots containing little bits and pieces Lara couldn't quite make out. The fourth wall was completely bare apart from a small rectangular opening without a door, through which bright light was shining.

Lara suddenly spotted Alexis's white shirt folded neatly on the adjoining bench near her feet. She looked down and realised for the first time that she was only wearing her underwear underneath the heavy layers of blankets that she was nestled in.

She felt a slight pang of embarrassment that someone must have removed her wet clothing at some point without her realising it. It was only short-lived however as she caught sight of the topmost blanket covering her; it had a definite raggedy look to it and was rough looking in patches. Around the edges loose threads were visible, threatening to unravel the whole thing. Most odd for a tourist hut in an exotic island resort...

Lara called upon her aching muscles to push herself up into a sitting position, leaning forward to grab the shirt and put it on. She buttoned it up hastily with one eye on the doorway, unsure if any of her rescuers would appear at any second to check on her.

She pulled back the collection of blankets and slowly put her feet on the makeshift floor. She still felt low on energy and her stomach rumbled now that she became active again.

There was a rustle as her foot brushed against something underneath the bed. She looked underneath. There seemed to be a silver, metallic-looking blanket folded neatly. It looked like something that would appear at the end of a disaster movie when the characters had overcome the major event and be wrapped up sipping cocoa. Lara had the feeling this had made up part of her pile of blankets at one point.

To the side of the blanket was a weathered glass jar. Lara didn't know why, but she reached out and picked it up without thinking. She lifted it up to eye-level to examine the contents. She realised with a sharp intake of breath that it seemed to contain a handful of human teeth.

Her heart hammered in her chest as she stared in horror at the contents of the jar in her hand. She glanced again at the doorway. Where was she? Why had she woken up on her own in an odd little hand-built hut?

She didn't know what else to do, so she hastily returned the jar to what she hoped was its exact position underneath the bed. Lara heard the contents clink unpleasantly against the jar over the sound of her heart pounding in her ears. She hoped nobody else was nearby enough to hear either of these noises.

Perturbed, she sat back up straight again and noticed the pillow her head had rested on whilst she had slept; it was almost completely flat, and the cover was as patchy and threadbare as the top blanket.

Lara surveyed the room again. This was

definitely a bizarre dwelling and not one she had expected to find when she had been frantically splashing towards the only bit of land in sight yesterday.

She suddenly had another image flash before her eyes; a pair of man's hands guiding a wooden cup of water towards her mouth. That must have been her rescuer. But where was he? Why hadn't he taken her to a hospital?

Lara drew together the energy to push herself up from the bed. She seemed to have pulled every muscle in her body. Her stiff legs loosened up a little as she hobbled over to the doorway where she was met with a view of the crystal-clear ocean she had crawled out of yesterday. The waves rolled noisily towards her over the white beach.

She descended the two steep steps of the hut and her bare feet sank into the soft sand.

Now that she was outside, blinking in the intensely bright sun she noticed that the hut was raised and set upon stilt-like legs.

She looked sideways in both directions, but couldn't see any sign of anyone.

She turned around and backed away from the makeshift building.

A span of dense trees lined the beach in both directions. After she had backed a few paces backwards another stick structure become visible to her left, except that this one was small and had a few items of clothing hung upon it. And there just beyond it, further along the beach two men sat opposite each other around a fire.

The flames flickered faintly in the bright light of the tropical day.

The men seemed to have been deep in conversation, but the grey-haired one facing Lara stopped and jumped up as soon as he saw her and rushed over.

The dark-haired man opposite him quickly span around before jumping up and following his friend as he jogged towards her.

The grey-haired man stopped in front of her. 'Hello!' he beamed brightly, peering at Lara as though judging her state of wellness. He seemed to be slightly worried that she was going to collapse.

Although he was white, his skin was well-tanned, as though he had been exposed to the sun too much. He was tall, with dark-grey curly hair that was slightly unkempt around the edges. His clothes were slightly tattered too and had been clearly patched up in several areas.

His attire didn't seem to suggest he was a rich tourist Lara would have expected to have found on such a scenic piece of paradise. His demeanour seemed friendly however, and his smile stretched to his bright blue eyes which seemed to have a warm sparkle about them.

His friend quickly appeared at his side looking at Lara in the same way, with expectant curiosity, although he seemed slightly more cautious and stood with his hands on his hips.

When Lara didn't respond straight away the first

man spoke again, as though to try and prompt a response out of her, 'Hey - you're awake!' He said it slightly louder and more slowly, his American accent more pronounced, as though concerned Lara wasn't hearing him. He went on, 'You had us worried there for a while, he gave a nervous half-laugh.

Lara recognised his voice from yesterday, he had been the man who had given her the water. She pulled herself together enough to answer him, 'Yes,' she said, not really knowing what to say, 'I was exhausted...I-I'd been in the ocean for a long time.' She noticed her voice sounded slightly unused

The man's shoulders seemed to relax a little and something like relief spread across his face, 'Oh great, you speak English!' he said brightly. He seemed genuinely delighted by this. He exchanged a glance with the man next to him, as if to say 'I told you so'.

'I guess that will make things easier,' the dark-haired man said. His voice was deeper and had a slightly rough quality to it, as though he hadn't used it for a while. He too was American and was decidedly more shabby than his friend. His clothes were so discoloured with dirt Lara couldn't tell what colour they had been originally and they were torn in several places, but no attempt had been made to repair them.

Although he was white too, his skin was darker than the first man's, as though he had taken even less care to stay out of the sun. His hair was speckled slightly with grey and was obviously uncared for, and it looked like he hadn't shaved for at least a few weeks.

If either of these men were rich businessmen on holiday, they certainly were eccentric, Lara thought to herself.

'How are you feeling?' the first man asked, looking at Lara slightly concerned again.

Lara searched within herself. She was hungry and thirsty, her pulled muscles ached and she felt low on energy, but other than that she felt normal. 'Fine, I guess...' she replied, shrugging her shoulders. Although in truth she would have felt much more comfortable if she had been wearing trousers. Instead, the full heat of the sun beamed down on her exposed legs. 'Just kind of hungry, and still a bit thirsty.' she added.

'Oh - of course. Hey, come and sit...' he said, gesturing towards the fire and the chunky wooden logs set around it. 'We'll get you some water. I thought you would be hungry too. We were just cooking breakfast.'

Lara led the way and sat beside the fire, the warmth it was giving off feeling unnecessary in addition to the blazing sun in the cloudless sky. Now that she was closer, she noticed the wooden frame above the flickering flames that supported a single stick through which three large fish had been speared.

'My name is Brandon by the way. Brandon

Wells.' said the first man cheerfully, holding out his hand and formally shaking Lara's.

'Lara Adams.' she said, trying to pull her shirt tails over her bare legs as best she could.

Brandon poured a wooden cup of water from a large container and handed it to Lara before he sat on the log to her right.

'This is Jace. Jace Dansinger.' he continued, indicating to his friend who sat on the log to Lara's left.

'Jace,' Lara said, looking towards the dark haired man. 'That's unusual. Is that short for Jason?'

'No.' he said, prodding the fire with a stick and giving a half-glance to Brandon.

'We think you might have had hypothermia when we found you yesterday,' Brandon told Lara as she drained the cup. 'I mean, neither of us are doctors or anything...but it's my best guess anyway. He continued staring at Lara, as though determined to make sure she wasn't going to start shivering again. 'You were ice-cold. We got every blanket we could find to cover you with and you warmed up eventually.

'Right, thanks.' Lara said feeling awkward. She didn't ask which one of them had removed her shirt. 'Well, I feel fine now. Its really hot here,' she added, with a slight gesture towards the sun.

'Isn't it just!' Brandon said, smiling and nodding his head in agreement.

Lara wasn't sure what to say next. She had been waiting for one of the men to tell her where they were and when she would be able to get out of here - wherever here was.

The problem was that they both seemed to be holding back. They were watching her as though they were waiting to hear her story first, as though hoping that she would tell them how she had come to be in the ocean for so long.

Lara decided to take a direct approach. 'So...erm, where are we exactly?' she asked, 'Is this one of the Cook Islands?

Jace gave a half-snigger, now prodding the fire pointlessly. He took his gaze away from Lara for a second to give an amused look to Brandon.

Lara was pleased to see that Brandon didn't return it.

'Umm, not exactly.' He looked awkward as he now slid a cooked fish onto a bowl that matched the water cup and handed it to Lara.

She took it, realising for the first time exactly how ravenous she was. She didn't start eating however. She looked from Brandon to Jace.

There was something odd about the situation here. Lara thought uncomfortably of the jar of teeth she had seen in the hut, but didn't dare mention them. What was going on? Why was Brandon so reluctant to tell her where she was?

'I kind of hoped that you would tell us where we are actually.' Brandon said, setting his own bowl on the log next to him, before handing the third one to Jace who had been watching Lara with close interest.

What did that mean? Why was Brandon so hesitant about telling her where she was? After all, she had a right to know...

'You must have been on board a boat right?' Brandon went on, looking for some confirmation from Lara. 'I mean, how else did you come to be in the water? Your boat - and there must have been a boat - it must have sailed nearby, and you...well...well - what happened exactly?'

Lara didn't say anything, she was feeling under pressure and was thinking fast. She had willingly gotten onto a yacht with two random strangers who had turned out to be part of a crew of drug couriers. Lara was sure that in itself was bound to be some kind of crime that surely carried a lengthy jail sentence, whether she had knowingly done it or not. She didn't want to think about the potential legal implications of such an action.

How was she to convince a judge, or anyone that she and Lizzy had unknowingly gotten onto that yacht? She felt a painful tug of heartache when she thought of Lizzy.

Lara didn't think that even she would have believed her own story. If Lara had heard of two female tourists doing what she and Lizzy had done, she wouldn't have believed that they had no idea what they were getting themselves into. Or else, she would have thought that they were simply self-serving, fortune-hunters looking for a taste of the high-life who had brought the events, no matter how horrific, upon themselves.

And then there was the fact that she had witnessed the rival gang murder her best friend in cold blood. She had seen their faces. She was a witness, and they had only let her escape because they thought she had foolishly jumped into the ocean in the middle of nowhere with no hope of rescue. They must have assumed that she would have drowned by now. Lara had even believed that she would have drowned herself until she had thankfully spotted land on the horizon.

If any of the rival gang found out that she had survived, they would surely make sure that they tied up that particular loose end.

Either way, it wouldn't be a good idea to tell the truth. And Lara thought she shouldn't reveal any incriminating details to the two men either side of her, who now sat waiting eagerly for her story. And anyway, why wouldn't Brandon tell her their location? Why did he want Lara to tell him where they were?

Lara decided to play along as far as they were concerned, but not reveal anything that would get her into any kind of trouble.

'I was on a boat,' she started slowly. 'My friend and me - we - we were travelling around New Zealand...And then we, hired a yacht,' Lara invented, changing details to suit her new story. 'We decided to make it a really memorable holiday and sail to the Cook Islands.'

'The Cook Islands,' Brandon repeated, nodding. 'You know how to sail?

'No,' Lara answered, 'We had a crew sailing for us. They came with the yacht.'

Jace shifted in his seat slightly and looked at Brandon, but his friend didn't respond.

'You had your own crew? That's the way to travel in style, I guess. It must have been a pretty big yacht?' Brandon said, looking impressed.

Lara nodded but didn't say anything.

'How did you end up in the water?' Brandon pressed on. 'You don't look like you just went for a swim.' he said glancing at the flimsy shirt she was wearing.

'No, I, um - fell overboard.' Lara said, feeling stupid. Now that she had said it out loud it sounded ridiculous.

'You fell overboard?' Jace repeated suddenly, looking at Lara incredulously with a slight smirk on his face.

Lara felt the heat rise in her face, but she had to stick with her lie - the alternative was worse.

'How did that happen?' Brandon asked gently. He had a much more tactful manner than Jace.

'Well, I was up on the top deck - I wanted to get some air. I was leaning over the railings at the back, and then I just - well - fell over. I must have lost my balance or something. I'm not exactly sure what happened. All I know is that I ended up in the water and the boat was sailing on without me.'

'Why didn't your friend have the boat stopped?' Brandon asked.

'I was on my own,' Lara replied. 'It was the

morning, and my friend was still asleep on the lower deck. I just went up to get some air and fell overboard.' Lara finished. Now that she justified her claim with more lies, it sounded more plausible. Why shouldn't they believe it?

'And no one from the crew saw you fall?' Jace asked her.

'No, they were in the control room,' sailing the yacht. Lara replied. She didn't like the disbelieving tone Jace was using. She even felt a little offended that he wasn't just accepting her story without question. 'Obviously they didn't see me, otherwise they wouldn't have sailed on without me would they?'

'Huh,' Jace said, looking thoughtfully at Lara for a moment, 'I think you should have hired a better crew.' he said with a further smirk.

Lara felt slightly annoyed that he found the fate of the version of herself in her made-up story so amusing, but she was relieved to feel that he seemed to believe it now.

'Then what happened?' Brandon asked.

'Well, I stayed where I was for a while...I thought maybe someone would notice that I was gone, and then come back for me.' Lara continued to invent.

It actually was easier to create an alternative version of the truth. It helped to distance her slightly from what really happened. She didn't have to tell them that her best friend had just been killed right in front of her for one thing. She felt like she would have been unable to find the words. 'But after a while...well...it seemed like hours had passed, and I was struggling to keep my head above the waves. I kept swallowing water - I realised that no one was going to help me...' Lara was a little too close to the truth now for her liking.

'No - you didn't stay where you were,' Brandon pointed out. 'The ocean - it moves you, without you realising it. You would have drifted quite far...' He looked out across the sea, the sunlight that illuminated the sand reflected in his bright blue eyes.

'I guess so. Well, I started swimming in the direction the boat had sailed in.' Lara started, immediately drawing Brandon's attention back to her. 'I thought maybe I could get somewhere, even if it was just a more heavily used yachting area...maybe nearer the Cook Islands... At least I would be doing something.

'And anyway, I was starting to get really cold. I thought moving would help keep me warmer. Then after a while - I don't remember how long I swam for, but I saw land in the distance. I swam towards it, and that's how I ended up here.'

Lara shrugged, as though to communicate that she had finished telling her tale.

Neither Brandon nor Jace said anything, they both seemed to be pondering what she had said.

Lara wondered if they didn't believe her.

She tried to change the subject, just in case. 'So,

where are we? You said this wasn't one of the Cook Islands?' Lara asked. 'Are you on holiday here?' She went on, although she could already tell that these two men weren't just enjoying a straightforward vacation here.

Brandon and Jace looked at each other across the fire. Jace resumed poking at it again for a moment, a dark smirk upon his face before he picked up his fish and started eating it without looking at the other two, as though he didn't want to listen to what Brandon was going to say next.

'No,' Brandon replied. 'We are not on vacation here,' he said with a slightly sad smile. 'We are here because we were shipwrecked.'

Lara's heart sank. She knew something had been off about the scenario she now found herself in, but she hadn't quite expected this revelation.

'Right...' she said, trying to take this information in and understand what it meant. It didn't help that she was still tired and hungry.

Instead of finding help on this island, she had unwittingly discovered people who were waiting for rescue themselves. 'I guess we're both waiting for rescue together then.' she said in a pitiful attempt to take the focus from the all-the-more-serious situation she now found herself in after Brandon's bombshell.

Brandon smiled and nodded, for some reason looking cheerful again. 'Yes, and hopefully it won't be too much longer now that you're here - I mean - don't get me wrong - I'm sorry that you had an accident, but you're all right now aren't you?-' he said, giving her another enquiring glance '-You know, even at this very second there will be people out looking for you. For sure, you will be officially missing by now.'

Lara could tell that Brandon and Jace had been discussing this at great length whilst she had been asleep.

'-A formal search will be started. The search party will go and retrace the boat's course and then...well, they should find us all here.' He looked at Jace. 'And then, we finally will be rescued. We can go home.' he said, a note of controlled excitement in his voice.

Jace allowed himself a small smile at these words, 'Amen to that,' he said, unwittingly using a phrase Lara often used.

Lara felt a strong stab of guilt in the pit of her stomach. She knew full well that no one would be looking for her, but there was no way that she could communicate this to the two people she had just injected with false hope. Not without backtracking on her lies, at least.

'Aren't you going to eat that?' Brandon asked her, indicating to the untouched fish in her bowl and starting on his own. 'You must be starving.'

Lara's guilt squirmed along with the hunger that burned in her stomach. She thought this would make eating difficult, but as soon as she took the first mouthful, Lara thought it was the tastiest thing she had ever eaten; it had cooled to the perfect temperature and crumbled into soft flakes that seemed to almost melt-in-her-mouth. In addition, it had been expertly de-boned, making it slip down easily. When she had finished the fish, Brandon handed her a banana for dessert.

Lara washed it all down with another cup of water handed to her by Brandon. Now that she was able to be more aware of her surroundings, she noticed that the cup in her hands was actually a hollowed out coconut shell.

'When it gets dark later, we're going to set up a couple more fires down the beach.' Brandon said, more to Lara than to Jace.

Lara presumed he had planned this with Jace already. She nodded, but didn't say anything.

'I'm also going to light up the SOS sign again like I did last night.' He pointed down the beach to where Lara could see some dark stones in a curved pattern that Lara presumed made up the letters of the sign.

'OK. That's a good idea.' Her insides again writhed with guilt.

'With any luck we could be spotted and out of here in just a matter of days,' Brandon said positively. He turned to Lara, 'Hey, now that you're done eating, we can give you a tour if you like? I mean - if you're feeling up to it that is?' He again tried to scrutinize her physical condition.

'Sure. That would be nice.' Lara replied, trying to mirror his upbeat tone.

'Great!' Brandon replied cheerily, getting up

from his log. 'I mean, you probably won't be here for very long. Someone should come across us soon, but it should give you a better sense of where we are.'

Lara got up too and started to follow Brandon away from the campfire.

Behind her, Jace got hastily to his feet and joined them, walking on Lara's other side.

To distract herself from her uncomfortable feeling of guilt, and to provide herself with a more logical point to add to her case in her mental argument that a totally unrelated boat would simply come across the island soon and rescue them, she asked, 'So how long have you two been here?'

Brandon slowed his already gentle pace and looked down at the sand as the three of them padded along the beach. He looked deep in thought.

'Uh, well...I'm not sure how long it has been exactly...' he said. He sounded uncomfortable all of a sudden.

Beside her, Jace gave a bitter laugh. 'Sure you do Brandon.' He turned to Lara, 'He keeps a record, you know. He has all these little bits of paper and he marks down each day in a tally chart.'

Brandon cheeks reddened slightly, but still kept staring at the ground. 'Thank you Jace.' There was a definite hint of irritation in his voice.

'No problem, my friend,' Jace smiled back at him.

Lara noticed that Jace's voice was losing its initial gravelly edge now as he went on. 'So how long has it been? Because I genuinely have lost track.'

'Well,' Brandon replied. 'Its something like s-'

'"Something like"!' repeated Jace amusedly. 'As if you don't know exactly how long its been! I've seen you with your little charts and-'

'Fifteen years, seven months and seven days if you want to be exact.' Brandon said calmly, quietening Jace immediately.

Lara's heart sank even further than it had earlier. All hope of an unprovoked rescue evaporated from her mind.

9
The Island

Lara walked with the two men at a slow pace along the shoreline, the latest shock revelation from Brandon weighing heavy on her mind as she tried to process this new piece of information.

She would never have guessed that Brandon and Jace had been waiting for rescue for almost sixteen years. Now that she thought about it however, it seemed to fit in with everything she had seen on the island so far. The makeshift hut, the threadbare blankets and clothes and the mostly unkempt condition of the two men all suggested that they weren't here through choice. She still had no idea why there was a jar of teeth in the hut, but she didn't quite know how to bring it up in casual conversation.

Brandon and Jace had ended up here through some kind of boating accident and it seemed that they had been forced to put their lives on hold, hoping that someone would eventually find them. And now, because of Lara, they were excitedly thinking that the time they had been dreaming about was now upon them.

Not only this, but now Lara was here too, and not through choice either. She couldn't see any way out of the situation she had gotten herself into. What was she supposed to say to them in a week's time when no search party turned up?

Admitting she had lied wasn't an option now. She was committed to her story and she was determined to stick to it, at least until she had a better idea.

'Are you all right?' Brandon asked, looking into her face as they strolled gently along.

'Er - yes.' Lara replied. 'I was just thinking,'

'It is um, well - that is to say - it isn't as bad as it sounds you know...Well, I mean it sounds like a long time, sure, but-'

'No - it's worse.' Jace added to Lara. 'I can't believe that's all it's been. I stopped counting after the first ten years,' he added with a sarcastic smile.

'Well, neither of us should have to count for much longer now Jace.' Brandon said.

Lara wished they would both somehow just forget about the idea that her being here suggested they were going to be rescued.

'God I hope so.' Jace said exasperatedly, looking around him. 'I'll be glad to see the back of this place for sure.'

No such luck, Lara thought to herself. She tried to change the subject. 'You said you two were shipwrecked?' she asked them. 'What happened exactly?'

'Well,' Brandon replied, 'We were on a kind of cruise of our own. We had hired a boat you see. We set off from the coast of Australia and set sail for Fiji. And - and, well it wasn't just the two of us.' His expression darkened slightly.

Jace seemed to stiffen somewhat at Lara's side

and he gazed towards the trees beside them as they walked.

'My father was with us - as well as my son. He was just five years old at the time-'

A feeling of dread sank into Lara's stomach, and she feared she was causing Brandon to recall what was sure to be a horrific and painful story.

'-My dad was really the best sailor of all of us. He used to be in the forces when he was younger...Anyway, we'd been sailing for a while - a couple of weeks. We hit some bad weather, but we were too far away from land and weren't close enough to Fiji yet. So we had no choice but to just carry on, and try to make it through the storm.

'Well, the boat didn't make it - it just wasn't big or strong enough, it was only a medium-sized fishing boat. It wasn't anything spectacular like the one you hired - I mean - it didn't have its own crew or anything, we just sailed the thing ourselves. Straight into a storm...

'It was really dark all of a sudden, it was raining even harder than earlier. So hard, it was actually hurting just to stand in it. We were all soaked through. The ocean was so violent and we were being thrown into one another by the aggressive waves. None of us could really see what we were doing, we were just sailing on and hoping the weather would clear up - trying to weather the storm, if you will. Jace and my dad were just dark outlines against the sea. My son was below deck in the cabin, and the three of us were sailing the boat as best we could.

'Anyway, I don't know how long we sailed on like that for - a couple of hours, perhaps? But without any warning the boat seemed to shudder and stop with so much force that we were all thrown off our feet.

'I'd hit my head, but I managed to get up. I found Jace nearby. He had dislocated his shoulder trying to hang onto the side railing during the impact. Then I realised my dad wasn't there. He had been thrown overboard by the force.' Brandon's voice broke slightly at this point and it seemed to take him more effort to speak. 'We - we couldn't find him in the dark. We came to the conclusion that - that, he must have been knocked unconscious when we lost him...We presume that sharks took his body. They're quite prevalent in this area as we've found out...'

Lara suddenly remembered the thing that had brushed against her leg yesterday, but she didn't say anything and neither did Jace. Lara thought it was best to let Brandon tell his story without asking any questions as they walked, so as to not further prolong any hurt she was causing him by getting him to recall this event.

'Well,' Brandon continued, 'As the sun rose, we could see that the boat was just about balanced upon some rocks. It was too badly damaged to hope to ever sail it again - it was letting in too much water, and there was a huge gash in the hull, bits and pieces from the galley were floating out and drifting away. As it got lighter, this island became visible in the distance, so the three of us rowed here in our inflatable dinghy.'

Lara forgot about her decision to not ask any questions. 'The three of you?' she asked surprised. 'You mean your son made it out of the boat too?'

Brandon looked at her. 'Oh yes. He was fine. A couple of cuts and bruises, but he came off the best out of all of us - luckily. I've just realised I haven't mentioned him at all have I? He is here too. In fact, we're just about to meet him. He has his own bit of island he likes to live in. I guess it's a castaway's version of a treehouse. We built this area for him when he was a teenager, so he could have a little more privacy, you know?'

'I wish I could get some privacy around here.' Jace muttered beside Lara.

'Don't worry Jace, we all wish you could.' Brandon retorted quickly back at him.

Once they had reached the end of the stretch of beach, Lara followed Brandon through a dense patch of trees which seemed to be loaded with bunches of green bananas, with Jace bringing up the rear.

Brandon explained that there were quite a few banana trees around the island now that they specifically encouraged them to grow. 'We also grow potatoes - well - some kind of vegetable that is pretty potato-like anyway. We're not sure what it is exactly.'

'But it's safe to eat?' Lara asked.

'Well, we've been eating it for apparently over fifteen years and we're all still alive.' Jace laughed from behind her. 'They certainly don't make good French-fries, but they don't taste that bad either.'

'It's a good source of carbohydrate,' Brandon added looking back before he ventured out of the trees and onto another sandy beach.

Lara stepped out onto the sand behind him and could see what looked like a tiny island in comparison to the one they were already standing on. It was attached by a small band of white sand which the colourless sea was almost threatening to envelop.

There was another hut on this island, just visible through the trees that surrounded it. This hut was smaller than the first, but was again set upon stilts, keeping it elevated from the ground beneath it.

Lara presumed this was for extra protection from the sea, perhaps for when stormier weather moved in.

Brandon led the three of them as they walked across the wet bank and approached the hut.

The dry sand of the mini-island stuck to Lara's wet feet as she stepped over a crisp, brown palm-tree leaf.

'Hey Jack,' Brandon called as they neared the door-less entrance.

A shirtless young man appeared almost immediately in the doorway. He froze as his eyes set upon Lara.

His taut skin was heavily tanned over the

contoured muscles of his arms and torso. He had bright blue eyes just like Brandon's, except that they were set in a more handsome face. His medium-length blonde hair was cut and styled in a way that made Lara think of nineties-boy bands.

For a moment, Lara was confused as to why they had been brought to this young man's hut when Brandon had said that they were going to visit his son, but then she realised that the attractive man in front of her was in fact his son. She mentally reprimanded herself for not realising that he wouldn't still be the faceless five-year-old boy she had pictured whilst listening to Brandon's story. Not after fifteen years on this island.

'We have a guest,' Brandon said, smiling at his son as he watched his reaction.

Jack stood frozen in the doorway staring at Lara, his look of surprise turning rapidly into a wide smile. 'We're rescued?!' he asked, grinning at his father, hardly able to believe it.

Lara inwardly groaned as another jolt of guilt gripped her insides.

'No, not yet,' Brandon replied, obviously trying not to get Jack over-excited. 'This is Lara Adams.' Brandon explained gesturing to Lara. 'She fell overboard when her boat sailed nearby some place. And now she's here, with us.'

Lara felt her cheeks flush slightly, but smiled and said hello to Jack, trying to keep her eyes on his face and not on his muscular physique. She again wished that she wasn't wearing just a shirt and clasped her hands in front of her in a pathetic attempt to cover her bare legs a little.

'So people are going to come looking for you now?' Jack said, catching on.

'That's what we are hoping is gonna happen,' Brandon said, nodding and smiling.

'I can't believe it!' Jack said, jumping down the two steps sending sand everywhere and rushing forward to hug his father, ecstatic.

He released Brandon and moved towards Lara as though he was going to hug her too, before stopping just in front of her and looking slightly awkward. 'I just can't believe you're here...' he said, shaking his head and slipping his thumbs into the pockets of his long shorts, seeming unable to think of anything else to say. Lara's arrival seemed to have put him into shock.

Lara thought she must have looked this way when she was just told that the men she was now hoping for rescue with had been waiting already for almost sixteen years.

'Yes, neither can I,' Lara said truthfully.

Both Brandon and Jace laughed.

'I bet you can't.' Jace said.

'It does take some getting used to.' Brandon agreed.

'Did you get here this morning?' Jack asked her, looking her up and down and taking note of her dry hair and shirt.

'No, um, yesterday evening I think.'

'That's right,' Brandon said, nodding. 'Just after

dinner.'

'And you waited until now to tell me?' Jack asked, aghast.

Jace looked amused at this. 'Well, we thought that if a rescue boat came from the north, we could all sneak onto it without you, and leave you here.' he said sarcastically, laughing and looking to Lara, inviting her to share the joke.

Lara smiled back politely.

For some reason, it seemed odd to her that Jace's mood was so light and jovial. The fine features of his face bore signs that they weren't used to being formed into a smile and it almost seemed unnatural when they did.

Brandon shook his head. 'We wanted to make sure we were in position if any boats did approach last night. We set up extra campfires along the beach and lit up the old SOS sign too. We made sure that if anybody came, they would see us.' Brandon explained. 'Don't worry, Jace and I had it covered and we weren't going to go anywhere without you.'

'That's good to hear.' Jack replied, although he still sounded slightly moody. 'So nobody came last night?'

Lara shifted uncomfortably where she stood.

'No. It's early days yet.' Brandon told him. 'It could take days, or even weeks for anyone to come across us. No one saw Lara fall, so they will probably have a pretty large area to cover, depending on how fast the yacht was going.' he looked at Lara. 'How fast would you say were going at the time?'

'You know, um, pretty fast,' Lara said. 'We wanted to get to where we were going as quickly as possible.' she added, in a flimsy attempt to dilute their hope by lessening the feasibility of her imaginary rescue party actually finding her.

'Hmm,' Brandon looked out to the sea again, thinking.

Lara was slightly relieved to see that her last comment had made some effect, but this relief was almost immediately quashed by Jack's boundless enthusiasm.

'They'll find us though right? I mean, they just have to.'

Brandon nodded. 'I want us all to carry on as normal though all right? No wasting anything, or using more of anything than usual. After all, we don't know how long it will be before the search party actually finds this place.'

'I'll go put the champagne back in the refrigerator then shall I?' Jace said, again looking to Lara and prompting another fake smile from her.

The four of them went together as they continued the tour of the island.

Lara felt slightly odd that she wasn't wearing shoes, but as she looked around her she noticed that no one else was either.

The island seemed to consist mainly of palm trees and fruit plants. Some of the palm trees in part of the island bore plentiful amounts of coconuts. The men showed Lara where they had deliberately planted rows and rows of the 'potatoes' and bananas which seemed to make up the bulk of their diet. Apparently the leaves of the potato plant were edible too and they ate them in seafood stews.

There was another hut nestled behind rows and rows of the potato plants. It was identical to the first one on the main beach in every detail. Jace identified this as the hut he lived in.

The south-eastern shore of the island had a smaller beach that was littered with rather chunky-looking crabs.

Jace explained that they caught the crabs from here and sometimes they found clams too at certain times of the year.

Lara had always hated crabs. She thought of them as the spiders of the ocean. She shuddered at the sight of them scuttling about and hoped Brandon hadn't seen so he wouldn't start worrying about her.

As Jace was talking, Brandon picked up a crab from the beach and Jack followed suit and picked up another announcing that they would be on the menu for lunch.

Lara didn't like the idea of all the claws and legs, but didn't say anything. Besides, she was already starting to get hungry again after the small breakfast she had eaten and wasn't going to turn down food in a place where supplies were limited.

They continued walking along this beach until it

abruptly ended. They then cut into the unexpectedly dense forest that ran alongside it.

It took Lara's eyes a few moments to adjust to the dark, greenish light after being on the pale, sunny sand. She noticed how surprisingly warm and humid it felt in here as she trod carefully on fallen palm tree leaves, concerned she might step bare-foot on any poisonous tropical insects that may be hiding in the rotting fronds.

Jace, who had been watching Lara closely, seemed to know exactly what she was worried about and allayed her fears, 'Don't worry. There's nothing too nasty hiding in here with us.' he said with a small wink.

The four of them came out of the trees long enough for Lara to see another, even smaller beach which was, she was pleased to notice, completely crab-free. It consisted of nothing but a stretch of pure, stoneless sand being lapped gently by small waves.

They returned back to the jungle for over ten minutes or so as Brandon was explaining the seasons they experienced on the island.

Lara noticed that the ground underfoot was becoming harder and rockier and there was a patch of green, fluffy moss that felt soft against Lara's toes as she stepped on them. The trees were becoming more sparse as they walked and it was starting to get lighter again.

The sound of running water reached Lara's ears as the four of them reached the end of the patch of trees. In the clearing ahead was what looked like a large, garden rockery; a small waterfall was cascading down onto large, almost perfectly flat, dark rocks.

Scattered here and there in the gaps in the stone were bright red flowers, adding to the idea that this was simply a water-feature in a beautiful garden. Rays of hazy sunshine from the sky above the clearing were filtering through the gaps in the trees on the whole scene, giving it a serene, golden glow.

Brandon explained that this is where they get most of their drinking water from and also where they wash sometimes. He told her it allowed them to give their skin a break from the harsh, salty water of the ocean.

'If you can stand the cold,' Jace pointed out. 'It's not exactly a premium experience.'

'I think it's beautiful.' Lara said, taking it all in. She thought all the scene needed was a few butterflies fluttering about for it to look like a picture in a luxury holiday brochure.

They moved on from this primitive shower facility and started walking up an abruptly steep slope to what Brandon explained was the most elevated area of the island.

Lara found her muscles protesting as she scaled the slope behind Brandon and Jack who were leading the way, with Jace behind her.

As soon as Lara reached the top, she was hit with a view of a huge expanse of bright-blue ocean which seemed to stretch out endlessly in front of her.

Near the edge of the cliff were three large, flat-topped rocks that were bordered with a palm tree on each side.

Jack dropped the crabs upside down on one of the rocks, before he turned to Lara. 'It-er...it's a beautiful view isn't it?' he said to her. He seemed somewhat nervous, but Lara couldn't think why.

'Yes...It's lovely.' Lara replied, yet again forcing a smile.

Although Lara recognised that the scene she now faced was beautiful, she was strongly reminded of her seemingly hopeless hours shivering alone and scared in the sea just yesterday. Although it seemed like much longer ago.

A rush of unexpected fear caused Lara to reach out and grip the palm tree nearest to her and she forced herself to look down at the grass her feet were nestled in to prove to herself that she was out of the water now. The grass was waving gently in the warm breeze. She was safe and on dry land.

'Lara, are you all right?' Brandon asked her suddenly.

'Yes, um, I'm fine.' Lara replied, as Jace quickly rushed forward and gripped her arm, steering her onto one of the rock seats next to her.

Brandon appeared, crouching in front of her and peering at her with a look of concern on his face like the one he'd had earlier. 'I thought you looked like you were struggling up the hill.' he said, sounding stressed. 'We will rest here for a while, and then we'll go back to the main beach. Get you some more to eat and drink.'

'I'm fine really, don't worry.' Lara said, trying to stop him from fretting. 'I just remembered how glad I am to be on dry land again, that's all.' she said with what she hoped was a reassuring smile, as she tried to avoid looking over Brandon's shoulder to where the crabs legs were flailing in the air, desperately trying to turn themselves the right way up again.

'Was the "beautiful view" too much for you?' Jace asked sarcastically, sitting next to Lara on the rock and throwing a mocking glance at Jack, who ignored him. Jace scoffed and turned back to Lara, 'The scenery is great and all, but I would die a very happy man if I never have to look at it again.'

Lara smiled weakly as she sat on the rock and took in the sweeping vista, trying to look at it objectively. Now she really thought she could have made use of her camera. That is, if it hadn't still been in her bag, which had most likely been cast off the boat and lying at the bottom of the sea by now.

The scene before her now was definitely what she could call picturesque. It occurred to her how ironic that here she was, along with three other people who were eagerly waiting for their opportunity to get away from such a beautiful place.

After a ten-minute rest Brandon insisted Lara took, they moved on. They descended the slope on the northern edge, which it transpired, was quite a bit rockier than it was on the jungle side. This made progress a little more difficult.

Again, Brandon and Jack took the lead and Jace followed along behind Lara. They walked carefully, feet turned sideways down the steep decline.

As they ventured down the steepest face of the hill, Lara twisted her ankle. Her heart plummeted as she lost her footing and slipped.

Lightning fast, Jace grabbed her by the wrist before she slipped further down the steep face, allowing her to scramble back onto her feet again.

'Thanks.' she said, slightly embarrassed.

'No problem.' he smiled.

As soon as they got back to the main camp, Jack tossed the crabs upside-down into the edge of the fire that was still burning.

Lara flinched as she noticed their many legs flailing even more frantically than they had before.

This didn't go unnoticed by Brandon. 'It's all right. They don't feel it for long.' he said reassuringly. 'It's one thing you get used to on this island-' he shrugged as he thought about it, '-I mean, we have to eat. It's only natural.'

The wind had picked up slightly and was blowing swirling smoke in the direction of the log Lara had sat on earlier; it stung her eyes and throat as she inhaled a small cloud of it, so instead she took a seat on the log that Jace had earlier.

There seemed to be a slight flurry as both Jace and Jack tried to sit in the free position next to her.

Jace won, and so Jack, looking slightly sulky, threw himself down onto the log opposite them where Brandon had earlier sat.

Brandon sat on the sand in front of Jack's log and leaned back on it whilst they were waiting for lunch to be cooked. Every few minutes he turned the crabs with a stick.

Lara, who had managed to complete twenty-six years without ever eating crab, was surprised to find that it wasn't all that bad. In fact, once she had grown accustomed to the flavour, she found she actually quite liked it. Of course, it helped that she was ravenous. She presumed that her body had used up far more energy than it usually had over the last day or two.

Brandon had this notion too, and he seemed determined that Lara should build her strength up by getting enough to eat and drink and avoiding doing anything strenuous. So after he had gotten her to eat another banana, she finished off the meal with the bright, white flesh from half a coconut. Brandon also got her to drink the milk he had siphoned out of it into one of their already existing coconut shell cups.

He then shared the other half of the flesh between himself, Jack and Jace.

They sat quietly eating for a minute, before Jack spoke. 'I'm definitely not going to miss the food when we get home.' he said, looking at the half-eaten piece of coconut in his hand. 'The first thing I'm gonna eat when we get rescued is a burger - with everything on it.' He looked suddenly thunderstruck as he looked up sharply to look at Lara, 'Hey Lara, er, do they still have McDonald's in the real world?'

Lara was caught off-guard by such an unexpected question and couldn't help a laugh bursting from her lips.

Jack seem to recoil and blush slightly, but he still waited for the answer to his question. He seemed to be avoiding looking at Jace for some reason.

Jace allowed himself a grin too, as he watched Lara for her answer.

'Um - sorry, yes. Yes, it still exists.' she said, composing herself again.

Brandon looked at his son. 'See Jack? The world isn't that different than it was before we left. You won't have missed much. Didn't I tell you, huh?' He stuffed the last piece of coconut into his mouth.

Lara thought that Brandon would be surprised if she told him exactly how much the world had changed in almost sixteen years, but she thought better of it. If there was one thing she didn't need, it was for the three people around her to start dreaming eagerly of a world they were expecting to be taken to in a matter of days, even though they had no idea that there was no conceivable way for them to get there.

However, it seemed she was out of luck. This time it was Jace who punctured the tiniest bubble of hope that had inflated in her chest that they might speak of something else.

'Is that really the first thing you would eat?' he asked Jack as he swallowed his last piece of coconut. 'That's ridiculous. But what would I expect from you?' he said, with a bitter kind of relish that Lara thought was totally unprovoked. 'You just have no taste in anything. And would it have hurt you to put a shirt on?' he finished with an irritated kind of flourish. 'Personally I would go for some *real* food,' he went on. 'Like - like a big, juicy steak...and some eggs - and bacon. And a huge pile of french fries,'

'Now I have to admit, that does sound appealing.' Brandon said, looking slightly dreamy with his elbows still behind him on his log. Apparently he didn't seem at all surprised by Jace's semi-outburst.

Now that Lara thought about it, she could imagine Jace using that kind of tone often.

'Well all right then, what's the first thing we're all going to *do* when we get back home?' Jack asked, obviously trying to talk about something that Jace wouldn't laugh at him for. 'You know, I can't wait to get my driver's license...' he said thoughtfully.

'I know what the first thing I want to do is when we get out of here...' Jace muttered.

Lara focused on eating her coconut, feeling the

conversation was descending into 'man talk'.

Jack looked somewhat awkward as he caught Lara's eye before hastily averting his gaze and looking into the fire.

Brandon rolled his eyes and cast his gaze into the fire, once again looking distant. He unconsciously fiddled with the tarnished, gold wedding ring on his finger as he stared into the flickering flames.

No one spoke for several, heavy moments.

Lara felt a slight tinge of annoyance that Jace had made such a vulgar statement and then made no attempt to change the subject, or even shown any remorse for what he had said.

Lara cast around for something to say. Perhaps she could steer them away from the topic of post-rescue to-do lists. Her thoughts fell on the well-built structure behind her and of the two others just like it on the island. 'You know, you've all done a good job with the huts you've built here. They look really sturdy.' she said.

'Thank you,' Jace said, looking pleased with himself. 'I designed them. I'm an architect - that is to say, I *was*. Back in the "real world" that is.' He looked over his shoulder to assess his creation. 'It's not exactly my best work.' he said with a scoff.

'I helped build them.' Jack pointed out, as though he didn't want to miss out on any credit Lara was giving out. 'W-we all built them together.' he added, somewhat nervously.

Jace sniggered slightly, making Jack look

awkward again.

Lara tried to gloss over this. 'Oh, well that was handy then. At least we have shelter, for when - when the weather isn't as nice.' Lara finished weakly, feeling rather silly since the sun was blazing so strongly it felt like it was shining straight through her. Ever since she had stepped out of the hut this morning, she felt like she had been squinting slightly the whole time and it was hard to imagine the weather being anything other than glorious.

'Oh don't worry, the weather does get bad.' Brandon chimed in. 'We're actually in the wet season right now, although you wouldn't guess it judging by today. It rains pretty often. And it can get really stormy here when it wants to.'

10
The Man in The Sand

The next few days followed pretty much the same pattern as the first. Lara went to sleep every night and awoke in the main hut every morning alone (Brandon had moved into Jace's hut near the food crops). She washed in the waterfall in the jungle rather than in the ocean, since the surrounding trees and dimmer lighting seemed to afford more privacy than a bright, open beach.

In addition, Jace had pointed out that there weren't any sharks in the waterfall.

Lara didn't think this was a very appropriate remark to make after hearing Brandon's story, but Brandon seemed more than used to Jace's harsh style of humour and simply ignored him.

Jace had made an obvious effort to smarten himself up before Lara saw him on the second day. He was clean shaven, had given himself a haircut and was wearing a set of clean clothes: a black shirt and dark grey cut-off trousers. He must have washed thoroughly too, since his skin looked brighter and his hair slightly darker. All of this seemed to contrast more with the rare colour of his grey eyes, making them stand out more. The transformation was quite remarkable, Lara thought he looked almost, well...handsome.

It transpired that Brandon had been right about the weather. The next few days seemed to well and truly make up for the first; it rained constantly and the four took shelter in the main hut a lot.

Lara answered their many questions about how the world had changed. She had talked until well past midnight to a captive audience that hung on her every word about how the internet had caught on (this had been Brandon's question). When her throat ached and her voice became audibly hoarse, Brandon had insisted that they all went to bed and let her get some sleep.

Lara quickly became aware that she was something of a novelty to the four of them. She could certainly see why however, since they had seen only each other and had no contact with the outside world for sixteen years.

Both Jack and Jace seemed to be particularly taken with her.

Jack always acted nervous around her. The conversation was stuttered and awkward. It reminded her of how it was when she had met Alan for the first time.

He didn't always seem sure of what to say, but he seemed determined that he wanted Lara's attention, especially when Jace had succeeded in getting it.

Jack, it seemed, had taken Jace's advice and worn a shirt every day, perhaps in an attempt to make himself look more presentable.

Lara was grateful for this. It certainly made talking back to him much easier, especially when she wasn't worried about where her eyes were wandering...

Jace seemed to be just as worried as Jack that Lara's attention was being drawn to the other man, although he was slightly more subtle in hiding it.

As well as keeping himself well-groomed and presentable, he seemed keen to try and win her over with his dark humour. Although it seemed to Lara that was possibly quite an angry person underneath it all.

On the fourth day, Brandon spent a large part of it fashioning Lara a pair of shorts from one of the blankets she had woken up underneath on the first morning. He painstakingly undid the stitching around the edges to retrieve enough thread to sew the shorts together. When he had finished, Lara couldn't believe that they had been crafted from the same blanket. She thanked Brandon and complimented his skills with a needle and thread ("I've had a lot of practice" he said).

The shorts were made from a dark brown, felt blanket and they came to just above her knee. Even though they were a simple garment, Lara loved them. She felt much more confident and less exposed now that she was a little more fully dressed. Although it had felt odd at first, she had also gotten more used to having no shoes or socks on by now. It helped that the others went bare-foot everywhere too.

Just as Lara was teaching them about life outside of the island, the men were teaching her about life on the island. She felt that she had the more difficult challenge, as they had been allowed sixteen years to learn the skills that seemed now almost second nature to them.

Adjusting to the life on the island was hard enough, but Lara also had her guilt to contend with. In fact, the only thing that weighed heavier than her guilt, was the feeling of hunger in her stomach. Her body was craving calories and they were hard to come by on the island. They had to be sought out, either caught or picked. No longer was it a simple case of walking to the refrigerator or cupboard any time Lara felt pangs of this sort.

On the fifth day, Brandon taught Lara how to use the fish-trap they had built, whilst he instructed Jace and Jack to collect fruit and renew the campfire.

Although he hadn't said anything, Lara had the feeling that Brandon had sent the other two on their errands to give her a rest from the constant attention they had been bestowing upon her.

Lara felt herself becoming anxious once she realised that the fishing process involved wading into the sea, even if they were only going to be waist-deep. She managed to convince herself that she was being irrational by appeasing-with-avoidance her newly-developed phobia of the ocean and that the only thing to fear was being far off shore with no form of boat. Not only this, but it took her mind of her current predicament as well as easing her conscience slightly to think that she was helping out with the island chores.

Lara steadied herself for a moment with a deep breath, before she followed Brandon who was carrying a coconut bowlful of slimy-looking bait, stepping into the warm, gentle waves that were so different from the violent, cold water she was adrift in before she arrived on the island.

The trap was a simple contraption which consisted of a large cage made up of a grid of thick sticks, tied together with strands of weedy looking, dark-green thread.

Brandon explained the concept: they lured fish into the open cage with small bits of clam and crab they had collected from the beach on the south of the island. Once a fish swam inside, they quickly lifted the cage from the water and emptied it onto the beach.

Unfortunately, Brandon explained, the commotion that ensues by lifting the cage from the water scares away any other fish that may have been tempted nearby by the bait, so usually only one fish would be caught at a time, making the process of gaining enough to feed several people quite time-consuming.

The two of them seemed to have been standing quite still, waiting in the water beside the cage for over twenty minutes with nothing to show for their time.

Brandon explained that this is a task that requires patience. 'That's why this chore usually falls to me. Jace isn't usually as enthusiastic about fishing as he was this morning.' he said, referring to how Jace had been insistent that he should be the one to teach Lara how to catch fish. Brandon looked thoughtful as he bent down slightly to look more closely at the water around them. 'It's nice to see him so upbeat for a change.'

'Upbeat?' Lara replied. That's not really the word she would have chosen to describe Jace's personality.

Brandon laughed. 'I know. But for Jace, he's positively joyful.'

'You mean he's not usually like that?' Lara asked.

'No, he's not. He's usually so hard to live with. It can wear a man down after a while.' Brandon replied suddenly sounding tired, confirming Lara's earlier thoughts of Jace having a darker side to him. 'You might even say he was a discomfort in the backside. But he's just been spirited so much by your arrival and the thought of finally being rescued. It's like he's become reanimated.'

Lara's leg gave an involuntary twitch beneath the water at being reminded once again of how her lies were giving people false hope, but she was confident that Brandon wouldn't have seen it. She was well and truly wishing that she had come up with a better story, one that didn't involve a likely rescue.

'You don't seem to be getting as animated though?' Lara asked him.

'No,' Brandon smiled. 'Believe me, the thought of getting out of here excites me more than anything - apart than seeing my wife again, of course. It's just that I want to set an example to Jack. There are many odds that stand between us and getting home. I don't want him to get his hopes up and then be disappointed if things take longer than we expected.'

Lara couldn't help but respect Brandon for taking such a sage approach to the subject, and she wished she hadn't been the one to give them all the idea that a boat would sail along any day and pick them up.

To help distract herself from the rising, hot guilt in her chest she changed the subject. 'How long have you been married?' she asked.

But Brandon didn't answer, instead he raised his finger to his lips indicating that Lara should be quiet.

She followed his gaze to where she could see a dark fish against the pale sand. Every detail was visible through the clear water as it glided quickly towards the open cage.

Lara felt a sudden thrill of excitement. She really hated the thought of having to kill a creature. She hated the cruelty of it all, but she knew that it was necessary. Their very survival relied upon them being able to capture whatever they could if they wanted to eat anything other than fruit, which wouldn't sustain them for very long.

Brandon slowly leaned down, his arms disappearing into the water until only his head and neck, which were still and stiff, were visible. His eyes were trained upon the fish, and he seemed to not even dare to blink.

Lara was strongly reminded of wildlife documentaries she had watched, when the predator focused intently upon its prey and never let it out of its sight.

Brandon had the same look in his eyes now.

Lara supposed that the men had been forced to revert slightly back to a more primitive way of life. Perhaps they had been forced to look within themselves and find that they had been born with the primal instincts and skills they now found themselves using, it had just been a case of learning how to use them.

Without warning, Brandon pulled the cage up out of the water with surprisingly little splash and started wading back to the shore with it. 'There we go.' he said, pleased with his haul, which consisted of two large fish thrashing wildly against the sides of the cage.

Lara was surprised as they waded back to the beach. She hadn't even seen the other fish swim into the cage. She felt a new wave of respect for Brandon's abilities and for the first time fully appreciated how long he had been doing this for.

Looking at the flapping creatures in the vessel in Brandon's arms, Lara was concerned that the fish were actually going to break the cage in their desperation to break free from their confinement.

She was relieved when Brandon tipped them out onto the beach, once they had gotten far enough from the shore. They were still flailing vigorously and disrupting the sand around them.

'You have to make sure that you only tip these guys out once you are far enough from the water,' Brandon explained. 'We had a couple of incidents in the early days where a couple of them got away. I can't tell you how demotivating that was.'

'I can imagine.' Lara replied, finding it hard to ignore the rumble of hunger in her stomach.

He stood back to appraise his catch. 'They're a decent size aren't they? I think we can call that a day,' He put the cage on a rock nearby to dry out. 'Twenty-four years.' he said, as though in response to a question.

Lara was confused, and she obviously looked it as Brandon laughed and prompted her, 'You asked me how long I've been married - it's twenty-four years. Twenty-five this year, actually.'

'Oh, right,' Lara replied, suddenly realising what he was talking about. 'That's nice,' she said. Then after a moment it occurred to her to ask, 'Why didn't your wife come with you on the trip?'

'Oh, her family were having some issues she wanted to help out with. She thought it would be nice if me and Jack could spend some time together - you know, father-son time? I used to spend a lot of time at the office and didn't get to see him all that much. Not as much as I would have liked anyway. I guess I've kinda made up for that now, haven't I?'

'What do - sorry - what did you used to do for a

living?'

Brandon laughed at Lara's choice of wording. 'Well, I *used* to be a lawyer. Maybe I will be again someday soon, huh?'

Lara didn't say anything.

'Yes, Helen - that's my wife's name - she flew out to stay with her sister whilst she was going through a messy divorce. She left the day before we did. Jack and I said goodbye to her, then a cab drove her to the airport.' He looked distant as he went on, 'That image of her waving through the cab window as it drove off is still so clear in my mind. I see it all the time in my dreams. I think my subconscious wants me to go back and stop her from leaving and for me and Jack to stay at home too. Slight details change when I dream of it, you know? Like sometimes she might drive herself to the airport, or it's raining instead of it being a perfectly beautiful sunny day, or she feeds our cat before she leaves. What is really stupid about that one, is that we don't even have a cat.' He laughed slightly to himself, fiddling with his wedding ring again. 'But it doesn't matter how it's different, because it's like Groundhog day - you know the movie?'

Lara nodded.

'I still wake up here-' he gestured around him '- on this island.'

'You'll see her again.' Lara said, before she could stop herself. This time she didn't regret attempting to improve Brandon's morale, because his story was just so heart-wrenching she just had to say something.

'No he won't.' Jace said flatly, suddenly appearing from the trees behind Brandon with a large bunch of green bananas in his arms.

Brandon flinched slightly, but didn't react much more than that. 'Jace, please don't start.' he said quietly, watching Jace out of the corner of his eye as he deposited the fruit on another nearby rock along with a pile of green coconuts.

Jace held up his hands in front of him to show he wasn't interested in starting conflict. 'Hey, I'm not starting anything. You know my views on the subject by now, anyway.' he said as he poured himself a cup of water from the container.

Jace dropped onto one of the logs beside the growing campfire with his back to it. 'If you were like me though, you would have thrown that-' he took a sip of water as he pointed to the ring on Brandon's finger, '-into the ocean years ago like I did with mine.'

Brandon shook his head before he answered. 'Well, thankfully Jace, I am not like you.' he said as he took his seat on the log opposite him.

Jace gave him a sarcastic smile.

Lara sat on the middle log again like she had on the first day as they waited for the fire to get up to a high enough temperature to cook the fish which were now still as Brandon rinsed them with fresh water before spearing onto a long stick

Jace turned to Lara. 'I was married too.' he said.

'But I don't cling onto the fantasy that my wife has waited for me all these years.'

Brandon's arm seemed to give a slight, involuntary spasm as he washed the fish, but he didn't look up from his task.

Lara felt a surge of anger towards Jace. She imagined that he had been making comments like this to Brandon and Jack for years from the way that Brandon was reacting, but it didn't do anything to quell the flow of rage she was suddenly feeling erupt within her.

Jace took another sip of water. 'No, my wife is long gone.' he went on. 'I guess I'm young, free and single as they say. Well, not so much free though, being stuck on this island...' he said, laughing and inviting Lara to join in.

'Not so much young either.' she said shortly to him.

Jace's face fell and he didn't seem to know what else to say to that.

Lara was surprised with herself for getting so angry, but when she saw that Brandon was trying to suppress a small smile, she felt satisfied that her remark, however snappy, was justified.

Before she knew it, Lara realised that she had been on the island for two weeks already. Every day, no matter how slow paced, was such a struggle for survival that the time seemed to pass by more quickly than she would have imagined.

Lara had thrown herself wholeheartedly into

helping the men with the chores involved in island life that she was surprised when she woke up on the fourteenth day and realised with a jolt as she was dressing that today was the day that she and Lizzy had been due to fly back to England from New Zealand.

Lara wasn't sure how to feel about this. On the one hand, it meant that her parents would soon realise that something had happened to her when she didn't arrive back in London Heathrow airport tomorrow. On the other hand, it didn't help her current predicament much. She had thought it through before she went to sleep each night.

First of all her and Lizzy's parents would report both of their children missing, then there would be some kind of search in New Zealand, where perhaps her and Lizzy's last movements would be traced. But then that is where the trail would come to a sudden and dead end. Even if the authorities managed to glean, from what Lara imagined would be bank statements, hotel staff testimony and vague CCTV footage, that she and her friend had gone to the Tauranga bay harbour that night, there was no way of their location being tracked beyond that. The boat they had boarded could have gone anywhere in the world as far as a third party, surveying the evidence from the outside was concerned.

No, the fact that people were now going to realise that she and Lizzy weren't going to step off the flight setting off today and set foot in England tomorrow didn't mean that she or the others were any closer to being rescued. All it meant was that her parents were now going to have to deal with the pain of her disappearance and there was absolutely nothing she could do to stop it, or communicate to them that she was alive.

Lara felt a rush of sympathy for Lizzy's family. They could only assume that Lizzy was missing, and they would have no idea what had really happened to her. Lara didn't know what had happened to Alexis and Matías, but she was quite confident that even if they had escaped the situation on the yacht, they wouldn't be willing to disclose the truth of the events of that day to anyone, least of all the authorities.

Only Lara knew the full story, but she had no way of telling it to the people that needed to hear it the most. She wondered if she would ever be able to speak to hers and Lizzy's family again. She wondered if she would ever see home again.

It seemed odd to think of her home on the other side of the world. It felt a million miles away from where she was now; at the mercy of the elements and a reliable source of food, with only a small, door-less wooden shack for shelter. She felt exposed and vulnerable being in such an unfamiliar environment and living a totally different type of life.

Additionally, her lies had emotionally isolated her from the others. She alone was carrying the truth within her, and she wasn't planning on sharing it with the men, no matter how anxious they would get.

After two weeks, the men were starting to get restless with the lack of any sign of rescue.

Brandon would light the campfires along the beach at the first sign of darkness and he constantly adjusted the SOS sign unnecessarily every day, as though he was starting to think that it perhaps wasn't clear enough to be visible by any would-be search party.

Lara finished getting dressed and left the hut, making her way towards the main campfire, where Brandon and Jace were already seated upon their usual logs. Jack wasn't there; as well as acting like a teenager, he also had the sleep pattern of one and liked to sleep late.

The day was already as hot as any summer Lara had known. The sun lit up the beach with its golden glow through small, lilac clouds spread here and there across the sky.

The other signal fires were smoking along the beach, having recently burned themselves out before dawn.

Lara joined the two men for a cup of water and a piece of coconut after bidding them good morning, before they all set off to go and catch some fish for breakfast.

Brandon had said that he was going to let Lara do the fishing this morning, whilst he supervised.

Jace tagged along with them. He had glossed over Lara's comment a week earlier and gone back to his previously jovial manner, although he seemed to be making an effort to keep his more harsh comments to himself.

Brandon told Lara that he thought he had seen a fish leaping out of the water a few minutes previously further along the shore than the area where they had fished in previous days, so they had set off to take advantage of this information.

Brandon carried the cage as they walked.

Jace walked beside Lara. He seemed determined he wouldn't miss out on today's fishing trip and a chance to talk to Lara without Jack being there. He asked Lara what her favourite food was.

Since they hadn't had breakfast yet, food was obviously on the forefront of their minds, but Lara wished that Jace hadn't asked her to think of something she really liked to eat when it was so inaccessible in their current situation.

Even though the thoughts only made her hungrier, Lara recalled her favourite dish, 'Well, I-' Lara was cut off mid-sentence by Brandon, who had stopped dead and thrown his arm out in front of her to stop her where she stood.

'What the hell are you doing?' Jace asked him confusedly before he followed his friend's gaze.

Lara followed it too. She cast her sight along the beach ahead of them to where the tide was lapping around a large, solid object upon the wet sand.

Lara immediately thought of a beached dolphin, but her logic almost immediately told her that the object she was looking at was too dark, and too

small to be one of those. Perhaps it was a seal?
'What is it?' she asked, completely perplexed.

Brandon didn't say anything.

Neither did Jace.

They glanced at each other and had both gone too quiet for Lara's liking.

'Wait here,' Jace said to her quietly, starting forward. He stopped and looked at Brandon, who hadn't moved. 'Aren't you coming?' he asked him.

Brandon shook his head and turned to Lara. 'Lara, I think you should go back to the camp.' he said, not quite meeting her eyes.

'Why?' she asked, confused. What was going on?

'It's just that - well - you can go and keep an eye on the campfire - make sure it gets hot enough.' He sounded thoroughly as though he was making this up as he went along. 'And if Jack is there, make sure he doesn't come this way either.' he added, as an afterthought.

'I thought I was going to be doing the fishing today - what's going on?' she asked, wondering what could have gotten both him and Jace so worried. She looked past Brandon to try and work out what the mysterious object was. The golden sunlight was shining down on whatever the thing was, but it didn't help Lara to identify it.

'Why don't you just go and wait at the camp, have some water, and we'll come and talk to you in a little while.' he said, turning her gently by the elbow and leading her in the direction of the camp.

Once he had walked her a few paces along the beach, Brandon turned and quickly trotted towards Jace.

The pair set off hurriedly towards the object on the beach, heads leaned sideways in to each other, muttering a rapid conversation back and forth they were determined that Lara wouldn't overhear.

Part of Lara wanted to do as Brandon had said. After all, he had done nothing but look after her since her arrival on the island, but something overrode her logical mind, and caused her to turn around and follow the two men's deep footsteps in the sand.

For some reason she couldn't explain she had a bad feeling about this object, even though she couldn't imagine what it could be. But Lara wasn't gong to simply wait around, she was going to find out exactly what was happening.

As she approached, a feeling of dread started creeping upon her with alarming speed. Now her logical mind was nagging at her to turn around, to follow Brandon's advice and not be disobedient; this surely was the right thing to do.

When she got there the two men were leaning over the dark shape in the sand, a mixture of horror and confusion on their faces.

Suddenly Lara realised with a thrill of horror what the object was - it was a body.

Now that she was closer, she realised that her inability to decipher exactly what the object was had been justified. For one thing, it wasn't complete. Large parts were missing and the edges that were left were jagged, almost like they had been severed. Lara couldn't see the face as it was lying downwards in the sand.

She thought wildly of Brandon's story of his father going missing from the deck of their fishing boat and how Brandon had thought that he had been taken by sharks.

Lara thought that it seemed Brandon had been right about the sharks, and this must be his father's body. How odd that it had washed up so long afterwards, she thought. And not long after Lara's arrival either...

But then, she thought, the remains of the man now lying in the sand didn't seem to match up with the image of Brandon's father that she had conjured up in her mind as Brandon had told his story. The father she had imagined for Brandon had grey hair, and he was much thinner and more frail looking than how the man in front of her appeared to have been.

Lara's attention was dawn to the remaining hand of the man. It was bloated and grey looking, but there were several thick rings upon it. Rings that were set with gleaming black jewels...

Lara realised with a sudden, now intense feeling of dread who the man in the sand was - it was Matías.

A loud gasp escaped her lips and she clasped her hands over her mouth, taking a step backwards.

Brandon and Jace looked around immediately,

only just realising she was there.

Brandon rushed forwards towards her. His hands grasped her firmly by the shoulders and turned her around, away from the scene. 'Lara, you shouldn't be here.' he said sombrely.

'I-I wanted to know what was going on.' she said, noticing how high pitched and odd her voice sounded.

'Come on,' he said, putting his hand on her back and leading her back towards the camp that she wished she had stayed at.

Lara felt strangely detached from herself as she started walking with Brandon. Her legs seemed to be carrying her, without her even noticing.

'Wait a second,' Jace called from behind them.

Brandon stopped, so did Lara. They turned back to look at Jace, who had stepped around Matías's remains and started towards them.

'Did you know him?' Jace asked looking at Lara, making an obvious effort to try and be delicate, although his brow was slightly furrowed.

Lara froze. She didn't know what to say. 'Um,' she said, as she quickly tried to think of how to answer Jace's question without jeopardising her story.

'Jace, let's not do this now. It can wait. She's had a shock.' Brandon reasoned to his friend, but Jace wasn't listening.

'You did, didn't you?' Jace went on, moving towards her and Brandon, looking intently at Lara's face.

'No,' she said, feeling the pressure. 'Well...not really.' Lara could feel the heat rising in her cheeks as Brandon turned to look at her now too.

'Which one is it?' Jace asked, forgetting about his softer tone now.

'What do you mean?'

'"No" or "not really"?' he clarified. 'Have you seen him before or not? Was he on your boat?' He watched Lara closely for her answer.

'Well...yes. He was on the boat.' Lara replied, not seeing how she could get out of this. They would surely never believe it if she told them it was a coincidence that a man's body had washed up on the island two weeks after she had. And besides, she hadn't been convincing enough with her "no" to ever hope to pull off a plausible lie now.

There was a very loaded pause where Lara felt that she could almost hear the thoughts whirring through the heads of the two men above the sound of the waves rolling beside them all.

Lara did nothing to dispel this silence. She was desperately trying to think of how this latest revelation could fit into her original story.

'So how is it that he has come to be here?' Brandon asked, still retaining his gentle tone.

'Did he fall overboard too?' Jace added quickly.

Lara didn't like the sarcastic tone of his voice, but she remained defiant as she answered, 'Perhaps...' she said slowly, 'After all, it happened to me didn't it? Or maybe he tried to go in after me...maybe - maybe he saw me fall, and jumped in to try and save me...and - and accidentally drowned himself...' She knew this all sounded completely implausible, but putting up what she hoped was an impassive expression anyway.

Jace gave a bitter laugh that he seemed to really have to force. 'That's completely absurd!' he said. 'That really isn't the standard procedure when someone falls overboard on a boat - not even close!' he said. 'Even the worst hired crew in the world would know that - no matter what type of boat you're on! And if it was a luxury yacht - like you say - then they would be more than familiar with what to do if someone went overboard. And it wouldn't be to jump in after them without raising the alarm first!' he finished, sounding irritated.

Lara really regretted having made such a suggestion. She folded her arms, feeling as though she was about to be interrogated.

'Jace, calm down.' Brandon said from next to Lara.

Jace took a deep breath and put his hands on his hips. He looked over his shoulder at Matías's body, before looking back to Lara and taking a few steps towards her and leaned in slightly, so that his deep voice came out in a low tone. 'And you know what else?' he said slowly, his grey eyes never leaving hers as he spoke. 'This man didn't drown.' He paused and scrutinised her face for a reaction.

Lara forced herself not to blink.

Jace leaned slightly closer and spoke even lower

still, 'He was shot.'

11
Caught

Jace's declaration seemed to ring in Lara's ears as she stood, still in front of him.

There was again silence.

Brandon didn't say anything, he was standing quietly at Lara's side.

Lara had the feeling that he was waiting for her to either defend herself further or confess, as was Jace.

Lara knew which one she had to do, but couldn't bring herself to do it, she didn't even know where to start.

Images of her and Lizzy meeting Alexis and Matías in the bar, getting onto the yacht, the other men boarding the boat, running away from the large man in the corridor, Lizzy getting shot, Lara alone in the sea trying to stay afloat all flooded into Lara's mind all at once. She then looked to where Matías's body was lying on the beach behind Jace.

Immediately the full horror of what had happened that day hit Lara with an overwhelming force. She suddenly felt that her chest was constricted, making it difficult to breathe, just as her eyes burned with tears. She took a step backwards, trying to find the words to make Jace and Brandon understand.

'I - I - we...we were on the boat.' Lara started

weakly, staring at the sand, still with her arms folded. She took a deep breath to steady herself enough to go on. 'It wasn't our boat. Lizzy - my friend and me, we were in a bar in New Zealand and these - these two men started talking to us. They told us they were businessmen - and we believed them,' Lara's noticed her voice became shaky here, so she took another deep breath before continuing, 'They invited us to sail on their yacht. Lizzy had always wanted to go to the Cook Islands. She was all for it...she said it was a good idea...and that it would be fine.' Lara looked up at Brandon and Jace, 'I didn't want to go...I should have never gotten on the boat. I should have insisted that we didn't go...I had a bad feeling about it, but I got talked into it like I always do.' For some reason, it seemed important for them to understand that she hadn't willingly boarded the yacht.

Brandon and Jace said nothing. They instead waited patiently for her to continue her story.

Jace's expression had softened slightly as he watched and waited for her to speak again.

Lara went on, speaking in a less expressive voice to try and avoid breaking off. She wanted to just give her confession and then never have to think about these events again. 'But we did get on the boat.' she said. The new flatter tone helped. It helped detach her from the images she saw in front of her eyes as she spoke. 'We sailed away from New Zealand. And after a few days, we...we...there was another boat. It caught up with ours. My friend woke me up - she was scared - really scared. She said they had guns. We heard shots being fired-'

Brandon opened his mouth to ask something, but Jace held up his hand and shook his head to stop him.

'- A man chased us - I couldn't see Lizzy - I thought she was right behind me, but when I looked around she wasn't there - I didn't know what to do - I hadn't even gotten dressed yet - I was just wearing this stupid shirt - then the men - they - they had her...' Lara's voice was panicked sounding, the pace quickening the more she talked and her chest felt constricted again. She struggled for breath as she tried to go on. 'And they - they shot her!' she gasped. 'They just shot her!' she repeated in barely more than a frantic whisper as her voice broke. Her shoulders shook as tears ran down her cheeks feeling wet and warm, even in the heat of the day. She slumped down into the sand and covered her face with her hands.

Lara couldn't remember ever crying so much before, and she had never done it in front of other people. She'd always kept her feelings well hidden until she was alone where she could manage them in private.

Through blurry eyes and around the sides of her hands, Lara saw Brandon kneel down beside her. His arm reached out and grasp her shoulder firmly, in an attempt to provide her with some comfort.

'Lara come on, it's all right. You're all right now. It's over.' Brandon said, gently, even though he seemed awkward and unsure of what to do. He clearly hadn't expected her to fall to pieces like this.

Jace didn't move. He was still standing with his hands upon his hips, brow furrowed, clearly thinking it all over.

After a few minutes, Lara felt the sobbing starting to subside. She managed to get control of her breathing again, feeling it gradually return to normal. She wiped her eyes on the back of her hands and took a deep breath.

Jace seemed to take this as a sign that he could continue his questioning. 'So how did you escape?' he asked. 'I mean, there was a group of armed men - and you're just one woman with no way of defending yourself...Did they throw you off the boat?'

Brandon looked annoyed with him. 'Jace, it doesn't matter!' he said firmly.

Lara didn't care. She might as well answer all of their questions now, and save herself having to go over it for as long as their curiosity lasted. 'No,' she said in a sort of quiet monotone, 'They didn't push me - I jumped.'

A sort of hush seemed to fall over both of them as she said these last words.

Lara saw Jace and Brandon look at each other, but they didn't say anything.

Lara decided to go on without any prompting.

'They were coming towards me and they were raising their guns. They stepped over Lizzy's body like-like she was nothing and they were about to shoot me too. I didn't even think...I just - jumped.'

Now there was nothing but the rolling waves beside them to be heard.

Lara was aware that Brandon had taken his hand from her shoulder. He had sunk into a sitting position next to her, his elbows on the tanned knees that were exposed below his cut-off trousers. Looking stressed, he ran his fingers through his hair, obviously thinking hard.

After a moment or two, Jace broke the intense quiet. 'So,' he said. 'Are we to glean from this little session, that we are indeed still waiting here in this - this place, with no hope of being rescued?' he continued, his voice loaded suddenly with what sounded like suppressed rage.

'Jace, come on.' Brandon said. 'Nothing has really changed. No harm has been done. We haven't lost anything.'

'Only hope!' Jace yelled back at him angrily.

'I think that you had lost that anyway.' Brandon retorted firmly. 'Lara didn't mean to mislead us, she had just been through a trauma, that's all.'

Lara felt overwhelmingly grateful for Brandon sticking up for her, but she somehow felt that Jace wasn't going to let it go so easily.

She was right.

'Why did you lie?' Jace shot at her.

'I'm sorry I lied to you.' she said imploringly to

both of them, thoroughly meaning what she said. 'I - I didn't realise that you were shipwrecked when I told you that I fell. I didn't know where I was when I woke up on this island. I thought I was somewhere normal, and that I was going to be taken to a hospital or a police station - or an embassy. I couldn't tell the truth in case the men that boarded the boat came after me. They wouldn't think twice about killing me - I was a witness. They killed my friend, they killed him-' Lara gestured towards Matías '- and I don't know how many other people they've killed.'

Jace seemed to have softened slightly when she looked at him, but he still stood on the spot and didn't say anything. He seemed deep in thought.

'I'm really sorry,' she said. 'I was just scared. I didn't know what to do.'

'It's all right,' Brandon said. 'We're not going to hold it against you. We will just forget about it. I'll talk to Jack a little later.' He smiled in an attempt to reassure her, but somehow he looked more strained than Lara had yet seen him. He glanced towards Matías's remains, 'I think in light of what's happened, we'll skip fish for breakfast. Maybe we'll just have some fruit instead.' He turned to Lara, 'Hey, Lara why don't you go back to camp and prepare some coconuts for us? You remember how to, don't you?'

Lara nodded.

'Great,' he replied cheerfully, clapping his hands together and standing up.

Lara rose too.

'We will, um, take care of things here...' he added quietly to her, with another attempt at a smile. This one however had a definite look of a grimace about it.

Lara turned and made her way back to the camp. Her legs felt a little wobbly still and she seemed to be finding it harder than usual to trek through the soft sand her heels sank into, although she was more than grateful to have been given an opportunity to get away from the sight of the man in the sand.

Lara had done as she was told this time. She had prepared fruit for the three of them (Jack still hadn't materialised) and had sat in front of the campfire until Jace and Brandon returned an hour later.

Lara hadn't asked what they had done with the body, but she presumed that they had buried it somewhere on the island.

They didn't speak of it again. Everyone seemed to have come to an unspoken agreement not to mention it and Lara had no intention of breaking this silent vow.

She had been concerned that Jace was going to hold a grudge against her. He had been so angry when he had discovered the truth that no one was coming to their aid.

And yes, for the first day he was much more quiet and subdued; he hardly spoke a word to anyone. But the next day he seemed to have recovered from his initial bout of sullenness and was almost as bright as he had been for the whole time.

Brandon seemed to be the most surprised by this, followed by Lara, who had decided rather early on that Jace was inherently an angry, bitter person. She supposed that perhaps he hadn't always been that way and his more positive demeanour was maybe a truer reflection of himself. Perhaps it was the case that the island had been an oppressing factor upon him, but Lara's unintentional promise of rescue had brought him back to life.

Whatever it was, he reverted back to making an effort, not only with his attitude but also with his appearance. He continued keeping himself clean-shaven and as smart as the conditions around him allowed.

Jack on the other hand took the news much harder. He initially seemed disappointed after Brandon's talk with him. This was followed by his retreat to his personal island, which lasted for no less than two weeks. Lara presumed he was sulking there, reminding her strongly of Alan.

During this fortnight she got to know Jace and Brandon much better.

Brandon's attitude towards Lara didn't change much, he was still polite and warm as ever, but something seemed to have broken in him. His spirit had definitely taken a hit from the infectious-now-evaporated hope he had absorbed from the other two men.

He had since ceased sleeping on the main beach near the campfires in anticipation of a boat being attracted by the bright flames. He had moved into Jace's hut by the potato plants for the time being.

Jace spent a whole afternoon complaining about how he sees enough of Brandon anyway without having to share quarters with him, but stopped quite abruptly when he noticed that it wasn't impressing Lara. He then went on to reminisce about his and Brandon's college years when they had shared a dormitory.

It turned out that they had been friends since they were children, having grown up together after Jace's parents moved next door to Brandon's.

Brandon took his few possessions with him to make his move to Jace's hut near the food crops. He rolled up all of his things in a blanket. This consisted of his clothes, and the jars from underneath the bed - including the mysterious jar of teeth.

One of the jars seemed to contain his personal items from his former life. He showed Lara his wallet before he added it to his bundle. It contained all of the usual things: credit cards, a library card, American dollars and a colourful photograph of a much younger looking Brandon and Jack. They were smiling broadly with an arm each around a woman with dark blonde hair, just like Jack's. Brandon had explained that this was his wife.

Since Brandon had the presence of mind to keep these things in a sealed jar which had protected them from the elements, everything was in pristine condition.

Everything was just as well preserved as the day they landed on the island.

Lara could have believed that Brandon had just taken his wallet out of his pocket in a bank queue back in civilisation.

Brandon was also keeping hold of Jace's wallet and passport in another jar. Apparently Jace had tried to burn them in a fit of rage during their eighth year on the island. Brandon had explained that he had rescued them from the flames before they had reached the contents.

Brandon had noticed the wary look Lara had given the jar of teeth as he wrapped that too in his blanket. He had laughed at her expression and explained that they were the milk teeth Jack had lost since they had become shipwrecked.

So now it was that the four were waiting for rescue together. Lara didn't want to think about how long the men had been waiting on the island to be saved. It was either the case that the others had endured the bulk of the sentence and rescue was due any day now, or as Lara anxiously suspected, this was simply proof that the island was so remote that they were unlikely to ever be found.

It had now been over two months since the tide

had ebbed away Lara's web of lies and brought her secret to the surface. She had slowly adjusted to life on the island, involving herself in all of the chores involved in the daily goal of survival.

She now felt quite adept at catching fish, collecting water and selecting the right fruit. She had gotten completely used to having to wash in the ocean or waterfall. Each wasn't ideal. The sea on an abandoned area of beach felt very exposed and didn't feel at all private; in addition the salt water was more harsh on Lara's skin, whilst the waterfall was chillier and the rocks she stood on felt precariously slippery.

Jack seemed to have come around now and was being just as friendly to Lara as he was before, perhaps even more so. He was now more confident speaking to, and in front of her. This was however in-between disappearing back to his private island for days at a time.

Lara didn't know why he did this, but Brandon reassured her this was normal. Lara presumed that Jack hadn't psychologically left his teenage years fully yet, and was still somewhat immature. This was something that Jace was more than willing to point out to Lara at every available opportunity.

Jace himself was more friendly than ever, and never missed an opportunity to help Lara with her tasks, or teach her a new skill, even when Brandon was prepared to do this himself.

Lara found that Jace was more often finding excuses to spend time with her and almost every time she turned around he would be there. This practice had gotten to such an extent that she was now starting to take extra care to make sure that she was definitely alone before she started to wash.

She presumed that this was because she was still something of a curiosity to him and he enjoyed having different company after all these years, but then again Brandon and Jack didn't seem as enthusiastic as Jace was at being in her presence.

That night Lara had one of her more successful fishing sessions. She was of course accompanied (as she usually was these days) by Jace who heavily complimented her on her catch of three large fish caught in one go all the way back to camp.

Dusk seemed to be the best time for poaching the most plentiful supplies of fish and darkness was falling as Lara and Jace made their way towards the campfire.

Open and endless lilac skies were turning rapidly into smoky blue ones dotted with the first bright stars of the night as they approached the glowing, orange flames.

With now experienced hands, Lara slid the fish onto the stick and despite their unusually heavy weight and slotted it onto the frame above the fire.

'First time's a charm with you, isn't it?' Jace said, complimenting her technique.

'I guess so...' Lara replied, not believing she had done anything to warrant such praise.

Brandon appeared just then, emerging from the

trees behind them. 'Wow, what a haul,' he said. 'In record time too. We are going to have to wait for the potatoes to bake, I'm afraid. I didn't realise you two would be so fast.' he added, setting down some 'potatoes' around the edge of the fire and taking a seat on the log behind him.

'We have Lara to thank for that,' Jace immediately volunteered. 'She's got the golden touch. Caught them all in one go.'

Lara felt the heat rise slightly in her cheeks, but didn't think that this was noticeable in the darkness that was creeping in rapidly around them. She tried to change the subject, 'Where's Jack?' she asked.

Brandon shook his head, 'He won't be joining us.' he said, helping himself to a cup of water. 'I'll take him some of this later,' he added, gesturing with his cup to the cooking food in front of them.

'What's he sulking about now?' Jace asked.

Brandon shook his head, but didn't answer.

Once they had eaten the fish, they moved onto the potatoes; these always surprised Lara by how similar they were to the ones she ate back home in England. The insides were soft and fluffy and the skin had been made crisp and smoky flavoured by the fire. She liked to think of this meal as being like fish and chips, a dish she had always enjoyed back home. Although thinking like this always gave her an aching pang, so she always tried to quash these thoughts as soon as she realised her mind was forming them.

They sat and talked as they digested their simple

meal.

Lara's stomach had learned to deal with the lesser quantities of food and she found that even smaller meals managed to just about satisfy her hunger now. Although, from the way her clothes hung a little more loosely on her body, they implied that she had used up some of her fat reserves.

'Well, that was a delicious dinner.' Brandon said, as he set down his bowl beside him.

'That's all down to the fish,' Jace said, turning to Lara. 'That was some technique you used. You'll have to teach me how to do that next time.'

'I don't know,' Lara said feeling slightly awkward again under Jace's over-enthusiastic praise, 'I'm not really sure what I did was that special, really...'

'You're being too modest,' Jace replied insistently, taking a sip of his water.

'Not really,' she replied with a shrug. 'I just saw them swim into the cage and then lifted it out of the water as quickly as I could.'

'That's the simple answer, for sure,' Jace replied, leaning forward on his log in his enthusiasm to pay her further compliment. 'But if you look deeper, it's all in the technique,' he went on. His voice took on a slightly seductive note as he reached towards her and gently lifted her hand, gently brushing the tops of her fingers with his rough, weather-toughened thumb. 'You have such beautiful hands, you see...'

Lara froze, she didn't quite know how to respond

to this.

Neither it seemed did Brandon, who also seemed to be all of a sudden a little suspended in his seat opposite Jace.

'Right, erm...thanks.' she said, slipping her hand back out of his light grip.

'You're welcome.' Jace said confidently in his deep voice, 'I can't argue with perfection, after all.'

Brandon decided to come to Lara's rescue. 'I think it's time we took this to Jack.' he said, pointing at the dinner they had wrapped in a leaf for him. Say, Lara, why don't you go and deliver it? Maybe you can even talk him into coming over here with us for a while? Stranger things have happened.'

'OK, sure.' Lara said, grabbing the food parcel and quickly standing up, stepping over her log in the direction of the Jack's hut.

'Hey, I'll take you.' Jace quickly volunteered.

'She knows where Jack's hut is, Jace.' Brandon said flatly.

'Well, it's dark...And I thought she might like some company-' Jace replied, getting to his feet.

'It's all right really. Like Brandon said, I know where Jack lives. I'll just be a few minutes.' Lara turned and walked quickly to deliver her parcel.

She was grateful to Brandon for allowing her to break away from the scene behind her. Jace was making her feel more than a little uncomfortable and she wasn't sure how to deal with him.

Once she was swallowed by the darkness

surrounding the campfire, she slowed her pace a little, trying to make her task take as long as possible. Hopefully Jace would have forgotten his train of thought by the time she got back.

Unfortunately, Jack's hut wasn't too far away and she reached it after just a couple of minutes. She found Jack sitting on the steps in the dark, having extinguished his fire, looking up at the bright, white stars which were now vividly clear above their heads.

From what she could see of his face, he registered some surprise at receiving his dinner from Lara and not his father. And unfortunately again, Jack was not in a talkative mood, so Lara had no choice but to return after a few minutes to the campfire with Jace and Brandon.

She took her time getting back to the main camp and even went the longer way through the food crops and past Jace's hut, before she passed slowly through the dark silhouettes of the trees near the main camp.

The campfire flickered through the gap in the trees ahead as she approached. Lara could now make out the two men's faces lit up orange on opposite sides of the campfire as she drew near; the darkness seemed to press in on them.

Just as she was emerging from the trees behind them, Lara became aware that they were moving animatedly, leaning towards each other and seemed to be having an argument.

'-because it's excruciating!-' Brandon hissed at

Jace

'-I don't know what you're talking about - you are imagining things!-' Jace hissed back, more vehemently.

'I wish I was! You are embarrassing everybody - most of all yourself!-'

As Lara stepped into the glow of the campfire, they both stopped arguing immediately and straightened up.

Jace looked flustered and agitated. He looked like he had been about to give Brandon another snappy retort before he became aware of Lara's presence.

Lara didn't need to ask what they had been arguing about. She thought it best to try and gloss over it as much as possible. She cast around for something to say, 'Jack's not feeling very sociable at the moment.' she said, shrugging in what she hoped was a casual manner. 'Speaking of which, I think I might go to bed too. I'm feeling quite tired now,' she lied, before bidding them goodnight and retiring to her hut for the night.

Once she had removed her shorts and shirt, Lara pulled on her sleeping t-shirt which happened to be an old, grey one that Jace had donated to her. Other than the shorts that Brandon had donated to her, she only had men's clothes to wear. She was glad that she had been wearing a bra, at least when she had jumped ship. She laid down under the few blankets that were required for sleeping and reflected upon the evening's events.

Jace certainly had made his intentions clear. Lara hadn't expected that at all. She had thought all along that Jace was just appreciative of different company, other than that he had experienced for over fifteen years. Lara had found herself quite surprised at this latest discovery.

She rolled onto her side and thought with a slight twinge of embarrassment at how naive she had been all this time. Surely now it seemed obvious when she thought back to all the compliments and attention Jace had showered upon her that he perhaps wanted more from her than just friendship.

She wasn't entirely sure how she felt about this either. She had been taken completely by surprise when he had grasped her hand earlier. But she had to admit that her heart had skipped a beat at that moment, and not out of shame or embarrassment either...

Lara avoided over-analysing her feelings too much as she lay thinking, because whatever she may or may not feel for him, Lara just wasn't ready to jump into any kind of relationship just yet. Even though so much had happened to her in the past few months, the memories of her previous relationship still felt as fresh and recent as if she had just stepped out of them.

The emotional taint Alan had left upon her still seemed to linger and she hadn't quite let go of them yet, despite being what felt like a million miles away, living a once completely unimaginable life.

Not only this, but she also felt emotionally drained and the idea of embarking upon a romantic relationship in the very near future daunted her. If anything, she just needed a rest from her love life, she just needed time to think.

She was confident in this thought as she allowed the consistent sound of the rolling waves outside to help her drift off to sleep.

The next day Lara awoke to the golden rays of sunshine streaming into the hut through the doorway. It was hard to sleep once it started to get light. Lara marvelled at how Jack managed to lie-in so regularly.

Once she left the hut, she noticed that no-one else seemed to be awake yet. The main camp was deserted and the camp-fire had burned itself out.

She ventured further down the beach to a more private area and washed briefly in the fresh, white waves. She then put on her underwear before fully dressing, allowing the already-warm morning wind to flow around her, drying her within mere minutes.

Afterwards Jace and Brandon emerged from the trees as she approached the camp. They greeted her brightly as usual before they sat and ate a simple breakfast of coconut and banana together.

Jack appeared after an hour and had a belated breakfast.

'That's the last of the coconuts.' Brandon said, as

he handed his son a portion.

Lara looked at where there usually sat a pile of green-coloured fruit, ripening beside them.

'We need to pick some more good ones.' Brandon went on, 'But not from these trees-' he gestured to the jungle behind him, '-These ones need a little longer to develop. I say we should use the ones from up the hill next.'

'You mean the ones from the cliff-top?' Lara asked.

Brandon nodded.

'I can go and get them if you like?' Lara volunteered, always keen to do her fair share of chores.

'Sure,' Brandon shrugged, 'I mean, if you feel up to it.'

Lara smiled, 'I think I can manage to carry a few coconuts back to camp. Anyway, I like helping out.'

Lara noticed that Jace was being uncharacteristically quiet. By this point he usually would have almost certainly offered his help or advice, but he just sat finishing his water and said nothing.

Perhaps what Brandon had said to him had sunk in, or he had reflected overnight upon Lara's less-than-enthusiastic response to his advances.

Just as Lara had this thought, Jace stood up and announced that he was going to take a shower in the waterfall.

Lara stayed and talked with Brandon and Jack

for a while, before she set off for the cliff-top to go and collect some coconuts for the camp.

It was a beautiful day, and there were few clouds in the sky. Lara had learned a lot about weather since she had arrived on the island. Today she could tell that it was unlikely to rain, judging from the bright blue sky and limited quantity of soft, white clouds. On the other hand, the wind was blowing more than usual, so that may bring in storm clouds later, but that wouldn't be for a good few hours, at least.

She was just approaching the base of the hill near the edge of the jungle, when Jace appeared from the trees up ahead.

'Hey Lara,' he said casually. 'I thought I would come and see if you wanted a hand? Brandon may leave you to struggle back to camp with a heap of fruit, but I'm not so harsh.'

'Erm, thanks.' Lara said, noticing that Jace didn't look like he had taken the shower he had excused himself for. His hair wasn't at all wet and Lara just had a nagging feeling in the back of her mind. She had the suspicion that he had been waiting in the jungle in order to avoid Brandon politely sabotaging any offer of help Jace may have offered to her.

'Many hands make light work, right?' he replied with a smile, 'Especially in this heat. No, I consider myself to be more of a gentleman than Brandon. I wouldn't send a beautiful woman off to go and fetch provisions for the whole camp alone.'

Lara had to inwardly smile at the fact Jace considered himself to be more well-mannered than Brandon, even before she felt a tinge of embarrassment that he was attempting to flatter her again.

They reached the top breathless and sweating slightly; it was a hotter day than usual and the wind was so warm and humid it didn't help cool them at all.

'Why don't we take a seat for a moment?' Jace said, panting slightly and dropping himself onto the biggest of the rocks overlooking the ocean. 'Catch our breath.'

Lara could feel herself overheating after scaling the hill, so she complied. She noticed that the tree beyond Jace was laden with ripe-looking coconuts as she sat on the other end of the rock.

After a minute of resting Jace spoke, 'Maybe the view from here isn't so bad after all.' He looked at Lara. 'But I guess it depends on the company you're keeping too,' he said with a wink.

'I guess...' Lara now had the sinking feeling that she was being drawn into a trap that Jace was setting. He had managed to get himself alone with her without the others realising.

Here they were in the most strikingly beautiful area of the island; in fact it was Lara's favourite place and they were now sitting admiring the view together.

How could she have allowed herself to get into this situation, when she knew that Jace had more than friendship on his mind?

Lara felt a jolt of nerves at being alone with Jace. It didn't help when she glanced across at him taking in the ocean vista, and noticed for the first time that he was actually really quite handsome.

His almond-shaped grey eyes, straight nose and pronounced cheekbones all made up the artful symmetry of his face. His hair was neatly swept back and the occasional flecks of grey even seemed to suit him. He was also still faithfully clean-shaven, as he had been every day since the day after Lara had arrived.

Lara thought about how she could get herself out of this situation as subtly as possible without hurting Jace, since they had to live in close quarters with each other along with any potential consequences on a small island.

Just as she was thinking this however, Jace slid smoothly across the rock so that he was sitting directly beside her, much too close for her liking.

'You know,' he said quietly, his deep voice a low rumble, barely audible over the waves crashing into the cliff-base below them, his eyes focused on hers, 'I do really enjoy spending time with you. I can't tell you how nice it is to speak to someone like you for a change.'

Lara wanted to shuffle further away from him, but she was already perched as far as she could go without falling on the ground. 'Someone like me?' she repeated, playing for time and wondering how she could let him down gently.

'You know - someone who has a great sense of humour, someone who is intelligent...beautiful...' His rough hand reached up to brush the hair from her face before he leaned in to kiss her.

Lara realised she wasn't going to find some tactful way to let Jace know that she wasn't looking for a boyfriend right this minute, so having run out of ideas, she jumped up and grabbed a fallen coconut near her feet, 'This'll get us started, won't it?' she said, a little more loudly than she meant to.

And ignoring the look of surprise (or maybe disappointment) on Jace's face, Lara turned on her heel and made her way swiftly down the hill and back to camp.

12
Wild

Brandon had registered some light-hearted surprise at seeing Lara return to the camp with just the one coconut in her hands. But Lara had laughed along with him, saying that she had forgotten to take a blanket with her to carry her bounty in.

More than anything, she was just glad to have escaped the situation with Jace up on the cliff-top. She hoped that Jace would not judge her actions as being too carelessly dismissive, and that he wasn't too offended. After all, she still had to exist in this place just as he did. They lived directly alongside each other and they saw each other all the time, especially around mealtimes; it was unavoidable. Hopefully he would understand and the atmosphere between them wouldn't be too strained.

Lara was slightly worried that Jace was hurt however when he didn't turn up for lunch, leaving Brandon, Jack and Lara to fish for their dinner alone that evening.

Lara thought for a while that Jace was going to skip dinner too before he arrived at the last minute, just as they had almost finished eating.

She took several tentative glances across the campfire at Jace as he ate his food.

He was quieter than usual, but still joked a little, even though he avoided her eye most of the time.

He didn't seem too angry or upset, which Lara ruled as a good sign. He would probably forget all about the incident in a couple of days like he had with her lies.

Jace's behaviour over the next few weeks reassured Lara that she had been right. He gradually returned to his usual self within a day or two and even went back to helping Lara out with the tasks she volunteered to complete.

He didn't once mention his advance towards her and Lara took his lead and avoided bringing up the subject too.

She took his skirting of the topic to mean that he didn't want to talk about it, and that was more than fine with Lara. She was definitely happy to avoid any conversation that would create any amount of awkwardness between them, and kept her silence.

It was simply easier to ignore the subject than to face it head-on and Lara assumed that his lack of discussion meant that Jace had got the message that she wasn't interested in any romantic entanglement and was simply trying to save face by not uttering a word about it.

How wrong she was.

Several weeks after their previous encounter, Lara once again found herself alone with Jace. And once again, the two of them were collecting food to take back to the main camp. This time, however, they were crouched next to each other in the potato plants.

The large, thick, vividly green leaves around them waved in the gentle breeze as they dug up the roots ready for dinner that night using a small makeshift trowel Jace had fashioned from a coconut shell.

Lara tossed another potato, still with the rest of the plant attached into their pile; the stems and leaves were to be eaten too. Nothing was wasted on the island.

'Hold it.' Jace said suddenly.

Lara looked up at him. 'What is it?'. She couldn't see anything wrong with her technique.

'You have a little mud-' he gestured to the side of her face, but before she could do anything about it, Jace had reached out and brushed it from her cheek.

'Um, thanks.' she said awkwardly.

Without warning, Jace leaned quickly forward in what Lara realised too late was another attempt at a kiss. This time however, the element of surprise allowed him to make contact and he pressed his warm lips against hers and taking her face firmly in his hand.

Since she was crouched in such an awkward position, Lara could only stop his advance by placing her hand tentatively on his chest to push him away.

He pulled away slightly and searched her face as he waited for her response.

Lara took her hand from where it had made contact with him; the bare sliver of chest his shirt didn't cover.

'Um, Jace,' she said in a half-whisper. 'I-I can't do this. I er - it's not you,' she pointed out quickly. 'It's just that, well...um. I have just come out of a long-term relationship and well...a lot has happened in the last few months. It's a lot for me to think about.' She hoped he would understand.

'I see...' he said quietly.

Lara was made a little uncomfortable by the fact that he said nothing else. They were still crouched together in the rows of plants and the atmosphere was more than a little strained.

Lara decided to try and brush over what had just happened by adding what she hoped was a positive slant on the topic, trying to ignore the aching feeling creeping through her muscles in her legs from remaining in a crouched position for longer than she had anticipated, 'You know...no one has to rush into doing anything reckless. We might all be rescued by this time next week.'

Lara thought she saw a muscle in Jace's cheek twitch, but she carried on anyway, 'A boat could just sail along any day and find us.' she said with a nervous shrug, trying to compensate for the awkward silence Jace was maintaining. 'It has to happen eventually though, doesn't it?' she went on. 'Why shouldn't it be tomorrow, or next month maybe?' She hoped Jace would join in and say something - anything. Anything that would relieve the palpable tension between them now.

Jace looked down at his hands, he seemed to be considering what Lara had just said.

Lara's legs were really burning now from staying crouched for so long, so she stood up and tried to add a final casual word to put an end to the matter, before she left for the camp. 'It's like Brandon said isn't it? Nothing has really been changed by me coming here. We've got just as much chance of being rescued as ever, and it's bound to happen sooner or later. It's just, well, we're all waiting here together now aren't we?'

Surely Jace would have to agree with this, Lara thought to herself as she turned around to leave.

It seemed that she had said the wrong thing however, in fact, Lara's words seemed to have hit a raw nerve with Jace and he was provoked into quickly standing up, grabbing her by the arm and pulling her sharply back to face him.

'Do you really think that nothing has changed here since you arrived?' he said in a dangerous whisper that shook with rage.

Lara looked back at him with wide eyes as his thick fingers pressed uncomfortably into her upper arm. She hadn't expected him to snap like this. What on earth had she said to him to make him respond this way? 'I - I don't know what you're-'

'You have no idea what you have done, do you?' Jace hissed at her.

'I really don't know what you mean.' Lara was genuinely scared now, Jace seemed to have gone crazy. She didn't know what he was talking about and wanted more than anything to get back to the camp where it was safe with the others.

Lara tried to wriggle her arm slowly from Jace's hold, at the same time she backed away, but it was no use.

Jace simply responded to this by pulling her closer still and tightening his grip.

His face was now so close to hers that when he spoke next, she could feel his breath upon her face, making the stray strands of hair around it flutter. 'You made me believe we were going to be saved. After all this time...' he went on. 'After all the waiting... So *many* years. *So many*, Lara. Finally - finally I thought we might get out of here...But you *lied*, didn't you?'

'I -I'm sorry,' she said, still trying to release herself from his iron grasp on her arm. Her fingers were starting to tingle uncomfortably now. 'I said I was sorry - I made a mistake. Please let go of me - you're hurting me.'

'"Sorry"' he repeated bitterly. 'Sorry is just a word! You can't just give us all false hope and then just destroy it!'

'Well - I really meant it!' Lara said, her voice rising now to match Jace's. She had thought that they had put this all behind them, she was annoyed to find that Jace was still harbouring a grudge. 'I'm sorry that I made up a story - which I don't think you really believed anyway - but I was scared that I was going to be found by a group of drug dealers that I had seen murder my best friend! I was scared OK? And I'm scared now! So why don't you just take your hands off me and leave me alone!'

In her anger, Lara managed to shove Jace's hand from her arm. But she hadn't finished setting him straight yet.

She stood and faced him firmly, the strength of her indignation empowering her. 'Look, you just need to let it go all right? I made a mistake, but you just need to get over it and just go back to how things were before I got here.'

'No. I can't go back. Certainly not now that you are here,' he continued, shaking his head.

'I don't know what you mean. What difference does it make to you whether I am here or not?'

Jace laughed out loud.

This did nothing more to Lara than to unnerve her further.

'You just don't get it, do you?' He took a step towards her.

Lara backed away half a step, but her back hit a tree, leaving her without escape just as Jace drew closer and closing the distance between them.

'You don't know that you being here is really hard for me,' he said, his face just inches from hers so that she could feel each of his words again. 'You have no idea what it is you're doing to me, do you?' he asked in the same seductive whisper he had used when he had grasped her hand by the campfire in front of Brandon.

Only now they were both quite alone, and Lara realised, with a flushing in her cheeks where this conversation was leading.

'You know...It has been such a long time since I was with a woman...' He spoke still in the same whisper, except that now Lara could hear a distinct pang of longing in his deep voice. His eyes never left hers.

Lara shook her head. She had no idea how to tactfully end the conversation and so stood rooted to the spot. She felt she shouldn't just run away from the situation this time.

'It's been too long...too long since I've kissed a woman. Too long since I've-' he faltered slightly as a muscle twitched again in his jaw '-made love to a woman...Felt her body against mine...' Jace moved in closer to Lara and pressed his firm body against hers gently. 'Too long since I've run my hands over her body...'

With the lightest of touch he placed his fingertips to her jawline and slowly traced down her neck.

Just as his fingers reached the collar of her white shirt, Lara came to her senses and grabbed his hand, stopping him. 'I'm sorry,' she said, sounding more flustered than she realised.

She was more than aware that her cheeks were still flushed; she hoped it wasn't visibly obvious to Jace. 'I already told you - I can't do this.' she said firmly.

And without another word, she slipped out of Jace's hold and swooped down to pick up the pile of potatoes before striding away.

This time she wasn't going to go back empty-handed to greet Brandon at the camp.

Dinner that evening was much easier than Lara had anticipated - mostly because Jace didn't make an appearance at all.

Lara had been dreading an awkward atmosphere that she feared she would have to explain to Brandon at some point, or else he would perceive it by himself.

Instead, Brandon remained oblivious to what had happened earlier between her and Jace and Lara wasn't going to update him. She assumed that Jace wouldn't either, when he eventually did re-emerge that was.

Jack was also missing from dinner, although this wasn't unusual and Lara and Brandon found themselves making up two food parcels to deliver later.

Brandon informed Lara that this wasn't as unusual as it seemed. He explained that before Lara had arrived, Jace had taken to keeping himself isolated from himself and Jack. He said that it wasn't unusual for him to not be seen for weeks on end, which was the complete opposite of how he had been behaving since Lara had arrived.

Lara was slightly concerned that she would have some explaining to do when Brandon wondered out loud about what had caused Jace to go back to his old ways, but he didn't question Lara about it, for which she was grateful.

When they had finished eating, Lara volunteered to take Jack's food parcel to him to avoid having to deliver Jace's.

Jack was his usual, difficult-to-talk-to self so Lara dropped off his dinner before returning to her hut for the night.

The pillow was so flat it was hard to get comfortable, especially when she had so much on her mind.

Lara eventually managed to relax on her back. She looked at the few stars that she could see in the strip of sky visible through the open doorway.

She was quite certain that she had done the right thing with Jace. Lara had to admit that he was certainly handsome, but she had to remind herself that he wasn't exactly close to her age. Then there was the fact that he was rude, bitter and angry. He was so very angry.

Lara had presumed that he had forgiven her for her lies from the way that he had been acting recently, but she had obviously been mistaken.

He still blamed her for giving him "false hope". It was bad enough that she criticised herself for having done this, she didn't need someone else doing it too.

After hours of going over everything in her head, Lara turned over onto her side and tried to forget about the other feelings Jace had accused her of stirring within him.

Breakfast the next day was another quiet affair.

Neither Jace nor Jack made an appearance and Lara and Brandon were left to fish, cook and eat by themselves.

Lara was a little concerned when Brandon casually mentioned the fact that Jace hadn't returned to their hut last night either; in fact, he hadn't seen him since yesterday lunchtime.

Brandon told her not worry, Jace was most likely just slipping into his old habits again.

It was a dark, cloudy day with intermittent light rain showers which made fishing more difficult. The water droplets spattered on the surface of the sea, ruining visibility and disturbing the fish.

In the end, Lara and Brandon got so hungry that they just settled for half a fish each. They decided that if Jace and Jack couldn't be bothered to turn up for the mealtime, then they shouldn't be dissatisfied with a serving of fruit for breakfast instead.

Brandon's annoyance towards his son faded after he had eaten, and his fatherly instincts caused him to wrap up the remainder of the coconut and a banana to take to Jack to make sure that he didn't go hungry.

His feeling of goodwill however, did not extend to Jace and he advised Lara to leave him to his own devices.

Lara was more than willing to do as she was told, happy to keep out of Jace's way for a while, although not for any reason Brandon was aware of.

Brandon seemed to take her quiet thoughtfulness on the matter as sign she was concerned about Jace, and he reassured her that he would go and find him after he had delivered Jack's breakfast.

Lara didn't tell him her real stance on the Jace situation and decided to go and take a quick shower in the waterfall.

Since there had been no sign of Jace or Jack at the main camp, Lara approached the tranquil clearing with some caution, hoping she wouldn't discover that either of them had thought of the same early morning activity as her.

Once she was happy the coast was clear, she undressed and slipped beneath the stream of lukewarm water. She washed quickly, thinking that she would get time to take a solitary walk around the island to clear her head a little before lunch had to be prepared.

A sudden *snap* from the dense trees to her right made all thoughts of alone-time disappear.

Lara froze and looked over her shoulder. As her gaze reached where she thought the sound had come from, she thought she could hear further rustling. She couldn't see anything untoward in the dark jungle however. From where she stood bathed in the bright sunlight that surrounded her it was hard to see anything further than a few feet in any direction, thanks to the vivid glow of the morning sun.

After a minute or two Lara came to the conclusion that perhaps one of the others had come up with the idea of a shower too and then realising their mistake had left again, although Lara couldn't shake the feeling that they had lingered in the trees longer than they should have done; she wondered which one it had been.

She decided to spend the rest of the morning up

on the cliff-top rocks. It looked like the rain would hold off for the time being, so Lara set off thinking that she could while away a few hours enjoying the scenery with her own company for a while.

There was nothing but a view of open and vast seas to accompany today's more gentle waves crashing against the base of the land from the cliff-top rock seats. The sky was a dramatic looking panorama of angry, blue-grey clouds that seemed to stretch on forever into the horizon softened by various different rain showers.

Here and there in the far-off distance there were beams of golden sunlight slanting onto the water's surface, turning it a unique shade of sea green and making the whole scene look eerie.

Lara was so engrossed in the view that seemed to change every minute and had forgotten herself completely, when a nearby rustling footstep brought her suddenly back to her immediate environment.

She span around in her seat to see who had come to pay her a visit; it was Jace.

He stood, rooted to the spot at the edge of the trees when he caught sight of her.

Lara was slightly taken aback when, in a seconds glance, she took in his appearance.

She thought he looked terrible. Other than her very first day on the island, Jace had made a deliberate effort to remain clean-shaven. Now however, there was a definite, unfamiliar shadow of stubble across his face which seemed to emphasise even further the dark circles underneath his eyes. In addition, he was still wearing the same dark blue shirt and khaki trousers he had been wearing yesterday.

Lara had the wild impression that Jace hadn't slept much, or even at all last night and imagined he had just been wandering around the island on his own. As Brandon had said, Jace hadn't returned to his hut last night, so this possibility didn't seem that wild at all.

Lara felt a little shade of regret at the fact she hadn't made more of an effort to let Jace down more gently. Her rejection had obviously hit him harder than she had expected.

There was a moment where they simply looked at each other, where Lara tried briefly to think of what she should say to him, before she realised that something was wrong.

As she looked at Jace, she realised that his expression was akin to the one she had seen him wear yesterday; the one of anger intermingled with desire. Only this time he seemed to project a much more menacing quality. He seemed to emanate an air that was more aggressive, dangerous even.

Lara felt a twinge of fear that she couldn't explain as Jace walked over to the rocks and sat on the one next to her. Usually he always opted to sit as close to her as possible to be able to readily engage her in conversation. Today he seemed to be breaking from this habit and, in Lara's opinion, was acting rather strangely.

He didn't say anything and stared out at the ominous ocean to avoid eye contact with her.

'Hi,' she said to him awkwardly as he continued to gaze off into the horizon.

She didn't get an answer, so she went on, trying to think of anything to talk about other than what had happened yesterday. 'If you're looking for Brandon, he took some food to Jack. You know - because he missed breakfast?'

She thought she sounded nervous. Why did she sound so nervous?

'I'm not looking for Brandon.' Jace said flatly. His voice was slightly hoarse, like he hadn't used it at all overnight, leaving Lara in no doubt that he hadn't spoken to anyone since their encounter yesterday afternoon.

'Oh...good, because he's not here.' Lara replied, realising with a cringe as the words left her mouth that she was merely stating the obvious, but she was struggling to think of what to say to a man she had so abruptly rejected during an unintentionally-intimate situation.

Silence fell once again. The only sound was that of the crashing waves against the base of the cliff.

Lara noticed that she wasn't the only one who felt nervous. Jace seemed to be showing signs of anxiety too. He was fiddling with his hands a little and seemed distracted. He still wouldn't make eye contact with her.

Lara had the nagging feeling that something wasn't right. She was anxious and unnerved but she couldn't say why.

She wanted more than anything to just get up and leave. Her instincts were telling her to run away, but social convention was making her stay put.

'I'm sorry.' he said quietly, as though he was forcing the words out against their will.

Lara looked at him sharply, she had no idea what he was referring to, but she there was a sudden feeling of dread creeping high in her chest. 'For what?' she asked, watching him cautiously for his response.

He was staring down at his hands, but looked as though he couldn't really see them.

He shook his head with some degree of sorrow, 'I can't do it. I can't wait another sixteen years on this island,' he said quietly. 'Not like this. Not without...a woman.' His voice had become quieter as he had spoken, until what he said next was in just a cracked whisper, barely audible above the waves down below, 'I didn't want it to have to come to this. I'm sorry...'

Lara wasn't aware that she had made the decision to stand up and make a run for the trees, but her body had acted automatically, and she found herself on the threshold of the jungle when Jace caught up with her. He grabbed her bodily around the torso, forcing her to a sudden stop and used her moment of imbalance to his advantage, pulling her to the ground.

Lara automatically put her hands out in front of

her as she hit the wild, untamed grass just beside the tree line. The summery smell of it was vividly impressed upon her senses as she tried to frantically scramble to her feet.

She felt the itchy blades prickle her face as Jace pressed his weight down on top of her, pushing her further into the ground as he tried to take control of her now flailing arms that were reaching back and attempting to shove him off her.

Lara suddenly found her voice, 'Jace!' she gasped, still struggling against him. 'What are you doing?!'

But Jace didn't respond.

For a few minutes, they were both arms and legs fighting each other as they fought on the ground.

'What are you doing?!' she repeated urgently, breathless from the struggle.

Jace ignored her and took hold of both of her wrists this time; his thick fingers closed around them, pushing them down into the grass above her head.

For the first time, he made eye contact with her.

What Lara saw as she looked into his steel-grey eyes filled her with dread; the look in them told her everything she needed to know. A rush of fear flooded through her as she realised what he was planning to do.

'Jace!' she gasped, still breathless, 'Jace - please don't do this!' she pleaded with him.

Jace adjusted his grip on her wrists, and for a fleeting second Lara thought he was going to release her. But then she realised that he was just shifting them into the grip of one of his hands to leave the other one free to proceed.

He didn't get very far however.

His free hand slid under her shirt, fumbling against her skin for the waistband of her shorts.

But then all of a sudden Jace's weight was abruptly pulled off her and he was thrown backwards and slammed into the grass a couple of yards away.

Lara didn't miss her opportunity. She sat up and scrabbled backwards on her hands as she looked to see where Jace had gone.

Brandon was there. His demeanour matched the dark stormy sky around him as he looked down at the crumpled form of Jace sprawled in the long grass. 'WHAT THE HELL ARE YOU DOING?!' he yelled at the defeated man at his feet.

Lara realised that it had been Brandon that had dragged Jace off her, and it seemed that with surprising strength he had thrown him to the ground.

Lara thought Brandon looked like he wanted to hit Jace. Or maybe he wanted to shake him and force him to answer his question.

Jace had initially looked angry and much like he wanted to hit Brandon back too, but now said nothing and sat with his head in his hands.

Lara didn't want to be anywhere near him at the moment. She didn't care if Brandon would hurt him or not. She wasn't going to wait and find out.

She quickly got to her feet and disappeared into the trees.

13
Unforgivable

Lara ran and ran. She didn't know where she was going, but she urged her legs to take her as far away from Jace as possible.

After descending the slope as fast as she could without falling, she tore through the thickly set trees of the jungle; her shoulders hit the odd one or two as she ploughed through them with little care.

The fine branches of the densely-set trees tugged at her shirt as she shoved through them, but Lara frantically batted them away and forced herself to continue.

She was breathless, she was aware that she was shaking and her legs felt weak, but still she did not stop. She didn't even hear the waterfall over the sound of her own frantic breathing as she burst from the trees where it stood in the clearing.

As beautiful as ever, the tranquil scene of trickling water seemed to contrast harshly with the aggressive act that had almost been forced upon her not far from here.

Lara continued past the waterfall and disappeared into the dense, dark forest opposite; the stormy day was making it far darker than she had ever seen it.

She didn't care that she was so out of breath she felt like collapsing against a nearby rock to steady her breathing, just as long as she was distancing herself from the man that she had just left and it wasn't his breath she could hear now in her ears.

Lara found herself irritatingly slowed down in this darker jungle. To her annoyance she had to navigate the thicker, more well established trees with a little more care.

But it wasn't for long however, as the trees became more sparse and the light grew brighter again. Lara picked up the pace and a few moments later her feet hit the sand of the smallest beach on the island.

She was disappointed that she couldn't just keep running. She just wanted to keep running forever, to never have to think of what had almost just happened to her and what she had just fled from, but there was nowhere to run.

Lara would have to settle for this tiny beach. She was grateful to find it completely deserted, she needed more than ever to be alone.

Now that she had stopped running and stood struggling to regain her breath, Lara's thoughts seemed to catch up with her. It was almost as though she had managed to outrun them for a few minutes as she had hastily made her way to her private retreat, but now they hit her with an overwhelming force.

She folded her arms in a fruitless attempt to try and comfort herself and sank onto her knees in the sand. Tears once again overcame her, just as they had when she had been forced to relive Lizzy's murder.

Lara was so angry with Jace for what he had planned to do to her. There was no excusing it. She knew that he had been forced to endure almost sixteen years of loneliness and frustration, but what he had attempted to make Lara endure was far worse.

How dare he ignore her wishes and decide to use her for his own ends like that? Lara had made herself more than clear, but he had decided he wouldn't take no for an answer, despite her protests.

Social convention had overruled her instincts and forced her to ignore them. She was as far away from civilisation as it was possible to get and yet she had almost been forced to endure an unexpected attack because she had been more afraid of hurting a man's feelings than she had been of him and what he could do to her.

All this, even though the island itself was wild, everything around her was alive and aggressive, fighting for survival.

No matter how hard Brandon tried to uphold a reasonably normal life here, nothing about this place was civilised. Maybe if Lara had been a little more wild herself and a little less civilised she could have gotten herself out of the situation if she had made a run for it sooner.

Lara felt slightly ashamed that she had only been spared the act that Jace had planned for her because Brandon had come to her rescue. She was angry with herself for having ended up at risk of coming under that sort of attack at all. But then, Lara thought that she wasn't the one to blame at all; it was Jace.

Jace had obviously slipped far over the edge of civil. He hadn't abandoned his instincts at all, he had given into them. Decency, respect and free will had all been forgotten about and he was giving precedence to his basic interests, no matter what the cost to those around him.

Lara wiped her eyes with the back of her hand and took several, steadying breaths in an attempt to get herself under control and thought bitterly of how she had gotten herself into this situation.

Lara sat in the sand for a long time, watching without really seeing the ever-changing clouds and distant rain showers in the dark, stormy sky just as she had done earlier that morning; although it seemed like a long time ago now. Gradually her tears ceased and without her realising it, her breathing returned to normal.

Lara had stayed on her private beach until she felt calm enough to think clearly again. After a while, she became anxious about where Jace was now. Had Brandon finished with him yet? She had no idea where he would be, but found it hard to imagine that he was still up on the cliff-top.

Lara had found herself glancing over her shoulder every few minutes and didn't feel safe alone, so she made sure that she was fully composed before she returned to the main camp.

There she found Brandon who had been waiting for her. He was concerned that Lara hadn't returned straight away and seemed even more so when he took in her appearance.

'I just needed some time alone.' she told him, taking her usual seat beside the dwindling fire.

As hard as Lara had tried, she still seemed to appear somehow slightly ruffled to Brandon, who repeatedly asked her if she was all right.

Lara had spent several hours trying to compose a brave face to present to the camp, and she was most disappointed with herself when it fell apart so quickly in front of Brandon. She tried, and failed, to hold back tears as she sat upon her log and tried to get herself under control.

Brandon sat himself beside her. He looked slightly awkward, as though he was wondering whether or not to put a consoling arm around her or not.

Instead he stared out at the ocean and shook his head as he tried to comprehend Jace's actions. 'I just can't believe he would try to do something like this...' he said. 'I mean, I know being here with just Jack and myself has hit him hard, I just...I didn't realise he was capable of trying something like this.'

'Neither did I.' Lara admitted, once again forcing the tears to stop.

'I mean, what the hell was he thinking?' Brandon said abruptly after a minute, as though a debate had been going on inside his head and he was now continuing it out loud. 'Did he-' Brandon faltered slightly, looking awkward again '-I mean - what did he say to you?' he asked delicately.

Lara shook her head as she stared out at the ocean. It was easier to face the blank stretch of grey water and sky, rather than Brandon as she spoke. 'Nothing,' she replied. 'He never spoke a word to me the whole time. He just said that he couldn't face being alone any more and-' now it was Lara's turn to falter '-and that he was sorry.' She finished quietly.

Brandon tutted and shook his head again, staring at the sand as he tried to piece together the facts in his mind. 'I never expected him to resort to this,' he said, still with an element of shock in his voice. 'I'm so sorry Lara,' he said, turning to face her. 'If I had known he would try something like this, I would have...well, I would have kept a closer watch over you.'

'It's all right,' Lara said, managing somehow to force a weak smile. 'I know it wasn't your fault.'

'I can only apologise on Jace's behalf too. I don't know what he could have been thinking. He must have completely lost his mind. I need to have a proper talk with him later. I couldn't reason with him up on the cliff-top earlier. I'll wait until he has calmed down a little. Then we need to have a little talk...' Brandon trailed off, looking as though he was thinking uncharacteristically angry thoughts.

'Listen, you're not going to go picking a fight with him are you?' Lara was concerned for

Brandon's safety, even though she had no care whatsoever for Jace's. In fact, she thought that she would be pleased to hear that Jace had received a beating, but didn't want Brandon to get injured as a result. 'I don't want you to get hurt just because of me.'

'Oh, don't worry about me,' he replied, with a weak smile. 'However I may appear, I can take pretty good care of myself. Besides, I really haven't decided what to do with Jace yet.'

'Just promise me you won't do anything silly.' She looked for confirmation from him.

'All right, I promise.' Although he still looked distracted and wouldn't meet her eyes.

Speaking with Brandon had calmed Lara much more than her time on the other beach. He had the demeanour of a kindly uncle, and Lara felt safe in his company.

When Brandon announced that he was going to find Jace and set things straight, Lara suddenly realised that she didn't want to be left alone. She felt anxious at the thought of being abandoned, not knowing whether Jace would turn up here whilst Brandon was out looking for him.

She thought she was probably being irrational, but had no idea how substantiated her fears were. After all, up until this morning she had assumed that she was safe in Jace's company and she had realised, too late, that she was not. What else was he potentially capable of? Would he come back for her to try again?

Lara didn't want to think of any of these possibilities right now, if ever. One thing she knew for certain was that she didn't want Brandon to leave her alone here with only her thoughts and fears for company.

Lara wasn't sure how to convey this to Brandon, but when she admitted to him that she wanted him to stay at the camp with her he seemed to understand the reason why.

She again felt a rush of gratitude towards her kindly uncle, and fitting to his role even more he insisted that Lara should get something to eat since she missed lunch.

Lara didn't feel much like eating, even though her stomach was telling her otherwise, but Brandon was determined. 'Come on Lara, we get so little to eat anyway, you can't afford to skip meals,' he said, handing her some fruit.

The rest of the day seemed to pass by quickly. Lara and Brandon ate an easy-to-prepare dinner of fish and fruit.

When it was time for bed, Brandon suggested that Lara should get an early night to recuperate after her stressful day.

She was suddenly reminded of when she had first arrived on the island, although now she felt even less secure than she had then - and that had been a very difficult day. 'Brandon?' she asked. 'Will you stay with me tonight? It's just, I really don't want to be on my own. I don't know if Jace will come back here or not.'

'Uh, sure...' Brandon said gently. 'I'll make sure Jace doesn't try anything.'

True to his word, Brandon made himself as comfortable as he could in the sand in front of the steps outside Lara's hut, using the spare blankets he kept stored there.

With Brandon sleeping out in the open on the main camp beach, it seemed even more like when Lara had first arrived.

She had difficulty settling when she had nestled herself under the blankets, even though she now realised for the first time how exhausted she was.

It had been more humid than usual all day and seemed even more so now that she was trying to get comfortable enough to sleep.

She tossed and turned a lot with many uncomfortable thoughts nagging at her, preventing her from relaxing in even the slightest.

The problem was that every time Lara closed her eyes, she saw images of the day's events flash before them. Now that she lay still and alone in the darkness she could almost feel Jace's hands on her again, almost as though he was there. It was hard to believe that it had happened earlier that same day; Lara thought it seemed like so much longer ago.

It wasn't until several restless and clammy hours later, that Lara finally found herself drifting off into an uneasy sleep.

She awoke later than usual the next day after a terrible night's sleep. After she finally had managed to doze off, she had been awoken by several vivid and disturbing nightmares and she had found it difficult to get back to sleep again. All in all, she was glad to have woken up to find it was the morning.

Lara sat up and reached for her shorts, trying not to think of how Jace had almost managed to remove them yesterday. She froze when she saw her arms; they were very obviously bruised. The impressions of Jace's hands from when he had held her down were very clearly marked upon her wrists.

Lara could feel the heat rising in her face at the thought of Brandon or Jack seeing them, so she rolled down the sleeves of her white shirt to hide them, fastening the cuffs before she left the hut.

Lara approached the campfire to find Jack sitting there alone, cooking fish and helping himself to a cup of water.

'Good morning,' she said as brightly as she could, thinking that it was unusual for Jack to be there before she was. Surely she hadn't slept so late that Jack had woken up before her. 'Where's your Dad?' she asked him nonchalantly as she approached. Now that she sat on her log opposite him, Lara could see that he had dark circles under his eyes and he looked decidedly sleep deprived, although not half as tired as Lara felt herself.

'Oh, uh, he went to find Jace,' he replied, looking awkward and avoiding her eyes, running his fingers nervously through his blonde hair.

His sly behaviour told Lara everything she needed to know. She now understood why Jack looked so tired and why he was acting so shiftily.

Brandon had obviously woken Jack up earlier this morning to take care of Lara, whilst he went off to find Jace and confront him.

Lara felt a stab of humiliation as she guessed that Brandon had told Jack what had happened. She also felt slightly betrayed that Brandon must have left her unguarded briefly whilst she was sleeping to go and fetch his son.

Jack didn't quite seem to know how to act around her, the awkwardness he usually displayed even more pronounced.

She tried to gloss over this as she took charge of the fish cooking on the fire and served it out. She made a great effort to maintain upbeat conversation as she did so. *As if it wasn't hard enough talking to Jack already*, she thought.

After they had eaten, Lara found that Jack was a little more relaxed in her company and was back to his usual level of social ineptitude around her. He had obviously decided that she was still the same person and he didn't need to act any differently around her, no matter what had happened between her and Jace.

After several hours of being alone in Jack's company, Lara almost jumped out of her skin when a rustling behind her in the trees caused her to stop mid-sentence.

She relaxed as soon as she saw that it was

Brandon emerging from the jungle and not Jace.

He looked more than a little strained, and Lara's attention was immediately drawn to the knuckles of his right hand, which were red and sore looking, making Lara think that he had broken his promise to her about not getting physical with Jace.

Brandon asked Jack to go and fetch enough potatoes for lunch for all four of them.

Lara must have given an involuntary reaction at Brandon's request, because he held up his hand and told her that it was okay; Jace wouldn't be joining them for lunch.

As Jack disappeared into the trees to complete his task, his father sat down on the log next to Lara and confirmed that he had successfully tracked down and spoken with Jace. He now relayed what they had talked about.

Apparently Jace had taken occupancy of the small beach that no one visited to avoid having to see her.

'It's lucky we don't go there anyway right?' Brandon said, with a half-hearted attempt at being upbeat.

Lara's heart sank slightly at finding out that one of her favourite haunts on the island had been rendered inaccessible, but didn't interrupt Brandon as he gave her his news update.

Brandon explained that he had arranged to take Jace food across to his new abode, so that they wouldn't have to eat meals together.

Lara was glad of this, but it felt like too much of

an easy option for Jace. She thought him a coward for finding somewhere to conveniently hide, instead of facing her. Not that she wanted to see him, so it was easier for her, but she doubted that was why he had chosen such an option.

Lara was annoyed too, because if nothing else, it meant that he was getting out of doing the island chores. She shook her head. 'So now he's got you waiting on him while he hides on the other side of the island?' she said incredulously. 'I don't know how you've put up with him for so long, what with him always bullying you and Jack.'

'Well, I don't know...' Brandon said, seemingly reluctant to dismiss Jace completely, even after everything, even though he had obviously had some kind of argument with him.

'Of course he does.' Lara said, realising Brandon did have some kind of loyalty reserved for Jace after all. This only served to annoy Lara, so she attempted to point out to Brandon how bad Jace was, 'He's always putting you down, with his stupid little comments. He has nothing nice to say about anyone - except about me, but that's just because it turned out he wanted something from me! His snide remarks are so incredibly childish and pointless. He's just horrible!' Lara finished angrily, looking at Brandon as though daring him to argue with her. She was feeling rather angry now and wanted to hit out at everyone, even though she couldn't specifically say why.

Lara was slightly disappointed that Brandon

would side with Jace. Brandon was always so sensible, he was always the voice of reason on the island.

But of course, she thought angrily to herself, he and Jace had been best friends forever. Oh, and there was also the fact that everyone she had ever met had sided with whoever was opposing her, including her own mother when Lara had left her boyfriend.

Brandon looked sympathetically at her. 'Lara, listen. Jace isn't a monster. He's not exactly the kind of guy who preys on women from behind the bushes-'

Lara thought of the rustle from the trees she had heard when she had been showering yesterday, but said nothing.

'-Jace is just a normal guy.' Brandon went on. 'He just...he has just been affected far more than me and Jack have, at least where - er - that subject is concerned.'

'I don't care.' Lara said harshly. 'That's his problem, he didn't have to drag me into it.'

'I know. I understand that, I do.'

'Really? Because it sounds like you think he did the right thing!'

'No, Lara of course that's not what I'm saying,' Brandon insisted. 'I just don't want you to have the wrong idea about Jace. You haven't been here that long, you haven't really gotten to know him-'

'I don't want to get to know him!'

'Well, I can understand how you might feel that

way, I really can. And I know that what Jace tried to do to you was inexcusable - he knows that for sure. I certainly don't condone his actions, not in the slightest. I abhor men who hurt women, but he isn't exactly one of them. I just want you to understand that he hasn't done anything like this before, this isn't who he is.'

Lara put up her hand to stop him. 'I don't care who he is. And I don't want to get to know him, because what he did,' she went on, sounding more calm now 'was unforgivable.'

14
Exile

True to his word, Jace avoided the main camp and didn't make an appearance again for the rest of the month.

Lara assumed that this was down to his guilt. She felt that if Brandon hadn't of interrupted him, then Jace wouldn't have stopped. Jace knew it too, and it seemed like he hadn't made any attempt to fight his corner or argue his case. He accepted his punishment of exile and banished himself completely to the other side of the island.

Lara was more than happy that he had upheld his side of the deal, so much so that she only felt a minor stab of annoyance every time she, Brandon and Jack were left to complete all of the island chores by themselves.

She detested having to pick fruit and potatoes and catch fish knowing that Jace would be benefiting from her hard work, but she did it without saying a word in protest.

Lara thought she could easily leave Jace to forage for his own food, but she completed the daily tasks alongside the other two knowing that by doing them without question she was actively keeping Jace at bay.

On the whole, Lara had managed to quell her fear of being on her own. She was satisfied that Jace would stay put and wouldn't dare attempt anything else.

Jace's good behaviour made Lara feel that he was perhaps, as Brandon had suggested, remorseful for his actions, but she didn't care. She was still just as angry with him as she had been directly after the event.

Lara felt she should make a determined effort to relieve Brandon of his guard duty at her doorstep for his own comfort, even though she knew that he would have stayed there as long as she asked him to. He slept in the hut he had previously shared with Jace again just over two weeks after the attack. Only now, he found himself alone there.

Now that she was spending more time with Brandon, Lara got to see inside this hut one day.

Lara could tell that it had formerly been Jace's residence. Not only did it seem to ooze his personality, but everywhere she looked there were signs that the person that had lived here had given up.

Years of dirt and grime seemed to cover everything and even though Brandon had obviously made an attempt to clean it up in more recent times, it was far too ingrained deep in the fibres of the wood that made up the shack to ever be truly cleansed.

Lara thought fiercely to herself that the place could have easily represented Jace's soul; too dark and full of despair to ever hope to be saved.

The hut itself had less sunlight streaming through the entrance due to the fact that it overlooked the crop of potatoes.

The layout was just the same as the main hut; it had a bench that ran all the way around the inside three of the walls. Brandon and Jace had evidently slept on opposite sides of the hut; the wood was a lighter shade and was depressed slightly where Lara presumed Jace had slept.

On Brandon's side of the shack, he seemed to have attempted to make his space more homely. He had arranged his collection of jars containing his personal belongings much as they had been in his former residence. The jar of teeth and his wallet seemed to take pride of place underneath his bed where Lara could see they were handled often.

Now that she and Brandon were talking as he was folding away his clean, dry washing Lara could see another container underneath Brandon's bed with what looked like some kind of small book inside.

Brandon seemed to become aware that Lara had not taken in whatever it was he had just said, noticing she was distracted, he looked to see what had caught her attention. He nodded to himself and stooped to pick it up. 'This is my diary,' he said, before he handed it to her to examine.

Lara paused with it in her hands and looked up at him. She hadn't expected it to be something so personal. Brandon smiled, 'It's all right,' he said, folding up a once-white shirt. 'There isn't anything too juicy in there. It's pretty empty actually. People always give me diaries for Christmas and I never write anything in them. Not unless you count the occasional dentist appointment.'

Lara flipped through the pages. She still felt awkward, but now that she had asked about the little book she now had in her hands, she felt she should at least give it a brief glance before handing it back to it's owner.

The cover was dark-green leather and didn't look like it had faded much, although it was worn around the corners. The curly golden numbers that curved around to form the year "1999" were missing some of their edges too.

As Brandon had said, he hadn't written too much in here and most of the pages were either blank or contained brief times scribbled down with an explanatory note like "dentist" or "soccer practice" jotted next to them.

As Lara quickly thumbed further through the diary she came across a page that was half-filled with the tiniest tally charts she had ever seen. Every page after that until the end of the book seemed to be filled with hundreds of the minuscule charts; they filled every millimetre of the paper. These pages no longer appeared mainly pale yellow as the previous pages had been, instead they had been made dark blue by the hundreds of marks made delicately upon them.

As she got closer to the end of the book the marks seemed to get slightly larger every time she turned a page.

With a renewed sense of doom, Lara suddenly

understood what they were. She was suddenly aware that Brandon was crouched next to her and was looking at the book too.

'I started off at the back of the diary, here look-' he pointed at the heading that said "Notes" at the top of the page. '-That wasn't long after we first got here. It was after the first few weeks. We thought we weren't going to be here that long, so I thought that the notes section would be sufficient to keep count of how many days we would be here.' Brandon looked slightly contemplative as he stared at the pages. 'But then, the days turned into weeks, and those turned into months...And anyway, you know the rest.' He got back and returned to sorting his laundry.

Lara's reinstated fear that she was going to spend the rest of her life on this island must have shown upon her face as she stayed sat on the floor staring at the ink-marked pages in her hands when Brandon glanced across at her.

He seemed to be trying to conjure some words of comfort. 'It isn't as bad as it looks, Lara.' Brandon said, adopting a slightly gentler tone.

'No, it's worse,' she said, closing the book and handing it back to him.

'Come on, it's not that bad at all,' Brandon replied, a slightly springy note in his voice. 'We've got everything we need here for now. Just think of this place as a private, luxury holiday resort.' He smiled at her.

Lara couldn't help but smile back at the positive

perspective Brandon always managed to put upon everything. 'Luxury holiday resorts have hot water in their showers.' she said.

Brandon laughed.

'And when it's dinner time, the fish come already on plates and don't swim away.' she added sarcastically.

Brandon nodded, 'True,' he said smiling. 'It's good to know you haven't lost your sense of humour. You don't want to lose that, or you'll end up like Jace.'

Lara felt a sudden, unpleasant ache at the unexpected sound of Jace's name. She hadn't been prepared for it, and this put an instant uncomfortable air on their light-hearted conversation.

Brandon looked apologetic. 'I'm sorry...' he said.

'It's all right, I know he lives on this island too. You're allowed to say his name.' She knew she really needed to get used to hearing his name, although she thought she was handling the situation rather well. Of course, it helped that she hadn't had to face Jace yet.

Lara thought he was doing a great job of staying out of the way. The only evidence that Jace still existed on the island was the fact that the three of them on this side were still having to prepare food for him.

It was always either Brandon or Jack that actually delivered his meals.

Lara never had any need to see Jace, and she

was grateful to the other two for taking her side. She knew that Jace and Brandon had been best friends since they were children. Brandon could easily have refused to acknowledge what Jace had done, or simply chosen to exclude Lara from the camp instead. But as it happened, Brandon had maintained the sense of law and morality that anyone would expect from normal society and left Jace exiled for his actions.

The next month the weather seemed to turn colder than Lara had ever known it on the island. The temperature was still well-and-truly as warm as an English summer, but compared to the intense tropical heat she had experienced so far during her time on the island, the air was now noticeably cooler.

Brandon explained that this was their "winter" period and the dropping temperatures were the lowest they encounter here.

Jace was still on his side of the island and Lara now spent most of her time with Brandon and Jack.

Jack seemed to have gained a little more confidence and was able to talk to Lara more freely now that Jace wasn't around to make any mocking comments towards him. He still treated her with some caution, however.

Lara presumed this was down to what had happened between her and Jace and Jack didn't know how to factor this into the way he treated her, rather than being attributed to the shyness he developed whenever she was around.

One day halfway through the month, Brandon informed her and Jack over lunch that the day marked sixteen years since himself, Jack and Jace had become shipwrecked on the island.

Lara was surprised to hear that they had reached the milestone already; it had still seemed a distance away when she had first arrived on the island.

The speed that time was passing here was slightly overwhelming to Lara. Most of the day was spent collecting and preparing food. Then there were the usual chores involved with living like washing clothes and keeping herself clean too, which was much more difficult (and uncomfortable) on the island.

Lara was still slightly nervous about washing, for that was the only time she was alone, other than when she slept at night. She found that she was more inclined to utilize the ocean to keep clean in, even if it was harsher on her skin.

Brandon decided that the three of them should mark the occasion by eating something slightly different for dinner. He pointed out that clams were sometimes found on the crab beach. Whilst they weren't really substantial enough on their own, he suggested that they could have them as a starter with dinner.

Jack volunteered to show Lara how to collect the clams from the beach and she agreed to go with him later.

When later came, the two of them set off around the island with their mission whilst Brandon collected the potatoes by himself.

Now that Jack had no hangups about talking to Lara, he spoke enthusiastically about the last summer he had spent in the "real world" as he called it.

She thought it was ironic that this is how Jack referred to civilisation. Everything was so easy and non-laborious back there. Lara thought that life on the island was far more real than anything she had ever experienced. Every day was a fight for survival. She was more than aware of how difficult it was to obtain enough food for them to eat when they each had to hunt, catch and prepare it all from scratch. Well, apart from Jace, who had somehow managed to get out of the daily struggle and have his food caught, cooked and delivered to him, without him having to do anything.

This still irked Lara, but she chose to do nothing to change it. After all, she was still satisfied that Jace stuck to his side of the island so that she wouldn't have to see him.

Jack was now talking about the bike he had owned when he had left for his and Brandon's trip and wondering out loud where it could be now, as the two of them walked along crab beach.

Lara tried to force calm upon herself as the chunky, shelled spiders-of-the-ocean scuttled around the beach, or else sat motionless and, in Lara's opinion, sinister in the sand around them.

She seemed to do a good job of hiding her disquiet however, as Jack appeared not to have noticed anything as he scanned the sand around them for clams.

Lara didn't have the chance to start looking around her for the small delicacies, for she had just noticed something moving nearby that made her forget all about food - it was Jace.

He seemed to notice her at exactly the same moment she had noticed him and froze where he stood shirtless and knee-deep in the sea.

Lara had completely missed him as she had approached, having been so engrossed in listening to Jack's in-depth description of his childhood bike that she hadn't looked any further ahead of herself than her own feet sinking into the sand with each step.

Neither, did it seem had Jack, who had frozen too next to Lara. He stood and glanced between her and Jace nervously.

Lara noticed that Jace looked worse than she had last seen him. His cheeks and neck were once again adorned with thick, grey stubble and his hair looked slightly unkempt again.

The surprise Jace's face registered told Lara that he wasn't expecting to see them as much as they weren't expecting to see him.

For a moment nobody moved or did anything. Then all of a sudden, like time had started again they all looked away from each other.

Jack resumed his searching for their starter and

Jace turned away and walked into the nearest part of jungle and disappeared quickly into the trees.

Lara hadn't been prepared to see Jace. She scolded herself mentally for not expecting to see him so close to the beach she knew he now occupied. Of course he wouldn't have confined himself to one, tiny stretch of beach. He would have to leave it sometimes, even just to get some exercise.

A few moments after Jace had gone, Jack looked at her. 'Are you all right?' he asked, quietly.

'Yes, fine,' Lara said, shaking her head with a forced smile. 'Everything's fine.'

Seeing Jace had taken the shine slightly from the occasion, but Lara thought it wasn't anything to celebrate anyway. She knew that Brandon was only trying to take the emphasis off the fact that they were all still waiting for rescue, but if the decision had been hers, Lara would have chosen not to mark the day at all.

Back at the main camp dinner unfolded much the way Lara had expected it to. Brandon was trying his best to keep the occasion upbeat and positive, implying that they shouldn't have to acknowledge too many more anniversaries on the island.

Jack was either doing a good job of playing along with his father, or he genuinely believed that they would be leaving the island behind in the near future.

Lara found herself forcing smiles and agreeing

with Brandon too, although she wondered how convincing her act was.

After they had followed their starter with a fish stew (which was made up of the usual fish, with potatoes, flavoured with coconut and simmered with potato leaves) and eaten a dessert of banana, Brandon decided to lead a toast.

'Well,' he said, holding his shell of coconut milk out in front of him formally. 'I always hated making toasts back home, for some reason everyone always expects me to do it though, so I won't break with tradition...'

It suddenly occurred to Lara that although she thought of Brandon as the leader of the camp, he may not have voluntarily taken up the role. Especially if his father had accompanied them on their trip, and not made it to the island. Brandon must have all of a sudden found himself the head of the family under very strained circumstances.

Lara could see the strain now that she looked closely at him. She could see it in the deep lines around his eyes and across his forehead. These surely were far more pronounced than when they had first arrived, and sixteen years of stress, strain and struggle for survival had scored them further.

'Well,' Brandon went on, 'As always, let us hope that rescue finds us soon. And we hope that we continue to be able to feed ourselves and stay safe until it does. May the fish and the potatoes be plentiful and good fortune remain with us.' He raised his cup and Jack and Lara knocked their cups against his, before they all took a sip.

Lara knew that rescue was a lot to hope for, but she wished for it with every fibre of her being as she drank along with the other two.

It had now been over three months since Brandon's toast, and Lara couldn't help but feel that he had jinxed them all slightly. Yes, the potatoes, bananas and coconuts were still as abundant as they ever were, but the fish were virtually nowhere to be seen.

Lara had only ever known the fish stocks to be more than ample. However, in recent weeks it had been hard to even catch just one fish a day. Since the fish were the bulkiest, most filling thing they ate, Lara knew how significant this change was for the four of them.

Even Brandon didn't do a good job of convincing her that it wasn't a serious issue, although he did put forward the argument that they could survive on everything else they had. Lara wasn't made to feel any better by the fact that they would be eating more crab to compensate for the difference in protein.

One particular day, Lara had inadvertently missed two chances to catch what she suspected was the same fish. On the first attempt, she had annoyingly lost her balance as she reached for the cage. And on the second attempt, there was frantic splashing as she made a grab for the cage too soon in her panic.

Brandon made the wise decision to allow his more skilled hands to take over the fishing for the evening and relieved Lara of her duty, diplomatically suggesting she could prepare the potatoes with Jack instead.

Lara trudged back through the water and threw herself dripping wet onto a log in front of the fire as dusk was falling. She was so angry with herself at missing two good opportunities. Mistakes just couldn't be made when the fish had now become so scarce. It had been days since they had even seen one, so she was doubly irritated. She had done better on her first attempt months ago.

Jack was piercing the last of the potatoes and placing them carefully on the rock beside the fire. 'Still no luck, huh?' he asked her, sliding the rock closer to the flames.

'No,' she replied, a little more harshly than she had intended to.

'I guess we're having crab again then. There won't be any left if we keep hammering them like we have been.'

'I almost had one,' Lara replied, staring into the glowing orange flames which were starting to look as striking as ever against the darkening sky beyond them. 'It just got away from me though.'

Jack shook his head, 'It's all right Lara. Don't beat yourself up. Fish come and go, they'll be back.' He smiled at her with only a hint of uncertainty.

'Have the fish ever disappeared like this before?'

She watched his eyes closely to see if he was being truthful.

He shrugged and looked into the fire, 'Uh, well, not really. Sometimes there are more than others, but they have never been so few for so long. But we shouldn't worry about it though, more will come. We just have to be patient and wait.'

Lara could see the optimism his father always spoke with had rubbed off onto Jack and he looked upon everything around him with it. She realised this must have been how he coped when he was a child. She could imagine Brandon had tried to preserve his innocence by sheltering him from the harsh realities around them by putting a positive slant upon everything. It suddenly occurred to Lara that this was probably the main reason why Brandon clung so desperately onto hope, even when Jace had lost his; it was because he didn't want his son to give up.

After over an hour, Brandon returned to the camp empty handed. He had been forced to admit defeat now that darkness had completely fallen around him and he couldn't see what he was doing.

The three of them ate a banana each, before Brandon quickly got up and hastily set off over to the other side of the island through the jungle to fetch a couple of crabs to complete their meal.

'I'd better get going,' he said, setting off after gulping down a whole cup of water. 'Jace will be wondering where the hell his dinner is.'

Lara said nothing. She was annoyed that Jace

wasn't experiencing the stress of their disappointing recent hauls. She imagined him sitting on his beach, relaxing and watching the sky as he waited for his food to be delivered to him.

Still, she reasoned with herself, it was better than him actually being here.

After their unexpected encounter a few months ago, Lara hadn't seen Jace at all. This was perhaps partly due to the fact that she now made sure she avoided the crab-beach in addition to the one that Jace had been living on.

Lara wasn't sure how she felt about Jace now. It had been over four months since the incident between them. The memories felt like they had faded slightly and now she felt no emotion when she rarely thought of them.

She felt like she now had a greater sense of the length of time and the desperation that the three men had experienced during their stay on the island compared to several months ago. But that didn't mean that she had, in any way, forgiven Jace. She still resented him almost as much as before, even if she had been given a greater sense of perspective on his motive. In her opinion, it still did not justify his actions and he was still guilty of losing his humanity a little and giving into the primal urges he should, as a human being, have had better control over.

The next day, Lara awoke to the familiar sunlight shining through the open doorway. She dressed as usual and started off down the steps to breakfast. But she slowed as her foot hit the sand and paused with the other still on the steps. Her attention had been drawn to Brandon, who was shoulder-deep in the ocean ahead of her with Jace similarly submerged by his side.

The two men appeared to be holding long sticks that were pointed on one end. They were discussing something intently, almost completely unaware of the height of the gentle waves around them.

Lara glanced towards the campfire and saw Jack sitting beside it, eating a large piece of coconut. He waved when he saw her and she went over to join him.

'Good morning,' she said, taking her usual seat facing the ocean. 'What's going on?' She asked, trying to keep her voice sounding casual, despite the fact Jace was unexpectedly within the vicinity of the main camp.

Jack swallowed his mouthful and replied, 'Dad thinks Jace might be able to help out with the, you know - fishing situation.' He shrugged and looked at her slightly tentatively. 'Jace was the one who came up with the cage system in the first place. They're trying out spears at the moment,' he added, nodding towards the pair. 'Jace has wanted to try that out for years, but Dad always said that it would be too hard to get their aim right, and it would make too much of a mess of the fish. But they're having a good go at it.' He looked out towards the sea, where Jace had just disappeared beneath the water. 'I think Dad's getting worried. He's willing to try anything.'

'Hmm,' Lara said in response, watching Jace resurface again and indicate with his spear to Brandon to follow him along the shore slightly.

After over two hours, Brandon and Jace strode from the water soaking wet and, apart from their spears, empty handed.

Lara realised too late that they were both approaching the campfire. She had no idea how to respond to Jace, so she tried to act as casually as possible. She picked up her empty cup of water and set her focus upon it, so she would have an excuse not to have to make eye contact with Jace.

'Morning Lara,' Brandon said as he arrived at the campfire. He set his spear to stand against his log to dry out in the sun, and Jace did the same thing.

'Yeah, good morning.' she replied, not looking up.

Jace didn't say anything, he remained stood on the other side of the fire from Lara.

She didn't dare look in his direction, but Lara could easily sense his uncomfortable body language. He seemed as though he didn't know whether he should take a seat or not.

Lara thought she saw Brandon prompt him silently into taking his formerly-usual position on the log next to Lara.

He did so, although carefully making sure he was on the furthest end from her.

There was an uncomfortable sort of stir in the air when Jace sat down, but Brandon being his usual bright self, tried his best to gloss over it. He had obviously decided that it was time for the four of them to be able to sit together just like old times.

Except it wasn't old times, and Lara felt so uncomfortable she wished that she could be the one to retreat to the other side of the island, rather than have to sit through it.

She had known, deep down that it was inevitable that she would have to spend time with Jace again at some point. After all, he was still a human being in this place just like they were and he was still Brandon's friend. Lara just hadn't managed to prepare herself for it at all. She just stared down at the empty cup in her hands, the heat rising in her cheeks slightly.

'I've asked Jace to help me figure out how we can start catching fish again.' Brandon said pleasantly before he drank from his coconut cup. 'It's a tough one, all right. There are hardly any fish out there. And the ones that are still around are way further out than we usually fish. Isn't that right Jace?' He added a little extra emphasis on the last part, he was obviously trying to prompt Jace into joining in the conversation.

Lara thought she felt Jace glare a little at Brandon before he answered in the familiar deep voice Lara hadn't heard for months, 'Yes,' he said slowly, 'It's not so much what we're doing that's wrong...there just isn't that much to catch. It's why we've had to move further afield, so to speak.'

Lara still didn't look up at Jace as he talked, and she knew without seeing that he was avoiding looking in her direction too.

'So Jace suggested using these spears.' Brandon added, picking his up from behind him and passing it to Lara to look at.

She took it, it was heavier than she had expected. It was made up from a long tree branch and one end had been roughly cut to a sharp point. Glancing across to the sand beyond Jace, she could see that his was almost identical. She passed it back to Brandon. 'Do they work?' she asked him with a tone of casual interest.

'Well, admittedly we don't know yet.' Brandon replied. 'We will give them a proper trial run for lunch. We know where to position ourselves now.' he assured Lara. 'Don't we?' He added, prompting Jace again.

'Yes...' Jace said after another slight pause. 'We're going to have to fish a little further down the beach, and much further out than we usually do.'

Lara nodded to acknowledge that she had taken in the information, but she refused to look in Jace's direction.

Brandon was determined to keep the conversation going, 'That's right. I think we've been given an easy time of it the first sixteen years. The fish have given up swimming right into our backyard pond now, and they want to give us more of a challenge!' He laughed briefly, and Lara smiled politely at him.

Jack did the same.

Lara didn't know what Jace did, because she didn't look, but after a moment he spoke again.

'I don't think they're challenging us, Brandon.' he said quietly. 'I think they have been scared off by something.'

Lara felt a slight chill as Jace said those last words. For a moment she forgot to continue staring at her cup and looked up at him.

He didn't say anything else, he just stared out at the water the way he did when he was deep in thought.

Several hours later, Jace and Brandon returned from the sea again. This time though, having refined their spearing technique they weren't empty handed, they had managed to catch a single fish. It wasn't much, and as Jack had said, the spear did make a large hole through the middle of it, but they shared it out between the four of them and Lara thought she would never take eating fish for granted again.

She spent the whole of lunch avoiding Jace's eyes and he seemed to do the same with her. She was careful not to speak to him, and again, he returned the gesture.

Later that day, Brandon helped Jace move his few possessions back into the hut by the potato crop so that the two once again shared quarters.

Lara was a little annoyed that Brandon had

decided to reintegrate Jace back into their tiny community without even consulting her first, but there was nothing she could really do about it.

She also found it difficult to get Brandon alone to speak with him on the matter, because either Jace or Jack was nearby whenever she thought about approaching him. And even if she could get him alone, she had no idea what to say to him. She couldn't exactly order Brandon to send Jace back to the other side of the island.

Maybe it was for the best that he was once again part of their group. Even Lara had to admit that Jace had been helpful in successfully managing to catch their first fish for over a week.

But then again, surely between herself, Jack and Brandon, one of them would surely have come up with a new system for collecting fish that was as good as a sharp stick? Lara concluded that Jace hadn't really done that much at all and she certainly wouldn't be giving him any credit for his so-called ingenuity.

Over the next few days the camp returned to something like normality with Jace's return, except that he and Lara still avoided looking at, or talking to each other.

Lara supposed that since the other two men had been delivering food to him all the while, nothing was really that different for them. They must still have spoken to him as they dropped off the parcels, and now all his return meant was that they had one less chore to complete at every meal time.

Lara thought that she was handling the situation gracefully and that her conclusion was that Jace was still a person that needed human company just like everyone else. It would have been perhaps a little too barbaric to have left him isolated on one part of the island, no matter how much she thought he deserved it.

She was surprised when just short of a week since Jace had re-joined the group Brandon wished him Happy Birthday over breakfast.

Jack did the same when he turned up part way through the simple meal of fruit.

Lara said nothing and continued eating. If Jace was expecting any well-wishing from her, he had another thing coming.

Brandon arranged a slightly more special dinner than usual, more like what they had eaten to mark sixteen-years, except that they only had one fish to share between them all. But they had crab and clams added to their stew along with the potatoes and green leaves which they ate as dusk was starting to fall around them.

Brandon had baked a single potato in the fire and Lara now realised why when he inserted a small stick into the top of it and set it alight; it was the best attempt he could make at a birthday cake and candle.

'You know the score,' Brandon said to Jace, setting it on a rock beside him. 'Make a wish.'

Jace looked soberly at it, 'You know what it's going to be,' he said flatly to Brandon. 'To finally see the back of this place.' He leaned down and extinguished the tiny flame with one puff.

Afterwards they all shared the potato. Lara felt she wanted Jace's wish to come true more than he probably did.

It didn't look like it was going to come to fruition yet though, as they ploughed into October before Lara knew it and nothing had really changed.

The weather was getting warmer again and sunset was later every day and was now setting after dinner each night.

Jace and Brandon were getting more proficient at using the spears. They managed to catch at least one fish quite regularly now even though the stocks were still low to none existent.

The only problem was that their new system was messy. The spear caused a cloud of blood to spread from the fish when it was caught and Lara thought it was, in some ways, even worse than leaving the fish to suffocate upon the sand.

The other fish that may have been within the vicinity when the first was caught fled and didn't return for a long time after the initial dark cloud had completely dispersed. This meant that catching more than one fish was rare to impossible. Jace had managed it twice so far. It was due to this that everyone now thought of him as being the most skilled fisherman.

Lara was annoyed that she hadn't managed to even catch anything so far using this method.

Jack had seemed to show similar talent to her on his first attempts, but then had been heavily congratulated by his father when he had managed to catch a rather large specimen for dinner last night.

Lara decided to leave the fishing to the men for while. She knew she would get better at it eventually, but this new technique needed practice and she didn't feel like spending too much time in Jace's company. Since he was the one who was demonstrating how to perform the technique to get the best results, Lara decided to avoid the fishing area for a while.

This particular day she volunteered to collect the potatoes for lunch.

Jack was just leaving for the other side of the island to collect a crab to supplement the single fish Brandon and Jace were expecting to catch, as they set off too, spears in hands in the direction of the ocean.

It was the warmest day Lara had known for a while and she walked more slowly towards the potato crop to try and avoid getting too overheated.

She was in no hurry. Jace and Brandon would be awhile before they actually managed to retrieve anything and Jack wouldn't arrive back too soon either. In any case it would allow her some time away from Jace's company for a little while.

The tension had eased only ever so slightly now, but they weren't even on speaking terms yet. Lara wondered how long it would take before they could even look each other in the eye again, let alone share a few words.

She took her time as she dug up the muddy roots. She was now so used to this task, that she found she did everything automatically without even having to think about it. She laid enough of the plants next to her before she gathered them up and took them back to camp.

She again walked slowly so that she wouldn't be back too soon. The trouble was that the distance between the crop and the camp wasn't that large and she arrived within five minutes, as she knew she would.

When her reluctant feet finally did reach the camp however, the first thing she noticed what that it was unexpectedly quiet.

There was still no sign of Jack, but Lara suspected that he often took the long way around too, so she hadn't expected him to be here.

But oddly there was no sign of Jace or Brandon in the ocean where she thought they would still be. Surely they hadn't caught anything that quickly? And if they had, then why weren't they around the campfire that was burning furiously away, preparing and cooking their catch?

Lara deposited the potatoes upon a rock beside the fire and looked both ways down the beach. The sense that something was wrong came very suddenly upon her.

Unpleasant butterflies rose inexplicably inside of her as she wandered down the beach towards the water. She couldn't think of any reason why Jace and Brandon wouldn't still be in sight in the ocean.

She had hardly taken a few steps past the unattended campfire when she saw something ahead of her that might suggest why the two men had abandoned their post.

Lara felt her stomach drop as she caught sight of the bright scarlet trail ahead of her that could only have been blood - it was leading towards the main hut.

15
Karma

Lara found herself strangely detached from her surroundings as her heavy legs stumbled forward towards the horrible trail emblazoned upon the bright, white sand.

She didn't want to see what it would lead to, but knew she had to follow it. Her body seemed to be drawn in its direction, even though the scared voice she could hear in her head was screaming for her to turn around and spare her the horror of what she was about to see.

Lara surprised herself as she approached the hut that her thoughts had any amount of logic applied to them in her state of utter panic. It occurred to her that for so much blood to be upon the sand, the person must be seriously injured.

She had only managed to take a few paces forward when she almost jumped out of her skin when she heard her name called.

'LARA!'

It was Brandon. His voice sounded distorted by a horrible blend of horror and fear.

Brandon's injured, Lara thought as she increased her pace.

Now that she had heard a cry for help, she seemed far more in control of her legs and she forced them to carry her as quickly as they could towards Brandon's voice.

He yelled again, 'LARA!'

He sounded nearby. Lara guessed he was in front of the main hut.

Her mind was racing and questions flashed to the forefront as she rushed towards where she expected him to be. How did Brandon get injured in the first place? What had happened to him to cause such a bad injury? And where had Jace disappeared to? Why wasn't he helping his friend?

Lara closed the last gap at a run. She tried, and failed, to brace herself as she rounded the corner.

Nothing could have prepared her for the scene that now lay in front of her.

Brandon was there. Lara's brain, even in its panicked state registered that Brandon wasn't injured, even though he was covered in a copious quantity of bright crimson blood. But the blood wasn't his; it belonged to Jace.

Jace was lying sprawled in the sand in front of Brandon, who was kneeling beside him with both his blood-soaked hands pressed down on his left side where his shirt was torn.

There was no need to ask what had happened, Jace had clearly been attacked by a shark.

Brandon's head spun around as Lara appeared behind him. He kept his hands firmly down in front of him.

Lara couldn't hear what he was saying over the rushing noise in her ears. But then all of a sudden his voice broke through, 'Lara!' he yelled, 'I need you here! NOW!' he shouted, summoning her forward.

Lara's heart was in her throat as she dropped to her knees beside him.

Brandon quickly took hold of her hands and pressed them firmly down on Jace's wound where his own had been a second before. 'I need you to press down here as hard as you can!' he shouted at her as he scrambled to his feet and started across the sand.

'Wait!' Lara shouted after him, 'Where are you going?!' She didn't want to be left alone in this horrific situation.

'I need to get some things! Just keep pressing down!' He yelled over his shoulder before turning and sprinting into the trees.

Now on her own with him, Lara looked at Jace's face.

He was still conscious, although Lara couldn't imagine how he could be, considering how much blood he had lost. He was pale and his breathing was erratic and he seemed very weak. He was shaking slightly as he stared at the sky above. His clothes were still soaking wet from having been in the ocean and his face was paler than usual in the mid-day sun.

Lara had no idea what to do. She had always known it was irresponsible to go through everyday life with absolutely no knowledge of first-aid and now it was more than obvious why.

She wondered if she should keep Jace talking. That sounded right, like something she had heard on television before. Isn't that what people were supposed to do in this situation? They needed to be kept conscious until the ambulance arrived. But in this case, there was no ambulance.

They were in the middle of nowhere without any kind of medical help.

Lara had never felt so isolated in the whole time she had been here. She wished Brandon would come back.

Almost as though he was responding to her thought, Brandon's hurried, sandy footsteps became audible and drew nearer.

He fell to his knees on the other side of Lara. She had never been more relieved to see him.

He dropped a bundle next to him on the sand and quickly unfolded it. There was a large, half-empty bottle of what looked like whiskey, a pen knife, scraps of different materials and a needle and thread. He now placed a cup of water on the corner of the unfolded blanket.

'All right,' Brandon said to himself, as though he was trying to think of what needed to be done next. 'All right Lara - I need you to do everything I say. Just follow my instructions exactly, you understand?'

Lara nodded. She found it was difficult to speak.

'Good,' Brandon said. He was looking a similar shade of white as Jace was and sounded extremely strained. 'All right, we need to move his shirt away.'

Brandon undid Jace's buttons carefully, before

carefully peeling his shredded shirt away from his body.

Lara moved her hands for the briefest of moments to allow the material to slip from underneath them. She made the mistake of looking down at the injury beneath her fingers and had to suppress a gasp as she saw the extent of it for the first time. The wound was a large, curved gash that ran half way up Jace's side. The flesh looked as though it had been literally torn.

'We're going to need to clean this up a little...' He looked more closely at Jace's wound.

Now that his shirt had been moved away, Lara was more than aware that she was all that was stopping Jace from bleeding to death; it felt like too much responsibility.

Brandon picked up the cup of water and poured it carefully around Lara's hands. He indicated that she should lift them up for a split second.

Brandon picked up the bottle of whiskey and opened it, pouring some into the coconut cup.

Jace turned his head now to see what Brandon was doing. 'Hey,' he said. He sounded like speaking was costing him great effort. 'Brandon, you've been holding out on us!' He somehow managed a small version of his characteristic laugh.

Brandon ignored him. He dropped the needle and thread into the cup, pushing the thread down so that it was completely submerged. He poured a little of the amber liquid out onto his hands and rubbed them together thoroughly. He picked up the needle and started trying to thread it as best as he could with shaking hands.

Lara realised that he was planning to stitch Jace's wound up right here as he lay in the sand. 'Shouldn't we move him?' she asked Brandon, looking at the hut beside them.

Brandon shook his head. 'It doesn't matter where we do it,' he said through taught lips. 'We need to get this wound sealed as quickly as we can, before the bacteria can really get at it. And besides - the two of us aren't going to move him now. I need Jack for that, but he sure as hell isn't here. We will just stitch him up first. At least it's bright out here - so we can see what we are doing.'

It didn't seem right somehow to be doing something so important out in the open like this, but Lara remained silent and was prepared to do as she was told.

After a few moments of hurried fumbling, Brandon managed to thread the needle and looked back down at his patient. 'Lara, I need you to press down harder than that!' he said firmly.

'Um, sorry...' Lara replied, quickly applying more pressure.

Jace suddenly laughed, making her jump. 'I don't think she's inclined to press down Brandon,' he said, looking directly at Lara's face. He rested his head back against the sand again, 'And who can blame her...' he added as he shut his eyes, as though his sudden outburst had weakened him.

Lara didn't know what to say to this, she instead focused on keeping enough pressure on the wound as Brandon poured the contents of the cup out onto it.

Jace screwed up his face as he did this and suppressed a whimper. His face now had a sheen of sweat across it.

Brandon didn't waste any time in making his first stitch.

Jace clenched his fists on his chest and took a sharp intake of breath. He opened his eyes and looked at the whiskey bottle next to Brandon. 'Aren't you going to give me some of that - for the pain?'

'No,' Brandon said firmly, focused on his task. 'We need it to keep the wound clean.'

Jace shook his head slightly. 'I can't believe you've had that all this time. Where the hell have you been hiding-' he took another sharp intake of breath '-it?'

He gave him a grim smile. 'I'm not going to tell. I was saving it for emergencies. I'd say this was an emergency.'

Brandon continued swiftly creating neat stitches until they completely covered the entire laceration. It took a while since the wound was so large.

When he had set his needle down, he poured a little more alcohol over the whole area again before picking up the rags and covering the wound. He fitted them securely around Jace's waist.

It was at this moment that Jack arrived looking shaken and scared. He had obviously done the same thing as Lara. She imagined he had set down his contribution to lunch over by the campfire and then when he had gone to investigate where everyone was, discovered the trail of blood leading to the scene of the three of them having just finished stitching Jace up.

Brandon explained what had happened to him.

Lara listened too, as Brandon explained how he and Jace had almost caught a fish. He described how the spear had injured it, before it managed to swim away. He supposed the blood must have attracted the shark, which had come out of nowhere and moved towards Jace who had reacted automatically by holding out his spear in front of him at the last second, stopping the sharks top jaws from sinking into his shoulder. 'It could have been a lot worse...' Brandon finished grimly, still looking stressed.

Jack looked horrified.

Brandon now orchestrated moving Jace from the beach and into the main hut which was just a few feet away. Brandon carried his top half and Jack took hold of his legs and they both lifted him carefully up the steps and into the hut.

Lara followed.

They placed Jace gingerly down on the bed where Lara usually slept and pulled one of the blankets over him.

'Are you warm enough?' Brandon asked him,

concerned.

'Of course I am.' Jace replied. 'I'm not an old person.'

'It's nice to know that you're grateful.' Brandon retorted. 'Listen, I'll go and get you some water.'

'I'll get some.' Lara quickly volunteered. She was glad of a reason to get away from things for a few minutes. She quickly turned on her heel and arrived at the water tank a few minutes later.

When she got there, she sank onto the nearest log and took a deep, steadying breath trying to take in what had just happened. The last hour or two had just passed in a flash of panic and chaos. The worst thing was that she hadn't been prepared for it. Why hadn't she thought of the possibility of sharks before now? She had washed in the sea so many times since she had arrived without any fear at all, especially recently.

Brandon had mentioned that he suspected his father's body was taken by sharks, and Lara herself had felt something brush her leg when she had been in the ocean for hours on end.

She suppressed an involuntary shudder as she thought of what would have happened if it had in fact been a shark she had felt beneath the waves that day.

Lara moved to put her face in her hands, but then she realised that they were covered in Jace's blood. She washed them in the ocean and tried to compose herself before she returned to the hut with a cup of water.

Now that the initial panic was over and Jace was resting, Brandon decided that they should all try and get something to eat.

Jack remembered that he had brought back two crabs and left them cooking in the campfire.

He and Lara went to retrieve them as Brandon helped Jace sip some water.

They split the overdone crab meat into four servings and prepared some coconut before taking it all back to the main hut where they all ate.

After a much later lunch than expected, Brandon announced that he was putting a ban on going into the ocean. No one was to fish, wash or even set one foot in the sea until he said otherwise. 'We don't know how far in the shark will come. I thought the water Jace and I were in earlier would be too shallow for a shark that size, but I guess was wrong. We will just have to forget about fish for a while, until I think of a better idea.'

Later they had a simple dinner of crab and potato as the sun was setting, casting a bright red glow over everything. Lara and Jack ate in almost-silence beside the campfire whilst Brandon helped Jace eat his in the hut.

Afterwards Lara moved her few possessions into Jace and Brandon's hut beside the potato crops. She and Jack then moved Brandon's and Jace's things into the main hut.

Brandon had decided that they should keep Jace where he was for now, since moving him was awkward and they had to be careful not to split his stitches. This meant an exchange of quarters and Lara found herself moving her few possessions into the hut in which Jace had spent most of his time on the island.

She didn't stay there to dwell too long however, as she returned to the beach camp a few minutes later. The sun had well and truly set now and the only light came from the moon and the fading campfire. Tonight the moon was large and full and the bright, white light that shone from it lit up the quietly rippling ocean.

It was a beautifully serene evening on the surface, it was just a shame it was a cruel juxtaposition for what was happening in their world; it made the darkness seem to press in everything in a far more sinister way than usual.

Lara tried to tell herself that this was just her imagination as she approached the main hut steps with a cup of fresh water. She found herself knocking awkwardly, before Brandon invited her in and she entered the hut in which she had spent the nights of her entire stay on the island.

The whole room was as dark as it always was and the shadowy outlines of Jack, Brandon and Jace were highlighted by the glow from the moon.

Brandon was sitting on the bed next to Jace who was still in the same position as earlier.

Jack was next to the doorway, he looked as though he was just about to leave.

'I just brought some more water...' Lara said, hovering in the middle of room as she realised that

Brandon already had a cup beside him, although he seemed to be using it to clean Jace's wound again.

'Thanks, Lara. Could you just set it down here?' Brandon said. He sounded weary and stressed.

Lara set the cup down on the bench next to Brandon.

She wanted to ask how Jace was doing, but didn't know how to word it considering he was right there and from what she could see of him, he didn't look too good. Even in the limited light from the moon, Lara could see the droplets of sweat on his forehead and he still seemed to be tensed with pain.

No one spoke for a moment, then Brandon broke the silence, 'Listen, why don't you two turn in for the night?-' He looked towards Lara and Jack '-I think we could all do with the rest.' He spoke politely and she knew that he only had their best interests at heart, but Lara took this more of an instruction than a suggestion; she had no choice but to follow it, even though she wasn't satisfied that her question had been fully answered.

After all, Brandon hadn't given them any indication of how serious Jace's injury was. Lara didn't even know if Brandon expected Jace to survive.

'Well, Goodnight then.' Jack said, moving past her.

Lara thought he seemed slightly relieved that he had been dismissed of any potential responsibility. With a stab of anger she was reminded of Alan, he always had the same air of alleviation whenever Lara had taken the burden of any unwanted chores for him.

Jack paused in the doorway and turned back. 'I'll see you all tomorrow.' he added, speaking mainly to his father and Jace before descending the stairs.

Lara felt she should leave now too, but didn't want to appear as dismissive as she felt Jack had been. 'Um, I'll say Goodnight too then...If you need anything, just let me know - and I'll be right over.'

Jace had gone slightly quiet as she said this, in a way that indicated he was listening, although he didn't say anything in response.

'Thanks Lara. I'll be sure to do that.' Brandon replied.

Lara walked the distance to the other hut in the darkness, alone. Jack was long gone.

The moon was still shining brightly, making it slightly easier for her to follow the more unfamiliar route to her new shelter.

Once inside, Lara rummaged in the pile of clothes and blankets she had dumped in here earlier for her sleeping t-shirt. It was only once she had slipped it on that she realised this was the one Jace had given her.

She made herself the best bed she could out of the blankets, careful to do this on Brandon's side of the hut. She couldn't tell in the dark whether her pillow had been mixed up with Brandon's in the move, but she didn't care, she was just grateful to lie down and be comfortable at last after such a nightmare day.

She lay and stared up at the ceiling and tried to make sense of everything that had happened.

Both her body and mind were exhausted, but she knew she wasn't going to get to sleep any time soon. Images from the day seemed to flash before her eyes and disturbing thoughts of what the next few days may hold haunted her as she lay in the darkness.

She couldn't believe that something so horrible had happened in such a beautiful place. For some reason Lara had forgotten all about the possibility of sharks lurking in the crystal, blue waters that surrounded the island. Until now she had thought of the sea as somewhere beautiful to fish and bathe. Now it was somewhere dangerous, to be avoided.

Lara felt a pang of fear as she thought of the number of times she had been in the same depth of water as Jace had been earlier, unaware of the danger that may have surrounded her without her knowing it. After all, it could have been her or Brandon or Jack that could have been the victim of an unprovoked, undeserved attack.

But Lara wondered if it was undeserved? Had Jace really done nothing to warrant something horrific happening to him? Maybe it was just...karma?

Lara felt a wave of disgust as she had this thought. What Jace had done was bad and she had been angry with him, but she had never wanted him to be seriously injured.

Lara hoped now, even more than she had all day, that Jace would be all right. She knew her conscience would never forgive her and she didn't think she could live with herself if anything bad happened to him after she'd had such a thought.

Lara tossed and turned for hours in her restless state. Despite the fact that her body ached and she was mentally and emotionally exhausted from the day, she still was nowhere near falling asleep.

Gradually the cabin grew lighter around her, and more of the details of the room were becoming visible again, meaning sunrise was approaching.

One thing occurred to her as the ceiling became clearer above her, was that as a result of his injury, Jace and Lara were now on speaking terms again. Even if it wasn't just like it was before, there was nothing like a near-fatal accident to break the ice.

16
Abandoned

Lara thought that she had managed to doze off briefly just before sunrise, but woke up at what seemed to be her usual time in the morning.

She immediately thought of Jace, wondering grimly if he had made it through the night. She found herself sitting fully dressed on top of her bed, trying to pluck up the courage to go over to the main hut and see if her fear was justified.

After half an hour, she became brave enough to venture over to the main camp where she found Brandon.

He looked as tired as Lara felt. He had both bags and dark circles under his eyes, and he looked terrible. He informed her that Jace was still the in the same condition. He had been awake several times in the night with the pain in his wound, but Brandon had cleaned it again this morning and now Jace was sleeping. 'The rest will do him good.' Brandon reassured her.

Again, Lara found she couldn't find the words to voice her fears for Jace's future, so she focused her efforts on preparing breakfast instead. Brandon looked like he needed it, so she insisted that he should get some rest himself while she took charge of his usual chores.

The next couple of days were difficult. Lara and Jack took up Brandon's duties so that he would have more time to care for Jace.

On top of their usual tasks, they now had to boil bandages every couple of hours too for Brandon to be able to change Jace's dressing to prevent infection.

They obeyed Brandon's rule and avoided the ocean completely. Neither Lara, nor Jack had any intention of breaking it and exposing themselves to the danger that they had discovered the hard way was lurking in the water just yards away from the shore. They now took turns on a schedule to wash in the waterfall.

Lara hadn't been there much in recent months due to the fact that it felt so isolated and she didn't like to be alone. Now she welcomed the solitude and quiet. She had forgotten how idyllic and peaceful the gently flowing water was.

She now liked going there to take her mind off how worried she was about Jace. That was another odd thing, it was only when she appreciated the peace of the waterfall, that she realised just how worried she was about Jace.

She was surprised that she cared so much about his fate. She would have thought that the animosity she had held for him for months would have prevented any concern she now found herself feeling towards him, and yet here she was feeling it.

Despite the protests of her cynical side, her anger had now evaporated and she found she didn't have the heart to hate Jace at the moment. She felt that his life was hanging so precariously in the balance, that if she now projected the hatred she had felt towards him from previous months upon him now, it might just tip him over the edge.

That was another thing that was keeping Lara awake and tossing and turning at night - she didn't know if Jace was going to make a full recovery. She still hadn't managed to find the right moment to ask Brandon, and even if she did, she wasn't sure that Brandon would even know the answer himself. And even if he did, Lara still wasn't sure that she wanted to hear his honest judgement.

From what she saw of Jace when she took him food and water and delivered clean bandages, she couldn't really tell if his condition was improving. He still seemed to be in as much pain as when he had first been stitched up.

Lara assumed that this was just part of the healing process and it would take more than a couple of days for him to show any real signs of recovery.

She had quickly gotten used to returning to her new cabin next to the potato crops at night, but she left it as long as possible before she retired every evening. For one thing, she knew she wouldn't be able to sleep if it was too early. It also seemed darker, gloomier and every inch of the place reminded her of Jace; the very walls seemed to speak of years of his loneliness and unhappiness.

Lara had made sure that she made her bed on the side that Brandon had been sleeping on; it just felt more proper to do this somehow. After what had happened a few months ago, it was hardly surprising she felt this way, although, she did suspect that Jace must have tried out more than one sleeping area during his sixteen-year stay here.

Other than when he helped out with essential chores, Jack seemed to be making himself rather scarce.

Lara got the sense that he was having a hard time dealing with the stress of Jace's condition, and as Lara had learned, his way of dealing with any difficult situation was to avoid it completely. He spent most of his time, in his own cabin. He was the first to retreat to it at night time, and he appeared to leave it as long as possible before he arrived in the morning.

On the third day Lara had initially thought she had overslept, but when she arrived at the main camp, she realised that she was actually the first to rise. Brandon appeared half an hour later to inform her that Jace was awake too and Lara started preparing a simple breakfast of fruit for them.

They were still well-and-truly avoiding fishing, and their only source of protein were the crabs and clams that they collected from the other beach which they ate for both their midday and evening meals.

Lara poured a cup of water from the tank, before she followed Brandon into the main hut with the breakfast.

As she entered, Jace was lying on his back in

bed. He greeted her as she walked in and set down the food and water, 'Morning,' he said, still sounding as though he had only just woken up.

'Good morning.' she said in response.

'Is it?' Jace replied with a brief laugh that he cut short with a grimace at the pain.

'Sorry,' Lara said with a sympathetic smile. 'How are you feeling?'

He smiled grimly. 'Like a big, huge monster has tried to take a chunk out of me because he thought I looked good to eat.' He winced again. 'I won't lie, I've been better.'

Brandon nodded, 'Huge,' he said. 'I can attest that isn't an exaggeration. It must have been easily, what - eight feet or so?'

'Amen to that, but you're forgetting the rest of it.' Jace said with a weak smile.

'Is there anything else I can get for you?' Lara asked him.

'I think I've got you running around after me enough.' He turned his head to face her. 'This is just the highlight of your time here isn't it? Having to wait on me constantly like this. You didn't see that in the brochure...'

'It's fine, really. I don't mind. It was an accident, it's not your fault.'

'Believe me, I'd rather we were all doing anything else right now.' Jace replied.

Brandon interjected, 'Are you ready to go to the bathroom yet, or do you want breakfast first?' He asked Jace.

'See Lara?' Jace turned to her again with a slight wince. 'It could be worse. Brandon is just getting all the best jobs isn't he?' he said sarcastically.

Lara thought Jace seemed to be doing a very good job of acting like his usual self. Even though he was clearly in a lot of pain, he was still managing to put on a brave face.

Later that evening however, Jace seemed to be struggling to keep it up. In the falling dusk, Lara could just make out the sheen on his face returning again.

She and Jack brought fresh bandages. Brandon cleaned his wound with water along with a sparing quantity of alcohol from the limited amount in the bottle, before applying the clean dressing.

Lara couldn't help but notice as Brandon removed the old bandage that he paused for the slightest of moments. His mouth tautened with stress the way that it did when he was deep in thought about something. A few minutes later, he announced that he thought Jace should get some rest and an early night was in order.

As she had expected, Jack was eager to leave and disappeared with a polite "Goodnight" almost as soon as Brandon had made this suggestion. This left Lara feeling pressured to make a swift departure too, without being able to invent a reason to talk to Brandon about Jace's state of well-being.

The next day Lara awoke early again and arrived at the main camp and was surprised to find

Brandon already seated on a log, staring into the fire he hadn't lit yet. He looked miles away. He didn't even notice Lara approaching and was only snapped out of his reverie as she took her usual seat facing the ocean.

'Good morning.' she said as she sat down. She watched Brandon closely for his response, wondering whether he had any update on Jace.

It turned out he did have some news to tell her, and it wasn't good. He informed her that Jace's wound was infected. He was still asleep at the moment, mainly due to the fact that he had awoken in the night having developed a fever and had only gotten back to sleep a short while ago.

Lara wasn't sure how to take this information, but she knew that it was bad news due to the fact they were isolated on this island, with no access to twenty-first century medicine.

She finally mustered the courage to ask the question she didn't really want to hear the answer to, 'Is he going to be OK?'

Brandon looked back at the bundle of fire-wood in front of him again and shook his head, subconsciously fiddling with his wedding ring. 'I don't know, Lara. It's not looking good for him at the moment...' His voice broke off and he stared out at the ocean.

Ironically it was a beautiful, sunny day with only a few clouds over the sea in the distance. The waves were rolling in gently and quietly along the shoreline.

They sat in silence for a while, both contemplating what this latest development could mean for Jace's future.

After twenty minutes she made a suggestion, 'Maybe you should try and get some sleep too.' She looked at Brandon, whose puffy eyes were still shadowed with heavy dark circles.

He shook his head. 'No, I can't sleep. I've tried all night to no avail. I can't stand looking at the ceiling any longer.'

Lara prepared them both breakfast. Just as they had finished eating, Jack turned up and Lara left him to make his own whilst she busied herself with the usual daily chores. She spent the morning collecting potatoes, gathering coconuts from the cliff-top and boiling and drying more bandages.

By the time Jace woke up, it was time for a late lunch.

Lara baked some potatoes in the fire, whilst Brandon took Jace water and went to change his bandages.

She had taken in Brandon's revelation enough to have prepared a strong, positive front when she took lunch for them all into the main hut. Unfortunately it didn't seem to do much good.

Jace was much less conscious than he had been just yesterday. He seemed to have deteriorated a lot even just overnight. He seemed tired still and his cheeks were flushed.

Brandon helped him eat his food and insisted that he should wash it down with an entire cup of water. 'You need to stay hydrated.' Brandon urged him.

'I think it's a little late for that.' Jace said, as Brandon lay him back down again.

Brandon ignored him.

Jack disappeared shortly after lunch, making an excuse that he was going to collect more bananas. 'I think I saw some really ripe ones over by the waterfall...' he said as he left.

Lara was more angry with Jack than ever for not being mature enough to stay around and handle the situation like an adult.

To Lara's astonishment, Brandon made a similar move around an hour later, although he was much more honest about his intentions. 'I think I'm going to go for a little walk. I'll pick up some crabs for dinner on the way back.' he said, avoiding eye contact with them and getting up to leave. He looked strained, like the weight of the world was on his shoulders and Lara understood that Jace's predicament was really taking its toll on him as he disappeared down the stairs.

Lara could forgive Brandon for his behaviour, but her good will did not extend to Jack who she was deeply annoyed with. It was evident that Brandon had been a pillar for the other two the whole time he had been on the island, but now he seemed to be finally crumbling at the thought of losing his childhood friend and member of their tiny community.

'Looks like we've been abandoned.' Jace said.

'Looks like it.' Lara replied, leaning back against the cabin wall.

'No one wants to sit here and wait for me to die.' he said with a less than half-hearted attempt at his old bitter laugh. He was also starting to shiver now.

'Don't say that.'

'Why not? Everyone knows it...Even Brandon has bailed on me. That's a bad sign, for sure...'

'He just needs some air, that's all...' she said reassuringly, although she knew she wasn't convincing either of them.

'You can leave too. I won't hold it against you, I promise.'

'I'm not going anywhere.' Lara replied defiantly, noticing Jace was shivering quite badly now.

Speaking seemed difficult for him with his jaw involuntarily clenched.

'Are you warm enough?' she asked, thinking of putting another blanket over him.

'Burning up.' he said, wincing with the pain in his wound.

'Here, have some more water.' She picked up the cup beside her on the bench.

'I don't n-need any more to drink. Brandon already forced two cups down me before you got here this morning.'

Lara didn't point out to him that it was actually the afternoon.

'Unless - you've g-got anything stronger?' There was a definite note of hope in his quivering voice.

'No,' Lara said firmly, putting the cup back down again. 'We need the whiskey for your injury.'

'Like it matters now,' Jace replied hopelessly. 'You might as well let me drink the rest of it. At least I'd die happy...'

'Please don't talk like that.' she said quietly, looking at the floor.

'Let's not pretend...I know the bite is infected. Brandon told me this morning.' He turned back to face the ceiling and closed his eyes. Beads of sweat were now visible, running from his forehead.

Lara didn't know what to say. She decided she would let him rest, but she felt she shouldn't leave, not when he felt the other two had abandoned him.

Lara didn't know how long for, but she watched the tide rolling placidly up and down the beach through the doorway. Usually there would be a slight breeze coming into the cabin through here, but today was very still and calm, it felt more humid than usual.

Lara wondered if this was a bad thing for Jace or not, considering that he felt hot already. But then again, a fever was just the illusion of heat wasn't it? Really the person could in fact feel cold to the touch. She again cursed her lack of first aid and medical knowledge.

She wondered if Jace was actually cold, and just felt like he was too hot. She didn't want him to deteriorate in her care. She had no idea when Brandon would come back. By the way he had looked earlier when he had left, Lara would be very surprised if they would see him any time soon.

She glanced across to Jace. His shivering had subsided slightly and he seemed quite calm. Lara couldn't tell if he was asleep or not. She decided to feel his forehead and put another blanket on him if she felt he needed it.

She kneeled on the floor beside the bed and reached the back of her hand to his damp forehead, he felt fine.

Jace opened his eyes.

Lara took a sharp intake of breath.

He turned to her. 'You checking I'm still a-alive?'

'I thought you were asleep. I just wanted to see if you were warm enough.'

'I'm surprised you're still here. Have Brandon or Jack been back yet?'

She shook her head. 'No. Anyway I told you, I'm not going to leave you.'

'That's very noble of you.' He closed his eyes again.

Lara thought that he was going to go back to sleep, and remained on the floor next to the bed until she was sure he had drifted off, so as to not disturb him.

After a few minutes, he spoke again, 'You know what I just can't believe?' He asked, opening his eyes again.

Lara shook her head.

'I can't believe I am going to die on this island.'

He made something like his characteristic scoff as best he could through his clenched jaw and shook his head. 'I never really believed it, you know?' His eyes looked more watery than normal as he looked back at the ceiling again. 'It was like...my mind t-told me that there was no hope of ever getting out of here. But somewhere deep inside - I still kept hope alive...' He took a deep breath. 'You know, I had to work away in Europe once. My wife gave me a watch as a going away present. She had it engraved with "It's Never Forever". She said that every time I looked at it, it would remind me that I would be closer to going back home to her, even if it was just a moment sooner...'

'That sounds nice...' Lara said, imagining the romantic sentiment in her mind.

Jace scoffed as much as he could through a wince of pain. 'She bought that on a shopping trip - when she also treated herself to a whole new wardrobe. She only got it so that she would have an excuse to go to an out-of-town mall right next to a day-spa...'

'I'm sure that wasn't the case at all, she probably put a lot of thought into it.'

'Oh yeah, she put a lot of thought into it all right. She always did carefully plan the best way to spend as much money as possible!'

'Jace, just relax!' Lara said, putting a hand on his clammy shoulder, willing him to lie still and rest.

Luckily Jace obeyed, and lay still for a moment with his eyes shut. After a few minutes, he opened them again, 'She never did care about me...' he said. 'She only married me for my money. She just used me to fund her lifestyle of salons and shopping. Why did I have to marry her...?' he trailed off thoughtfully. 'Still, it doesn't m-matter now d-does it? She'll have inherited everything because the world thinks I'm dead - she's probably had the spree of her life. And now here I am - about to make it true!'

'Stop it! Just stop talking like that! I don't want to hear it.'

Jace smiled and fell silent. 'You know, that watch came in handy here on the island. For the first few years I would get it out and look at it every now and then, to remind myself that I wouldn't be here forever. I clung onto the hope for years that eventually someone would find us...'

'There's still time.' Lara insisted urgently.

He looked at her with a grim smile, 'Not for me.'

Lara felt her eyes sting with tears. 'Don't say that!' She said firmly, getting frustrated. 'You are going to be OK. You just need some time to recover, that's all. You didn't deserve this to happen to you. You'll be fine. Just believe it and you'll get better!'

He was quiet for a moment, considering what she had just said. 'You really think I don't deserve this?' He said in barely more than a whisper.

Lara looked at the floor again. 'Of course not. This was just a bad accident. It could have happened to any of us. You were just in the wrong place at the wrong time.'

'But it h-happened to me. And I'm OK with that. I'm glad it was me. I do deserve this...'

'No! I don't think that. I never wanted anything bad to happen to you...' Lara tried to suppress the tears that were welling in her eyes. She looked at the floor again and tried to blink them away. She wiped them on the back of her hand and looked up at him again.

Jace made a sudden motion with his hand.

Lara thought he was having an involuntary movement, but then she thought he looked like he had been about to reach out and stroke her face, but then stopped himself. He rested his hand on his chest. He settled for studying her features instead, as though he thought they were going to be parted and was trying to remember every detail.

'Lara, there's something I have to s-say to you,' he said quietly, the words seemed to be costing him an even greater effort now.

Lara knew what was coming. She knew he wanted to apologise to her and clear his conscience, absolve himself of his sins before his body gave up and couldn't fight any more.

She decided she didn't want to hear it. She couldn't stand the thought that he wouldn't survive. Even if everyone else had given up hope, Lara wasn't going to let go of it. It felt like if she still refused to believe that Jace would do anything other than make a full recovery, then it wouldn't happen. He would be all right, he just had to be.

'I'm s-sorry,' he uttered through his tense jaw. 'I need you to know-'

'No! Just stop it. You don't need to say this now.'

'But I really do-'

'No, you don't. Just save it!' The tears burned in her eyes again. 'If you want to apologise then you can do it when you're better. Not in here, not now. Right now you just need to rest, so you can recover.'

This just seemed to frustrate Jace. 'L-Lara, please! Why can't you accept that I w-won't make it that l-long!' The exertion of raising his voice made him wince.

Lara took hold of his lost hand that had wanted to reach out for her and squeezed it firmly. 'I just can't accept that. I want you to be OK...'

Jace's eyes seemed to shine slightly again as he looked back at her defiant face. He didn't say anything.

Either he had come around to her way of thinking, or he didn't have any energy left to argue with her, Lara couldn't tell.

'You should get some rest.' she said to him gently now, still holding his hand.

He turned his head back to the ceiling and shut his eyes.

Lara thought he looked quite worn out. She presumed the constant shivering must be sapping his energy; after just a few minutes it subsided as his breathing changed, telling Lara that he had fallen asleep.

She knelt for a long while on the floor next to Jace, still holding his hand. The hand that belonged to the pair that had forcefully held her down a few months ago. It had been so strong then, but now it felt so weak and helpless in hers.

When she was satisfied that he was in a deep enough sleep, Lara slowly slipped her hand from his. She rested his own hand on his chest and gingerly lifted the blanket up over it.

Brandon arrived just as she was getting to her feet. She looked around at him, her initial reaction was that he looked like he had done some crying too.

'Has he just fallen asleep?' he asked her in a gentle whisper, his eyes looking even puffier than they had earlier.

'Yes.' she whispered back, moving away from Jace to the doorway where Brandon was.

The sun was starting to set outside, casting the same ominous, red glow as yesterday across the beach.

'Dinner will be ready soon, if you're hungry?'

'That sounds good.' she lied. Food was the last thing on her mind right now, but she thought it would do Brandon good at least to have some sense of normality.

They both paused as Jace made a sudden noise and shifted in his sleep slightly.

Lara wondered if he was having a nightmare.

After a moment, Brandon whispered, 'Come on.'

Lara followed him back to camp where Jack

already was. They all sat down and Jack served their dinner of crab and potatoes as dusk was falling. Lara didn't bother attempting to make small talk with Jack. She was still angry with him for unceremoniously abandoning her in the main hut earlier like a child.

Instead, she focused her energy on wrapping Jace's serving in a potato leaf for when he woke up later.

Jace didn't wake until much later that night.

Lara thought it must have been past midnight when he finally woke up from his nap.

Brandon had suggested that he would stay awake and tend to him, whilst Lara and Jack went to bed. Not surprisingly, Jack took this offer as soon as it was dispensed, but Lara insisted on staying to help his father. Not only did Brandon look exhausted, but Lara wanted Jace to know that she wanted to make sure that he was OK and she wasn't going to just leave him.

Even though she felt drained and exhausted herself, Lara made sure that Jace had clean bandages for Brandon to apply. She also took him several cups of drinking water.

When Brandon removed Jace's bandages, she could see that his wound was swollen and more red looking, even in the moonlight.

Lara could also see that Brandon used more water, as well as more alcohol than usual when he cleaned the area. Jace winced and suppressed a grunt in his throat as the dark liquid stung his damaged skin.

When she was satisfied that Jace had been well cared for and when she and Brandon had spoken to him for a while until he seemed tired and ready for another sleep, Lara decided that it was time for her to retire to her cabin too.

She bid them both goodnight, and made the now-familiar journey to her cabin alone. The moonlight lit her path as she passed out of the trees and through the beginning of the potato crops. Everywhere seemed to be made up of dark-blue shadows, moving gently in the refreshing breeze that had materialised in the last few hours.

As soon as she crossed the threshold into the cabin, Lara threw herself down onto the bed and curled up in the blankets without getting undressed.

She had expected to be asleep fairly soon after she had laid down, but after almost an hour she found she was still awake.

Lara decided to get changed into her night t-shirt and remove her shorts to try and make herself more comfortable. She tossed them carelessly onto the floor instead of folding them neatly on the adjoining bench like she usually did.

She looked at where they lay in a small heap on the cabin floor, thinking that she had just created a job for herself when she woke up tomorrow. Her eyes moved above the heap and she looked at the bed opposite where Jace had slept for years.

Lara couldn't explain why she did it, but she got

up from her restless space on Brandon's side of the hut with her pillow and blankets and set them up on Jace's side instead.

She felt comforted as the curves of her body fitted satisfyingly into the slight indents left behind by Jace. She felt slightly comforted lying here, and she tried to analyse why. She came up with the conclusion that by being in this space, she felt somehow closer to him.

A rush of sudden unexpected tears threatened to well up in her eyes and not for the first time today; she fought them back. To cry would mean that she thought something bad was about to happen to Jace; but it wasn't, it just couldn't. There was no way that she was going to allow herself to believe in that possibility.

Not long afterwards, exhaustion got the better of her and her new bed helped her finally drift off into sleep.

When Lara woke up the next morning, she instantly realised that she had well-and-truly overslept.

She got dressed quickly and made her way to the main camp.

Brandon was there, although he looked like he had only just got there himself, and was pouring a cup of water.

'Morning,' he said.

Now that Lara was closer, she noticed that Brandon looked like he'd had a better night's sleep than in previous days.

'Good morning,' she said. Without any pause she asked, 'How is he?'

Brandon shrugged. 'He's still sleeping.' When he saw Lara's look of disappointment he added, 'That's the best thing for him at this stage. He'll - He'll get over the infection faster if he gets plenty of rest.'

Lara nodded.

She and Brandon had a breakfast of fruit, and as with the previous day they were joined towards the end by Jack, who was again left to prepare his own meal.

Afterwards Lara went to wash in the waterfall, before she returned to the camp.

Jack volunteered to go and fetch the crabs for lunch with her.

Lara thought he seemed to be making an effort to help out more, but she wasn't ready to forgive him yet.

Jack tried to engage her in conversation throughout the crab-collection process, but she didn't really pay much attention. She was too busy wondering how Jace would be today when he woke up, as well as thinking about their conversation yesterday.

She thought about when she had stopped Jace mid-apology. The look of sincerity on his face had haunted her all last night before she had gone to sleep. What he said hadn't just seemed like a dying man simply clearing his conscience, he had seemed to really mean it.

Jace had woken up not long after lunch. He wasn't shivering today and it seemed that his appetite was better than it had been yesterday. He even managed to finish his meal more easily and with less encouragement from Brandon.

Lara paid close attention when Brandon changed Jace's dressing and wasn't sure if she was imagining that it looked much better than it had last night. Although Lara was aware that it had been dark last night, but she was quite confident that the wound had improved overnight.

Brandon seemed to be using the alcohol more liberally when cleaning Jace's injury and she thought that this might have something to do with her impression of his recovery. Hopefully they would have enough to get him clear of the infection.

Brandon himself seemed much more like his usual upbeat self again today. He didn't do a Jack-style disappearance and seemed determined to stay with Jace all day.

Lara was much happier about leaving Jace when she retired to bed that night. He seemed much more conscious and didn't dispense a single self-pitying comment.

The bright sunshine continued for yet another day and it greeted Lara as she walked through the potato plants towards the camp the next day.

She felt so much more positive than she had done in the previous week and she suddenly became aware of the beautiful scenery and weather that surrounded her as she approached the campfire.

As she went to pour a cup of water however, her good mood evaporated faster than she could have imagined when she saw what sat at the side of the water tank - it was the empty bottle of whiskey.

Her heart sank as she realised that Jace was now left to fight the infection without it.

It seemed to take an age for Brandon to appear that morning, even though she knew it can't have been that long in reality.

He seemed happy enough, and Lara didn't want to dispel his slightly lighter mindset by adding undue stress to it, so she simply asked how Jace was.

Brandon told her that he had slept all through the night and he his fever seemed to have broken.

Lara scrutinised Jace closely when he woke up just after breakfast. He did indeed look much better than yesterday. She watched him carefully throughout the day for signs of any returning fever, but there were none to be seen.

Brandon still religiously washed his injury, but using only water now, since that was all they had. Lara still supplied fresh dressings regularly. She was glad to have this job, it made her feel like she was actively doing something to help Jace recover.

Lara still analysed Jace's well-being before she bid him and Brandon goodnight, but she was satisfied that he was showing signs of being on the road to recovery.

Over the next week it became apparent that Jace had managed to fight the infection and was recovering quickly. Brandon had removed his stitches smoothly, and the wound was noticeably healing day by day.

When Lara went to see him one morning a week later, he was sitting up without Brandon's assistance and was drinking water by himself.

A few days later, she saw that he was only being loosely supported by Brandon when he was taken to the bathroom and seemed to be doing a good job of taking his own weight, even though he was still wincing slightly.

That evening, he managed to talk Brandon into letting him have dinner by the campfire.

Brandon supported him as he usually did, with Jace's arm around his neck. Brandon in turn had his arm around Jace's waist as he hobbled over to his usual log next to Lara.

He sat down and seemed to be relishing the breeze around him.

He noted that he would never take fresh air for granted again and how nice it was to be out of the four walls to get a change of scenery.

'I didn't ever think there would ever be a time when I would call sitting by this campfire a "change of scenery",' he laughed.

They all ate a special dinner of crab and baked potatoes before a dessert of banana and coconut. Although no one had officially said it, this felt like a celebratory meal. It marked the recovery they were all glad Jace had made, even when it had all looked so hopeless.

The four ate and drank together and were so busy talking that they didn't notice darkness falling around them. Even Jack joined in more than usual. Now that Jace was definitely on the mend, he seemed to have relaxed and was happily interacting normally with them again. Well, as normally as Jack did interact anyway.

They all talked like they had done when Lara had first arrived, before her story had been exposed and the men were under the impression that rescue was looming on the horizon.

Now it didn't matter that there was no promise of an imminent rescue, they were all just glad to be alive, and together.

It was past midnight when Brandon insisted that they should all go to bed.

Although Jace looked happy, he also looked tired, and Brandon insisted that he shouldn't over-do it and get some more rest.

'All I have been doing is resting!' Jace protested to his friend, but after a few moments he agreed and put his arm around Brandon's neck and allowed himself to be helped back to his hut, bidding Lara and Jack goodnight over his shoulder.

Lara finished her water and set her cup down. 'Well, I'm going to head off to bed too. Goodnight Jack.' She got up to leave and to her surprise, Jack quickly stood up too.

'Hey, uh, don't you want to stay up a little longer?' He asked.

'No, I'm pretty tired actually. I think I could do with the sleep too.' she replied honestly.

'Do you want me to walk you to your cabin?' he asked awkwardly, stepping over his log and closer to her.

Lara was slightly taken aback by this, 'No, it's OK. I know it's dark, but it's not far.' she said light-heartedly. 'Well, goodnight then.'

'Yeah, goodnight.' For some reason he looked slightly disappointed.

She smiled at him, before turning on her heel and slipping into the dark trees. Her thoughts again turned to Jace.

Jace continued getting better over the next fortnight. Lara noticed him getting gradually more animated and his movements more fluid as the weeks went by. He seemed so much stronger, full of life and raring to go, even though Brandon constantly urged him to rest until he was completely healed. This was difficult for Brandon to enforce, as Jace was eager not to be confined within the walls of the cabin.

It was only when he looked so much more like himself, that Lara allowed herself to feel a sense of relief. She suddenly became aware that there had been a constant tension in her shoulders since the initial accident and now it was being released with every passing day.

There was one thing that had come from the accident that had surprised Lara. She had all but mentally dismissed Jace as an angry, bitter and resentful person that had, in some ways, reverted back to a more selfish, primal state.

For a short period of time at least over the last few weeks, she had seen a glimpse of another side of him; one that was much more endearing. Lara suspected that this was perhaps the real Jace, the one that had lain guarded underneath a tough, defensive layer built up through years of hopelessness and despair. The real Jace seemed like someone she could get along with. He was much more appealing.

17
Confessions

Lara had been so preoccupied with worrying about and helping take care of Jace, as well as performing most of Brandon's chores, that she was surprised when she found out that it was November already.

It was safe to say that Jace had made a full recovery and was walking around now without any assistance, although Brandon insisted that he shouldn't take up his old chores again for another week, just to make sure his health had been completely restored.

Jace had been slightly frustrated by this, but had agreed. This hadn't stopped him from helping out with food preparation from his log-seat beside the campfire, however, as Brandon couldn't argue with this.

Jace seemed to be filled with a new lease of life and wasn't making as many bitter remarks as he had once done, now only his characteristic dark, sarcastic ones. His good mood was infectious. One day, he regaled Lara and Jack with a mischievous tale from his and Brandon's childhood.

Lara couldn't help an insuppressible giggle bursting from her as Jace delivered the punchline.

Jack on the other hand, did not seem amused.

Lara couldn't understand why, but thought nothing more of it afterwards. Jack always seemed to be able to slip quickly into a sulky mood with no warning; this was sometimes accompanied by his trademark disappearing act.

Brandon seemed happier than ever once his set time-frame had expired and Jace had returned to his usual duties. Only then did he seem confident that he definitely had his friend back.

He and Jace were now in discussions on the topic of how they could start catching fish again.

Although he didn't say it, Lara got the impression that Jace seemed to have a phobia of stepping foot in the ocean again, even if it was just a foot deep.

She didn't blame him. She was having similar thoughts herself, but also knew that this wasn't conducive to providing the group with fish, a much needed source of sustenance.

Jace suggested some kind of trap that they could operate from the safety of the beach, but was stuck as to what they could use as the building material.

'What about line-fishing?' Jack suggested as the discussion continued over breakfast one morning.

Brandon shrugged after thinking about it with a furrowed brow for a moment, 'Jack, we've talked about that before. It would be very hit and miss. You can't be sure you would catch anything every day.'

'Why not?' Jack insisted, fighting his corner. 'We've caught stuff before like that when we used to go fishing with Grandpa.'

Brandon shook his head. 'That was different.

The lakes we fished in were manually stocked with fish by the landowners. You'd have been hard pressed not to have caught anything.'

Jack looked slightly crestfallen at this, as though this was the first time he had considered this fact.

'We can't afford not to catch anything, Jack.' His father went on, 'If we didn't catch anything at the lakes when you were a kid, then we just didn't have anything to brag to your mother about. But things are different here. If we don't catch a fish here, we don't eat.'

Jack looked suddenly irritated by this. 'I know that - I'm not a child!' Jack retorted shortly, with a hint of temper that was out of character for him.

Lara expected him to disappear shortly after this outburst, but to his credit he didn't, which was also out of character for Jack.

Mainly because they had no better ideas, rather than to humour Jack, they decided to attempt fishing from the safety of the shore using a fishing line they had crafted out of some worn, old rope that had once made up part of their initial makeshift shelter when they had first become shipwrecked.

Jace explained to Lara how at first, when they had thought that their stay was only temporary, they built a small sort of tent out of their inflatable dinghy and some loose branches, binding the whole thing together with the rope. The three of them had spent several months sleeping in this tent together, until they decided it was time to consider other arrangements.

'How times have changed, huh?' he mused to Brandon. He turned back to Lara, 'What we live in now is the height of luxury in comparison.'

'It feels like it.' Lara smiled back at him.

'Hey!' Brandon interjected, with a smile and mock offence. 'You were glad of our tent when it poured down with rain for three days in a row.'

Jace carved a small, sharp hook from a palm tree branch and tied it to the end of the rope.

Brandon slid some crab meat onto the end of the hook and cast the whole thing into the water. 'Here goes nothing...' he said as the hook splashed far out in the deeper water.

Since there was nothing else to do, the four of them sat in a row in the sand just before the tide line.

After over forty minutes, Brandon suddenly became animated and jumped to his feet. 'I got something.' he said.

Everyone else jumped up too, in tense support, eager to see if their new technique was going to work.

Brandon quickly reeled in the rope and seemed as though he was holding his breath in concentration. As he pulled, small ripples of erratic splashing drew nearer with each tug.

The last length of rope was pulled clear of the water now and on the end was a frantically flapping fish, trying to escape back underneath the waves it had just been dragged from.

They all let out an excited cheer as they saw their catch. This was the first fish they had managed to get hold of for over two months.

Like Brandon had said, back in civilisation where fishing was a mere hobby, a fish was simply a prize to be bragged about. But here, it meant real nourishment and an excellent source of protein. Not to mention it tasted much better than the crab too.

They tried for a further hour and a half to catch another fish, but had no takers for their bait. They even added more to the end of the line, stuffing the hook with as much as it could hold, but it didn't make any difference. Instead they prepared and ate their single catch and split it between the four of them, along with some baked potatoes.

Lara thought it was the most delicious thing she had eaten since being on the island. It was even better than the fish she had been served on her first day.

After their initial, mild success with the line-fishing method, Brandon and Jace tried again the next day using the same technique. But after two whole hours with nothing to show for it, they decided to move further afield and try out different areas of the beach. When that didn't work, they were forced to give up for the day and revert to another crab-based dinner instead.

The next few days bore similar results. After a week, they had yet to catch a second fish using their line.

One day, all four of them ventured along the ridge of rocks that Lara had avoided when she had swum to the island, determined that the deeper water should yield something. It was somewhat slippery towards the furthest end and felt slightly precarious.

Lara watched her footing carefully as they all took their time arriving at the furthest point.

Jack and Brandon had far greater success here and after just minutes they found that they were easily pulling in a fish every ten minutes or so.

Jack was most proud that his idea had turned out so well. He seemed intent on being credited with it too, fishing for compliments as well as for food.

When both Lara and Jace had their turns with the line, they found that they weren't as lucky and hadn't caught anything after half an hour.

Jace had implied that this was down to the fact that the fish wouldn't linger too long and allow themselves to be caught so easily. Although, Brandon had quashed this theory when he had taken hold of the line again, and managed to catch another shortly afterwards.

Both Jace and Lara had to admit defeat at this point and gracefully acknowledged that the other two had managed to develop the right technique.

In preparation for lunch the next day, the four took their line back to the rocky ridge to find out if it wasn't simply a fluke that they had caught something yesterday.

Lara and Jace took a slight back seat to see if

they could learn the correct method the other two seemed to have success with.

They stepped aside and allowed father and son to gather the fish. They decided that for now it was just good to have a supply of them again, and in time they would master this effective technique too.

Feeling a little redundant as Jack had pulled his second fish from the line, Lara pointed out that someone should go and restock the coconut supplies back at the camp and excused herself.

She stepped off the last rock and onto the sandy beach again, turning right and reaching the base of the steep hill that lead up to the cliff-top.

Once she had arrived at the top of the cliff, she didn't immediately rush to collect the fruit, instead she took in the view she had only seen once for months on end. Since her experience with Jace up here, she had only visited once and that had been with Jack as they both briefly collected coconuts together.

This was the first time she had been back alone, and she realised how much she had missed the beautiful view that spanned far and wide across the ocean. In her opinion, it was the nicest part of the island and she was glad to see it again.

She strolled forward slowly and took a seat on one of the rocks in between the two palm trees, intending to spend a few minutes alone before she went back to the main camp.

He solitude didn't last long however, as after

several minutes Jace emerged from the top of the slope Lara had not long ago just scaled herself.

He stood a few yards away with his hands on his hips and was slightly breathless from the steep walk as he explained his unexpected arrival, 'They're uh, they're struggling with the fourth one. It's rather elusive,' he said, nodding his head in the general direction of the rocks jutting out to sea. 'But I'll be damned if I can do any better.'

'Me neither. I'm sure we'll get the hang of it, though.'

'Yeah, if Jack would let anyone else have a go. He is determined to catch every last one by himself, for some reason.' Jace shook his head and shrugged.

'I thought I would leave them to it and make myself useful somewhere else.' Lara said, gesturing towards the untouched coconuts that lay scattered around the base of the tree.

'Really? It looks like you're sitting back and admiring the view to me.' he said, with a trace of his familiar smirk.

Lara smiled back at him, 'I'm just about to get started.'

Jace shook his head. 'Actually, I'm glad you came up here. I've been waiting for a chance to talk to you alone.'

'Oh?'

'Yes, it's been harder than I thought actually. Brandon is always around - or Jack. He seems to be trying his best to spend more time with you lately.'

Lara was suddenly aware that the last time she and Jace were alone together on the cliff-top was when he attempted his attack. She didn't feel nervous, she was confused and trying to think of why Jace needed to talk to her when she was by herself.

'There are things I need to say to you,' Jace went on, 'I just wondered, will you hear my confession now?'

Lara suddenly understood what he was talking about - he wanted to make the apology she had denied him in the cabin, when he thought he wasn't going to survive.

Jace looked at her inquiringly and took a tentative step forward, 'May I join you? You said you wanted to wait until I had recovered, so here I am.'

'Yes, you can. But it - it doesn't matter. Let's just put it behind us. We don't have to talk about it...'

'I think we do have to talk about it. And it does matter, Lara. It matters to me. I can only imagine what you must think of me.'

'Well, all right then...' she said awkwardly, shifting on her rock slightly to face him as he sat on the rock beside her. Lara hadn't expected this, she thought they had already left any uncomfortable atmosphere behind them. She decided to let him say what he felt he had to say, clear his conscience and get it over and done with.

Jace paused for a moment, obviously choosing

his words carefully. 'I want you to know why I did what I did - what drove me to it.' He looked at Lara with insistent sincerity as he went on, 'I'm not looking to excuse my behaviour. I certainly can't justify it, and I wouldn't want to. You didn't deserve that, and every time I think about it I'm mortified of what I put you through.'

Lara suddenly found that her throat was slightly constricted, which would have made speaking difficult. And she thought that even if it wasn't, she didn't want to stop Jace from continuing with what was evidently an apology he had thought long and hard about. So she simply nodded.

'Like I told you...it's been hard for me to be on this island alone. I mean, yes - I was here with Brandon and Jack - two other men. But they, well, they have each other - being father and son and all. I guess all these years I've always felt like I'm on the outside - alone. And even if I wasn't, their company could only do so much...

'In the last few years, I know I've treated them badly. I avoided them, and when I didn't - I insulted them. I didn't really consider that being here was hard for them too. I think I may have blamed them for me being here. Of course, it wasn't their fault at all. I chose to go with them on the trip, they didn't force me...

Anyway, I'd almost completely alienated myself from them. I only spoke to them during chores and when we ate if I could help it. We went on for a couple of years like that. Brandon tried his best and still stuck by me, but I always rejected his attempts to communicate. For all I knew, he was as lonely as I was, but I didn't think about that. All I knew was my own loneliness. I wallowed in it. It was like a constant ache inside me. From the second I woke up, to the second I went to sleep at night it was all I knew...'

He shook his head. 'And then one day, you washed up - and it had to be you. Right on the beach next to the main camp. I thought that everything was about to change. I thought we were going to be rescued, and that finally I wouldn't have to endure the daily torment any more. But then - then...

'Then you found out I had lied.' Lara said quietly.

Jace nodded, 'Yes. I won't lie - that hit me pretty hard. I had known there was something about your story that didn't feel right, but I couldn't figure out what at the time. I couldn't think of a reason why you would lie to us.'

Lara felt the ghost of the regret she had felt at having raised and dashed the hopes of the men, but let Jace go on with his story.

'At that point I decided that everything was just the same as it had been before you arrived. We were no closer to being rescued than we had been for years and it wasn't going to change. I just knew that we were all back to facing years - possibly forever on this island. Except that now - you were here with us.' There was a pause where Jace shifted and looked down at his hands, before he continued, speaking more quietly now. 'I wanted you. I'd known that as soon we first met-' He now fiddled with his hands slightly as he spoke down at them '-I felt an attraction I'd never known...I had never felt that way about anyone before. Then I realised I had fallen for you-'

Lara was taken aback by this, but didn't interrupt.

'-I tried to get your attention - tried making the most foolish passes at you-' He gritted his teeth slightly in embarrassment as he thought about them '-But I knew you weren't interested. If you hadn't have told me so yourself, then your body language said it for you...That was hard for me to deal with. I tried to forget about the way I felt...push it aside and ignore it, but I couldn't...It didn't help that you were the most attractive woman I'd ever met-'

Lara had to scoff at that, forgetting about letting him have any easy confession.

Jace looked taken aback. He looked up at her with something like astonishment before he said, 'I don't think you realise just how beautiful you are...'

After a few moments where they looked at each other, Lara had to pull her eyes away from his and now it was her turn to look at her hands as she felt the heat rising in her cheeks.

Jace returned to his story, 'Well, it was so hard for me being around you every day with the way that I felt, knowing that you didn't feel the same way. You had rejected my advances and I couldn't imagine going through the years before me, living out my life alone without...without any physical, human contact.' He looked across at her, 'You probably can't imagine this - since you haven't been here that long, and being a woman and all - but it's hard to be a man in this situation...Urges are hard to ignore.'

Lara wanted to point out that women have "urges" too, but didn't think it was appropriate.

Jace paused for a moment, before what he said next in his most sober tone yet, 'Then one day, it all just came to a head. I didn't even think about what I was doing. I just planned to find you, make sure you were alone...'

Lara tried to make it easier for the both of them by avoiding eye contact with Jace as he spoke now, more than aware that the incident he was now speaking of had happened not far behind where they currently sat.

'I wanted you so badly I just got overcome with desire... I couldn't control myself. It was like - like I was watching myself do it. It was like something took control of me and I was going through the motions and all the time my head was screaming at my body to stop, but I couldn't.'

He cringed with shame and he stared at his hands as he added, 'I really hated that I was going to hurt you.'

Lara felt an uncomfortable tug in her chest. She was aware of the anguish and guilt in Jace's voice as he spoke and knew it was genuine.

'I've never tried anything like that before - it's not who I am,' he said insistently. 'And I want you to understand - as soon as...' He faltered and looked a little more awkward. 'As soon as Brandon stopped me, reality sank down on me like a stone - and I realised what I had done. I know it might be hard for you to imagine, but I hated myself far more than you were hating me.'

Lara found that her throat felt constricted again. She wanted to tell Jace that she hadn't hated him, but the truth was that she had been so angry with him at that point. Now however, since his accident, she just hadn't had the heart to hate him. She had realised that she didn't want him to be hurt, and she certainly didn't want him to die, and she had found that any bad feelings she had towards him had dissipated. She didn't know how to convey this to Jace, so she nodded again.

'Lara,' he said, now shifting in his seat so that they were face to face. 'I know that I don't deserve your forgiveness, but I want you to hear my apology. I want you to know that I'm truly sorry-'

'No,' Lara said, suddenly finding her voice. 'I forgive you. I know you're sorry.' She shook her head, trying to conjure the words to explain how she felt, but couldn't find any. 'It's all right, I forgive you.' she repeated, accepting his apology.

The relief that fell upon Jace was quite visible. His conscience now allowed the tension in his shoulders to ease a little. He nodded too. Now they both knew that the matter was concluded and neither of them needed to say any more as they both looked out at the sunlight sparkling on the endless ocean before them in the midday sun.

The thoughts of Jace's confession were still with Lara as she got into bed that night. She pulled the blankets up over herself and stared at the glow of the moonlight on the wall.

So Jace had been genuinely remorseful just seconds after their encounter. She thought of the brief glimpse of him with his head in his hands she had taken in before she had made her escape. She now tried to piece together her memories of their meeting months before, with what Jace had told her today.

Lara now knew that a powerful internal battle had been raging within Jace before he had given in to his feelings. Now that she thought back, she could see it. She remembered the look on his face as he had approached and sat beside her that day; remembered how he seemed to be within himself and deep in thought as he had tried to fight his desire.

His desire...Lara thought now of the way he had looked when he was trying to explain the way that he had felt about her. He said that he'd fallen for her...What did that mean? Was he trying to tell her that he had been in love with her? And why was he speaking in past tense when he talked about his feelings? If he had felt that way at the time, then did that mean that this was the way he felt about her now?

Lara felt confused by this, but also by her own feelings. She had been surprised that she felt so strongly for Jace when she had feared for his life. She surely wasn't supposed to feel that way about him? Not after what he had tried to do, anyway. But then, he was genuinely remorseful for his actions. He hadn't lived a normal life for the past sixteen years at all, and his mindset had obviously been affected. Lara had definitely forgiven him for his temporary loss of control.

She tried to analyse her own feelings as she lay in the dark, staring at the wall.

After a while, Lara concluded that even if she did have feelings towards Jace, then she was under no obligation to act upon them.

Yes, she felt initially happy with that conclusion. Although in truth, she was trying to avoid admitting that she really did feel an attraction towards Jace - a very strong attraction such as she had never felt before.

18
The Storm

The beautiful, calm days of the previous few months were now rapidly transforming into hotter and stormier ones. It was December, the beginning of the wet season was approaching which meant that hot, wet days and frequent storms were becoming commonplace. And as the others had told Lara, it was only going to get worse over the next few months.

Other than the increasingly turbulent weather, everything was going well. Lara and Jace were getting on as well as ever, perhaps even better than her first few months here. She felt that she understood him better now, and could see why the other two had taken his insults with only the slightest reaction.

Now however, she noticed that he wasn't dispensing his cutting remarks as much as he had in the past. Perhaps he had thought about all of his past misdeeds as he had lain in the hut during the weeks of his recovery.

Lara inwardly berated herself for not asking Jace whether he still had feelings for her during their talk whilst it was still relevant. And despite how desperately she wanted to know, it didn't feel appropriate to ask him now. She knew she could not simply bring it up in casual conversation, and she felt she had missed her chance.

Besides, even if she could gather the courage together, she found that she couldn't get to be alone with Jace since Jack always seemed to be around. Jace had been right, it was difficult to find a time when she was alone, and this was mainly down to Jack.

He seemed determined that he wouldn't miss an opportunity to spend time with her. It had become obvious to her now why he did this; he had a crush on her. But she felt uncomfortable about the matter and she did not return his feelings. He may be handsome and close to her age, but his array of immature habits reminded her too much of Alan. Lara wondered if she should talk to him about the attachment he had formed, but didn't want to sound condescending.

Despite the fact that she never seemed to get an opportunity to be alone with Jace, she still enjoyed his company far more than that of Brandon and Jack.

Brandon was attractive in his own way, but Lara thought upon him more of a kindly relative and he remained faithful to the thought of his wife. As for Jack, he was young and good-looking, but Lara had long since deemed him immature; surprisingly so, considering how hard life had been for him growing up on the island. She would have expected this upbringing to have aged him faster.

No, Jace was the one of the three that captured Lara's interest. As the days went by, Lara noticed more and more how attractive he was. For the first time, she fully appreciated his handsome features; how his defined cheekbones seemed to draw her attention to the eyes that were such an unusual icy grey. Lara thought that every time she observed this and Jace looked in her direction, he could tell what she was thinking as though her thoughts were plain for him to see.

Despite his grey-flecked hair, he was still young-looking. The tanned skin of his face, arms and legs looked firm and smooth above the well-defined muscles of his body. And even though he had been so badly injured, he seemed to have fully recovered and was as strong as ever.

Every time she was near Jace, Lara found she experienced the most intense feelings towards him; far more than just a simple case of butterflies.

During the time that they spent together she would cast him the occasional glance, trying to judge from the little information her eyes stole, whether he felt the same way. Lara genuinely couldn't tell if his feelings for her remained intact or if they had dissipated.

Perhaps it was just wishful thinking on her part that an interest in her still burned inside him. But was it wishful thinking? What was she actually hoping was going to happen? Her cynical side told her that she couldn't start a relationship with him after what had happened between them, even if it was just purely out of principle. On the other hand, her heart was telling her something completely different.

Her attraction to Jace was the strongest she had ever felt towards anyone, and it was becoming very difficult to fight. At night, it was the first thing she thought about when she got into bed alone.

Lara spent countless hours staring at the ceiling in the dark, going over it all in her mind.

Try as she might, she couldn't stop her mind straying to the part of Jace's apology when he had confessed that he had fallen in love with her. She mentally replayed it often. But then, he had also been speaking in retrospect.

Lara wondered if he still felt this way, and what it would mean if he did.

Did he think of her at night, the way that she thought of him? In the silent darkness of the midnight hours, Lara often found her mind wandering over to the main hut where Jace still slept, and wondering if he was thinking about her too. With a slight nervous thrill, she contemplated the idea that if her thoughts of him became too intense then he might feel it. But maybe, she wanted him to…

Lara struggled with her feelings through the month as the weather increasingly became more turbulent around her. She was surprised when she went to breakfast one morning and Brandon wished her 'Merry Christmas'.

In light of such a significant day, Brandon arranged for them to have a more special dinner than usual. He took charge of making the more labour-intensive fish stew, and even prepared some entrées for them all to enjoy while they waited for it to cook. Granted, these little morsels weren't made up from anything different than they usually ate, but it helped make the day stand out from the rest.

It had been noticeably breezy all day, and now that darkness had completely fallen, it seemed that the wind was picking up.

It was now very hard to sit around the campfire due to the fact that the swirling wind was blowing it in all directions, making it difficult to avoid the clouds of smoke that were gusting everywhere. Not only this, but conversation was tricky too and Lara found herself having to shout slightly to be heard over the roaring wind.

In the end, they all finished their food quickly as twilight was falling and extinguished the campfire to avoid the possibility that the nearby trees might catch alight.

Lara had thought this was Brandon being slightly over-cautious until just a minute after the flames had gone out, when a piece of charred firewood flew in the direction of the jungle.

They all worked together, scrabbling about and frantically securing anything in the main camp that wasn't attached to anything and could potentially be taken by the wind.

Once this was done Brandon suggested, half-yelling to be heard above the raging gale around them, that they should collect any loose fruit or vegetables on the island perimeter that hadn't been gathered yet, to make sure that they didn't lose it to the sea because of the storm. They didn't want to end up short on food for the next month, especially if they couldn't fish if the bad weather continued.

'But, be careful! Watch your footing, especially if you're up on the cliff!' Brandon yelled as they all scattered in different directions to complete their task.

Jack had offered to go and fetch any remaining cliff-top coconuts that dropped to the ground, whilst Brandon himself went to secure the fishing equipment, as well as the smaller rocks that made up the SOS sign. Lara and Jace both volunteered to go and collect any loose and ready to fall bananas. This task required two people, since the banana trees bore the most fruit of anything on the island; they were also very close to the sea on one side of the crop.

Lara and Jace jogged along the beach as far as they could before they disappeared into the gap in the trees. There was less beach than usual because the sea was being driven so far up the sandy slope that areas where they could usually walk had been completely dissolved by the surging water.

It was obvious what needed to be done as soon as they arrived amidst the banana trees, as several loose bananas dropped from their position straight away.

Now huge droplets of cool rain were driven

against them as they sprung into action.

The two worked quickly, gathering up what they could into a small pile in a corner that was the most sheltered from the wind.

After a few minutes of this, Jace frantically dug a hole in the soft ground with his bare hands. The pair then started moving the pile of fruit into the hole as quickly as they could.

The wind and rain were being forced down on them with such force, that Lara found it hard to stay on her feet. She had to throw herself against the gale to move in it and she could barely see where she was going as she chased after stray pieces of fruit before they could be blown too far from the trees.

She could hear Jace yelling to her, but couldn't hear what he was saying. She also couldn't see where he was with the growing darkness that was falling rapidly around them. It didn't help that her hair was flying wildly in front of her face.

Lara had never been in the middle of a storm before, and realised that it was now dangerous, and they needed to complete their task quickly and seek shelter somewhere.

She started towards several stray bright-yellow pieces of fruit that blew just past her feet, when she suddenly heard a loud CRACK nearby.

In the almost complete darkness Lara couldn't immediately identify where it came from, and realised too late that it actually had emanated from the largest tree in front of her that was rapidly getting nearer.

Lara froze. She knew that in the second it had taken her to decide what to do that her time was up.

One thought formed in her mind - she was about to be crushed.

Lara abruptly found herself on her side amongst the moist, fallen leaves that made up the jungle floor. She was suddenly aware that the tree that had been just feet away from her a second ago, fell with a large thump that she felt vibrate through the ground beside her.

Confused, she looked over her shoulder at Jace lying beside her - he had launched himself forwards and pulled her out of the way of the falling wood just in time.

He quickly got up and pulled her to her feet. Taking hold of her hand, he dragged her over to the small gap between two sturdy trees that seemed to provide some degree of shelter.

They both squeezed into it, crouched back to chest in the same direction with Lara at the front.

They both shielded their heads from the raging wind with their arms, as small bits of unseen debris flew at them in the dark.

Lara wanted to thank Jace for saving her from the tree, but knew she wouldn't make herself heard over the roaring wind, so she remained sat pressed against him. The warmth from his body emphasised how cool the ferocious rain was that pelted down upon the parts of her that weren't in contact with him.

Lara hadn't been this close to Jace, since their cliff-top encounter all those months ago. She thought it was ironic that she thought of that now. Now the situation was completely different and he had saved her. Now he was protecting her, and she felt safe against his firm body as they both crouched in their shelter together and waited for the storm to pass.

Lara and Jace stayed together in their gap between the trees until the storm blew itself out rather suddenly in the early hours of the morning. The usually calm air returned, leaving only a gentle breeze swaying the leaves of the trees around them.

Jace declared that the storm was over as he surveyed the scene around them, and they both went back to their separate cabins to get some sleep.

When the group did reconvene in the harsh light of day the next morning, it was obvious how much damage had been done to their environment. There was debris; leaves, branches and tree bark was littered everywhere along the beach, ruining its usual pristine appearance. The sand itself had been swept with some force, far into the trees.

What little of the SOS sign Brandon had left, had been scattered out of place and now was illegible.

Brandon had initially declared that the large,

heavy pan they used for cooking had been taken by the storm, until Lara got a shock when she stepped on it; it had been almost completely buried in the sand near the edge of the tide.

Lara was impressed that the main hut had remained virtually intact. Only one of the struts that elevated it from the sand was in need of a slight repair.

They spent the next few days clearing up the beach and moving the debris back into the jungle. They had to completely rebuild a new campfire since they couldn't even find most of the pieces that had made up the old one. They also eventually found the water tank the next day; the wind had driven it into the branches of a tree. It was only when Jace heard a heavy rain shower hitting it, that it was discovered.

Once they had the main camp under control, they moved into the jungle. It took the four of them to work together to lift the tree that had almost fallen on Lara out of the way of the other banana trees.

Once it had been moved, Lara saw the large dent it had made in the earth it was driven into. She now fully appreciated the force that had been behind it and knew that if Jace hadn't pulled her out of the way, then she surely would have been killed.

Lara thought that perhaps she should thank Jace for his quick reflexes, but she wasn't quite sure how to say it. And still, she never seemed to have a chance to speak to him alone as Jack still never missed an opportunity to be around her.

After the clean-up operation, New Year's Eve was upon them all before Lara knew it. This time the celebration seemed more earned, due to the fact they had worked so had to restore normality in their settlement.

Again, Brandon made an effort to make the dinner more special with slightly altered dishes.

When it came time for the toast, Brandon, as usual, took charge of making the speech in the twilight that was falling around them.

They all raised their cups of coconut milk in a toast, and took turns knocking them with each other. Lara and Jace were the last to do this, and as they did so Lara thought that it wasn't her imagination that the glance that they shared as their cups connected was far from meaningless.

Brandon suggested that they should all make New Year's resolutions as Lara was getting up to wash the empty stew pot in the sea.

She was glad that she had left at that moment, because she wouldn't have been able to think of anything she should share. The obvious answer was rescue, but since that didn't look likely at the moment she didn't want to say it out loud and put a dampener on the celebration.

Lara straightened up and shook the last drops of salt water from the pan as she looked out across the darkening ocean. The last streaks of gold from the sunset in the cooling sky highlighted patches of sea in the distance and stars were emerging with every passing minute.

Lara cast around for something to hope for in the new year, and was surprised at how quickly her thoughts fell on Jace.

Lara looked over her shoulder for him around the campfire. When her eyes found his face reflecting the orange flames, she was certain he had been looking in her direction just a moment before, but now he seemed engrossed in stoking the fire.

It was true that she had never felt the way she did about Jace before, not about anyone, and certainly not about Alan. Lara had been aware now for some weeks that her feelings for Jace weren't just a simple crush. And she knew that sooner or later, she was going to take a chance on those feelings and discover first-hand if Jace felt the same way about her.

19
It's Never Forever

Although she had known it was coming, Lara felt slightly anxious and overwhelmed that her birthday was approaching. For that meant that it was almost a year since she had arrived on the island. Of course, they still appeared no closer to rescue than they had been back then.

Lara hoped that her insecurity wasn't showing to the others, she didn't want to bring the mood down in the camp. Despite the weather becoming more wild as they moved further into storm season, everyone seemed in relatively good spirits.

She had thought she had faltered slightly one day when she was fishing with Jack and Jace, when Jack pointed out that it was almost the anniversary of her arrival. She had become quite proficient at the line-fishing method and had just pulled in a second fish within fifteen minutes of the first one, when Jack had made the observation that left her subdued for the rest of the day. Neither Jack, nor Jace had said anything however, so Lara felt secure that she had gotten away with it.

When it came to the big day, Brandon arranged for them to partake in the same dinner they had eaten for Christmas and new year; with the addition of an extra baked potato with a makeshift candle within it, which acted as Lara's birthday cake.

'Go on then, make a wish.' Jace said, placing it down in front of Lara and giving her a smile that brought his handsome features together in a pleasingly symmetrical way.

Lara took a deep breath and easily extinguished the candle, hoping for the same thing she had on New Year's Eve.

The four spent the rest of the evening talking as complete darkness fell around them, leaving them all illuminated by the orange glow of the campfire. An almost-full moon glittered brightly on the relatively calm, low tide a distance away from them.

It was well past midnight, and technically not Lara's birthday any more when they all went their separate ways to bed.

Realising how tired she was now, Lara walked through the moonlit jungle towards her cabin thinking enthusiastically about sleep.

Although on her last birthday, she never would have expected to spend her next one like this, Lara thought it was actually OK considering the circumstances. The others had done a good job of keeping her mind off the sinking feeling she experienced when contemplating the thought of spending the rest of her life on the island. Now that she was alone however, she found these thoughts creeping out of the darkness to haunt her during her night time solitude.

When she sat down on her bed to get changed into her sleeping shirt, she became aware of a small, roughly wrapped package beside her on top of the blankets. Bemused, her hand automatically moved towards it and picked it up. She moved over and sat on the top step of her hut, allowing the cool moonlight to illuminate the item in her hands.

It was wrapped in lined paper and bound in a bow with a weathered piece of string.

Lara hadn't expected any gifts, and she couldn't imagine which of the three men would have left this on her bed for her without saying anything.

Unable to contain her curiosity any longer, Lara tugged at the string and the small, heavy item slipped from its makeshift wrapping and into her hand. It was a men's watch.

Lara lifted it up closer to her face. It wasn't working any more, but from what she could see of it, it looked in good condition; it had a metallic, silver strap and the face was relatively unscratched. There weren't any numbers, only numerals. She knew nothing of watches, but thought it was probably expensive when new.

She turned it over to look at the back. The back plate seemed to have something scratched into it.

Lara lifted it up closer still to her face and inspected it. She tilted it to see it better in the limited moonlight. Now she noticed that it was actually engraved. The words read "It's Never Forever".

Being so tired the previous night when she had

gone to bed, Lara had thought she would have easily fallen asleep. Once she had unwrapped her surprise gift however, she found that her mind was unexpectedly occupied, making her thoughts of sleep evaporate.

As soon as she had read the engraving, she had realised who had left her an unexpected birthday present.

She realised now that she hadn't gotten away with keeping her concerns to herself about having been on the island for almost a year. One of the two men she had been with the other day when this thought had hit her had noticed her reaction. And when she thought about it, she wasn't surprised that it wasn't Jack.

The one thing that stayed with Lara the most was the amount of thought Jace had put into his gift. Not only had he been perceptive enough to have noticed that Lara was uneasy about her impending, unwanted anniversary when no one else had, he had also come up with a thoughtful way to comfort her. And it was discreet too, avoiding any unwanted fussing and sympathy from Brandon and Jack.

If Lara hadn't of been struggling with her secret attraction to Jace, then she would have woken up feeling much more relieved.

His gift may have allayed her fears on the matter of there being no promise of rescue in the near future, but he had unintentionally drawn her focus even more towards himself.

Lara thought back to the gifts Alan had given her for the four birthday's she had experienced with him. All of which, were hastily thrown together at the last minute when he had remembered the day before. As a result of this, she was usually presented with the same box of chocolates and bunch of supermarket flowers she got every year. Apart from the second year of their relationship, where he had forgotten completely.

Jace had put more thought into this one gift, than the man she had spent five years of her life with. Why was she letting immature nerves, doubts and principles get in the way of what could potentially be an incredible relationship with Jace?

If presenting her with such a thoughtful present wasn't a sign that he cared for her, then what was? There was also the fact that just a few weeks ago he had risked his life to save her from a falling tree.

But perhaps he didn't care for her as much as she hoped he did? Maybe, he only wanted to be friends with her, and he thought the watch was a nice gift for a woman he only wanted a platonic relationship with? And maybe he hadn't really thought about throwing himself forward to push her out of the way during the storm. Perhaps he had just acted out of instinct, and would have done that for either of the others?

Lara was confused and frustrated at her lack of certainty about anything, so she vowed to herself to find out the truth, one way or another. With startling conviction as she got out of bed and got dressed, she made a decision. As soon as she had an available opportunity, she would push aside her fear of rejection and bring up the subject with Jace.

Getting some alone time with Jace was harder than Lara had thought. Of course, she had expected Jack to continue to attach himself to her as much as he could, but she would have thought that it would have been easier to give him the slip. As it happened, it wasn't so easy. After several failed attempts at making a variety of excuses to be alone with Jace, Lara found that she had to resolve to make another potentially awkward exchange; she decided to have a talk with Jack.

She spent several days trying to work out exactly what to say to Jack to set him straight, whilst at the same time, saying it in a way that wouldn't offend him. Lara had nothing against Jack, apart from the fact that he could be immensely childish sometimes. But she was also very aware that they would both still have to live within a very small geographical area of each other and would inevitably see each other on a regular basis. She didn't want to create another situation where one member of their tiny community was living in isolation, and they were having to deliver him food every meal time.

Lara managed to get Jack alone when they went out fishing together one day on the rocks jutting out to sea.

They talked, or rather, Lara talked and Jack listened as she explained that she didn't return his affection in the kindest way she could think of. She managed to tell him everything she had rehearsed in her head, mainly because Jack didn't say much back whilst he reeled in fish in the midst of a light rain shower.

Afterwards, as Lara had expected, Jack disappeared onto his island for the rest of the day, leaving Brandon and Jace slightly bemused as to why he had done this.

With a pang of guilt Lara told them she had no idea, although she noticed Jace looked at her slightly strangely as she spoke.

Brandon went to visit Jack on his island later that day to find out what was happening with him.

Lara hoped he wouldn't be upset with her for crushing Jack's feelings too much as she watched Brandon disappear around the corner of the beach.

To her surprise, Brandon returned a few hours later for dinner that evening with Jack in tow. And although Jack didn't speak to Lara directly, he was actually behaving pretty much as he usually did.

Brandon didn't seem to harbour any bad feeling towards her either, and Lara had the sense that he and his son had partaken in a man-to-man chat that had enabled Jack to rejoin the group with his dignity intact.

Lara was relieved by this, and actually thought that affirming Jack on their relationship had gone better than she had imagined.

Now there was just one more relationship she wanted to affirm...

Lara couldn't remember ever feeling more nervous. She was confident that now Jack wasn't tailing her all the time, she should be able to get Jace alone at some point; she just wasn't sure what to do with him once she did.

Lara spent the next couple of nights going over different scenario's in her mind, playing them out and analysing the imagined outcome. She tried to work out what she wanted to say to Jace that would best communicate how she felt, whilst still trying to save some face if she had completely misjudged the situation.

For if he didn't return her affection, then just as was the case with Jack, she still had to see Jace on a daily basis. She thought that if he totally rejected her and was completely offended by her advances, then she might end up being the one moving to live in isolation on the smallest beach on the island. This thought did nothing to improve her nervous state of mind.

As it happened, it was the smallest beach where Lara managed to find Jace alone several days later.

Lara had left Jack and Brandon on the opposite side of the island, where they were just setting off to go fishing. Brandon had asked Lara if she would like to accompany them, but she declined, saying she might go and take a shower instead. If nothing else, she had thought that Jack might appreciate some bonus time away from her.

She had entered the jungle and approached the waterfall, but carried on straight past it and through the dense jungle to the other side. She had listened as Jace mentioned he was going to fetch coconuts from the trees near the smallest beach, and set off in this direction as soon as she knew that Brandon and Jack were going to be occupied for a while.

She now emerged onto the sandy, curved beach which at the moment was bathed in the full midday sunshine.

It was a hot day. The weather recently had been getting increasingly warmer and stormier, but at the present moment in time there was no sign of rain to be seen.

A gentle breeze lifted Lara's hair from her shoulders slightly as she walked towards where Jace was collecting loose coconuts from the small cluster of trees at the end of the small stretch of beach.

He had his back to her and the gently crashing waves covered any noise of her approach.

She hoped that he would turn around and notice her before she got there, she still had no idea how to start this encounter. For all the thinking and planning in her head, she was still none the wiser as to how to convey her feelings to Jace without any potential embarrassment.

She was almost right behind him now, and she suddenly had a wave of panic fill her chest. *What am I doing?*, she thought to herself. *I can't do this...I'm about to ruin our friendship forever...*

Lara suddenly had the urge to abort her plan and throw a casual spin on the situation, making an excuse to leave again quickly. But before she could think of a subtle escape plan, Jace suddenly turned around, causing all logical thoughts to leave her mind. She now stood before him without the cooperation of her usually quite rational brain.

'Hey Lara,' Jace said with his usual smile. 'I thought you would be going fishing with the other two.' He bent down and grabbed another coconut to add to his pile on the grass next to him.

'No, I, um - well I thought I would let Jack and Brandon have some time alone.' Simply because she didn't know what else to do, Lara stepped casually up onto the grass too. A little too casually in her opinion.

Jace seemed to take notice of her unusually nonchalant body language, but he didn't mention it and turned back to his fruit collection. 'Oh yeah,' he said, starting to smirk now. 'Brandon mentioned that you shot Jack down in flames...'

Lara was so taken aback by this, she forgot about her nerves for a moment, 'I didn't shoot him down in flames!' she objected. 'I-I just may have said that, well, that I wasn't interested in him.'

'Right...' Jace replied, sceptical.

'There's - well, there's no point in letting him think that I might like him back. It's best just to be honest isn't it?' Lara glimpsed her opportunity.

'Don't you think so? I mean, if people know how each other feel, then...well, they can act on it can't they?'

Jace gave her a glance, but continued with his chore and didn't say anything.

'Or, you know...they might not...' Lara went on. She cringed slightly at how vague that sounded. It wasn't getting any response from Jace either. *Time to be a little more direct*, she thought.

'I mean,' she said, feeling a little more daring now, 'If two people know that there is something between them, then maybe they should do something about it...'

Jace gave her a slightly inquisitive look as he cut a bad section from a coconut, before he looked away and tossed it into the pile.

Lara was sure she saw a flash of understanding in his eyes and realised that she was virtually holding her breath in anticipation of his response. Surely, Jace had to have picked up that hint?

'I think I'm going to take these over to our beach.' he said after a moment, nodding his head to the small fruit harvest near his feet.

Lara felt deflated. She had been expecting an answer to what she had been wondering for so many nights alone in her cabin. Either way, she just wanted to know the truth. She had been building up the courage to find out for so long, she wasn't going to just let him walk away now.

She took a few steps towards him, closing the gap between them slightly. 'Jace,' she said, trying to draw his attention away from his task.

It worked. He straightened up and turned to face her before he managed to gather up his haul.

'There's something I need to talk to you about.'

Jace seemed to know what was coming, even though he still didn't actively respond. Lara could see the recognition in his eyes. And now that she was closer, that was not all she could see in them. The bright sun beating down from high in the sky illuminated their steel-grey, making all the intricate details and patterns visible.

Lara was now more than aware that she had never felt this way about anyone before. It was a completely different experience actually being genuinely and passionately attracted to someone, and not simply going through the motions as she had done in the past.

She felt thoroughly alive and excited. She had the worst case of butterflies she had ever known. Her heart was pounding and she wondered if Jace noticed how slightly breathless she sounded when she continued to speak, 'I'm, er, I'm not sure how to say this but...'

Lara faltered. She really wasn't sure how she was going to say this. In every one of the situations she had played out in her head, she had always gotten more of a response from Jace. But now he was in front of her, he seemed unwilling to give her any kind of indication of his stance. Surely he knew where she was going with this?

Stuck for inspiration, Lara thought of how she

had felt when she had feared for his life after his accident.

With a tentative hand, she reached out and touched her fingertips to his side where his wound had been. She hadn't seen it for months, and wondered how it had healed. She rubbed the area gently through the material of his dark blue shirt. 'You know, I was really worried about you when you got hurt,' she said softly, still slightly breathless. 'It surprised me how strongly I felt. Every night, I would go back to my cabin and I couldn't sleep because I was thinking about you.'

Jace looked at her but he waited for her to go on, and still remained silent.

'And when you got better,' Lara went on in a low voice that was barely audible above the sound of the nearby ocean. 'I still went back to my cabin at night, and couldn't stop thinking about you...'

Lara allowed her fingers to slide from where Jace had been injured, running them slowly up his stomach and onto his chest.

Jace, who had watched her hand travel upwards, now made a sudden movement and grabbed her wandering hand firmly with his.

Lara looked up at him and he firmly met her gaze now. His breathing had changed slightly, it was heavier, but his expression remained impassive.

Lara didn't pull away from his rough, warm grip. She could really see the desire in his eyes now, but couldn't understand why he wasn't responding to her obvious advances. Then it suddenly occurred to her; he didn't want to overstep the mark, and wanted more definite reassurance from her that she wanted this.

Lara decided to show him she was willing, and moved her body closer to his, so they were only separated by mere inches.

Jace seemed to take this as the confirmation he was waiting for. With his other hand, he reached up and tenderly stroked her cheek, brushing his thumb gently against her lips.

Without relinquishing his grip on her hand, or his touch on her face, Jace moved in closer, closing any gap there was between them.

Lara could feel the warmth from his body, even in the intense heat of the day.

Tentatively, Jace leaned in to kiss her, closing his eyes as he did so.

Lara instinctively closed hers too, expecting to feel his lips touch hers. But Jace stopped just short of the kiss she was sure was about to happen and paused, his mouth barely an inch from hers as though expecting her to stop him as she had previously.

Aching with anticipation, Lara decided to quash any doubts and met his lips firmly with hers. He returned her kiss gently, but passionately, brushing his thumb along her cheekbone.

Realizing Jace had let go of her earlier exploratory hand, Lara brought both of them up to cup his face, running her own thumbs over the trace of stubble along his jaw.

Even with her eyes shut, Lara was vaguely aware of the swaying palm leaves of the trees above her and Jace. They cast dancing shadows across the two people embraced beneath the fluid fronds, as the couple intensified the kiss.

In her cabin, Lara reflected on how the afternoon had gone. She had finally been brave enough to make a move with Jace, and the result was even better than she had hoped. She had kissed him and he had kissed her back.

Lara smiled to herself as she thought what a good kisser Jace was as she tucked her shirt into the waistband of her shorts.

He had invited her to join him for dinner on the smallest beach they had been on earlier, and now she was getting ready to meet him. Granted, being on the island there wasn't much that Lara could do to prepare herself for a date. That was, other than comb her hair as she did every day anyway. She had decided to tuck her shirt in, and hoped that this would perhaps give her a more formal 'evening look'.

She set the comb down and looked down at herself. Without a mirror, this was the only way that she could judge her appearance. Lara was satisfied it was the best she could do and decided that she would have to meet Jace as she was.

She felt quite confident however. Since she had spent almost a year on the island, she knew that for better and worse, Jace well-and-truly knew what she looked like by now.

So she set off through the jungle and made her way towards the smallest beach on the island.

It was still a very hot day and the air was more humid than earlier. The sun was setting, and casting its orange glow through the gaps in the trees. The waterfall had the same dramatic lighting effect upon it, making it look quite magical. Lara didn't stop to admire it however, she was excited, and also increasingly nervous about her date with Jace.

Lara knew she shouldn't be nervous. After all, Jace had already acknowledged his affection. She presumed her fresh case of butterflies was all down to the fact that she had only ever been on a few dates in her life. She tried to calm herself with logic, telling herself that she had technically had dinner with Jace almost every day, although, never alone before...

The trees were thinning now and more orange sunset was flooding the area around her, covering the jungle floor and trees with its luminous glow.

Just as the evening beach became visible through the gaps in the trees, Jace suddenly entered the wood ahead of her. He smiled when he saw her.

Lara noticed that he had made an effort in the interlude too. He had combed his dark hair, and attempted to style it too; it was swept back more than usual and still looked slightly wet as he approached. He was still wearing the same dark blue shirt as he was earlier, but had opted to tuck it in just as Lara had, in an attempt to look more formal.

As he reached her, he leaned in quickly and gave her a brief kiss on the cheek, leaving Lara with a waft of cologne. 'Good evening.' he said with a smile.

'Good evening,' Lara replied smiling too, wondering where on earth he had managed to find cologne from. 'You smell nice.'

'Thank you. I dug out an old bottle Brandon unceremoniously used up to light the campfires during our first month here. I spent a good ten minutes adding water to the bottle to extract the last little traces out of it this afternoon. So make the most of it, because that's all I can get out.' He paused for a moment, before he said in a slightly more husky voice, 'You look very beautiful tonight.'

Lara shrugged slightly at her almost-everyday appearance, 'I don't really look any different than normal.'

'I know. You always look beautiful.' He smiled as he looked into her eyes and took hold of her hand. 'Come on.' he said and led her to the edge of the trees.

Before they stepped out onto the beach, Jace stopped and turned around to face her, blocking her view from the rest of the beach behind him. 'I want you to close your eyes.'

Lara smiled, curious. 'Why?'

'Just trust me, close them.'

Lara did as she was told.

Jace took hold of her other hand too.

Lara was more aware of the soft warmth of the sand beneath her bare feet, as Jace led her carefully down the beach. She kept her eyes firmly shut, but she could still see the bright glow of the sunset. She thought that she could now feel more heat immediately in front of her, in addition to the intense warmth the evening sun was beaming down on them.

She was aware of the crackle and scent of a campfire as Jace brought her to a standstill.

'OK then,' he said, his voice close to her ear. 'You can open them now.'

Lara opened her eyes. There was indeed a campfire near by, but her attention was immediately drawn in front of her to where a large circle of candles surrounded a couple of blankets, upon which two wooden cups and a pierced coconut sat.

'Oh, it's beautiful.' she said, smiling at him.

Jace took hold of her hand again and bent his back slightly as he guided her allowing her to step over the lit circle. 'My lady...' he said with a smirk.

Lara laughed.

They sat down together and Jace poured them both some coconut water.

'Thank you.' Lara said, accepting hers and taking a sip. She looked around at the glowing circle around her. Now that she was closer, she recognised the 'candles' to be the same as the ones that got inserted into the island birthday potato.

After a moment Jace set his cup down thoughtfully and spoke, 'You know, I have to say I'm quite surprised that we're actually here doing this. I mean - I'm pleased, just surprised.'

'Not as surprised as Brandon was when we told him we were having dinner alone.'

Jace laughed at this. 'I know right? He didn't see that one coming...' His smile faded as he looked at her again, more serious, 'If I'm honest, I had the impression that you were thinking about us-' he shook his head slightly. 'But I didn't know if that was just wishful thinking or not. And even if it wasn't - I thought you might not give into it.'

Lara set down her cup too. 'You're right, I'm pretty stubborn. And I did try to ignore the way I felt...I was confused at first. I really wanted you to be OK when you got injured. But then, I realised that I was attracted to you. I wasn't sure that I should do anything about it though...I didn't know if you felt the same way still, but...' Lara felt herself blushing, and hoped Jace wouldn't notice, even though he had already proven himself to be very perceptive of her innermost thoughts.

'But I was just too irresistible?' Jace suggested with his trademark smirk.

'Something like that...' Lara felt slightly awkward at laying her feelings bare like this. Even though Jace now knew how she felt towards him, there was a definite tension between them and this line of conversation was flustering her slightly.

Jace leaned over and took hold of her hand. 'You don't have to worry, Lara. I still feel the same way...'

After a few minutes, Jace got up to serve them dinner. It was Lara's favourite island dish, grilled fish and a baked potato.

Lara appreciated for a moment how much effort Jace had put into this evening as they started to eat. She conveyed her feelings to Jace of how, in England, fish and chips was a popular meal.

'I've always wanted to go to England,' he said. 'It's all so...English.'

Lara laughed. 'Yes it is. It's certainly a far cry from this place.'

'That sounds great,'

'Does it? It's all just grey and it can get really cold there.'

'Perfect.'

'And when people say it's always raining, they're not far wrong. Especially in recent years.'

'It sounds delightful. When do we set sail?' He smiled at her. 'Seriously though, you will have to show me around when we go there someday.'

'Well if you're that keen, then yes I will.'

'I'll look forward to it.'

Dusk started to fall around them as they went onto their dessert course, causing the candles to really show off their full effect now. The flickering shadows they caused to fall over the two of them really added to the ambience as they talked about their hopes and desires from past and present.

Lara felt like she was learning so much more about Jace as they talked. From what he talked about, Lara now fully appreciated how creative Jace was. She now thought that the angrier side she had previously seen of him was perhaps just his artistic temperament that had been suspended here, unable to be put to its full use.

In turn, Lara confided in Jace things she never could have imagined telling anyone. She confessed how she had let other people rule her life; how she had spent years with a man she had secretly despised; how she had been frustrated at being held back from her dream job in Paris years before, and how this had made her resent the people she should have cared about the most.

To Lara's surprise, Jace managed to ease the anguish at the biggest disappointment of her life with just a few sentences.

'You know, I'm glad that you didn't get that job in Paris.' he said.

Lara was so taken aback by this, she swallowed a much larger mouthful of coconut water than she had intended to and choked slightly. 'Why?' she asked him, trying to dab her chin as subtly as she could.

'Because if you had of been satisfied there,' Jace said, his face illuminated in the shadowy glow of the candles. 'Then you wouldn't have gone searching for something more on the other side of the world...And then you wouldn't be sitting here talking to me right now.'

Lara thought about this for a moment. 'Then I made the right choice.' she said looking at him.

He held her gaze, and leaned in to kiss her. His lips pressed against hers and for a moment, she enjoyed how soft they felt against hers, before she returned the kiss.

He kissed her slowly and firmly, the warm, rough fingers of his hand stroking her face gently.

Lara was happy that after so much wanting of him, here they both were, locked in a sure embrace.

Jace deepened the kiss slightly, his movements becoming more intense. His hand now traced down her jawline and onto her neck, caressing it gently.

Lara pulled back and broke their contact. She stroked his cheek to show that she had liked it, but didn't want him to get carried away.

'I'm sorry,' he said. 'I'm going too fast-'

'Just a little,' she admitted.

'It's all right. Just take your time. I can wait.' He adjusted his position so he was sitting beside her and put his arm around her slightly tentatively.

Lara snuggled up to him, to show that she wanted his touch and he seemed to relax a little. He rubbed his thumb against her shoulder gently as they sat and looked out at the last streaks of light in the rapidly darkening, star-filled sky.

That night, Lara replayed her favourite moments

from her date with Jace in her head as she lay in her dark cabin.

They'd had a wonderful evening together. They had talked and gotten to know each other much better. Lara had been surprised that there was so much to find out about Jace, and she was sure there was much more to find out if tonight had been anything to go by. She was now really looking forward to their second date which they had arranged this evening.

When it had gotten late, darkness had been completely upon them as the candles were starting to burn into the sand, they had said goodnight. They had shared one more kiss before they had parted ways.

Lara looked at the ceiling in her cabin and reflected that today really had changed everything for the both of them. The day had gone so well that she had to replay each individual moment to remind herself that it had been real.

She rolled over onto her side and had a sudden hit of the traces of cologne his contact had left upon her hair, making him feel closer. She gladly inhaled his scent as she drifted off into a contended sleep, hoping that thoughts of him would perhaps inspire her dreams.

20
Brave

If Lara had thought that Jack was going to be the most taken aback by the announcement that her and Jace were now dating, then she would have been wrong. Brandon was having a hard time accepting the fact too.

The two of them had broken the news over breakfast the next day when they had greeted each other with a brief good-morning kiss. And when Lara had gone to sit in her usual log-seat, Jace had taken hold of her hand and guided her beside him onto his instead.

Lara had ideally liked to have avoided this sort of behaviour directly in front of Jack, but Jace didn't seemed to have this concern; in fact, he seemed to slightly revel in it.

Brandon had appeared to have gone through quite a range of emotions once the realisation had hit him. At first he had seemed surprised, then a slight state of what looked like disbelief had washed over him, before this finally morphed into a sort of scepticism about the seriousness of their relationship.

Later that day, Brandon had managed to get Lara on her own long enough to have a five-minute conversation as they did the dinner-dishes in the ocean together at sunset.

Brandon had questioned whether Lara had really

wanted to start the relationship with Jace, and whether she had simply done it because she had felt pressured. He had even questioned whether Jace had made any more assertive advances towards her again. Lara had been quick to assure him that this wasn't the case; that she had thought long and hard before making her decision, that she was happy and that she had actually been the one to initiate her and Jace's change in status.

Brandon had seemed satisfied enough with his line of enquiry to continue the evening as normal. Lara noticed however, that he still threw the odd curious glance towards her and Jace as they sat together on the same log.

Brandon had remained quietened into private wondering it seemed, until the next day when he had invented a badly disguised reason to be alone with Jace.

Lara was slightly annoyed that Brandon couldn't just accept their news without question. She could only imagine that he had discussed the subject with Jace last night too, since they were still sharing the same quarters and hoped that Jace didn't feel too harassed.

In Lara's opinion, Jack was handling the revelation in a much better fashion and didn't say a word on the matter. He didn't even sulk too much either. He was pretty much just carrying on with his routine as usual. He was even maintaining his civil attitude towards Lara, even though he wasn't as bright and cheerful as he had previously been before her rejection. Whatever Brandon had said to him during their talk, it was effective.

Lara and Jack returned from their task that day of collecting a crab to add to their dinner of fish stew to find that Brandon and Jace seemed to have finished their not-so-covert talk.

One thing that Lara noticed now was that Brandon now must be satisfied with the validity and foundation of her and Jace's relationship, because he seemed to have given up questioning it. He had even stopped glancing between the two of them with an inquisitive expression.

Lara wondered what Jace must have said to his friend to quell his curiosity.

The next day Lara and Jace arranged to have dinner together again.

Jace again put in a lot of effort into setting up a circle of candles in which they dined together, looking out across the ocean beyond the small stretch of white sand in front of them.

They had earlier managed to dodge a rain storm that had threatened to soak them if they had partaken in their dinner plans at their pre-agreed time. They now were having a slightly later meal, after they had taken shelter in the trees of the jungle at the seam of the beach.

It was still wet season and rain storms were frequent, even if they lasted just a few minutes.

They now finished their main course just as a typically beautiful sunset graced the open ocean before them.

Lara sipped her drink as she pondered how Brandon had reacted over the last few days, 'Brandon seemed a little sceptical about us, didn't he?' she wondered out loud as she watched the mauve, gold-lined clouds drift across the sky far in the distance.

'Hmm,' Jace said, draining the last of the coconut into his cup. 'He was. He thought that I was still a little too unstable to be around you and behave myself,' he said with a faint scoff.

'I told him that it was me that came onto you, not the other way around.'

'I know, he told me that this afternoon,' Jace nodded, leaning back on his elbows.

Lara found her curiosity piqued. 'What else did he say to you?'

'Oh...He just questioned me a little. *Grilled* was more the word, I'd say.'

'But he looked like he was OK after you talked to him...?' Lara encouraged.

'Yes, he gets it now. After what I told him.' Jace continued to stare out across the sea unwilling to expand upon his comment without further nudging, so Lara decided she should be a little more direct if she wanted more details.

'And what did you tell him?' she asked, wondering how he was going to dodge this one.

Jace continued to face the beautiful scenery in front of him, but Lara had the impression that he wasn't appreciating the view. He shrugged. 'I told him what I told you - up on the cliff-top. About how I feel about you...' he said quietly.

Lara leaned over and wrapped her arms around him, kissing him on the cheek in an attempt to put him at ease slightly. For now she understood why Jace had suddenly appeared a little shy.

Even though they both had admitted their mutual affection and this was out in the open, there was still a palpable tension between the two of them.

Lara even thought that perhaps their honest confessions of the intensity of their feelings for one another made the atmosphere even more highly charged.

Over the next few weeks Lara and Jace continued meeting each other for their dates. Lara found herself spending all day looking forward to having some alone time with Jace. She found his company the most soothing in comparison to that of the other two and found that she ached for it more and more.

She relished the fact that she had found a kindred spirit in him that she could retreat to at the end of the day.

Jace had stuck to his word to allow Lara time and continued to be a true gentlemen. He walked Lara back to her cabin every night and they parted with a kiss and good-night sentiments, even though Lara knew from his longing touch and the almost imperceptible look in his eyes that he wanted more.

Lara didn't want to keep him waiting on purpose, but felt she needed a little more time. They were taking things slowly, moving at her pace and she was satisfied with that. And even if Jace seemed slightly frustrated at times, he didn't push her or even voice it.

Lara was continually surprised on a daily basis how romantic Jace was. He put a great amount of thought into each of their dates and tried to be creative with each one.

One particular day Lara woke up and left her cabin one morning to find two of the colourful waterfall flowers had been planted on either side of the steps outside.

Jace had later explained over breakfast that he thought it would brighten up her space a little and she would think of him as soon as she saw them in the morning.

Lara pointed out that he was the first thing that she thought about in the morning anyway.

Jack, who had been getting himself a cup of water nearby at the time, seemed to cringe slightly and had swiftly left without saying anything.

On another day when the pair had been eating lunch with Brandon and Jack, Lara was surprised to find that Jace had cut the potato leaves in the fish stew into little heart shapes.

She felt her cheeks flush slightly that the other two had to witness this, but she appreciated the sentiment from Jace.

No matter how much effort Jace put in however

to ensure that each of the dates he arranged were magical, he had no control over the weather. And since it was still the wet season, it wasn't always certain that a downpour wouldn't be unleashed upon them without warning.

This made their private dinners on the smallest beach a little more difficult to plan however.

When the four of them usually found themselves beneath a sudden shower in the main camp, they would all retreat into the hut beside them and take shelter. They would often stay there too, long after the shower had ceased to avoid having to return to their sodden seats.

Luckily Jace came up with a solution that didn't involve having to build a cabin on this beach. Instead, he once again crafted his tent from the solitary months he had spent alone here before his accident.

Lara had been a little sceptical when he had first suggested this idea, especially when she had seen the remnants of his makeshift shelter in a heap in the jungle where they had been abandoned.

When Jace had finished constructing it however, Lara thought it was actually quite ideal for what they wanted it for.

The roof and one of the 'walls' was made from what was clearly an inflatable dinghy, except that now it was faded and slightly green from age in places. Strong beams supported the weight of the thick, rubber craft in a semi circle and thick sheets made up the rest of the shelter, protecting the inside from the elements.

When Jace gave her the "grand tour", Lara thought that it was rather cosy once they were inside. The sheets at the front could be lifted up to reveal the ocean vista they usually enjoyed from out in the open.

Jace not only went out of his way to make their dates special, he also put all his effort into helping Lara with her chores too. This even extended to him helping her put away her clean, dry laundry one day after he had rescued it from a sudden, heavy rain shower. She had suggested that she didn't really need any assistance with it, but he had insisted.

They were both in her cabin and the same rain cloud was pelting its vast quantity of water noisily against the roof with some force. Inside Lara folded her clothes neatly into piles.

Jace had delivered the bundle of clothes to her cabin safely dry. Unlike himself however, since he had been rather drenched thanks to his chivalry and had peeled off his soaking wet shirt before Lara hung it up to dry.

Lara then managed to convince him that she was capable of folding and putting away her own clothes; not that there were really that many to take care of, anyway.

Confident that Lara had her limited wardrobe under control, a now-shirtless Jace lay back on her bed and looked around the room critically. 'You know, this place feels different now that you're living in it. When I was here it seemed so much darker...'

'That was just your attitude,' she smiled over her shoulder as she tried to focus on folding her only other pair of shorts instead of Jace's naked torso. 'It's really not that bad,' she went on. 'The view of the potato plants is nice. I like it.'

She looked past Jace's hanging shirt and out of the open doorway where the luscious, green plants were dripping wet and looking slightly defeated as they continued to get pelted with rain. On a sunny day they looked much more attractive.

'Even the bed feels different.' Jace said, shuffling his bare-back against the blankets.

'Maybe I've finally broken it in for you. Or maybe it's just your imagination...'

'Broken it in for me?' Jace asked, a smirk spreading across his face. 'My bed is currently opposite my dear old friend Brandon's in the other hut - unless you plan on letting me sleep here...?'

Lara quickly realised what she had said and felt herself blushing. She wished she hadn't of run out of clothes to fold. 'I just meant that, um...'

She was suddenly aware of a wicked glint in Jace's steel eyes as he swung his legs onto the cabin floor and crossed the room towards her.

He moved behind her and placed his hands upon her shoulders. When he spoke next, his mouth was directly beside her ear, 'I hope we weren't having impure thoughts Miss Adams?' he said seductively, before adding in a whisper, 'Or are you feeling brave?'

Lara attempted to suppress the involuntary shudder that his voice had sent through her body, but knew that Jace had felt it.

He ran his hands over her arms and slid them around her waist, pressing his bare torso against her back.

Lara could feel the heat of his skin against hers through the thin material of her shirt as he gently kissed her neck.

It occurred to her that the situation was getting very quickly out of control without her meaning it to. Was she ready yet? She didn't want her and Jace's first time together to be something that she regretted, and she wasn't sure that it wasn't too soon.

With a wrench, Lara managed to find the strength to stop Jace's hand as it slid slowly downwards over her stomach.

He took the hint immediately and it seemed to take him some strength too to let go of her and sink onto the bed again with his back against the wall. He looked rather rejected, but didn't say another word on the matter.

Lara was grateful to him when he managed to change the subject so swiftly, 'You know, I think it is going to be a nice day tomorrow. You still want to have dinner with me?'

'Of course I do,' Lara replied reassuringly. She wanted to explain to Jace that she just needed more time before they took things to the next level, but she thought it might be better just to follow Jace's lead and talk about something else instead, 'I'm looking forward to it.'

'You should be, I've been thinking about it a lot.'

Lara once again appreciated how much effort he put into planning their time together.

'You may not realise it, you know - being a woman and all, but tomorrow is a really big day for a man. It's a lot of pressure.'

Lara frowned slightly at this. What was Jace talking about? She all of a sudden had the feeling that he thought that the next day was some kind of special event she should already know about.

It had only just been her birthday recently, so she knew that Jace couldn't think it was tomorrow.

Lara sat down on the bed beside him and decided to just admit her ignorance, 'What's the occasion?' she asked him.

Jace laughed aloud. 'And I thought it was men that were supposed to forget that kind of thing?' he said with an amused smile.

Lara was bemused as to what she was supposed to have forgotten, but thought that it was good that Jace found it so amusing that he seemed to have forgotten about her rejection. If nothing else, she thought, it had lightened the atmosphere. 'All right, I confess - I have no idea what you are talking about. Are you going to tell me what tomorrow is, or what?'

Jace shrugged, 'It's Valentines Day. I thought

you already knew.'

'Oh.' Lara said, quite taken aback that it had come around so quickly.

It had seemed like she had celebrated her birthday very recently, but now she realised that must have been a little over a month ago now; almost the same amount of time as she had been dating Jace. No wonder he was keen to take their relationship forward.

'I didn't realise the time had gone so fast...' she told him thoughtfully.

'I only know what day it is because of Brandon. He keeps his diary without fail every day. The first thing he does in the morning is let me know the date.' Jace reached forward and stroked her face gently. 'But it is true. Time flies when you are having a good time.' He winked.

Yes, Lara thought the days certainly were flying by. She thought that it must have been Jace that was keeping her mind from straying to thoughts of how quickly the days were passing. But she found she didn't mind, in fact she was happier than she could ever remember being before.

When Lara left her cabin the next day, she was surprised to find that Jace had planted more flowers to accompany the first two. They now formed a vibrant row on each side of the steps.

When she joined the others for breakfast Jace had insisted on giving her an intensely heartfelt good-morning kiss, despite the fact they weren't alone around the campfire.

Lara had tried to give Brandon and Jack some kind of apology for Jace's over-zealous acts of affection he displayed in front of them when he went to cut her heart-shaped pieces of coconut, but didn't have enough time before he returned.

Brandon had understood what she was trying to say however, and seemed mostly amused by Jace's behaviour.

Even Jack appeared to be somewhat entertained by what Jace was doing, although this appeared to be in spite of himself.

Jace kept showering Lara with caring gestures all day. He insisted that she shouldn't have to do any of her usual chores and completed them all for her.

Lara understood that Jace did all of this out of love, but she felt just a little redundant at not really having anything to do, although she enjoyed spending time with Jace all the same.

The weather kept flitting from bright sunshine to rain and just as it always was, very changeable. One thing that was consistent however was the intense, humid heat that clung to the island inhabitants.

When the evening came, Jace left to prepare for their dinner date earlier than usual, and as he had all day, he insisted on not accepting her help with it.

Lara said goodbye to him with a brief kiss, before he set off quickly towards their beach.

Looking up at the sky above the jungle, she wasn't sure that the rain would hold off long enough for them to cook dinner on the campfire, and hoped Jace wouldn't be too disappointed if whatever he was planning didn't quite work out like he imagined.

When it came time for their date Lara, as usual, did her best to make herself look good before she set off to meet Jace.

Even though the intermittent clouds had allowed the sunset to illuminate everything around them with its deep, red glow, they still lingered and the sand was still wet from an earlier downpour.

Jace led Lara to the now-familiar circle of candles surrounding the blankets on which she had spent her evenings together with him; talking, laughing and getting to know him better than any other person she had ever met.

He handed her a cup of what he explained was a banana and coconut smoothie as he started cooking their starter.

Lara took a sip; it was actually surprisingly delicious for such few ingredients. She wondered why they didn't have it more often. Then she realised it probably took quite a lot of effort to blend a banana to a complete smooth pulp by hand, fully appreciating how much time and effort Jace was putting into all of this. She wanted to tell him that he didn't have to try so hard, they could just enjoy their usual fare and she was content to simply be with him. She didn't want to seem ungrateful however, so she didn't mention it.

She thought to herself that she could drop some hints to him over the next year in preparation for next Valentine's Day. She could let him know subtly that she would be happy just to spend the day with him, without him feeling under pressure. Then she took a moment to marvel at the fact she was already planning the next year with Jace so far in advance. She couldn't remember ever doing that with anyone else before...

As Lara had predicted, the weather was so erratic that part way through their dessert they were forced to take shelter in their tent at the end of the beach from a very sudden and ferocious downpour. It was so bad, that they had to utilise all sides of the tent, including the front sheets in order to protect themselves from the rain. 'So much for watching the sunset,' Jace said with a slight note of disappointment, as he finished off his serving of the fruit dessert he had made for them both.

'Well, we saw most of it.' Lara pointed out, finishing hers too. 'It was beautiful.' she added, getting up and placing her bowl on top of his in the corner.

She sat back down beside Jace on top of the patchwork of blankets that made up the floor of the tent and listened to the sound of the rain pelting its way against the rubber roof outside. It was relentless, but even so it did nothing to ease the intense heat of the day.

Lara couldn't see that it was going to stop any

time soon. She had spent too long on the island to believe that this was just a brief shower and so resided herself to the fact that it would be dark by the time it finished.

Jace seemed to have had this thought too and seemed slightly offended the weather hadn't been more compliant with his plans for the perfect Valentine's evening.

'At least it's cosy.' Lara said somewhat playfully, trying to distract Jace from his woes. This wasn't a lie. The blankets they sat upon were dry, and just as the ones outside, provided a barrier between themselves and the beach. They still allowed the sand to mould comfortably to the shape of their bodies, and the vivid glow from the sunset outside was still managing to penetrate the sheets that made up the walls around them.

'Hmm. I think it is safe to say that we can assume the campfire will have gone out by now.' Jace said, picturing the scene outside they had hastily left now that the rain had taken over it.

'It doesn't matter though does it?' Lara tried to assure him. 'We had almost finished eating and it was all lovely.'

When he still didn't seem convinced, Lara decided to use humour to try and cheer him up, 'I'm sorry Jace, if I hadn't of spent so long on my makeup and choosing which outfit to wear, then we probably would have been completely finished.'

Jace couldn't help but smile at this, which

seemed to put his disappointment into perspective before it was extinguished. 'I guess we'll just have to make our own entertainment then.' he said, leaning back on his hands.

She smiled at him. 'Thank you for doing all of this, and for everything you've done today. It's been really special. Although every day is special anyway - with you...'

Jace smiled. 'Are you getting all sentimental on me?' he asked, putting an arm around her and kissing her cheek.

'Maybe I am.'

'That surprises me. It isn't like you to just come out and say it like that.'

'I guess I just feel brave tonight,' Lara said looking Jace straight in the eyes, hoping he would remember how he had worded his attempt at seducing her yesterday.

It seemed he had however, as he searched her eyes now for confirmation that she had just said what he thought she had. 'Do you feel brave?' he asked quietly.

Lara nodded.

There was a pause, before he leaned forward slowly and met her lips with his.

The pace quickened before long however as their kiss turned ever more passionate.

Jace moved his hands from where they cupped her face and began running them slowly down her back and over her sides.

Lara thought she had never been touched like

this before; it was so intimate. In the past, her only other partner had always run through the same, bare-minimum motions. Jace actually put so much passion into each movement, that she knew he must genuinely mean it.

Each garment was replaced with tender kisses, until both of them were completely undressed together.

Lara pulled Jace on top of her as they lay back on the blanketed sand and embraced their affection for each other beneath the rain-battered roof.

21
Worth the Wait

A sudden rush of pleasant memories hit Lara the next morning before anything else. She lay for a moment nestled snugly in the blankets, allowing the thoughts of last night to come rushing back to her in a warm haze.

With her eyes still shut, she reached her arm forward to find Jace in the cosy nest, but he wasn't there.

Lara sat up and rested on her elbow, looking around the tent. There was no sign of him.

She could still see his pile of clothes nearby, so thought that he couldn't be far.

Lara lay back down again, but after a few minutes got impatient and wrapping a single sheet around herself under her arms, ventured through the now-dry hanging tent door.

As soon as she stepped into the glowing, warm sunshine outside, she saw Jace; he was tending to a new campfire he had started further down the small beach, and appeared to be only wearing his underwear.

He noticed Lara as she approached him and immediately got up from where he had been stoking the flames. 'Good morning beautiful,' he said, greeting her with a heartfelt kiss and hug.

'Good morning.' she said, smiling back at him and squinting slightly in the already-bright, morning sunshine.

Jace stood back and appraised what she was wearing, 'You look like an angel...' he said, tilting his head to the side.

Lara laughed. Now that she imagined it from Jace's perspective, she could see how he could think this. The golden sunlight was beaming down upon the flowing, white sheet she had hastily wrapped around herself; it made her think of the romantic, draping dresses ancient-Greek women wore. The sheet flowed to the bright, white sand beneath her feet where it billowed slightly in the gentle breeze. 'It's just a little something I threw on,' she said sarcastically, with a casual wave of her hand.

He paused for a moment, as if he was trying to store how she looked in this moment to his permanent memory, before he took hold of her hand. 'I was just making breakfast,' he said, leading her to the now dried-out set of blankets.

Jace added a large crab to the fire, before he started preparing some fruit to accompany it.

Lara sat down still in her sheet. She half-thought that she should go and put some clothes on, but was enjoying the feel of the warm air upon her bare shoulders. Besides, Jace seemed to be quite comfortable how he was, in just his underwear.

She smiled to herself as she watched him working.

He handed her a cup of water and caught sight of her expression, 'What is it?' he asked, returning her smile with interest.

Lara shrugged. 'Just you...' she replied. 'You know I...I really enjoyed last night...'

Jace shuffled over on his knees and sat next to her, 'So did I.' He took hold of her hand and brushed it with his thumb. 'It was incredible.'

'I know...Sorry I made you wait so long.'

Jace smiled. 'Well, you were definitely worth the wait.' he said surely, leaning forward and kissing her again.

During the times over the next few months when all four of the island occupants were together, Lara found herself more often wanting to spend the time solely with Jace. She still enjoyed the company of the others to a certain extent, but she found that even just after a short while, she longed to be alone with her boyfriend again. She often found herself daydreaming about the time they had spent together after joining Brandon and Jack for a fishing trip or to gather fruit, or to complete any of the other island chores they still had to do on a daily basis.

Lara hardly noticed that she was doing them any more however, as her mind was always on other things she found her hands working automatically.

If she found anything even the slightest bit tedious, she would simply tell herself that she would be seeing Jace in a short while and then she would forget anything mundane. Whenever she had these thoughts she would look around to see where Jace was, and often found that he was looking for her too.

Whilst Lara thought it was romantic that they thought of each other at the same moment, she was aware that perhaps they weren't being very subtle. Lara had every intention of not flaunting their relationship in front of the other two, in particular Jack. However, she didn't think that her and Jace were doing a very good job.

Jace just shrugged and told her not to worry about it whenever she mentioned it to him, but Lara wanted to avoid displaying too much affection towards each other whenever Jack was around.

Lara was impressed that Jack was handling the situation in such an adult way. Since she had arrived on the island, she felt that he had matured enough to deal with more complicated social situations than he had been used to for most of his life here.

Recently he only retreated to his island hut when he seemed to find Lara and Jace particularly difficult to deal with. For the rest of the time, he treated them with mostly indifference, attempting to ignore their hand-holding, or the fact that they were sat so close together on a single log seat.

Brandon seemed happy that the two of them had found love together. He appeared very encouraged that Jace now looked more recognisable as the old friend he had once known. Indeed, the only concern he seemed to have was whether Lara was taking the relationship as seriously as Jace was. She tried to assure him one day that she shared Jace's feelings once she guessed that this troubled him.

Lara lay naked and nestled under the blankets on the tent floor as she watched Jace slip out of them and pull on his trousers. They had met each other before sunset. Once they were alone on their private beach they had enthusiastically kissed each other in greeting. A little too enthusiastically, in fact. They had originally planned to have dinner together, but once their lips had connected, they had realised that they had missed each other so much during the day and quickly found that they couldn't stop.

Several hours later, it was now completely dark apart from the limited light the moon was managing to project through the walls of blankets around them. They were both very hungry and Jace had managed to tear himself away from Lara for long enough to go and get dinner started.

Lara decided that she would like to get some air after being in the tent for so long, so she gathered up her blanket around her and followed behind Jace as he left the tent towards the glowing campfire. The bright orange flames glowed and flickered, throwing its light over the sand and highlighting some of the trees on the edge of the jungle.

A full moon was positioned high in the sky,

reflecting upon the quietly rippling water and adding to the serene calm of the scene. Lara thought back to one night when Jace was injured, it was a night similar to this one in the way that the surroundings looked. Of course, the circumstances had changed a lot since then, and she realised with a smile that she was so glad that they had.

Lara carefully stepped over the few remaining candles that were still burning in their circle with her blanket. She lay down and got comfortable, shifting her body so that the sand shifted its shape to accommodate her figure.

Jace finished spearing the fish onto a stick and balanced them over the frame of the fire, before coming to join her, leaning back on his elbows. 'So much for a romantic, candlelit dinner...' he said with a smirk, gesturing towards the perimeter of the circle.

'I know...They lasted a pretty long time though didn't they? I mean, it's gone totally dark since we got here,' she shrugged. 'They don't usually last for hours, do they?'

Jace frowned slightly at this. 'No, they don't. I just meant that we got a little more carried away than I expected - it isn't that late.'

'Isn't it?' Lara replied, looking up at the moon and full sky of stars above them. 'It's gone completely dark though hasn't it? That doesn't usually happen early until the summer months in middle of the year.'

Jace looked across at her, as though making a

judgement of her sanity. 'Lara, it *is* the summer months. You do know what month it is, don't you?'

Lara had to pause for a second. 'Erm, well it was Valentine's day...and then it was Jack's birthday...' She shrugged. 'So, it should have been April a week or two ago?'

Jace shook his head in amazement, 'No sweetie, we're coming up to the end of May now.'

Lara thought that Jace must be using his access to Brandon's diary to his advantage to pull her leg a bit. She had to admit that she had lost track of time, but there was no way that she was that far out. 'You're joking,' she said.

'No, I'm not. Haven't you noticed that the weather has been calming down again? The wet season is over, and the crazy heat is starting to lay off us for a while.'

'Not really...' Lara was trying to adjust to this new bit of information. It didn't really change anything. It just showed how preoccupied she had been with Jace. She had even forgotten all about being rescued for a while, she had been so happy.

It now occurred to her that she had been together with Jace for over four months now without realising it. It hardly seemed like any time had passed at all, but then on the other hand, it felt like she had known Jace forever; it was quite an odd feeling.

Lara looked at Jace, and realised that he was still looking slightly marvelled that she had no idea what time of year it was. She smiled at him, before remembering something he had said once, 'I guess time really does fly when you are enjoying yourself...' she said to him, running a hand down his chest.

'Hey, I thought you were hungry?' he said. 'I know I am. You're going to have to give me a while to recover if you want another round.' He smirked cheekily at her as he went to check on dinner, obviously worried that he wasn't going to get it if he lingered too long.

Luckily for Jace, it was ready.

They both gratefully ate their food and washed it down with a cup of water each, before lying down together in the now completely dark circle and facing the vast sky of stars above them.

They stared for a while at the dark glittering expanse above them; it seemed that more twinkling lights popped out of the infinite darkness the more Lara gazed at it.

It suddenly occurred to Lara that her and Jace were in similar attire to the morning after their first night together; Lara in a blanket and a shirtless Jace. She smiled at the thought of this.

Jace must have felt the curve of her lips against the skin of his bare chest. 'What is it?' he asked her, smiling himself.

'I was just thinking of our first time together,' she said, finding his hand to intertwine their fingers.

'Huh...I know, it was great wasn't it? I even amazed myself.' Lara didn't have to look at his face to know that there was a smirk across it.

She laughed. 'That's not what I meant! I just meant that us being here like this reminds me of it.' She rested her head on his shoulder. 'Being with you has been the best few months of my life,' she said honestly and without thinking she added, 'I love you.'

The words sort of hung in the air for a moment and she wondered if she should have uttered them at all, even though it had felt natural.

Jace didn't leave it long however, before he replied with 'I love you too, Lara.'

Lara lifted her head from his chest and rested on her elbow so that she could search his eyes. She was confident that he wholeheartedly meant it.

She leaned into him and kissed him.

He kissed her back, quickly deepening the kiss.

Lara moved onto her back again so that the stars were visible beyond Jace as he moved on top of her. She opened the blanket and enclosed it again behind his back, which she for the first time noticed that the lower temperatures of the May evening had cooled slightly, as they continued their embrace underneath the sea of bright lights glowing out of the dark above them.

22
Three

Lara had resolved to try and keep better track of time, but she had ended up breaking her resolution soon after making it when she found that she had lost a couple of weeks without realising it. She blamed the same routine that they were all forced to follow on a daily basis, criticising it for having little differentiation from one day to the next.

Lara could see why Brandon had insisted on strictly keeping his diary for so many years. There were a surprising amount of distractions on the island, and Lara was still very aware that they relied heavily on a number of factors to stay in exact harmony just to provide them with food.

The incident nine months ago when the fish had become scarce proved how much they relied on the surrounding sea to be stocked with a decent supply of food on a regular basis.

This still concerned Lara. After a lifetime of having an unlimited quantity of anything she desired available at the nearest supermarket, she still felt that their resources were precariously perched on a knife edge, and she worried that one strong tropical gale could tip the odds against them at any moment.

No wonder she couldn't keep track of time if she was always thinking of the bigger picture like this. She reminded herself, as she sat beside Jace on their log and she made her way through her grilled fish and baked potato, that the others must worry about this too, even though they didn't say anything.

It was also hard to remember what day it was, Lara thought, when the food was always the same.

They tried to vary the dishes as much as was possible with just a few ingredients, but to little avail. It always tasted the same. Lately this seemed to bother Lara more than ever.

She knew there was nothing she could do about it, and was grateful to actually have anything to eat, especially recently. Lara's appetite had initially shrunk as her body had adjusted to the island's modest portions, now however it seemed to be returning with a vengeance. She chewed a mouthful of char-grilled potato skin and wondered why this was, but couldn't think of a satisfactory explanation.

Maybe they were catching smaller fish, or harvesting smaller potatoes without her having noticed? Somehow she didn't think this was it, and continued eating her lunch. Or at least, she tried to. Eating seemed to be taking her longer than usual. Lara thought it tasted funny, like it had a flavour to it that she had never noticed before.

She looked up to where Brandon and Jack sat opposite her on their respective logs.

Jack had already finished his and was leaning forward, his elbows on his knees, looking out across the ocean like his father did sometimes.

Brandon was still chewing his last mouthful of food and leaning over to stack his empty bowl with Jack's in the sand by his feet. Neither of them appeared to have had a problem with their meals.

Lara tried to force the rest of it down. Both the fish and the potato tasted odd to her, and she reasoned that there couldn't be anything wrong with both of the elements, so she tried to finish it.

Beside her, Jace finished too and stacked his bowl before fetching himself a cup of water and sitting back down beside her. 'I thought you were starving?' he said to her after gulping a mouthful of his drink.

'So did I...' she replied, swallowing another mouthful. This was hard, since her mouth seemed to have stopped producing saliva. She was determined to force it down however, since food wasn't exactly in over-abundance here. Besides, before she had started eating she had been ravenous.

'Are you feeling OK?' he asked, looking slightly concerned.

'Yes, I think so.' Although now that she thought about it, she did feel a little queasy. But she just wanted to get what was left in her bowl eaten so that she wouldn't have to look at it any more. The remnants looked so unappealing that she would be glad not to have to see them for much longer.

All four of the islanders were still careful not to set foot into the ocean. None of them had seen any trace of the shark that had attacked Jace last year. What had happened to him that fateful day had shaken them all too deeply for anyone to dare to venture into the seemingly beautiful, enticing depths. They were all too aware that a shark was master of its domain and could be lurking in any area of water surrounding the island.

They still fished using the line method; it kept them safely out of the water and it was effective at ensuring that they consistently caught something.

Brandon often remarked that they should have been using it for years.

Lara and Jace were in charge of fishing for the evening's dinner just as the sun was starting to set. They found this was a great time to catch the bigger fish, since they seemed to come out to hunt the smaller fish by the dusky light.

The pair were now very proficient at catching fish and Jace managed to pull in two fine, large specimens for the group to share.

She found that she struggled to watch as Jace unhooked the fish from its trap. She was surprised by this, she had thought that she had long ago managed to put aside her squeamish side; she was taken aback to see it resurface again now.

Once they sat down for dinner half an hour later, Lara found that she was disappointed that their catch, along with a potato each, was all they had for dinner.

She was so ravenous that she felt she would be so truly grateful for some more substantial food.

Something satisfying that she hadn't enjoyed for over a year and a half now would be so greatly appreciated. In particular, she was craving a large, juicy burger.

If she had known that she was going to be half-starved on an island for the rest of her life, then she would have made the most of being able to eat anything in the world. She berated herself for not having taken advantage of unlimited choice when it had been available, even though she reasoned to herself that she had no way of knowing that she wouldn't have access to the tasty treats she was now fantasising about.

Lara wished she hadn't of indulged her thoughts in the glorious memories of dishes gone by now that she was lovingly handed the usual grilled fish by Jace. Before she had arrived on the island, Lara had usually avoided fish. She had eaten it only occasionally when in the mood for something healthy, and mentally congratulated herself on such a wholesome choice, forgetting all about it until the next time she had such a thought.

Lara picked up an end piece from the fish from her bowl and it easily flaked just as it usually did. She tried to tell herself that it was nicely cooked just as it had always been and she should just eat it. Perhaps trying to get it down quickly would get it out of the way, she thought. She put the whole piece in her mouth and instantly regretted it. The salty, slightly fishy, unpleasant scent of the sea suddenly filled her senses. She had got a slight whiff of it about a split second before the morsel had reached her mouth, but by then she had been committed. She sat as inconspicuously as possible and tried to chew without tasting. This was the worst fish she had ever tasted. What was going on? And why weren't any of the men complaining of the same thing. She glanced around at them as she finally swallowed the first bite. None of them even seemed to notice that there was anything different about the meal. What on earth was wrong with her all of a sudden?

She took another bite of fish, but felt that she honestly couldn't face another. The taste was such an assault on her senses, she thought she might actually be sick if she tried to force it down.

The potato was a little easier to eat, even though the smoky-flavour was much stronger than usual that it left Lara feeling as though she had chewed on one of the pieces of wood that made up the actual campfire itself. It took her longer than usual, but she managed to finish it before she offered the remaining fish around to the others.

Jace couldn't understand why Lara didn't want it, but he helpfully took it off her hands and she was glad when it was gone within a minute.

Jace handed her a cup of water and encouraged her to take a few sips of it before he and Jack went down to the water's edge and washed the dishes in the ocean.

It was a dark evening and there wasn't any trace of moonlight behind the thick bands of clouds that had hung around the island all day. The only light came from the campfire, and Lara couldn't see Jack and Jace past the orange glow as they disappeared from view.

For a moment, Lara and Brandon sat quietly in the wake of Jack and Jace's departure. The only sound was that of the quietly spitting fire between them.

Brandon seemed to have been waiting for the other two to leave before he spoke to Lara, 'You're not feeling too good lately, huh?'

She shook her head, 'Not really, no. I think I've got a bit of an upset stomach, that's all. Hopefully I'll feel better in a couple of days.' Lara tried to play down her bug to Brandon, who she was sure would immediately order her to rest in bed if he thought that she was in any way unwell. She was surprised when he didn't question her as intently as she had expected.

'Have you got any other symptoms?'

Lara thought about it for a second. 'No, I don't think so - except I feel quite tired...' There was something odd about the way that Brandon was looking at her. She couldn't explain why, but it made her feel uneasy. Was she exhibiting signs of some kind of tropical disease that Brandon recognised and he wasn't telling her?

Brandon just replied with a 'Hmm,' still looking at her in consideration, whilst twirling the wedding ring on his finger. That was never a good sign.

She decided to test the water, 'Brandon,' she

asked, 'Do you think I've caught some kind of disease?'

'I wouldn't say so, no.' He shook his head slightly and looked into the fire, before he added, 'You don't think there is any possibility that you are pregnant?'

Lara hadn't expected that. She felt winded by this revelation.

She opened her mouth to respond to this, but had no idea where to start. 'I-' she started, but was interrupted at that moment by Jace and Jack arriving back with the clean dishes.

Lara realised that Brandon had used discretion when bringing up the subject, in order to let Lara come to terms with the thought before she broached the subject with Jace.

She wasn't sure if she was grateful to him for this or not, since she had to sit for the rest of the evening with the thought nagging at her. She also could hear that last word ringing in her ears as she tried to project the façade of her usual, bright self. It was difficult however, and she thought afterwards she had probably done a terrible job of it. Jace seemed able to tell that something was wrong.

In the end, she told them that she was tired and she would go and have an early night, sleep off her "upset stomach".

Jace accompanied Lara to bed in her cabin and tucked her into the blankets, before lying down behind her with his arm around her waist.

Lara had ideally liked to have had some alone time to think about what Brandon had said, but she couldn't think of a plausible excuse to provide to Jace. So instead she just stared at the wall in front of her in the dark and let her mind race.

Lara was now fully aware of how much she had lost track of time. The reality had hit her with full force after her brief words with Brandon earlier.

She knew that she had neglected the monitoring of her menstrual cycle like she had used to. But even now that she realised it, she knew that it was far too late to do anything about it now.

As soon as Brandon had said the word, she had known that he was right.

How could she have been so stupid as to think that her digestive system was what was causing her trouble? She felt a slight pang of shame that it had actually taken another person to point the actual cause out to her.

She had no idea how she felt about it if it did turn out to be true. The fear crept into her from out of the darkness, even though Jace's warm body was so close and she usually would have felt so safe in his arms. She didn't dare mention her secret worry to him. How would he react? Would he blame her for being so reckless with her carefree attitude towards time?

Lara could hardly believe that she could be pregnant. For some reason the notion that she was infertile had been lodged somewhere in the back of her mind. Now that she thought about it, this had been so foolish; she'd had no logic or reasoning for this thought, so why would she think it? Did she really have such little faith in her body that she thought it didn't know how to create life?

So many questions flowed through Lara's mind as she lay with Jace in the dark. She hoped that she didn't appear restless to him when she had said she'd wanted an early night. She didn't want any awkward questions.

Eventually however, the unusual tiredness that she had felt all day took over her and she drifted into an uneasy sleep.

Lara woke up the next day still far more tired than she usually was. Last night she had felt so very tired, and there was something that had been troubling her...She struggled to remember what it was...Then it hit her. All of her woes from last night came flooding back to the forefront of her mind as she opened her eyes.

She looked over her shoulder for Jace, but he wasn't there. Lara lay in bed for a while trying to muster the energy to get up and face the day. It was difficult, because she had no idea how it would pan out. Should she talk to Jace? She had no idea what to say to him if she did.

An overwhelmingly strong, burning hunger erupted in the bottom of her stomach forcing her to think that she should probably go and get something to eat.

She sat up in bed, savouring the warmth of the now-necessary blankets since the weather had turned significantly cooler.

Just as she did so, Jace appeared in the doorway, his arms laden with bowls of breakfast and cups of water. Lara gasped loudly at his sudden arrival.

'I didn't mean to startle you,' he said, smiling at her unusual reaction.

'I'm sorry,' she said, 'I didn't expect you to just turn up like that.' She tried to will her heart rate back to normal.

Jace came and sat down next to her on the bed, handing her a bowl of fruit.

Lara felt her stomach contract unpleasantly as she felt slightly nauseated by the thought of food. She felt she needed to be eased into the day more gradually than that. 'Maybe, I'll have that in a minute,' she said gently to Jace.

'All right,' he said, replacing it for water. 'I think you should try and eat it though, you know, keep your strength up.'

Lara looked up at him. She could tell immediately from his eyes that he had been speaking to Brandon. She sighed. 'You've been having a little chat with your friend, I see.' Lara surprised herself by how harsh this sounded.

'Hey, come on,' Jace said, setting his own cup of water down and putting his arms around her, kissing her on the cheek. 'I was worried about you. And I noticed you'd suddenly changed when I came back from doing the dishes last night...I wanted to know what the problem was. You can't blame me for that.'

Lara could feel her eyes welling up with tears as she picked unnecessarily at her cup. 'Well...?' she said, tentatively.

'Well, what?'

'Well, what do you think?'

Jace shook his head. 'Well we don't know for certain yet...but it sounds like you could be. I mean, Brandon said that Helen - his wife - he said that she was just the same when she first...well, when she was expecting Jack. She suddenly went off food. She was hungry, but she couldn't eat... I mean, even if it - if you-' he seemed to be scared to say the word '-well...if you are *pregnant*, then it's great news.'

Lara looked at him through her watery eyes. 'Really? You're pleased?'

Jace shuffled closer to her on the bed and hugged her tightly, kissing her neck. 'Of course I am. Lara I love you. Surely you know that by now?'

Lara wiped her eyes on the back of her hand. 'I guess so.' she replied quietly.

'I love you more than anything. I just can't imagine life without you.'

'Really?' She found she really needed reassuring right now.

'Of course. I mean, we're stuck on the same desert island together aren't we? I'm not going anywhere, for sure...' He smiled at her.

Lara found a laugh burst from her unexpectedly, ending her upset state. She felt better now that her predicament was out in the open and felt reassured that Jace wasn't averse to the idea.

She shook her head, 'Jace, what are we going to do? I can't have a baby on this island. I just can't...'

'It's all right,' he said, stroking her hair. 'We don't even know that you are even going to have one yet...Let's just take things one step at a time.'

Lara felt comforted by Jace's attitude, but felt that he may be wasting his time by trying to calm her down when she just knew in her heart that the two of them weren't really 'two' any more; they were three.

23
Hope

When Lara had first heard that Brandon was counting the days he had spent on the island with his diary, she had thought that he was unnecessarily torturing himself. Now however, she saw the full value of keeping hold of the little green book as she thumbed through it, attempting to work out where she should be in her menstrual cycle.

Jace was sitting beside her on his bed in the main cabin. At least, it used to be his bed. Recently though he hadn't slept in it much, always choosing to spend the night with Lara instead; whether in her cabin or in their tent on their private beach.

Lara's heart sank as she used the miniature calendar in the front pages of the diary and did the calculation. She was four weeks late already.

How could she have managed to go so long without noticing this? Lara felt a fresh wave of shame that it hadn't even been her that had noticed; it had been Brandon that had recognised her symptoms and spelled it out to her in her blissfully-oblivious state. She was more than a little annoyed with herself that she couldn't have worked this out on her own.

Lara could feel that Jace was getting impatient by her side, looking at the tiny calendar in her hands and then back up at her face.

'So how long has it been?' he prompted her eagerly.

Lara checked it again before she gave her answer, 'I should have had one four weeks ago.' She put the book down beside her and sunk back against the wall. She could see through the open doorway that it was a beautiful sunny day outside, albeit a little on the cooler side than usual.

'So...' Jace said slowly. 'That makes you - what - six weeks pregnant already?'

'I guess so...' Lara replied thoughtfully.

She thought that she must be pregnant. She was never late. Besides, she just knew from searching within herself that it was true. She couldn't explain how, but she just knew.

She cast her thoughts back through all of the times she and Jace had been together in the time-frame they had just identified.

For some reason, her mind kept proffering one particular memory to the forefront above all the others. Images of the evening they had spent together under the stars all came flashing through her mind now like she was seeing a snapshot summary of it before her eyes as she stared at the sliver of sparkling ocean out of the doorway. That had been the night when Lara had been amazed to find that it had already been the summer months without knowing it, no wonder this had happened if she had been so negligent with her time keeping.

'Are you all right?' the present-moment Jace asked her, snapping her back to the here and now.

Lara looked at him.

He was watching her closely, as though trying to figure out what she was thinking.

She smiled back at him reassuringly. 'Yes, I'm fine. I was just thinking about when this could have happened, that's all.'

Jace grasped her hand firmly. 'You are happy about this, aren't you?'

'Yes, of course I am,' she insisted. She shook her head, 'Why wouldn't I be?'

'Lara,' he smiled, 'You are saying yes, but shaking your head.'

'Well, I'm happy...I just can't imagine having to give birth here, on the island. What if something goes wrong?'

Jace shook his head defiantly, and pulled her into a firm hug. 'Nothing will go wrong,' he said. 'You'll be fine. I'm not going to let anything happen to you. I promise.'

Lara closed her eyes and enjoyed the feel of him against her cheek. The rough material of his shirt was comforting. She genuinely appreciated Jace's promise, but felt that he was slightly reckless in making it, since he really had no control over whether he kept it or not.

'Come on,' Jace said after a few minutes. 'We should go and get you some lunch. You need to eat plenty - you're eating for two now, don't forget.'

No, she couldn't forget.

As the two walked hand-in-hand towards the campfire, Lara saw that Brandon and Jack were already seated around it and seemed to be deep in conversation. She was glad to see that they already had a pot of fish stew already upon it. She thought that maybe it would taste a little better than the usual fare she now couldn't seem to stomach.

As Brandon caught sight of the couple now approaching them he quickly broke off whatever he was saying and straightened up from where he had been leaning towards Jack.

Lara had the definite sense that he didn't want her and Jace to hear what he had been saying. Nor did he seem at all willing to divulge the subject of their secret discussion, as he hastily tried to detract from it by commenting on how Lara looked like she could do with a good meal.

Twenty minutes later, Jace handed Lara a bowl of stew. 'Hopefully this will go down a bit more easily...' he said, kissing her forehead.

Lara was pleased to find that he was right. The hot liquid slipped down her throat with little effort. The tender morsels of fish and potato had been slow cooked and required little chewing. And whilst Lara had always found the bland flavour of this dish boring, she now welcomed it, fully appreciating how smooth and tasteless it was.

Lara drained her bowl thinking that she had never been so appreciative of a meal in her whole life. She followed this with a banana for desert. Somehow the enjoyment of their previous course had made the sweet fruit even easier to eat.

Brandon had finished his food too and took

Lara's empty bowl from her, stacking it beside him before he asked, 'So, did we work out a date?'

'Yes,' Lara said. 'We think it must have been around about the end of May. The conception date I mean...'

Brandon nodded, looking thoughtful. His brow was furrowed for a second before he spoke, 'So, we're looking at a due date in early February then?'

'It's looking like it,' Jace said, failing to hide his excitement as he stacked his own bowl with Brandon's and starting on a banana.

Jack was sitting on his usual log. Brandon had kept his silence and allowed Lara and Jace to break the news to him themselves. Lara thought there had been little point in keeping it from him since he was bound to find out sooner or later. He had been taken aback at the revelation and had even looked slightly disappointed for a second, but was now listening quietly to the conversation.

'All right,' Brandon replied slowly, still thinking. 'Well, that should mean that we should miss a good chunk of the storm season. If we get all the bad weather out of the way earlier in the season...Well, it's not unheard of... So with any luck you two should be taking care of the baby in more stable weather...' Brandon continued talking, but Lara couldn't hear what he was saying.

The Baby. That phrase suddenly hit home to Lara. Hearing it said like that made her realise that she was carrying a person and not just a pregnancy. Now it all seemed so very real. She was going to have a child. She was going to have Jace's child.

Excitement flooded her. She immediately found herself wondering if the baby she was growing inside her even at this very minute was a boy or girl; what colour hair he or she would have; whose eyes their son or daughter would inherit. It was overwhelming, but she suddenly knew that she was happy after all.

Brandon picked up his cup and raised it in a toast. 'Well,' he said. 'I suppose congratulations is in order.'

He raised his cup and the others did the same, knocking their drinks together.

'Congratulations.' Jack said briefly as he clunked his cup against Lara's and then Jace's.

Lara reached across for Jace's hand and intertwined her fingers with his and smiled at him.

He looked pleasantly surprised at her sudden show of affection towards him and gripped her hand back.

Other the next week Lara found herself struggling even more to keep food down.

This meant that the group had to change its eating habits slightly. Fish stew was now made on a daily basis and although she felt that the others were slightly disappointed to see grilled fish cast off the menu, Lara was grateful for it.

She thought that the term 'morning sickness' wasn't really apt to describe the phase she was currently going through. She couldn't imagine why it had ever been called this, when it lasted all day.

At the times when the nausea was at its worst, Lara retreated to her bed with Jace holding her hand and keeping her company. He did his best to take her mind from her queasy state by talking to her about baby-related matters.

Lara thought it helped slightly that he did this and he only left her side to take over her chores for her while she rested.

Another thing that she was glad of was the cooler weather. She didn't know how she would have coped if she'd had to have dealt with the intensely hot wet season. She sincerely hoped that the hot flushes she currently experienced on a regular basis would have subsided by the time the weather warmed again.

Jace was insistent on treating Lara like a delicate flower all of a sudden, determined that she should "rest" in her cabin and avoid over-exerting herself.

Whilst Lara mainly agreed with this, she didn't think that taking a simple stroll around the island was too much of a strain. Especially since she had been following her usual routine as little as a week and a half ago.

This frustrated her, and one day when she complained about being confined to her cabin for periods of the day, Jace pointed out that he had been forced to rest in his cabin when he had been injured.

Lara had started a retort based on the fact that this was a totally different situation, but didn't want to have an argument with Jace, so she stopped part way through. She had remained obediently in her cabin, whilst Jace had gone to gather potatoes for dinner in the crop outside. Although Lara moved the pillows to the other end of the bed so that she could watch him through the doorway.

It was actually nicer at this end, she thought. A gentle, cool breeze that managed to waft into the cabin was noticeable on her face where she lay now.

Lara watched Jace crouched over a potato plant on the far end of the crop until she found herself becoming drowsy. Despite the fact that she had been asleep all night, she found now that drowsiness was starting to wash over her.

She had been ridiculously tired lately. Lara supposed it was just the changes that her body was undergoing. She tried to imagine herself in a few months time when she was further along, wondering how big she was going to get. She hoped that Jace wouldn't find her less attractive when she got to that stage...

Lara suddenly felt she was falling. She jerked awake. Realising she had actually fallen asleep, she shifted in bed and then looked through the open doorway for Jace. He wasn't there any more.

Lara thought he must have taken his harvest to the main camp. How long had she been asleep for? Was it dinner time soon? Based on the feeling in her stomach, she thought it couldn't be too far off so she got up out of bed. She thought that Jace would probably come to fetch her when the food was ready, but she wasn't going to wait here for him. She didn't need to be waited on constantly. Surely she was allowed to walk around at least.

Lara found the cooler air outside the cabin refreshing as she made her way towards the main camp. She decided to take it slowly, she didn't need Jace telling her off for "rushing around".

Lara emerged from the trees and stepped onto the cool, shaded sand. The last remnants of sunlight ran between the shadows that stretched far along the beach. The glowing, orange flames matched its colour, but was soon to be the only light remaining once the sun disappeared behind the rocky ridge for the day.

As Lara approached the campfire, she became aware that all three men were huddled slightly around it. They were leaning forward, elbows on their knees, just as Jack and Brandon had been a week ago. They were obviously deep in serious conversation and hadn't noticed Lara approaching in the reddening glow of the oncoming sunset.

Jack had just said something Lara couldn't hear as she drew nearer, still unnoticed.

Brandon shook his head to this and when he spoke, Lara could just make out his words above the high tide nearby, '-it has to be before November - December at the very latest-' Brandon abruptly stopped talking as he caught sight of Lara who had just emerged from the trees to the left. He sat up straight and tried to clear his face of his grave expression. 'Hey Lara! Er - you're awake!' he said, clearly unsure as to how much of the conversation Lara had heard.

Jack's body language was a clone of his father's. He sat up straight too, attempting to adopt a look of nonchalance that aroused Lara's suspicion more than quashing it.

Jace jumped up from his log and rushed over to greet Lara with a kiss. 'I thought you were asleep,' he said, before he took hold of her hand and guided her over to their shared log. He fetched her a cup of water and sat beside her, stroking her back gently. 'How are you feeling?' he asked softly.

'Fine,' she said. 'A little better actually.' She looked around at Jack and Brandon. Both of them seemed aware that she had heard them discussing something they didn't want her to hear.

What were they all talking about that they didn't want Lara to know about? It was obviously something to do with the baby, so surely she had the right to know what it was? How dare they keep her out of it.

Perhaps they were wondering how she was going to give birth on the island? They had looked rather strained when she had caught them all talking about her.

They obviously thought that she wasn't up to it...That her body was strong enough to make a baby, but not to deliver it...Or maybe they had come to the conclusion that she just wouldn't survive it. Lara felt her heart sink at this thought. After all, wasn't it commonplace for women to die in childbirth without twenty-first century intervention?

She decided she wasn't going to mess around with niceties. No matter what the outcome was going to be, Lara was going to go into labour in less than eight months time and had no desire to waste time with small talk. 'So,' she said. 'What were you all talking about before I got here? You think I can't do it, don't you? That I'm just too weak to have a baby on my own without a hospital.'

She glared around at them all. 'I don't really care that you all think that. It's just that you don't all have to sneak around whispering about it when you think I can't see you!-'

'Lara,' Jace interrupted, looking quite startled. 'Lara - that wasn't what we were saying at all.'

'No?' she replied, still slightly hotly. 'Well, what were you talking about that you thought I'm not good enough to hear?'

Jace shook his head and took hold of her hand, squeezing it gently. 'Lara,' he said quietly, 'We were just discussing the possibility of trying to get some help - some off-island help.'

'Oh,' she replied, feeling a little sheepish. It wasn't like her to have an outburst like that. She assumed this must have something to do with hormones.

Brandon decided to offer his piece, 'You know

Lara, we have discussed this before - a long time ago. In the past we have talked a lot about the possibility of sailing out on the inflatable boat and trying to find rescue ourselves.' He shook his head, his brow furrowed. 'We never got brave enough to try out our theories on where we are exactly. We took the dinghy out as far as we dared a couple of times, but never far enough away from the island to find any sign of other land.'

'We always came back when this place started disappearing from view,' Jace added. 'Land could be as little as a hundred miles away for all we know.'

'But until we do go out there,' Brandon said, 'Well, we just don't know for sure. We could finally get out of here if we sail out soon...We could find rescue, and you could have your baby in a hospital. It is much safer...'

'But that dinghy...' Lara said, thinking of how it made up the roof of the tent that her and Jace had potentially conceived their baby under, 'It's really old now. All the letters have faded off it. It's not safe - it would probably leak...'

Brandon shook his head with a smile. 'Oh no, we know that we can't use that now. Like you said, it is just too old and damaged. No, I don't doubt for a second that it isn't seaworthy any more.'

'They want to build a raft.' Jack suddenly interjected from his log.

'A raft?' Lara repeated. 'Out of what?'

'That's the easy part,' Jace said, prodding the fire

the way he always did when he was deep in thought. 'We've got plenty of building materials. We will just use the same old wood we used for the cabins. It's definitely strong enough. We just need to build something big and tough enough to withstand the full force of whatever the Pacific ocean can throw at it.'

Lara shook her head. They couldn't really be thinking about this...It was crazy. But they had obviously given it a lot of thought and were all discussing it calmly like it was a simple thing to do. 'Who is going to sail the raft, if you build one?' she looked at Jace, hoping he hadn't volunteered himself. But he shook his head slightly and gripped her hand more tightly.

'We decided it should be me,' Brandon said from across the campfire. 'After all, I've got the most experience of sailing. I would stand the highest chance of making it.'

'You can't seriously be considering this...' Lara said. 'It's just crazy. You'll get yourself killed. You can't just sail out on a little wooden raft into the middle of the ocean and just hope that you'll come across land.'

'I don't see what else we are going to do,' Jace said. 'We're just not equipped to deal with this out here. I only just scraped through after my accident. We just don't have what we need.'

Brandon nodded. 'Jace is right. Childbirth is risky at the best of times. We should do our best now to prevent any likelihood of complications arising.'

Lara looked across the campfire at Brandon. He was completely serious about doing this. He was willing to risk his own life in one last-ditch attempt to get them all out of here, potentially saving Lara's life.

Lara shook her head, 'I can't let you do this,' she said. 'It's too dangerous.'

'Now Lara-' Brandon started, but Jace interrupted.

'Lara, we need to do this,' Jace said. 'We can't stay here. Not now. We planned this all out years ago - which route to take to have the best chance, which season, which weather conditions. We didn't take our chance before, but if there was ever a time to do it - it's now.'

'Well maybe you're not supposed to do it. If any of you had thought that it was genuinely a good idea, then you would have done it already!' Lara said, getting upset by the thought of Brandon sailing off into the middle of the sea on his own.

'No one is saying that there isn't an element of risk,' Brandon agreed. 'But I just don't think that staying here is sensible, what with your condition.'

'I don't have a condition!' Lara pointed out firmly. 'I'm having a baby, that's all. Women around the world do it all the time without any medical help - and some of them are in far worse places than this!'

'I understand what you are saying-' Brandon started, but this time it was Lara that interrupted him.

'I don't think you do,' she said. 'You've got it into your head that you are going to sail off into the sunset on your hand-made raft - you'll probably take a load of food and water with you - because you will have planned it all out nicely. Then a storm will come out of nowhere and you'll drown.' Lara drew a breath before she went on. 'I've been out in the sea on my own without a boat. It's so hard just to keep your head above the water. You wouldn't last more than half a day - that's if you don't get eaten by sharks first!'

Brandon seemed to be slightly disconcerted by this. 'Lara, I have taken these things into consideration.'

'You know what you haven't taken into consideration?' Lara asked him.

All three men waited for her answer.

'You haven't considered how I would feel if something happened to you - just because you are trying to let me have my baby in "the real world". I would never forgive myself - I don't want that on my conscience forever.'

She looked around at them all. They all seemed to have been quietened by this last statement.

'And besides, I think I would like you to be here when I go into labour.' Lara went on, 'I'm assuming that you're the only person here who has ever been present at a birth?'

Brandon nodded, glancing across at Jack who was listening intently to the conversation and looking more strained and deep in thought than Lara had ever seen him. He looked older all of a sudden.

'Well then,' she said trying to sound more upbeat now. 'You've got to be here when it happens. I don't want the only person who knows what to do to drown himself - and especially not because of me. If you still want to follow your plan and make a try for it, then you are welcome to *after* you've delivered our baby.' Lara squeezed Jace's hand slightly harder as she said this, because she didn't feel as brave as she sounded.

Still, her speech seemed to have had the desired effect. Brandon looked defeated, and nodded in agreement. 'All right,' he said. 'If that is what you want, then I'll stay.'

'Good. I don't want to hear any more about it.' She cast around, eager to move on and change the subject. 'Is this stew ready yet? I'm starving.'

That night, as Lara got into bed in her cabin with Jace by her side, she thought about what she had said at dinner and still stood by it. She knew that it was the right thing to do to stop Brandon from going on some kind of silly mission that could get him killed.

In her mind's eye she could see him setting off into the horizon on a flimsy, too-small raft with the version of Lara on the beach watching him go knowing that none of them would ever see him again. It was absurd.

She didn't know how three sensible people could

have come up with such a feeble plan between them. She supposed they were just desperate. And if she was honest with herself, Lara felt pretty desperate too.

    She took some comfort in the hope that perhaps there was still a faint chance that they could still be rescued at some point in the coming months, before it was too late.

24
Gone

Lara looked down at her developing bump, running her hands over it. She was now in her fifth month of the pregnancy and it was starting to show, even through her baggy clothes.

She was alarmed by how quickly the pregnancy was progressing. It hadn't seemed that long since she had found out that she was going to have Jace's child, and now it was more real than ever. She could hardly ignore the fact when she was now sporting a noticeable bump.

Time hadn't slowed down at all since the news. In fact, it was flashing by even more quickly than it had done in her first year. The added apprehension at the thought of giving birth on the island on top of the usual woes of worrying about their non-existent rescue seemed to spur time on even further than ever before.

Lara still clung on to the possibility that a passing boat could sail by any day, although she never shared this with the others, not even Jace. Perhaps this was because deep down she knew that it was hopeless.

No vessel had chanced by this place in over seventeen years, it was unlikely that one would pass by within the next four months to save her from the horror of a wild birth.

When she was alone, Lara often found herself

wondering if she had let Brandon go ahead with his quest for rescue, whether he would have been successful by now. She convinced herself that he wouldn't have been, and that she would have been forced to go into labour on the island either way. Lara had to remind herself that she needed Brandon here, since he was going to be crucial when the time came to take charge of delivering the baby.

Lara felt a twinge of embarrassment at the thought of this, but tried to cast it from her mind. She suspected that when she would need him to do this, any awkwardness between them would be the last thing on her mind.

On the other hand, her morning sickness was gone, leaving her only with an insatiable appetite that the limited island diet struggled to satisfy.

Although the others didn't say it, Lara felt that they were secretly quite pleased when they realised they didn't have to sit down each evening to a bowl of fish stew.

Lara was happy to enjoy their ocean haul grilled again. Really, she was happy to eat anything these days. Well apart from coconut, since this had started irritating her gums recently, causing them to itch and bleed. The lack of toothpaste and mouthwash didn't do anything to help the problem. Whilst Lara had been craving her favourite foods for months, she thought that her overwhelming desire for access to dental products might now outweigh her cravings for macaroni cheese.

Jack had gone back to his old ways somewhat. He appeared at mealtimes and to do his usual chores, but then he disappeared to his private island again shortly afterwards to spend the rest of his time.

Lara felt she and Jace were probably responsible for this. Jack had seemed to struggle to deal with the fact that she and Jace were in a relationship together. She had thought that he had all but accepted the fact, but the news that they were going to have a baby together seemed to have been just too much for him to handle.

Just a few days after they had broken the news to him, Jack had retreated to his island in what seemed to be a bid to avoid them. He didn't seem to want any visitors either, which was a little more unusual. Lara hadn't tried to make a trip herself, but apparently Jack was currently uncharacteristically short with any guests that ventured over to his island to check on him.

Jace's birthday sneaked up on them all before long. A lot had certainly happened since his last, and Lara wouldn't have blamed him for wishing for a more peaceful, uneventful year ahead of him.

As unspoken birthday protocol dictated, Lara did not ask him what he actually had wished for, but he looked much happier than he had done when he had blown out his last birthday potato candle. He extinguished the flame with a slight smile in his eyes.

Brandon picked up his cup and started to make a toast.

The others followed suit and picked up their cups of coconut water, raising them slightly in anticipation.

'Well,' Brandon said searching for the right words. 'This past year has certainly been eventful, for so many reasons. I would like to take a moment to express how pleased I am that two of my friends have found love with each other-'

Jack seemed to shuffle agitatedly at this.

'-I hope that they enjoy a long and good life together. And may they have a healthy, happy child to enjoy it with them. So, here's to a good year ahead, and many more to come...' He raised his cup and started clunking into everyone else's.

Lara had raised her cup in anticipation of the toast, but had lowered it again when she had experienced an odd sensation in her belly.

Jace suddenly noticed that Lara had frozen next to him. 'What is it?' he asked urgently, setting down his drink.

'I don't know,' Lara said, putting a hand above the strange feeling. It was the most bizarre thing she had ever felt; it was like a fluttering that was moving slowly around her abdomen.

Then there was an unmistakable kick.

Lara smiled. 'I think the baby is kicking.'

Jace quickly applied his hand to where Lara's was.

Lara adjusted it for him to the exact spot the

baby had kicked her. There were several moments of waiting, before Jace felt it too.

He smiled broadly. 'Hey, I can feel it!' he said excitedly. 'It's really strong. Hey Brandon, come and feel it,' he called loudly towards his friend, despite the fact he was only on the other side of the campfire.

Brandon looked a little awkward. 'Er, may I?' he said as he knelt next to Lara.

'Um, yes go ahead,' she said, feeling slightly embarrassed herself as his hand waited for a little kick too.

He looked overjoyed when he got one. 'I'd forgotten what it's like,' he said. He turned to Jack who was still on his log, 'That takes me back,' he said, looking fondly at his son and reminiscing.

Brandon went back to his seat. 'Hey, you two will have to start thinking about names soon you know. The baby will be here before you know it. Have you got any thoughts?'

Jack drained his cup and stacked it with his father's. Lara sensed an imminent disappearance from him.

Lara and Jace glanced at each other. 'No, not yet,' Lara said. 'We haven't really talked about it yet.'

'It isn't like we know what it's going to be yet either,' Jace pointed out, looking thoughtful. 'I bet it's a boy.' he said after a moment.

This seemed to prove too much for Jack who said goodnight, telling them he was tired and going to get an early night, despite the fact the sun was still in the process of setting behind the lilac clouds that scattered the sky above the trees behind them.

'I'm surprised you're always so tired when you get so much sleep!' Brandon called after him. But Jack just waved in response as he set off into the dimming, red light.

'How about Austin?' Jace suggested.

'Is that for a boy or girl?' Lara asked him.

Jace looked offended. 'A boy, obviously.'

'And what if it's a girl?'

Jace shrugged and smirked. 'Come on Lara, we both know that it's going to be a boy.'

'Austin Dansinger...Hmm. I'll think about it.'

'Aww, that's a "no" isn't it? Well, we'll have to stick with that one until you can come up with something better.'

Lara hoped that she would come up with something better than Jace's suggestion. There was nothing wrong with the name, but it just hadn't resonated with her like she would have expected hearing her child's name for the first time to have done. She was confident that when she did hear it, then she would know it was the right one.

Over the next week Jack seemed to put in an effort to avoid Lara and Jace completely. Although, from what Brandon had said, he seemed to be trying his best not to see his father either.

Lara wondered if she should go and talk to him. Jace didn't seem keen on this idea however, and

Brandon thought it wouldn't do much good either.

'He will come around,' Brandon said when Lara suggested this idea. 'He always does.'

Lara had been sceptical, but a few days after this however, it appeared that Brandon had been right.

Jack re-emerged for breakfast one morning and although everyone had expected him to vanish again after finishing the dishes, he stayed around and was happy to engage them all in conversation.

He was as talkative as ever and was even completely friendly to both Lara and Jace. He had often treated Jace with some amount of disdain and even jealousy since he had started dating Lara, but now he seemed happy to simply push that aside.

Lara couldn't imagine what had happened to bring about his sudden change in attitude, but was pleased that he wasn't in any way resentful to her and Jace any more, even if it was just for his sake. It surely wasn't good for him to brood, or to live in self-induced solitude.

Jack stayed around for lunch and the rest of the afternoon, he even announced that he had a surprise for the couple that he would reveal at dinnertime. Neither of them could imagine what this was going to be, since it was so unexpected.

When dinnertime came however, Jack unveiled a gift he had made for them. In the main camp beside the hut he drew back a sheet from a wooden crib he had made.

Lara felt slightly overwhelmed by this and found that she had tears in her eyes when she threw her arms around Jack's neck and hugged him tightly. 'Thank you,' she said as she drew back from him.

He had been rather taken aback and embarrassed by this, but he looked pleased that he had made her so happy.

Jace was delighted too, but shook Jack's hand instead of bursting into tears and pulling him in for a cuddle, for which Jack seemed grateful.

Jack remained sociable for the rest of the evening and Lara breathed a sigh of relief that her concern about Jack isolating himself was dispelled. She was confident that he wouldn't feel the need to retreat to his island again after the wonderful evening they had all had together.

Lara kept glancing over her shoulder at the present Jack had thoughtfully crafted for her and Jace's unborn child as she ate. He had clearly put a lot of effort into it and it was definitely sturdy. Lara couldn't imagine how it had been made, but she knew that it must have taken Jack a lot of time.

Perhaps that's what he was doing in all of those lonely hours, she thought. Maybe he hadn't been sulking at all? Maybe whenever the baby was mentioned, it simply reminded Jack of how little time there was to make preparations for the birth, spurring him on to get his secret project finished?

Yes, that was probably it, Lara thought as she watched Jack now happily laughing along with a joke Jace was telling. He didn't seem resentful at all. He was happy.

Although, when she looked really closely at him

Lara could sense a slight ache. As though there was a tinge of sadness around him. Even though he was laughing along with his father at what Jace was talking about, Jack's eyes seemed to be sad somehow. Almost as though there was something that was troubling him under the surface that the laughter wasn't really reaching. And although his smile was wide, his eyes weren't managing to keep up the pretence quite so well.

The four stayed up talking and laughing until well into the early hours of the morning when Lara announced that she was exhausted and couldn't stay awake any longer.

Jace was quick to accompany her, picking up the crib with another "thank you", leaving Jack and Brandon by the fireside.

As they left, Jack said a more formal goodnight to them than usual which struck Lara as odd, although, she was too tired to think any more of it tonight.

She was grateful to get into bed a few minutes later and nestle under the blankets with Jace. It wasn't a warm evening and she enjoyed the warmth washing over her almost at the same time that sleep did.

Bright sunshine poured into the cabin the next morning as Lara woke up. Jace was still asleep and she lay for a while enjoying the warmth that was still left over from sleep until Jace woke up too.

He greeted her with a heartfelt kiss, and as he

usually did lately, felt for a little kick from her bump. They dressed and went to breakfast once Jace was satisfied that he had felt enough of them.

They walked hand-in-hand through the trees, emerging onto the main camp beach.

The first thing that Lara noticed was that Brandon wasn't here. He was nowhere to be seen.

This was unusual. The whole time Lara had been here, Brandon was almost always the first to rise, apart from the shaky period when Jace had been injured. But he could be forgiven for that.

Jace took charge of making breakfast.

Lara ate her fruit rather hurriedly, since she was as ravenous as she usually was at this point in the morning lately.

Once Jace had eaten too and half an hour had passed, Lara looked around. Nether Brandon nor Jack had showed up. Something didn't feel right. Lara was sure they should have been here by now.

Jace agreed with her. He went to check the main cabin while Lara waited on her log seat anxiously.

When Jace didn't return within a few minutes or make any attempt to communicate with her, Lara went after him to see what was happening.

She climbed the steps that led up to the hut. The gloriously bright sunshine flooded the room so Lara could see exactly the scene in front of her.

Jace was looking grim crouched beside Brandon on the floor, who was sitting with his head in his right hand and a scrap of paper in the other.

Lara was taken aback by the fact that he had

obviously been crying at some point. His eyes were red and puffy still, as he shook his head at the paper in his left hand.

'What-What's going on?' Lara asked tentatively from the doorway.

Jace opened his mouth, but it was Brandon who answered. 'It's Jack,' he said quietly. 'He's gone.'

25
The Letter

'Gone?' she repeated blankly, thinking wildly that there had been another shark attack. But then, what was the paper in Brandon's hand about? 'What do you mean he's gone?'

Brandon shook his head. 'He sailed away this morning.'

'Sailed? I don't understand...?'

Jace slid the slip of paper carefully out of Brandon's hand and passed it to Lara delicately, as though he was trying to handle the situation as gently as possible for Brandon's sake. 'Jack left a note,' he said, as Lara accepted the letter from him.

The bright sunlight illuminated the paper that on closer inspection appeared to have been taken from Brandon's diary. Lara could see that 'pick up dry cleaning' was written in Brandon's handwriting on the back.

Minute handwriting covered the front of the page, and Lara presumed that it was Jack's, even though she had never seen his written words before. She read the block of words silently:

Dear Dad,

By the time you are reading this, I'll probably have already set off and will be too far from the island for you to reach me - so I don't want you to try. I have a confession to make: I have been building a raft in the trees behind my hut for the past couple of months. It's just like we talked about, I built it to the same design Jace planned years ago. It looks rock solid, you would be proud of me, I bet.

Don't worry about me. I'm going to sail North. I was listening to everything you said when you were planning to do this journey yourself. And I still remember everything you taught me about sailing when I was a kid. I'm following your plan and I'm using your sailing lessons, so I figure I should be able to get as far as you could.

I didn't tell you I was planning this because I knew you would just try and stop me. Lara needs you to be on the island. That's another thing Dad, I don't want you to blame Lara for me leaving. I would have gone anyway - I thought about it loads before she even arrived. I've known for ages that I can't stay on the island the rest of my life. I don't want you to blame Jace either - seeing him and Lara together makes me want to find what they have someday, but I already knew that before they got together too. So who knows Dad, maybe that "someday" will be soon?

I want to say that you're the best Dad anyone could hope for. You did so much for me and Mom before we left. And you never stopped looking out for me, never let me stop hoping, even when Jace lost it. I never stopped believing because of you. I hope someday I can be as good a father as you have always been to me.

I'm going to stop writing now because I need to get going before you all wake up (and I'm running out of paper).

P.s I'm sorry I ripped this page out of your diary, but I think Jace already took some sheets to wrap a birthday gift for Lara.

Jack

Lara finished reading Jack's note in silence, now however it was stunned. 'He left?' she asked the room in general, bewildered. 'How could he do that in secret? I didn't know he was even planning it...'

'I figure he must have left in the early hours...' Brandon said flatly, still on the floor, now with his head in both of his hands.

Lara couldn't just accept the fact that Jack was gone. The scrap of paper in her hand must be lying. He can't have just taken off in the middle of the night without saying anything to them all. That just...*wasn't his style?* said a mean voice in her head.

Now that she thought about it, that was exactly Jack's style. He would always disappear to his private island whenever he wanted. And lately he had been spending almost the whole day there, alone. He could have been doing anything for all they knew. So he had built a raft...

Still, the stubborn side within Lara wouldn't let it drop. 'Well...' she said, not sure where she was going with this, 'Well - maybe he hasn't gotten that far yet. Maybe he just - Maybe we could get the dinghy and go after him and perhaps we can still get him back?' Lara finished hopefully.

Brandon shook his head again, staring at the floor. 'I already went up to the cliff-top as soon as I found his note. There isn't any sign of him. Like he said - he left in the night. He's long gone by now.'

'But-' Lara looked at Jace for backup, but he shook his head warningly at her, telling her to leave it.

Lara felt slightly let down at this. She thought Jace should have said something to help her argue her point, but she couldn't imagine what it would have been. Brandon had already realised it before she had - Jack was long gone, he was not going to come back.

She had no idea what to say, so she looked back at the letter and re-read it, as though something she found within it would hold the solution, or at the very least, could provide some words of comfort for the father who had just been abandoned by his son.

When she came to the end of it, Lara noticed that there was an inky mark underneath where Jack had signed his name; Lara found her attention drawn to it. It was just slightly larger than a comma.

It looked like Jack had paused, pen in hand, to add a further sentiment here but then decided against it.

She wondered vaguely what it was going to be, but there were too many other questions still flooding her mind from every direction for her to ponder it any longer.

She looked back up at Brandon again, unsure of what to say. 'Listen, um. Is there anything we can do?' she said, cringing inwardly at how useless her words sounded in the face of such a serious turn of events.

Brandon shook his head, then unexpectedly his shoulders seemed to shake slightly and he moved his hands over his face.

Jace knelt down next to him and put his arm around his friend, pulling him into an awkward looking half-embrace on the floor. 'Hey Lara, I'll take it from here sweetie. Why don't you go and get some air?'

Lara decided to leave the two of them alone, they had known each other forever, so she was confident that if anyone could console Brandon it would be Jace.

Lara left the main cabin and set off down the beach, intending to take her usual walk around the island. When she got to the stretch of beach that ran next to Jack's island however, she decided to go over there and see his empty cabin. She felt she needed some kind of confirmation that Jack wasn't just sulking in his usual solitude and wasn't going to just turn up for his next meal at any moment.

Lara paddled through the clear, shallow water and onto the sand of Jack's private island. She immediately noticed fresh, frantic footprints, spaced far apart that she presumed belonged to Brandon. Lara imagined he must have made them when he had first read the letter and gone to see for himself if he could stop his only child from embarking on a dangerous mission to save them all.

From the front of the cabin everything looked just as it always did. The dazzling sunshine was raining down upon the wooden building in front of her and the palm trees around it were waving merrily away, unaware that the single inhabitant of their mini-island had left it forever.

It was only when Lara stepped around the back of the cabin where she had never been before, that Lara fully believed Jack's departure to be genuine.

The trees here had been completely hacked away in a strip that lead down to the sea at the bottom of the mound. There were deep drag-marks in the sand, where something large and heavy had obviously been pulled and set afloat in the blue, crystal ocean that lapped gently around the edges.

Again, Lara saw hurried footprints where Brandon had clearly run through Jack's departure process. They ran back on themselves, and Lara could see in her mind's eye where Brandon had run from here, straight up to the cliff-top to take advantage of the panoramic views in a desperate attempt to spot any sign of his son.

But there had been none to be had. Jack had planned it that way. He had already planned it all out to make sure that he could be far too far across the ocean to be seen. He had planned it all out in complete secrecy, confiding in none of them. Lara was offended, even slightly annoyed that Jack had been so devious and had fooled them all into thinking that everything was as it always had been and that he was simply hiding in his tropical "treehouse". She'd had no idea that Jack had been organising a bold attempt to take responsibility for rescue into his own hands; neither had Brandon nor Jace it seemed. They had all been hit by this as hard as each other.

Brandon remained quiet for the rest of the day. He was deep in thought and Lara and Jace's words of comfort couldn't reach him.

Jace had managed to console him enough to eat at mealtimes. Although he did so in silence and was clearly not focused on what he was doing. Lara was relieved that he was keeping his strength up however. She didn't know what the coming days or weeks held. She could only hope that the tide wouldn't bring them bad news. She didn't think she could stand it if Jack washed up on the beach like Matías had, and she knew that Brandon would be completely crushed if this came to fruition.

Lara wished she hadn't listed all of the things that could go wrong with Brandon's plan to build a raft and sail out into the unforgiving sea to go and find help.

If she recalled correctly, she had told him that if he went through with it he would have been in high danger from drowning and shark attacks. Her heart sank when she thought about this now.

She really hoped that Brandon had forgotten this particular element of their conversation, but somehow she just knew that he hadn't. As a result, when Lara offered words of comfort she felt that Brandon paid little attention, imagining that she had sparked nightmare images in his mind that he could not forget about easily.

Jace offered his words of comfort too and both he and Lara tried their best to take Brandon's mind from the matter. But this was virtually impossible, since Jack's departure had blown a tremendous hole through their tiny community, one that they simply couldn't ignore.

The couple now felt compelled to spend time with Brandon since they were now his only company. They knew that the last thing they should do was to leave him on his own.

They spent the whole day with him, offering consoling words and dropping in hopeful comments for the future. Although, if they were honest, they didn't really believe them to be true, but they both knew that Brandon could not afford to lose hope, certainly not now.

One day, when Brandon had obviously grown claustrophobic and tired of Lara and Jace's care as they sat around the campfire after lunch, he announced that he was going for a walk.

The two couldn't really find a valid reason to stop him, so they let him go.

Lara was reminded of when Jace had been injured and he had taken a turn for the worse. She supposed that this was just Brandon's way of dealing with things when they got really bad.

Lara watched Brandon's back disappear around the corner. She assumed that he was going to Jack's cabin, perhaps to get some time alone or perhaps in an attempt to feel closer to his son.

Lara looked at Jace, he looked as stressed as she felt.

He ran his fingers through his hair and took a deep breath before draining his cup of water.

'I still can't believe it.' Lara said, still struggling to come to terms with the idea.

'I know. It's crazy.' Jace said, setting his empty cup down.

'I guess that was why he was so nice to us that day. When he came back and built the crib for us...He knew he was leaving the next day. He was planning it the whole time. Like he thought he wouldn't see us again...' Lara paused. 'Do you think we will see him again?'

Jace looked grim and wouldn't return her gaze. 'I

don't know...' He looked down at the sand. 'I just don't know...' he said with a slight shrug, almost as if he was trying not to think about it.

Jace's reaction didn't do much to make Lara feel any better; she put this down to him being worried about Jack too. Or maybe he thought that Jack wouldn't make it, and didn't want to admit it to her.

Lara wondered if Jace would be able to ease the uncomfortable feeling of guilt that she couldn't shake when she considered Jack's true motives for leaving. 'Do you believe what he said?' she asked tentatively, 'About him not being affected by us?'

Jace thought about it for a few moments, staring out at the ocean although not really seeing it. 'I don't know.' he said.

Helpful, Lara thought.

But Jace went on after thinking about it, the sun reflecting in his grey eyes as they gazed across the cerulean ocean, 'Jack was a young guy,' he shrugged. 'He was just a little kid when we landed here. He has never had a girlfriend...I guess he would have gone and done something like this someday.'

Lara didn't like his use of past tense. 'But do you think that if we hadn't of gotten together, he wouldn't have gone?' she pressed, looking for some kind of reassurance that the two of them weren't to blame for this.

Jace looked sharply across at her. 'Do you regret us?'

Lara was taken aback by this. That hadn't been

at all what she was getting at. 'No, of course not. I just...I just wondered if you think this was our fault?'

'No. I don't think that. My bet is, he would have gone anyway - even if it would have taken him longer to come up with the idea.'

Lara felt comforted by this, but now wanted reassurance on another matter, 'You don't regret us, do you?' she asked quietly.

It was Jace's turn to look taken aback. 'No. No, I don't,' he said, putting his arm around her and pulling her into a hug so that they faced the sparkling ocean together. 'You are my world, Lara. I love you more than anything.' He lifted her chin and pressed his lips against hers firmly.

Now Lara felt more reassured.

Jace seemed to be too. He nodded, 'You know what? I bet Jack will be OK,' he said in a confident tone that lifted Lara's spirits further. 'Like he wrote in his letter - he knows how to sail,' he went on, 'Brandon taught him when he was a kid.'

Lara didn't want to point out that it was Brandon's sailing skills that had brought the three of them to the island in the first place.

Lara went through a range of emotions over the next month. At times she was angry with Jack for leaving them all here with nothing much else to think about other than his dramatic departure. Other times she was just stricken with worry about his safety. Perhaps it was the fact that she had spent one of the longest days of her life adrift alone in the middle of the ocean herself, but Lara couldn't imagine anything worse. She sincerely hoped Jack knew what he was doing, wherever he was.

It took Brandon several weeks to come out of his reverie enough to be aware of his surroundings again. He refused to let Lara and Jace do his chores for him and in the end, they decided that perhaps it was good for him to be doing them. If nothing else, these everyday tasks took Brandon's mind away from his woes for short periods during the day.

Although it was clear that Brandon's mind wasn't completely drawn away from thoughts of his missing son; this was apparent from the number of accidents he kept having. On one fishing trip, he caught his finger on the fishing hook, drawing blood. Another day he had a slightly worse mishap when cutting open a coconut. Luckily it wasn't too bad, but Jace had been forced to take over the task whilst Lara took care of his cut.

That same day, he also forgot to light the campfire for dinner, causing them to be delayed by an hour.

But apart from these few, minor incidents Lara was impressed with how Brandon was managing to carry on at all.

Lara herself was starting to find that she was having difficulty with her chores too, although for very different reasons. Her bump seemed to be growing larger with each passing day, and she was now finding that it got in the way slightly when she tried to go about her everyday tasks. Not only this, but her whole body ached and she also found that her legs swelled up if she stood on them for too long.

Lara was thankful that the intense heat and humidity of the wet season wasn't upon them, although it was approaching.

Jace told her nearly every day that she should slow down and take it easy, but Lara didn't want to listen to his considerate words, no matter how good the intentions. She had hated being confined to her cabin during her morning sickness phase. Now that was thankfully behind her, she wasn't going to willingly be sent back to it so easily, leaving Jace and Brandon to do everything.

That was another thing, with Jack gone all of the work had to be split between three of them and not four. Lara was determined to make sure that it wasn't going to be shared between two.

One morning, after she had hotly debated with Jace who should go and fetch the coconuts from the high cliff, Lara walked along the main beach in the direction of the vantage point. She had won the argument, allowing her some semblance of independence as she walked along the white sands sparkling in the early, golden light.

She knew that she was going to be dependant on the other two men when it was time to deliver the baby, but that wasn't for another two-and-a half-months.

Until then, she was going to make the most of being able to have some alone-time whilst she still could. This morning she was enjoying the heat of the sun warming her through a gentle breeze.

The sunlight was glowing through the gaps in the waving palm leaves and playing upon the sand. Here and there were patches of light and shade; Lara watched them changing as she walked. Her ankles sank deep into the moist sand the tide was slowly leaving behind.

She slowed her pace as she approached an odd-looking object the tide was leaving. It was unusual to see anything on this stretch of beach. They rarely saw shellfish or even stones on this side of the island.

Lara squinted at whatever it was, trying to work out what it could be. She was automatically wary, since this was the beach that Matías's body had washed up on. Perhaps this was why she had a strange, foreboding feeling now.

She stopped and crouched in front of the object that was as long as she was high; her growing bump made this difficult.

Then she suddenly realised what the object was; it was a section of tree; it had clearly been deliberately cut on both ends.

Lara felt the dread rising within her as she realised what this must be. There was no mistaking it. This was obviously part of Jack's raft.

26
Promises

Lara's numb brain struggled to comprehend what she was looking at. If this was part of the raft, then where was the rest of it? Was she about to make a grisly discovery further along the beach?

She felt a wave of fear wash over her. Had the tide brought Jack's body back here too?

Lara straightened up, still staring at the soaking bit of wood in front of her that could mean only bad news. As she stood up her eyes were automatically drawn further ahead. There were similar looking pieces strewn far along the beach, as far as she could see.

Lara trotted frantically onwards, glancing at all the dark objects that were interrupting the pristine whiteness of the otherwise idyllic-looking sand. She was really starting to panic now. What was she about to find?

Lara didn't want to think about what she might see at the end of this unwelcome trail, but her heavy legs were carrying her along it anyway, almost against her will. She had to know what it would lead her to.

But it didn't lead her to anything. The beach around her was littered with broken pieces of raft, but nothing else had washed up with them. Lara didn't know what this meant. Should she be relieved or not?

But were these pieces broken? Lara thought as she stooped down to pick one up. It looked completely intact now that she looked more closely at it. It hadn't been broken apart with the force of some rough wave; the edges were sharp and undamaged; and there was no sign of any bite marks embedded within it.

A tiny flutter of hope rose in her chest at this realisation, but it was almost immediately dampened when she realised that she now needed to go and tell the others about this.

Lara knew it wouldn't go down well, and it would only cause Brandon to become completely withdrawn with worry again.

She couldn't even imagine how she would bring up the subject with him. How on earth was she supposed to break this news to him?

Before Lara could think about it any further however, she suddenly became aware of movement behind her and realised that she wouldn't have much time to form the most perfectly tactful conversation in her head before she actually had to engage in it for real.

Lara turned around. To her relief, it was Jace that was now approaching her.

He caught sight of her stressed body language, and her face must have belied some amount of concern too, because he seemed to assume that she was upset about him encroaching on the alone-time she had been planning on relishing.

He caught up with her, and attempted to reassure

her that he wasn't being overly-protective, 'I know what you are going to say,' he said, placing his hands upon her shoulders affectionately. 'I just don't think you should be carrying a bunch of heavy fruit around in your condition.'

Lara opened her mouth to speak.

'I know. I know. You don't like me calling it that, but how else am I supposed to describe it. You're just a bit delicate right now - that is nothing to be ashamed of.'

'Jace-'

'I know, but it's like you said before. Loads of women have to go through this - but they don't all go lugging coconuts around a desert island by themselves, do they?'

'Jace, I'm not upset about that! Look...' She pointed.

He looked at where she was gesturing, stepping past her for a closer look.

'I think it might be Jack's raft,' she said, following him.

Jace was quiet for a few minutes whilst he examined a few of the pieces with a slight frown. He seemed to be going through the same thought processes Lara had. Although, it was often hard to tell what Jace was thinking sometimes before he formed his thoughts into words. 'Has Brandon seen this yet?' he asked.

'No. I only just found it all before you arrived.'

Jace nodded, looking out at the ocean. 'All right,' he said, almost to himself. 'Lara, help me gather up all the pieces you can find. Just get them and put them in a pile in the jungle over there.' He pointed.

'Why?' Lara asked, taken aback. 'Don't we need to show them to Brandon?'

Jace shook his head as he grabbed a piece in each hand and strode over to the jungle, 'The last thing Brandon needs right now is to see this. He has only just got over the shock of Jack taking off. We will just hide all of this for now, before he comes down here and finds all of this.'

Lara hesitated.

'Lara, you trust me don't you? I've known Brandon for most of his life. He is already at breaking point - I've never seen him like this before. If he thinks something has happened to Jack, it would just tip him over the edge. Please - help me...'

'All right, I trust you.' Lara said, as she swooped down on the nearest strip and hurried it over to the pile Jace had started under the cover of the trees.

The pair worked together until they had gathered all of the stray debris that hinted at Jack's demise.

Their movements became more frantic and panicked towards the end as they both feared that they would be caught by Brandon at any moment, in the midst of their deception.

Lara noticed that the baby was kicking erratically at this point. She wondered if this was because he or she could feel their mothers guilt at hiding something so potentially important from a friend. But then her logical side told her she was being silly and that it was most likely because she was moving so frantically herself. She hoped she wasn't causing the baby distress, whatever the cause. She avoided mentioning this to Jace, and just focussed on finishing the task.

When they had finished, Jace quickly dug a shallow hole in the soft ground with his bare hands, allowing them to deposit the pile of damp wood into it. They pushed the earth back over it all and pressed down, hoping it would be enough for it to stay hidden.

As they washed their muddy hands in the sea afterwards, Lara wondered if she and Jace had really done the right thing. Really she thought that Brandon should be told, but she also thought that Jace was right too.

Lara had never known Brandon to act the way he had done in the last few weeks. He had been so withdrawn. The stress was quite apparent in every fibre of him. She thought that the only thing that kept him going every day was the thought of hearing some news about Jack. But she knew that the secret she and Jace had just buried was not the kind of news that Brandon was hoping for.

The couple decided before they went back to the main camp that they would watch and wait for any more indication of Jack's fate washed upon the beach. They would try and get here before Brandon each day to save him any potentially unnecessary heartache.

Jace had declared that what they had found this

morning was not necessarily bad news; it could just mean that Jack had experienced some structural issues with his raft. The fact that they hadn't found more of it was encouraging; this meant that the most part of the vessel was most likely still intact, wherever it was.

Lara went along with this; it seemed like the sensible and tactful thing to do.

She couldn't imagine how Brandon would react if he was to imagine that something had happened to his son, but she was confident that he was probably better off not having to deal with the knowledge. At least, not yet.

Almost two months later, Lara was confident that her and Jace's decision to uphold the deception had been the right thing to do. Brandon was still oblivious to the bits of raft that had washed up on the island. It seemed that they had managed to keep their secret buried within the confines of the jungle, along with the parts of the craft themselves.

A few stray pieces of Jack's vessel had washed up on the same shore during that same week, only for Jace to hastily bury them along with the first lot.

Now it seemed that no news was good news on the Jack front. Contrary to Lara's fears that they might make a fearful discovery on the beach one day, they hadn't, and there was no indication that one was still to come.

Lara was happy to believe that Jack was still

safe, but she couldn't understand that if nothing bad had happened to him, why they had not heard anything at all from him? Surely he should have reached somewhere by now? The supply of food and water he had set off with would surely have run out by this point. And unless he had turned to the sea to provide him with food and he was surviving on rainwater, then Jack would be in bad shape indeed.

Lara voiced these worries to Jace, who managed to make her feel better by providing a logical answer to all of them. He told her that Jack was perfectly capable of living from the sea. He knew how to collect rainwater to drink and that it was definitely possible to survive purely on things he could catch from the ocean.

He also told her that if Jack had made it to land, then it would still take a while for a search party to actually find the island. Jack could only direct them so far, since none of them actually knew their exact location.

'So there is still time for a rescue boat to come and pick us up, and you can have our baby in a hospital.' Jace said, squeezing her hand.

'I'll believe it when I see it.' Lara replied, although sincerely hoping that Jace was right.

The three of the remaining island inhabitants were all in a slight state of disbelief one day when Brandon announced that it was Christmas Day. No one had expected this, since Brandon had become more casual with his time-keeping using his diary.

These days he only checked it once every week or so. This had allowed Christmas to creep up on them.

More because they all thought that it would take their minds of things for a while, rather than actually feeling the need to celebrate, the three all worked on making a special dinner; the one they always prepared for birthdays or the festive season.

Once they were about to enjoy their starters and a pot of fish stew with added crab and clams was simmering away, Brandon surprised Lara and Jace when he made a toast.

He raised his cup of coconut water, 'Don't worry - I'll keep it short. I know that we all feel Jack's absence. But, well, let's just hope and pray that he makes it somewhere soon - if he hasn't already, that is-' Lara and Jace glanced at each other '-I'm sure that wherever Jack is, he is thinking of us right now. So, let's make a toast to his success...'

Lara and Jace joined in and their cups all connected before they drank.

As Lara had expected, the celebration was subdued in comparison to the way it usually was when all four of them had been together. But all in all she was surprised to find that it seemed to lift the spirit of the camp. Even Brandon seemed to come out of himself a little and Lara thought that his mind was at least momentarily taken off his woes on a number of occasions.

The last thing that Lara had expected was for Brandon to present her with gifts, but this is what he did once they had finished dinner.

'It's just a little something you will find useful soon enough.' he said, handing her the bundle of material.

Lara unfolded it to find what she recognised as a baby carrier Brandon had crafted and stitched together himself. He had also made a patchwork blanket to match.

Lara was a little overwhelmed by this and it suddenly hit her that the baby was due to arrive in just over a month's time. She had thought in the back of her mind that since the baby was coming next year, then she had more time to prepare herself for it. Also in the back of her mind was the hope that the rescue boat she had been waiting so long for could still sail by and save her before it was too late. But now that the new year was almost upon them, she knew that the time was going to evaporate before she knew it.

The new year arrived with less haste than the last one. Lara thought this was typical since now she wanted time to progress quickly. She was excited about the baby's arrival, and just as much, she was eager to not be pregnant any more.

To Lara, it had felt like she had been carrying the baby forever. How much longer did it have to take? She already felt overly large and found it difficult to carry out her everyday chores which, much to Jace's annoyance, she still insisted on doing, even in the increasing heat and humidity.

Surely she wasn't going to get any bigger than she already was now?

There was now no room left for Jace on the narrow bed next to her in their cabin. He had been forced to set up his own bed on the adjacent bench. However, they had arranged it so that their pillows were in the same corner, so at least, their heads were near each other. This provided more of a semblance of companionship, even if they couldn't sleep exactly side by side.

Even if they could have still shared the same bed, Lara didn't think that it would make that much difference anyway, since she felt too huge to really be up to much in the way of physical contact. She pointed this out to Jace and although he seemed a little disappointed, he didn't voice it. He simply accepted her assurance that it was only temporary. 'I know,' he said, kissing her on the cheek and holding her to him before they said goodnight for the evening. 'It's never forever.'

Lara found that she and Jace had little time alone these days anyway, since they felt that they shouldn't leave Brandon on his own too much to dwell on what may have become of his son. He seemed to appreciate this gesture and was more positive now than he had been when the realisation that Jack had gone had first hit him.

There was more on the island to take his mind off things than usual since the start of the new year seemed to bring with it more wind and rain than Lara had ever known.

There had been several storms already, and they only seemed to be getting worse as the weeks went on. The last one had been severe and had obliterated Lara and Jace's tent on their private beach. They had been assured by Brandon one evening that he wanted some time alone, so they had obliged and taken the opportunity to arrange to have dinner since the weather had calmed slightly.

However, once they had arrived on the beach they had realised that they didn't have a shelter, so they continued with their dinner plans before a rain shower forced them back to their cabin for the rest of the evening.

Jace told her that they would have a better evening a week later to mark the anniversary of their relationship, no matter what the weather was doing. Lara didn't mind what they were doing, just as long as they were together. What was really worrying her was that in a few weeks time she would have to give birth. And since no sign of rescue was on the horizon, it looked like the turbulent island climate would surround her as she did so. Lara sincerely wished that the storms would subside before the baby came.

Somehow, the weather had improved for Lara and Jace's anniversary. Despite the fact that there had been some violently windy, wet days on the approach, today the sun seemed to have the upper hand on the storms that had kept it under their cover so much lately.

Lara thought as she sat down in the circle of candles that perhaps it was Jace's absolute determination that the two of them would have a special evening together that had kept it at bay. It had felt like a long time since they had last had dinner like this. She didn't count their meal last week, which had been rather hurried in an attempt to beat the oncoming downpour they had seen approaching from across the ocean.

Today however the imminent sunset was casting its light across the fluffy and unusually dry sand of the beach. The azure ocean waves were rolling in gently, glittering with orange with no sign of wanting to surge high up the beach to engulf their serene dining experience within its aggressive tide.

Lara had no idea what the coming weeks would bring upon them but she was becoming increasingly concerned about whether she would make it through the childbirth alive.

This was something she hadn't expressed to Jace, and she often found this was the subject of her worries in the middle of the night. Lately she hadn't been sleeping well due to the fact it was so difficult to get comfortable. It didn't seem to matter which way she turned, something was inevitably crushed or aching in every position she turned in.

As much as Lara wished that she would have the baby soon, she was desperately fearful of what would happen once she went into labour. She feared not only for herself, but also for Jace too. She didn't want to imagine what would happen to him if he was suddenly left without her. She imagined that the island camp would be very lonely indeed if the population was reduced further to just two.

Lara also found that her sleep was disturbed not only by nightmares, but also with the enthusiastic kicking of her son or daughter. That was another thing, Lara was aching to know if their baby was a boy or girl. She just couldn't decide either way, despite Jace's insistence that it had to be a boy because the kicks were so strong, and because he just "knew" that they were to have a son.

As she sat appreciating the view, Jace poured her a cup of coconut water and handed it to her, before adding the fish to the fire and pouring a drink for himself and sitting down too. Lara noticed there was something slightly different about the way he did this. His movements were slightly stiff and jerky and he almost knocked his cup over before he took his place next to her on the blanket. He seemed to be almost...nervous.

'Are you OK?' she asked him, sliding her free arm around his waist.

'What?' He looked surprised at her question. 'Of course. I'm fine. Everything is fine.' He put his free arm around her and pulled her closer as they together faced the ocean glinting in the evening sun.

Lara definitely saw a flash of anxiety in him now. She wondered if something had happened that he wasn't telling her about. Her thoughts fell on the main beach and she wondered if he had seen some hint of Jack's fate and he was trying to hide it from her. She couldn't imagine what else he would be keeping from her... 'Are you sure everything is all right?' she asked tentatively. 'There isn't anything you need to tell me, is there?'

Jace shook his head. 'I just, well - I wanted to make tonight extra special, that's all.'

Lara smiled, resting her head on his shoulder. 'You don't have to worry about making special dinners, you know. I think we will be too busy soon, what with the baby and everything. At least, it sounds like it from what Brandon says.'

'I realise that,' Jace said, setting his empty cup down. He had been taking large sips almost unconsciously and had finished the whole thing in the space of a few minutes.

Lara noted this as unusual. There was definitely something bothering him.

'I think that is why we should make the most of tonight.' he added, wiping the palm of his free hand on the leg of his long shorts.

Lara thought this was odd. Was he too troubled by the same worries that kept her awake at night? Did he think that she wasn't going to make it past the birth of their child when the time came? 'All right,' she said. 'Then that is what we'll do...'

If they really were on this subject, then there were things she felt she had to say to him whilst she had the chance, although Lara wasn't entirely sure that they were thinking the same thing. Jace was acting oddly, but she didn't feel that this was perhaps why.

But if in fact Jace worried that he was going to lose her in a few weeks time, then she thought that now was a good opportunity to express some sentiments to him, 'Um, Jace,' she said, unsure of where to start. 'I know that childbirth is dangerous, and there is a chance that I won't get through it. Not out here anyway-' she gestured at their surroundings '-so I just want to say a few things-'

'Lara - what are you talking about?' Jace said sharply, leaning forward from their linkage to look at her face. 'I already told you before that you would be fine. I'm not going to let anything happen to you. I made you a promise, remember?'

Lara set her cup down too. 'I know you did, but you can't really control what happens when the baby comes - and that could be any day now really. Anything could happen...I thought that was why you said you wanted tonight to be special...I thought that you felt that this could be the last night we get to have together?'

Jace looked flabbergasted, and moved in front of her so that they could talk properly, face to face. 'No, Lara. That is not what I was thinking when I brought you out here tonight. It's our anniversary. We haven't seen each other much lately - well we haven't had much alone time anyway. I thought it would be nice to do this. Especially since we managed to get a day where it isn't pouring down with rain...'

'Oh...'

'And what makes you think that you won't make it anyway? I said that you will be fine - you should believe me. Brandon will be there too - he's smart. He alone would get you through it. He got me through the incident with the shark, and I thought I was dead for sure.' He grasped her hands and gave them a comforting squeeze. 'I can't believe you thought that I was thinking that...' He looked slightly perturbed. 'Anyway, I don't break my promises. You should know that by now.'

Lara smiled. 'I guess so. I just thought you seemed nervous this evening. I couldn't think why...'

'You noticed, huh?' He looked thoughtfully at her for a moment.

'Of course I did. Like you said, I definitely know you by now...'

'Hmm. Well, you got me there. I guess I am a little nervous,' he said, looking slightly shifty.

'But why, though?'

'Well, I know I said that I wanted to make our anniversary special,' he said, standing up and tugging her hands gently to guide her into doing the same thing.

They now stood face to face, still holding hands in the circle of candles, the deepening light of the sunset glowing around them.

'But I wanted to make tonight special for another reason.' He searched her eyes. His mouth seemed to twitch slightly nervously now too.

Lara wondered what he meant. She released a split second later with a flutter of excitement where he was going with this, as he now got down on one knee in front of her.

'Lara Adams,' he said, 'Will you do me the honour of becoming my wife?'

Lara was aware that her heart was pounding very hard in her chest all of a sudden. She hadn't expected this when she accompanied Jace for dinner tonight. She couldn't imagine saying anything else when she gave her answer, 'Yes.' she said, causing Jace's face to light up with a broad smile.

He looked as delighted as she felt. He stood up and kissed her enthusiastically, cupping her face in his hands.

Brandon was equally happy about their news when they saw him before they went to bed that night, although Lara noticed that he didn't do a good job of acting surprised. She suspected that Jace may have discussed his proposal with his best friend first.

Brandon seemed to feel compelled to make a toast around the fading campfire before they all retired for the night. Lara felt that she had never been so happy in her life. She thought that she had been giddy enough when she had first started her relationship with Jace, but now she was positively ecstatic.

She had found the man she loved in the most

unlikely of places, and now she was not only marrying him, but she was also going to have his child. Lara didn't mind whether they had a son or daughter, she only hoped that the two of them would both be safe when it was all over in a month's time.

Lara felt she didn't need to be familiar with the early hours of the morning, but they had become something of a regular acquaintance.

Lara now lay awake in the dark in her and Jace's cabin by the potato crop. Judging from the amount of light in the room, it was surely the early hours of the morning. She couldn't have been asleep that long and now she knew that she was going to be awake for a good while, hoping to become comfortable and drowsy enough to get back to sleep again. The problem was that it was impossible to get comfortable because now she was very heavily pregnant. The baby was due in less than a week now according to Brandon's calculations and there seemed to be nowhere to turn to avoid pressure, aches and discomfort from everywhere. Every way she moved, the baby seemed to weigh down on her.

Now that she was awake, Lara noticed that the wind had picked up outside and it sounded like quite a gale. She could hear creaking and ominous snapping noises above the roar of the tropical gusts that were raging outside. It had been breezy as she was falling asleep with Jace earlier, but now it seemed that there was definitely a storm building. Lara hoped that it wouldn't get too bad.

She took a deep breath and wondered which would be the best way to roll to ease the weight of the baby. She didn't feel like she would go to sleep for a good while. Some nights it was easier than others, but at the moment she seemed to feel more restless and even slightly anxious for some reason.

Of course, this was probably because of the impending storm that was building outside. Lara could now hear heavy raindrops lashing against the leaves of the plants and trees outside as well as against the roof. She wondered how Jace could sleep through all of this.

Then she felt it. An intense cramping feeling erupted in her abdomen. Lara didn't need to wonder what it was - it was unmistakably a contraction.

27
Lizzy

Lara took a sharp intake of breath as the contraction faded. She reached over and grasped Jace's shoulder, waking him. 'Jace,' she said loudly, trying to make him realise the seriousness of the situation, even through his drowsy state. 'It's happening.'

As she hoped, this made Jace sit up quickly in his bed. Even in the pitch black, Lara could sense that he was almost instantly wide awake and ready for action. 'All right,' he said, kneeling on the floor in front of her and holding her hand. 'All right, just - just wait here and I'll go and get Brandon.' He raced off through the door and Lara could see his outline briefly as he vanished into the dark, stormy night.

Jace returned with a drowsy sounding Brandon just a few minutes later. Lara had the impression that Jace had dragged him here before he had been given the chance to fully wake up yet. But as ever, he was taking charge of a serious situation with his full focus.

'Well Lara, it's finally time,' Brandon said. 'How far apart are your contractions?' he asked, obviously trying to get things straight in his mind.

'Well, I just had one a few minutes ago, and I think one may have happened whilst I was asleep, but I'm not sure.' Lara felt a little stupid as she said this, but she hoped that neither Jace nor Brandon would notice this in the almost total darkness that they were all immersed in.

'All right...' Brandon replied, sounding thoughtful. 'I had hoped that this would happen in the daylight. But then again, I also hoped that it wouldn't happen during a storm, but there you are.'

The wind was really roaring outside now and Lara thought she had heard a snap not far away outside. Not for the first time recently, she hoped that the cabin would remain intact.

'Well, the contractions don't seem to be coming in thick and fast at the moment, so hopefully it will have gotten light again before we need to see what we are doing.' Brandon said. 'Lara - I need you to let me know when you have another contraction. We need to measure the time between them.'

'All right,' Lara said, still resting up on her elbows.

'You might want to lie back too,' Brandon added. 'You'll need to conserve your energy. You might as well try and get as much rest as possible.'

'What do I do?' Jace asked next to him.

'Just sit down, you just need to sit tight for a while. 'I'm just going to run back and get some things from my cabin, all right?'

Jace sat down on the bed beside Lara, and gripped her hand reassuringly. 'Are you excited as I am?' he asked her.

Lara smiled, before she realised that Jace couldn't actually see this. 'I'll be happy when it's all over,' she said.

Jace leaned down and pressed his lips against hers firmly. 'It will be all right - I promise.'

Brandon returned ten minutes later. Lara saw from his silhouette when he walked through the door that he was carrying a large bundle with him, although she couldn't tell what it comprised of. 'How are we doing with those contractions?' he asked.

'I haven't had any more yet.'

'All right,' he said.

Lara could see him sinking down onto the cabin floor. 'I think we are going to have a long night ahead of us.'

And they did.

Lara had to wait for hours until the contractions were frequent enough for the next stage. The later stages of sunrise were beginning when Brandon could see what he was doing enough to tell her that she was ready to push.

Lara was in such intense pain by this point that she didn't care much for her modesty as Brandon looked for the indication that she needed to do this. She just desperately wanted to get the baby out so that the pain would stop.

Lara hardly even noticed that the storm outside was getting louder, or that the rain was being driven so hard into the cabin by the ferocious wind that she even felt a little of it on her face; if anything it was even slightly refreshing.

Lara didn't count how many times she had to

push before she heard the first cry of her and Jace's baby.

Brandon lifted the baby onto Lara's chest whilst wiping the infant gently with a towel. 'It's a girl.' he said.

She calmed as she was placed close to her mother.

Lara was only half-aware of Brandon as he prepared to cut the umbilical cord, she was too busy taking in how her daughter looked. She was tiny, and yet, Lara couldn't believe that she had been carrying this miniature person inside her in recent weeks.

Jace put his arm around his fiancée as she held their child. He kissed Lara on the cheek and squeezed her firmly in a hug, 'You did so well,' he said softly.

'Thanks,' she said, closing her eyes and allowing herself to lie back and rest for the first time all night.

Several weeks had passed since Lara had managed to safely deliver her baby daughter into the world. Lara couldn't remember much of this period, she had been too exhausted. But now Lara and Jace had gotten into a routine of looking after her, grateful for plenty of help from Brandon.

If Lara had thought that she was the happiest she could have been when Jace had proposed to her, then she now would have realised that she was wrong.

Everything was perfect Lara decided as she held her sleeping daughter in her arms as she sat in the sand facing the ocean and away from the smoky campfire.

The storms had subsided again and had held off for several days. The afternoon sun was now shining brightly and Lara suspected that the storm season was now over for another year. She took a moment to appreciate the irony of this; she could have done with this weather one night a few weeks ago.

Jace sat down beside her with a cup of water in his hands. 'Don't forget to take care of yourself too,' he said, enjoying the sight of his family and offering Lara the cup.

'I'll have it in a minute.'

Jace set the drink down in the sand in front of them. 'You said that half an hour ago. Let me hold her for a little while. You can eat your lunch then too.'

Brandon was behind them at the campfire. He was preparing Lara's favourite meal of grilled fish and baked potato.

'All right,' Lara said. She handed the bundle over to Jace. They had called her Elizabeth, in honour of Lizzy.

Baby Lizzy stirred slightly as she settled into her father's arms.

Lara suddenly became aware that Brandon was seating himself on her other side as she drained her cup.

'I never imagined that anyone could manage without all the stuff you think you need to buy when you know you're going to have a baby,' Brandon said, looking thoughtfully at Lizzy. 'My wife and I, we bought so much when we were expecting Jack...' He trailed off and looked out at the ocean.

Lara suddenly noticed that he looked close to tears. 'It will be all right,' she said. 'Jack learned everything he knows from you, didn't he?'

Brandon nodded, still staring out at the ocean, the light reflecting in his eyes.

Lara was reminded of her first conversation with Brandon after her arrival on the island. 'Then I would say that wherever he is, he is safe.' She said, thinking about how he had managed to get her and Lizzy through the birth.

Brandon nodded again, 'Thank you.' He got up and went to serve lunch.

Lara looked to her other side, to check if Jace was still OK for her to go and get her food first with Brandon.

The first thing that Lara noticed was that Jace was smiling, but he wasn't looking down at Lizzy in his arms, he was looking out at the ocean.

Lara followed his gaze to the furthest point, where just around the corner a boat had just become visible. It was large and grey and had writing on the side that Lara couldn't read.

It was approaching quickly. As it came closer, Lara became aware of the silhouettes of men standing upon the deck, some of them leaning on the rails.

As they came closer, Lara could see that they were all wearing the same uniform and were all dark-haired. That was, except for one of them, whose blonde hair now became visible in the bright sunshine as the vessel drew nearer still.

'Hey Brandon!' Jace called quietly over his shoulder. 'I have to hand it to your son,' Jace said in a quiet voice that couldn't suppress the intense sarcasm. He smiled broadly as Brandon came over to watch the approaching vessel in a state of awe, 'His timing is excellent.'

Author's Note

First of all I want to thank my friends and family for being supportive during the writing of this novel. Without your help, I don't know where I would be. And thanks most of all to my husband who has been very patient during this process!

To my readers. If you liked *All Washed Up and Nowhere to Run*, then you might like to leave a review. I love hearing from readers who have enjoyed my book and it helps other people discover Lara & Jace's story.

You can also visit my website RosamundSnow.com for more information and to be exclusively notified of new releases. Sign up for the mailing list and be the first to hear when a new book is out.

Made in the USA
Lexington, KY
14 October 2018